W9-ALW-183

Captive Passions

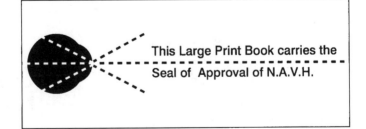

Captive Passions

Fern Michaels

G.K. Hall & Co. • Thorndike, Maine

Published in 1999 by arrangement with Ballantine Books,
a division of Random House, Inc.

G.K. Hall Large Print Romance Series.

The text of this Large Print edition is unabridged.
Other aspects of the book may vary from the original edition.

Set in 16 pt. Plantin.

Printed in the United States on permanent paper.

Library of Congress Cataloging in Publication Data

Michaels, Fern.
    Captive passions / Fern Michaels.
        p.   cm.
    ISBN 0-7838-8585-7 (lg. print : hc : alk. paper)
    1. Large type books.   I. Title.
[PS3563.I27C376   1999]
813′.54—dc21   99-18675

To my husband

Prologue

Tropical night breezes, fragrant with oleander and cloves, cooled by a gently ebbing sea, filtered through lacy, silk draperies into a softly lit bedroom of deep rose and pale beige. The candles in their brass sconces cast wavering shadows onto the low, wide bed. Pale pink satin coverlets rustled, the only sound in the hushed, sultry atmosphere.

Gretchen trailed long, tapered fingers across his glistening, sun-bronzed skin. "Take me, Regan," she breathed, as she raked her fingers across his chest, etching tiny red rivulets.

He grabbed her, crushing her softness in his hands. She moaned with the sounds of his passion and dug her nails into the hard muscles of his back. The moistness of drawn blood quickened her breathing as she became a wild jungle animal in the instinctive, abandoned throes of passion.

"Damn you, Regan," she panted as she struggled to free her breasts from his imprisoning grasp. "Stop playing with me! Don't make me wait any longer!" His answer was to slide his hands to her groin, never breaking the rhythm of his movements. He sought for and found the soft indentation where her thighs ended.

Thrusting, the giant astride her brought his

7

hands downwards, crushing her arched body flat against the bed. A wild shriek tore through the room as Gretchen moved against the pressure of the man atop her.

Spent, Gretchen lay still, her breathing ragged. She spoke harshly: "I've seen you perform better, Regan. I've bedded schoolboys that could do what you just did. Where's the expertise the Javanese women credit you with?" she asked mockingly.

Regan van der Rhys leaned on one elbow and looked into her changeling, hazel eyes; at her splendiferous pale gold hair as smooth and glossy as the satin pillows. Her passion satisfied — for the moment — she resembled a sleepy-eyed tigress. "Javanese women don't demand these . . . these little cruelties you like to inflict. There are other ways to satisfy passion."

His tone was light and easy, and Gretchen was chagrined that her sharp criticisms had little effect on him. He was so completely certain of his magnetism, so entirely confident of his prowess, he vexed her. Regan's cool, phlegmatic composure constantly infuriated her. That he remained unaffected by her scathing remarks was testimony to his superficial feelings for her. It rankled that she meant so little to him. Her full, pouting lips curled in frustration, her chameleon-like eyes darkening to a hazy brown.

"Bah! You men are all alike! Let it suffice to say you enjoyed it. Must we constantly play these games?" She smiled fetchingly, even teeth flashing against her reddened, kiss-bruised lips. "The women of Java know nothing of sensuous delights. Where is the passion? They lay like slugs for men

8

like you; and men like you come to women like myself to satisfy what they really want. Why lie, Regan?" she taunted.

"A bitch in heat," Regan muttered coldly, his handsome features stony and enigmatic.

"Bitch in heat, am I? How many times, Mynheer van der Rhys, have you mounted me when at the end we were both smeared with blood?" she asked derisively. "It was you who sought me! I'm your only release for whatever drives you! This inner burning, this intangible compulsion of yours! You come to me to exorcise yourself. But I don't mind," she said, stretching luxuriously, her eyes on the golden hair on Regan's chest. "Tell me," she coaxed, as her slender hands caressed her full, round breasts, "what would you do without me?"

She moved so that her taut bosom touched his nakedness. Narrowing his eyes, Regan grasped the soft flesh of her haunches and twisted it, pinching viciously.

Gretchen drew in her breath and writhed sensuously, her body glistening with a veil of perspiration. Pressing Regan back onto the mound of satin pillows, she straddled him. Clutching a handful of his hair, she shook his head wildly. "Love me, Regan, love me!"

He reached behind her, seized her round, white buttocks, and savagely brought her to him.

Lust blazed as their bodies sought to quench the flames engulfing them.

Gretchen watched Regan as he dressed, enjoying his unhurried, fluid movements. He was masculinely graceful, like an athlete. Wide broad

9

chest, muscular arms, proud leonine head — all tapering to a flat stomach and slim hips atop long, well-developed legs. His handsome, sun-darkened face; his piercing blue eyes, cold and aloof one moment, igniting to the sharp glare of a lynx the next. A sheaf of white-blond hair fell crisply over his wide and intelligent forehead. But it was his sinewy, muscular body that made her pulses throb.

He swung about to face her as he finished buttoning his lawn shirt, his cold, chiseled features expressionless.

"What are you thinking, Regan? I can never see behind your mask."

"I was wondering what you'll do for diversion, Gretchen. Our being together won't be so frequent after a certain ship arrives from Spain."

"Why not?" she pouted, eyes darkening, betraying her posed indifference.

"I've a bride arriving," he stated simply, enjoying the fleeting pain in her eyes.

"Your humor is in poor taste, Regan. I don't appreciate it!"

"I'm speaking the truth. The wedding will take place shortly after Señorita Córdez arrives." He flashed her a winning, boyish smile, mischievous but tinged with embarrassment. Seeing no trace of mockery behind it, Gretchen became alarmed. It was true!

"Córdez? A Spaniard? A Dutchman marrying a Spaniard!" she laughed shrilly. "Don't tease, Regan."

He saw she was verging on hysterics but ignored this. He had chosen tonight to tell her, so she

10

wouldn't do or say anything intentionally insulting when Señorita Córdez arrived. He hoped by that time Gretchen would be over the shock and at least try to act like a lady. Society, being quite limited here in Batavia, would soon throw her into company with the newly married couple.

Gretchen Lindenreich, a widow now, had been brought to Java in 1606 by her husband, a German sea captain; she had been but twenty years old. The Hamburg mercantile company for which Captain Peter Lindenreich sailed had encouraged him to take his brash and amoral new wife out of Saxony, to where her deviltry and disconcerting behavior would not reflect on the trading organization. Lindenreich, in love and beguiled by young Gretchen's beauty, readily agreed. And did more. He relinquished his German captaincy and accepted a new — and stationary — position with the recently formed Dutch East India Company, for he had long had friends in Holland. He was glad they were to be sent to the Spice Islands, for he too wanted his passionate wife away from the temptations of Hamburg society, and believed and hoped that in a more isolated environment she would settle into placidity and perhaps bless his old age with children.

Gretchen had no choice but to accompany her sixtyish husband. But the renunciation of his captaincy greatly depleted his earnings. Captains received a healthy share of cargo profits, but as a D.E.I. Official in Java Peter merely earned a yearly salary with a promise of pension. Five years later, having showered Gretchen with as many luxuries of the rich East Indian trade as he could

11

afford, Peter Lindenreich died poor and childless. He never knew of the three times his wife had visited an old native crone who used witchcraft and herbs to abort her.

Although free of Peter, Gretchen could not leave Java. She would receive her husband's East India Company pension only if she stayed on the island. This she accepted in a conciliatory manner, for she had by then met Regan van der Rhys and meant one day to marry him, when he should be free.

Regan had, unfortunately for Gretchen, cast his eyes on the youngest daughter of a Javanese tribal chief some three years following his arrival in the islands in 1607, and had married her. Tita's soft, quiet manner and brown-skinned beauty had fully captured his fancy; and their marriage had been in addition a diplomatic coup for the Dutch in their rivalry with mercantile competitors — and predecessors — in the Spice Islands: the Portuguese and Spanish, united at the time under one crown, that of Philip III of Spain. The marriage had furthermore been a feather in the cap of Regan's father, Vincent van der Rhys, D.E.I. Chief Pensioner since his coming to Java in 1603.

"I'm not teasing, Gretchen. It's been arranged and I'm going through with it. I'm marrying Señorita Córdez!"

"I stood by once before and watched you marry that mincing tribal virgin! If she were still alive she'd be fat and toothless by now!"

Gretchen gasped as she saw Regan stiffen. The words had burst from her and now she realized she must suffer the consequences.

Their eyes locked, cold chills danced up her spine. She almost wished he would strike her — anything instead of this frigid fury.

"Whatever her appearance, she would have remained a good and faithful wife, a loving mother to my son. Now she'll always be beautiful and young in my memory." His eyes bored into Gretchen's. "How old are you, my dear? Thirty-six? Thirty-seven? It won't be many years before I see *you* become a toothless hag."

"I'm no such age, Regan, and you know it. I'm years younger than you —" He turned his back on her, cutting her words off as with the sharp edge of a knife. Goaded by frustration, she attacked again. "And just where did you meet this Spaniard? On a pirate ship? In Spanish prison? In a Lisbon or Cádiz brothel?"

"No," he answered, his back still turned. "My father arranged the marriage a little more than three years ago, before my return. I've, well, not set eyes on her."

"Now I know you're lying! No father makes a marriage contract for a grown son, and one that's a widower besides! Do you take me for a complete fool?"

"Think what you like! It was a condition of my release from Spain — and one you doubtless did not know!" A shadow crossed Regan's eyes at the thought of this unwanted marriage, and his brows drew downwards like thick, golden hoods.

"I find it hard to believe your father would have been so presumptuous as to arrange this," Gretchen persisted angrily. "I won't stand by and let you do this! When you married Tita, Peter was

13

still alive. We're both free now. There's been nothing to stop us, these past three years. You've led me to believe we would eventually be mar—"

"Married?" he finished for her coldly. "There was never a mention of marriage. And, I won't betray my father's honor, though he has been dead these twelve months and more. When Señorita Córdez arrives in Batavia our wedding will take place." The serious, scolding tone of his voice lifted, and he mocked, "You *will* come, won't you?" His eyes slid over the expanse of her creamy skin.

"I'll kill you!" Gretchen shrieked as she sprang from the bed, heedless of her nakedness. She raised her clenched fists and pounded his chest, her breasts heaving with outrage.

Savagely, Regan seized her to him and brought his mouth cruelly down upon hers. Her anger melted and she moaned in renewed desire. Brutally, he shoved her backwards onto the satin pillows. She sprawled grotesquely, hair spilling across her face.

"Bitch in heat!" Regan snarled.

Her initial shock abated, Gretchen straightened herself on the silken coverlet and slightly parted her legs. She had never met a man with a greater capacity for brutality than this one. It always caused her some surprise, for she knew he wasn't that way with the Javanese women, nor had he been with Tita, his native wife. Only with Gretchen, and she loved it! She shivered — but not with fear.

She smiled, vulture-like. "We shall see, Mynheer van der Rhys, if you come back to me after a

14

few nights with the Spaniard. I understand they say a rosary during lovemaking." Sensuously moving her legs on the coverlet, her quivering breasts small mountains of white cream, she stretched her arms above her head.

Regan moved to the elegantly appointed bed with its silken hangings and threw down a pouch of gold coins. Gretchen eyed the pouch and spat on it. "There isn't enough gold to buy me, Regan. But then you aren't buying me, are you? You're paying me off! Bring me her rosary, that will be all the payment I need!" she laughed as he quietly left the room, softly closing the door behind him.

Gretchen sprawled over onto her stomach, the pouch of gold held tightly in her hand. Regan belonged to her and no Spanish slut would take him away! After all the planning and . . . She would have to speak to Chaezar. Did he know of Regan's little Spanish bride? Not likely; Chaezar told her everything. When he discovered what an adept pupil she was in the use of the whip, she had been able to glean any and all kinds of information from him — confidences that were soon forgotten in the throes of his passion.

Chaezar would help her as he had before. Her eyes turned murky as she remembered. If Regan ever discovered . . . he would kill her!

But first, she knew, he would see her suffer.

Regan mounted his horse and rode out of the cobblestoned courtyard. He was troubled. Gretchen had accepted the gold and given in too easily. She would play fast and loose and the Devil take all! He almost felt sorry for Señorita Córdez.

15

Señorita Córdez . . . He didn't even know her first name. He recalled the terms of the marriage agreement: ". . . that Regan van der Rhys, widowed these several years, shall take to wife, on my death or when she shall reach twenty years of age, my eldest daughter."

The contract itself had puzzled him, these three years since his return to Batavia. Why should Don Antonio Córdez y Savar, of Cádiz, have wished to marry his daughter not only to a Dutchman but to a Protestant — and a man he had never seen — as the condition for obtaining Regan's release from the Spanish prison? She was probably a snaggle-toothed, pockmarked shrew.

He wanted this marriage even less than Gretchen did — if that was possible. He had never had much use for the Spanish. Furthermore, Gretchen's words now came back to taunt him. He too had heard of the piety of Spanish women, that they hung a rosary about their necks and prayed constantly to God to see them through their wifely "duty." Would this one do that? Then perhaps it would be just as well if she were as homely as he suspected. She would doubtless smell of an unwashed body beneath her many layers of clothing and more than likely reek of garlic. Perhaps her father had merely wanted her out of his sight . . .

As his horse cantered along toward home, Regan turned his thoughts to the Javanese women he found so entrancing. Their comely looks, the clean and fresh scent of the sea hanging about them like an aura . . . *They* at least appreciated a man. They sought his favors and actually thanked

16

him for "honoring" them.

Ha. He knew that it was mainly because they felt it to be good luck to sleep with a white man; nevertheless, they were so uncomplicated . . . so refreshing . . .

Like Tita . . .

He decided he would not bed the Spanish woman if he didn't like her looks. He would lock her away in the chapel and forget about her. Then it immediately dawned upon him that he did not have a chapel. He must see that one was built immediately!

What a far cry from Gretchen Señorita Córdez was sure to be. Brutal, fiery Gretchen, who had long wanted to marry him. As if he would marry her! She amused him, pleasured him, he would never take her to wife. She was useful when his pent-up frustrations and hatreds began to get the better of him. Gretchen could take it, and could mete out some furies of her own! He laughed at himself as his horse quickened its pace, instinctively knowing it was nearing home.

He ought to pack off Señorita Córdez to Chaezar Alvarez, he thought. To that damned Spaniard!

Chaezar Alvarez held much the same position for the Spanish-Portuguese Crown in the Indies as Vincent van der Rhys had once held for the Dutch East India Company. Now Regan occupied that position. Based in Batavia, both men were responsible for the trade of their respective nations among the vast archipelago — Sumatra, Celebes, Borneo, Timor, Bali, New Guinea, and thousands of smaller islands, as well as Java —

17

sometimes called the Spice Islands. Theirs were positions of great responsibility: charting courses, warehousing cargoes, cataloging every yard of silk and pound of spice . . . in addition to keeping diplomatic channels open with the many inland chiefs and sultans.

Before Regan's father had come to take up his post on Java some twenty years before, the Dutch had not been faring well against the Spanish and Portuguese. The Netherlanders were too businesslike and aggressive to suit the gentle ways of the natives, whereas the Hispanic traders, educated by more than a century of world exploration, took the time to bring gifts and make friends with the tribes of the various islands. But the Dutch were determined to beat the Spanish and Portuguese at their own game. The efficient but personable Vincent van der Rhys, an established D.E.I. official in Amsterdam for some years, was sent out to manage the East Indian trade. A highly popular man and a born adapter, he succeeded marvelously well in his new post.

But Vincent van der Rhys's early days on Java had been lonely ones. Not only had his only child, Regan, been left behind with an aunt in Amsterdam in order to complete his education, but Irish-born Maureen, Vincent's ailing wife, had died en route to the islands. The middle-aged Dutchman was left only with his task of diplomat/ trader. Nevertheless, a few years after his arrival in Java it became clear to all that the Dutch dominated the Spice Island trade at last.

Seventeen-year-old Regan van der Rhys sailed into what was later to be known as Batavia four

18

years after his father, and set himself to the task of learning the business. At about that time a slick, sophisticated Spaniard only a few years older than Regan arrived in the harbor: Chaezar Alvarez, son of an impoverished Malágan don.

Regan had never liked the darkly handsome Chaezar, but the ratio of Europeans to native islanders in Batavia was so low that it behooved the small trading colony — officials of the two Crowns, sea captains, and merchants, and their wives — to band together, if not for safety, at least for social commerce and friendship in this island paradise so far from their homelands. Such friendships as did develop, however, did not begin until after business hours, for the days were spent in an aggressive competition for trade.

Regan's distaste for Chaezar Alvarez was based less on his Dutch dislike of the Spaniard's affected grandeur and suave pretense than on the iniquitous role Alvarez had played in ruining Vincent van der Rhys . . .

In 1615, when Regan's son was four years old, he embarked with the child and his wife, Tita, on a voyage home — to the Netherlands. It was to be a sentimental journey as well as one made for business reasons of his father's; it was to be a voyage of discovery and enlightenment for Tita and their child. But it was never to be completed. Before their ship, the *Tita*, captained by an old friend of Vincent van der Rhys, reached Capetown for reprovisioning, it was attacked by a shipful of Spanish-speaking pirates. Tita was murdered before Regan's own eyes, by the quick thrust of a Spanish broadsword, and the last time he saw his son — before he himself was prostrated by the butt of a Hispanic musket — the screaming boy's chubby hands were gripping the ship's wheel as a filthy bandanaed heathen lifted him to his battle-bloodied shoulders. Regan's memories of those scenes were indelible. As indelible as his enduring puzzlement that he, of all the crew, should have been singled out for survival — provided, indeed, with food and drink and set adrift in the ship's dinghy while the other passengers and the captain, dead or dying, were pitched overboard mercilessly. Someday, perhaps, he would learn the reason.

Two days later, or three — for his memory of the hours adrift was unclear now, eight long years after — Regan had the good fortune to be spotted by a brigantine, again Spanish, but one of the merchant ships out of Java and bound for Cádiz. His good fortune lasted only until he was aboardships. Accused of being one of the crew of a recently demolished Dutch pirateer which had preyed on Portuguese and Spanish vessels approaching the African coast, he was manacled, impressed in the gallows of the ship, and taken to Spain — where, imprisoned without trial, he spent almost six years in a hellhole of a dungeon in Seville.

For nearly five years, the grief-stricken D.E.I. Chief Pensioner had given his son up for dead — butchered along with Tita and his grandson. Until, one day, a merchant ship out of Rotterdam reached Batavia with the news that a Dutchman of Regan's description was an inmate at one of Philip III's infamous prisons in Seville or Cádiz — he was not certain which.

The news, however vague, aroused the elder van der Rhys. Further inquiries, made warily by one of his captains who, anchored at Cádiz for imaginary repairs and unnecessary reprovisioning, elucidated that a "Vanderrí," as the contact called him, was prisoner in Seville. And that, yes, the man was probably twenty-eight or -nine and blond-headed.

On receipt of this further information, Vincent van der Rhys made an unpleasant but necessary visit to the offices of the Spanish Crown in Batavia.

Yes, Chaezar Alvarez said, he would do all that he could; he was only too happy to know that his competitor's son still lived. But, he went on, inviting the aging Dutchman to a velvet-upholstered chair, there would be expenses . . . strings to pull . . . And, what was more, he confided to van der Rhys, Spanish trade had been hurt substantially over the past few years by the competence and persistence of the Dutch, and he, Chaezar, would welcome some of that trade. Or some of the profit from that trade. It would enhance his own position with his masters in Spain, might earn him a promotion, a return to the homeland . . .

Hundreds of thousands of gold sovereigns and a good portion of the Dutch trade later (Dutch ships were delayed by van der Rhys and reached their rendezvous with island chieftains later than the Spanish and Portuguese merchants), Chaezar Alvarez sent a letter to his godfather, Don Antonio Córdez, in Cádiz in the hope that the old statesman and shipbuilder might sway Philip . . .

Now, four years later, Regan had repaired his

father's losses, his personal fortune, and had re-established the Dutch East India Company as leader in the Indies — all the while concealing his father's shady dealings with the Spaniard, Alvarez. But the strain had been too much for the older man. His son regained, his honor and name untarnished, Vincent van der Rhys died.

"Alvarez!" Regan muttered, almost as an oath, as he reached his front gate. He knew Gretchen had amused herself with the slick Spaniard while he sat rotting in that Spanish jail! Alvarez . . . Regan's jaw contracted into tight knots just thinking of that Spanish swine.

Chapter One

The sleek, three-masted frigate seemed to scrape the late afternoon heavens of the South Pacific with her topsail, as she skipped and frolicked before the playful persuasion of the easterly trade winds. With flair and grace the pride of the Córdez Shipbuilding Line was skillfully demonstrating her prowess in this her maiden voyage, to the proud pleasure of her owner, the young and vivacious Sirena Córdez. Named for the Greek goddess of the sea, the *Rana* sported fresh decks scrupulously scoured with holy stones and a stern-castle whose varnish had not yet dulled from the salt spray.

Sirena impatiently paced the deck, her bottle-green eyes on the sails. "If *I* were skippering the *Rana* I'd steer her two points into the wind. The sail would draw fuller! What do you think, Tio Juan?" Sirena turned to her uncle, a tall, graying, elegant gentleman of the Spanish aristocracy.

He knew this impetuous niece of his had no need for his opinion; she was a better sailor than he would ever be. She was deferring to his age and experience out of love and respect. "What do I think? That you'd better allow the captain to sail this ship! He's complained to me of how you interfere with his orders. I wouldn't care to have a mutinous captain on my hands, Sirena."

"Spare me, Tio," Sirena laughed, her chin lifting with a hint of her stubbornness and head-strong character. "If I hadn't taken some matters into my own hands, we would have lost days! Didn't I tell you it was best to sacrifice cargo for speed? I've no doubt we'll set a new record for the distance between Spain and Java."

"Sirena," Don Juan Córdez said in an indulgent tone, "has it ever occurred to you the empty cargo holds are the reason behind Captain López's black moods? He's a hard businessman and has no time for dalliance. Yet you insisted your *Rana* carry little cargo. That cuts his profits from this journey in half."

"He's being compensated," Sirena answered hotly, her full mouth forming a pout. "This is my ship! The captain is a grog-soaked drunk! I'll never understand why you commissioned him to sail my ship in the first place. And his ablebodied seamen! Straight from the dregs of Hell! They're poor beasts who have been press-ganged from the worst ports on earth. They handle my ship roughly and I won't have it!" Sirena stamped her narrow-booted foot for emphasis. "The *Rana* is mine and I intend to get her to port in one piece, even if I have to throw the crew overboard!"

Juan Córdez watched his niece with an expression that contained equal amounts of admiration and awe. Her wide green eyes glittered fiercely when she spoke of the *Rana*; her dark, unruly hair now billowed free of its pins.

"It was unwise of your father to take you with him on his sea voyages. And to teach you the art of the cutlass and rapier!" He hesitated, throwing his long, slim arms up in a gesture of hopelessness.

"Sirena, you should be thinking of marriage and children. You're past eighteen, you should be settling down . . ." He shook his iron-gray aristocratic head forlornly. "I only want what's best for you, child."

"As you know, Tio Juan, the good sisters at the convent adored Isabel, but despaired of me," Sirena laughed, a glimmer of remembered mischief lighting her eyes, "and father felt that only he could guide my youthful energy."

"And now you're going to tell me about wise old de Silva, your late father's master-at-arms, who took such a motherly interest in you, seeing to your studies in geography, science, Dutch, English, French, and Latin, sitting up with you when you had the croup, and" — he pierced her with a disapproving stare — "teaching you the use of the cutlass, the rapier, the scabbard —"

With lynx-like grace she spun about. Quicker than the eye could see, she had Juan's scabbard in her hand, the point pressed firmly against his ribs. Her head thrown back, revealing the long, graceful arch of her throat, her hair spilling down her back, she laughed again — the silvery, tinkling tones dancing over the waves. "De Silva was the best damn teacher in all of Spain and you know it, Tio Juan!"

Córdez pretended shock as he looked at her reprovingly. "And that's not all de Silva taught you. Your speech is as salty and briny as his own. Am I doomed to watch you become a sinewy old spinster, who for want of a cool nature and a sweet tongue loses all chance for marriage and children?"

"Why do you chastise me, Tio? Is it perhaps because you're jealous of my talents?" she teased lightly, her eyes softening as she gazed fondly at the man who had assumed responsibility for herself and her sister, Isabel, on Don Antonio's death not quite a year ago.

"It's true, Sirena, that you have an expertise few men possess, but it's not a sport for a gentlewoman."

"Then I am the first! Please, Tio Juan, I've heard this all before. That I'm a woman and although I do possess some talent in the art of fencing I overestimate myself — I'd be useless opposing a man who really meant me harm." She sighed with repressed vexation. "As for marriage, I've yet to meet a man I would prefer to my ship. I've only to look at Isabel and how she dreads this ridiculous marriage our father arranged before his death. She wants only to join a convent. She has a genuine calling for the order and you know it, Tio. Perhaps when we reach Java you'll speak to Señor van der Rhys and tell him Isabel wants only to be left to her prayers." Sirena grasped his arm earnestly. "Say that you'll speak to him, try to buy him off, anything!"

"Child, you speak of our family honor! Your sister has been promised to Regan van der Rhys and it will not be changed! Isabel hasn't your verve and resilience but she's strong in a way you could never be. She accepts life, and endures."

"You may think I am obsessed with my sister. I'm not, I assure you, but I know her better than you do. I love her and it saddens me to know she's being denied what she wants most, to become a nun. She wants to be close to God! Can you deny her that?"

"Your protection of Isabel is most admirable, but quite unnecessary."

Sirena accepted his gentle admonishment quietly. Great green eyes brightened by tears looked up at him. "I shall never understand why Father promised her to anyone — much less a Dutchman and Protestant."

"I am as uncertain of Don Antonio's motives as you are, my dear, although I know Regan van der Rhys's mother was a Catholic. Perhaps one day we shall discover them. Though, with the elder van der Rhys dead, I have little reason to believe we shall."

"The Dutch nation breeds milky-skinned barbarians. And this van der Rhys is with the East India Company, a competitor of the Spanish Crown! How could Father do such a thing?"

"You make your father sound like a criminal, Sirena. And I will not have that! Sirena, your father was more than a Spanish grandee, he was above all a man of business — with a sound head for it. You, more than anyone, know to what extent he succeeded, since it is to you he left the bulk of his fortune and all of his shipyards and vessels. Perhaps — and I am but guessing — his mind worked this way: he had two daughters, one of them independent-minded, the other pliable if over-religious. He had little hope of ensuring *your* future by marriage; your husband will be of your own choosing, when and if you wilt. He therefore left his wealth to you. Isabel he knew he could marry — and doubtless *wanted* to marry, for he

27

had little belief that convent life would make his elder daughter happy, regardless of what you seem to think. The favor he did for Chaezar Alvarez afforded Don Antonio the opportunity of arranging a prosperous marriage for Isabel, *and* of sending her far from our Inquisition-hounded Spain, with its cloisters and black gowns!"

Usually a man of few words, Don Juan Córdez exhibited his pent-up exasperation with Sirena through this long dissertation.

Sirena wanted to remain on good terms with her uncle. Together they enjoyed an open, loving relationship. She also knew him to be a man of strong convictions and a deep sense of duty. At the moment, he saw it as his duty to marry Isabel to Mynheer van der Rhys. She knew it irked him that he would probably never be able to arrange a marriage for herself — her energy and independence were an embarrassment to him. Quickly, Sirena stood on tiptoe, kissed Juan's leathery cheek, and fled down the deck to the sterncastle, where she and her sister shared quarters.

The red glow of the setting sun reflected off the calm, azure sea through the sterncastle's mullioned window. Isabel was utilizing the last light of day to read her prayer book. Upon Sirena's entrance, she dropped her slim hands to her lap and glanced up, her liquid-brown eyes gentle and doe-like.

Isabel's composure irritated Sirena, who would have much preferred to find her sister spent from crying, eyes red and swollen with tears. Uncle Juan had been correct in his remarks about twenty-year-old Isabel's inner strength. At times Sirena believed that she was more upset about Isabel's thwarted vocation than Isabel was.

It seemed to her that Isabel had always been destined to join the Order. When the girls' mother had died in childbirth with Sirena, Don Antonio, having no close female relative to see to their upbringing, placed one-year-old Isabel with the holy sisters and had one of his young servant maids midwife the infant Sirena before confiding her in turn to the sisters a few months later. Isabel fit very well, from the first, into the quiet and restricted life of the convent, while Sirena, from the time she first walked, was into one kind of mischief or another. By the age of ten she was incorrigible — demanding, to the sisters' astonishment, to know why girls must either join a convent or marry and have babies, whereas boys were encouraged to seek exciting lives as warriors, explorers, and sailors. Having no answer to Sirena's demanding questions, the piqued Mother Superior immediately sent word to Don Antonio Córdez, pleading with him to come and take away his inquisitive daughter.

Córdez first cajoled, then pleaded, and finally begged the Mother Superior to revoke her decision. The sister, nevertheless, held out. So that at last, with a wary glance at his exuberant daughter — sitting curiously inactive and composed across the dark-walled visitor's room of the convent — he found himself not merely a wealthy shipbuilder and a father, but also a mother.

In addition to his shipyards, Don Antonio possessed a tidy fleet of trading vessels that sailed between West Africa and Cádiz. On one of three ships, retired from active service to become the don's private pleasure boat, Isabel rejoined her sister for several weeks each summer. Although the older girl appeared to enjoy these excursions along Spain's Atlantic coast and in the Mediterranean, her behavior was always so proper and decorous that it sometimes prompted Sirena to pull at Isabel's hair and tease her unmercifully. Isabel endured all this, saying, "I shall pray for you, Sirena."

"What has Captain López done this time, Sirena?" As was everything else about her, Isabel Córdez's voice was gently modulated and unhurried.

"Nothing. If you must know, it's you! Why don't you put up a fight? You don't want this marriage and you've resigned yourself to it! If you'd only kick and scream, I know Tio Juan would listen. But no, here you sit while I'm on deck pleading your case with Tio Juan." Swiftly, she dropped to her knees and buried her head in her sister's lap. "Isabel, I don't want you out on the edge of nowhere, dependent on the whims of a barbaric Dutchman!"

Isabel lightly touched Sirena's lustrous dark hair. "You silly! Don't torment yourself so. We have no reason to suspect Señor — er, Mynheer van der Rhys is a barbarian. Besides, even if I did not marry him we wouldn't be together any longer. It was my intention to join a cloistered order. Sirena, it's time to put childhood behind us!"

The younger girl jumped to her feet. Were she a cat, Isabel could have imagined her snarling and baring her claws. Her words came fast and furious. "Is that what you think? That I want to prolong our childhood? That I want us to cling together like a pair of marmoset monkeys? Isabel, it would benefit you to hear me well! I don't give one twit how you spend the rest of your days as long as it's of your own choosing! If you want to be a nun, then you should *be* one. If you want to be a whore, then so should you be! What I object to is your being forced into a life you don't want. You can't fool me, Isabel, I hear you crying in the night. I see the aversion in your eyes when one of the crew looks at you the way men will look at a comely woman. Do you really expect me to believe you're so strong that you could sleep with a man and let him have his way with you night after night, and not go crazy?"

"I like men . . . well enough, Sirena. I love Tio Juan," Isabel protested.

"I've no doubt of that, Isabel," Sirena went on, her voice calmer, softer. It was unbearable to hurt her sister this way, but it must be done. "But I also have no doubt that you have already committed yourself body and soul to God! In a way only one who seeks the religious order can understand. Please, Isabel, go to Tio and make him understand. If God has truly sent you the calling, perhaps He wants you to protest this marriage and He will grant you Divine Intervention."

"Sirena dear, I know that I hear the call to become a nun. It is true, what you have said. And," she sighed, smiling contentedly, "my faith in God is so strong that I know He will intervene somehow . . . and that this marriage will never come to pass."

31

Isabel had spoken softly, her piquant face glowing with an inner faith. Sirena's eyes lit up happily. So . . . Isabel had *not* given in to their father's whim after all. She hoped to be saved from the approaching marriage.

Impetuously, Sirena hugged her sister tightly — not yet knowing that her sister's words about God's intervention would haunt her till the end of her days.

"Sail ho!" a loud cry rang out from high in the ship's rigging. "Sail ho!"

"Where away?" the captain shouted.

Sirena, excitement heightening her vivid coloring, released Isabel from her embrace and ran out the door and up on to the deck.

A cry in the rigging answered the captain. "Directly astern, sir!"

"What flag does she fly?"

"No flag, Captain."

Sirena swiveled about to face the stern, her hands to her forehead in order to shield her eyes. A brigantine was approaching them from the north, the crimson light of sunset giving it a black, spectral appearance. A chill penetrated Sirena as she peered into the distance.

Slipping up beside Juan Córdez, she said, "I don't like her looks, Tio. Captain López! Loosen sail and full speed away," Sirena shouted. "I see her sail and she gains on us!"

The captain shot her a disapproving look and ignored her command. "Swing those yardarms. Look lively, men. Heave to!"

"How dare you!" Sirena exploded. "This is my ship! Can't you see she flies no flag? Do as I say!

32

Full speed ahead!"

"Send Señorita Córdez to her quarters, Senor Córdez, or I'll not be responsible for the men's actions." The captain's voice was thick with warning — and, Sirena thought furiously, with grog.

"Sirena, you heard the captain. Go below with Isabel."

"I won't! The *Rana* is mine! Isabel is fine." Turning again to face the captain, she commanded, "I won't warn you again, Captain López. Full speed ahead!"

"She flies a distress flag on her foretopmast!" came the clear call of Caleb, the young cabin boy, who had climbed into the rigging for a look at the vessel.

"It's a trick, I tell you!" Sirena implored her uncle. "She doesn't appear to be in distress, her speed is too great. She gains on us by the minute and that fool of a captain won't listen!"

"Sirena, I insist you join your sister." The determination in Juan's eyes pierced her. Nimbly but sulkily, she stepped over a coil of rigging and headed for the sterncastle.

Isabel was sitting quietly, her hands folded in prayer, eyes downcast. Noticing Sirena's presence, she crossed herself and looked up. "What's all the shouting? Is something wrong?"

Sirena forced a smile in order to abate the alarm that widened her sister's dark, long-lashed eyes, flushed her pale olive complexion and accentuated her still girlish heart-shaped face. "Everything is fine," Sirena said, her hand going to Isabel's gleaming black hair. "Go back to your prayers."

An eternity crawled by as Sirena compelled herself to sit on her ornate but narrow bed listening intently for sounds out on deck. She felt the *Rana*'s slow pace; she was merely drifting. She heard the sounds of the crew slowing her ship and the angry shouts of Captain López. Then, finally, the bump and scrape of a second ship nestling up to *Rana*.

Startled, Isabel looked up at her sister, a questioning expression arching her brows. Sirena was unable to be still any longer.

"Stay here and don't come out on deck!"

She reached for her rapier, which hung near the bed. Encumbered by her long skirts, she stumbled. With the rapier, Sirena tore the hem of her gown, then ripped upward to the level of her knees and crosswise, until she had made a short, tattered skirt. It allowed her free movement.

Cautiously and quietly, she closed the door behind her and moved up the steps toward the open deck, anger constricting her breast. Distress! In a pig's eye! she thought. Wasn't she her father's daughter and hadn't he schooled her well? And to think this stupid wretch of a captain had ignored her orders and allowed an assault on her *Rana*. There was no room for fear, only white-hot anger. If her father had been aboard he would have seen through the ruse. Now it must be left to her. She stood barely breathing, listening to the shouts on the mid-deck.

Creeping out further, to see what was happening, her heart pounded fiercely in surprise — the second ship was lashed slackly to her *Rana*. What

34

was that in its rigging . . . A glint? God! she screamed silently. Her father had told her of marauding ships and of the harquebusiers who stood in their riggings sniping at the crew of their victim ships. She knew that first they would pick off the captain and then down the crew one by one.

Sirena, herself, had never seen it done, but instinct told her this was the situation. The square-rigged sails hid the marksmen from view; it would be as easy as shooting unsuspecting birds.

The ship was broadside to the *Rana*, and Sirena could see its captain standing on deck. Naked to the waist, his broad, deep chest was covered with a mat of thick brown hair. Cupping his hands to his mouth, he shouted, "Do you have a man versed in medicine aboard? I have wounded men! We were attacked by pirates at sunup!"

The man spoke in English! Sirena noted with surprise. That cursed language of those old enemies of Spain, and the aiders and abettors of the Dutch in their war to gain independence from the Spanish.

Seeing that López did not understand him, the man began to use Spanish — but a garbled Spanish it was.

"We carry none!" came Captain López's reply. He was unsteady on his feet and Sirena guessed that he was well on the way to intoxication — again! "How many wounded? Can your ship make port?"

From her position Sirena could see the crew of the brigantine. They had gathered behind their captain, evil sneers marking their faces. Cannons were jutting from the ship's ports. What did they

35

want? Couldn't they see how high her *Rana* rode the waves? They must know she carried in her holds little more than what was necessary for the journey.

Anger blazed in Sirena's eyes as the brigantine's crew abruptly, and without warning, threw grappling hooks across the *Rana*'s deck rails. The result was instant chaos.

The *Rana* rocked from the force of a burst of cannon shot from her enemy while her crew hacked frantically with short-handled axes at the lines attached to the hooks embedded in their deck rails. The marauder's crew now scrambled aboard the *Rana* and as Sirena raised her eyes she saw that she had been frighteningly correct. There were men in the brigantine's rigging, their flintlock pistols aimed directly below. The *Rana* was outnumbered and outmaneuvered; her beautiful frigate would be totally disarmed within minutes.

Panic seized her, choking off all reason. She wouldn't allow this, she couldn't! She must fight for her ship, for her life!

Sirena moved out onto the deck, her rapier in hand. Taking a moment to orient herself, she ran to her uncle's aid. He was fighting for his life, but was no match for the near-naked crewman of the brigantine, whose cutlass was swinging so widely and wickedly.

She advanced a step, and her eyes spewed flames as she thrust her sword at the surprised crewman, bringing up the weapon with a forceful motion to knock the attacker's arm awry, and bringing it down again with such force that the quarterdeck rail received a gash an inch deep. In that second the crewman lost his advantage and Juan pierced the man's chest with his cutlass. Blood spurted from the wound and streamed from his open, gaping mouth.

Averting her eyes from the gore, Sirena swung about. Where was her crew? Hiding below decks, she would wager. "All hands to repel boarders!" she shouted, her voice ringing over the waters. "Fight, damn your eyes!" she yelled as she directed a high-flying swing at one of the pirates. Taken by surprise by a woman bent on cutting him down, he was sent off his stride.

Sirena's arm flashed in the twilight, her unruly, sable hair billowing out behind her. "You dare to assault my *Rana*! I'll *kill* you first!" Her rapier flashed and jabbed, feinting to the right with a lithe movement, slashing at the pirate's arm. Wildly, in frantic defense of her ship, she parried his advances. Unbridled savageness raging within her, she forgot the rules of the polite art of fencing: she had become a tumultuous barbarian defending herself and her own. When with one final slash she saw the pirate's arm roll along the deck, instead of shock she felt herself near to elation. Could she have gone mad? Was this Sirena Córdez laughing cruelly at the bewildered, wounded pirate and calling, "Pick up your arm, dog."

As he lay howling on the deck, Sirena snatched up his cutlass, which lay near the severed arm. Then she swung about — a blade now in each hand — to see how young Caleb was faring; she'd heard his voice a moment before. The half-grown lad had abandoned an English ship some months ago in Cádiz and had signed on to sail with

Sirena's small fleet of merchant vessels. She'd taken a great liking to the boy.

Within seconds, she found herself back to back with the boy — facing a new opponent. With a lunge and a jab, Sirena quickly had the man pinned to the ship's rail, however, and without further ado she wiped the wet, crimson blade of her cutlass on her short, ragged-edged skirt.

Turning, she saw that Caleb was fighting far more valiantly than any twelve-year-old could be expected to do. But he was no match for his brawny attacker. Her head thrown back and her long legs apart, she shouted in order to be heard above the bedlam around her. "Caleb, push off the bow! If they fire into us again they'll smash us to pieces! I'll take this man for you."

The boy gone, she attacked the man with her rapier, shrieking, "You had no right to board my ship! Now you'll fight and die! I'll not ask for quarter, nor do I give any!"

"I'll cut your heart out and hang it from the topsail," the pirate spat. "But first I'll have my way with you, same as every man aboard this ship."

For answer, Sirena brought up her cutlass.

The man was jarred from his feet as it caught his arm. Clumsily, he tried to regain his footing, but Sirena was too quick for him. In a lightning motion she struck once, then twice, forcing the pirate backwards. A fierce left jab — and he was pinned to a mast, his nostrils quivering in fear.

In a last frantic effort, he lashed out at her. For defense she plunged forward with the cutlass, sinking it in his chest but at the same time feeling a stinging sensation down her left arm. In surprise she saw red soaking through the sleeve of her tattered gown. Gasping with pain, she turned about, only to see her Uncle Juan's body topple to the deck. The frigate's crewmen were lying about now like slaughtered cattle. Rivers of blood ran everywhere.

"Quarter! Quarter!" the *Rana*'s crew were shouting. They fell silent, backing away, as the pirates picked their way among the dead bodies and came to stand before them awaiting their captain's orders.

"Throw the stinking flesh overboard!" he roared in English. His command was instantly obeyed. Jeering obscenely, the pirate's crew fell to their task. The sound of the dead and the half-dead hitting the water rang hideously in Sirena's ears. Fighting back hot tears, she stood mute near the sterncastle, her shaking hand cupping the elbow of her injured arm.

"Spare *one*," the pirate captain growled loudly. "The pretty one there by the sterncastle! I'll have plans for her later," he chortled, leering lewdly in Sirena's direction. "But tie her hands. That young woman is too handy with a weapon!"

"Pray God they don't find Isabel! Not alive . . ." Sirena whispered as two tall brigands strode towards her.

The pirate captain then set his crew to the task of emptying the hold. Within a half-hour nearly everything of real value was transferred to the brigantine, save food and water. Evidently they were not going to destroy the ship . . . *her* ship, Sirena mused as she stood, hands tied behind her, near the foremast.

The cruel shock of the twilight attack on the *Rana*, her *Rana*, had begun to wear off, however. Now Sirena trembled uncontrollably, her thoughts only on her sister Isabel's fate. She grieved, too, for her uncle — he who had protected her for the past year. But he had died like a man; of that she was glad. Then her thoughts turned to her own part in the defense of the ship. Had that fighting, shrieking animal really been Sirena Córdez? Could she have been so merciless, so barbaric? But she had been compelled to it — to defend her ship and her family. It *had* to be done! She had been taught the art of self-defense, and to have done any less would have been idiocy. She had been like a tigress who defends her cubs, but she had not enjoyed taking men's lives . . .

A hoarse shout suddenly broke the air as one of the pirates dragged Isabel Córdez onto the deck. "The prize! See the prize! And she *prays!* What do you think, men, does she pray for salvation or does she pray for —"

"Pig!" Sirena shouted, her eyes spitting fire. "Leave her alone! She is promised to God, she's to join a convent!"

Raucous shouts of laughter greeted her statement. "A convent! When we finish with her, there's not a convent that'll have her!"

The pirate leader called for order. "Take her below and let the men have their sport. Look lively now, we've many leagues to travel. *This* wench," he said, roughly pulling Sirena against his sweating, hairy chest, "is mine. Only when I'm done with her is she yours!"

40

Outrage seized Sirena, fear gripped her innards. "Isabel! Isabel!" she screamed.

This couldn't be happening! But it was, and the reality was paralyzing. Isabel, her sweet, gentle sister, who wanted only to be a bride of Christ, was writhing, struggling to be free of the brawny monster who pawed her roughly, intimately, heedless of her gasping sounds of protest, pitiful pleadings, and pale, terror-stricken face.

Laughing and sneering derisively, the lusty captain untied Sirena's hands, dragged her across the frigate's blood-slick deck, and threw her down near her sister. She struggled to get up, and kicked — her long legs aiming to strike a vulnerable mark. She screamed in protest, obscene oaths she hadn't realized she knew, torn from her throat along with low, heart-wracked sobs for mercy for Isabel and herself. She wrestled laboriously beneath the captain's brute strength, her fingers stretching into curving, talon-like claws and punctuating her screams with swift, violent slashes at her attacker's amused and jeering face.

He straddled her, his bulk pressing her back against the deck. Writhing and fighting, Sirena yet struggled to escape him. Suddenly, her hand made contact with the knife stuck in his wide belt. Clutching its handle, she whipped it forth, a murderous intent contributing to her strength and agility. But for all his bulk, the pirate was a nimble warrior. He adroitly dodged the swift slash of the knife and retaliated by delivering a stunning blow to the side of Sirena's head. The amusement disappeared from his coarse features; in its stead was a dark, malicious, purposeful light.

He called to one of his men, who now knelt near Sirena's head and stretched her arms above her, holding them fast to the deck. The captain, still straddling her legs, retrieved his fallen weapon and cut and tore her clothing from her body. His hands touched her shrinking flesh, his weight pressed her downward. Her breath came in painful rasps.

Sirena's head ached from the blow he had dealt her. Her wounded arm felt leaden and numb. She fought against the dim shadow of blessed unconsciousness, the sweet oblivion that could take her away from this horror and blanket her in sheltering, dark folds.

Isabel's pleadings brought her back from the edge of night.

Clenching her teeth, Sirena compelled herself to fight the beckoning blackness, determined to remain alert for any opportunity to escape.

She was naked now, exposed to the pirates' salacious stares, and her knees were forced apart and the captain fell upon her. Heedless of her virginity, he thrust himself forcefully upon the girl again and again, enjoying her screams of outrage and pain. Again and again he tore his way through her unwilling, recoiling body.

Hoarse animal shrieks spilled from her lips, paroxysms of burning anguish.

Isabel's screams echoed Sirena's as a pirate drove his way into her with animal brutality. The crew had ignored their captain and had not taken her below. They were raping her alongside her sister!

Sometime during the attack, her resolve weakened and Sirena momentarily lost consciousness. When she was roughly slapped to her senses she looked for Isabel. It was almost with relief that she heard her sister's screams. She lived! Thank God, she lived!

But another of the pirates was upon Sirena, his shoulders blocking Isabel from her view. Shock and humiliation flooded her senses, bringing a kind of detachment. Everything seemed to be happening in slow motion and she viewed the man a-top her as though through heavy gauze. Then an alarming cry from Isabel commanded her attention. Fuzzily, Sirena saw a pirate with a hook for a hand throw himself upon her sister's naked body. As he was raping her, he placed his hook at the base of the girl's throat and scored her tender, naked flesh, drawing the hook down the length of her torso and leaving in its wake a scarlet ribbon of torn flesh and oozing blood. Deformed and depraved, he laughed sadistically, the sight of Isabel's bleeding intensifying his lust.

Sirena's conscious mind rebelled and she swooned, only to be slapped awake again after what must have been eons of time. Almost immediately Sirena saw that Isabel was no longer on deck — the girl's terrified screams were coming from below. The ordeal was evidently not over, for as soon as one man was done with her another took his place. At some point, however, Sirena realized that Isabel's screams had long since ended.

When the men were done with Sirena, they left her shivering, naked, exposed to the chill night air. She lay on the deck, staring blindly up at the stars;

then she painfully pulled her battered body up to a sitting position, as her eyes searched for something to cover her nakedness. It was the boy Caleb who brought her a torn and dirty shirt. — Compassion for her humiliation shone from his dark eyes. For a fleeting moment, she was ashamed for Caleb to see her condition, but his pained expression was so mature in its understanding that her embarrassment abated.

The ship was curiously quiet now, with only a few drunken pirates softly singing, aloft near the ship's vessel. The *Rana* was like a ghost ship; yet the marauder's brigantine still clutched the frigate's sides.

Buttoning the front of the shirt, which came only halfway to her knees, she stumbled toward the hatch that led below. "Isabel, I must see Isabel!" she whispered hoarsely.

Caleb, his eye on the open hatch, quickly spun Sirena around. "Don't look," he pleaded. "Please, Señorita Córdez, don't look!"

Alarmed, she struggled free of his grasp, in time to see two of the pirates carry her sister's slim, battered body up through the open hatchway.

"Isabel!" the cry ripped from her, bringing with it all the pain and torment that had welled up inside her. Frantic, she pushed her way forward, her eyes straining to look upon her sister's face. But the long, red gash running the length of her body was all she could comprehend, all her eyes would focus on . . .

The men carrying Isabel swore at Sirena and brutally shoved her away, fighting off her groping hands. As she collapsed, sprawling on the deck, horror choking her, she watched them hoist Isabel's body over the rail and drop it into the greedy arms of the sea.

Caleb came to her side and helped her to stand. "She was dead, Señorita. I heard them say so as they came above. She was dead long before they stopped —" He caught himself, his black eyes mournful.

But it was too late. Sirena had heard his last words. "Oh my God! Isabel! Isabel! *Isabel!*" she sobbed. Then, heaving, she leaned weakly over the ship's rail and retched.

Chapter Two

It was nearly a week now since the pirates had commandeered the *Rana* and began sailing it with a skeleton crew under their captain, Dick Blackheart — he who had so cruelly raped Sirena. The pirate brigantine sailed close by, in the wake of the frigate. Tonight Sirena lay in the hold of the rocking, pitching ship and was numbly thankful for the storm that raged about them. All hands were needed to secure the frigate, and there would be no time for any of the brigands to ravage her yet again.

"Dear God," she moaned miserably, "how much more can I take?"

Weakly, Sirena turned over on her side and looked with vague interest at the raw, festering wound on her left arm. A greenish pus already oozed from it. She would probably lose the arm, she thought with alarm, the first emotion she had felt since seeing Isabel's poor ravaged corpse thrown into the sea.

She held her throbbing arm carefully and attempted to gain her feet, but the pitching and rolling of the *Rana* drove her back to her knees, causing her to knock her injured arm against a sack of rice. Pain shot through her body, doubling her over. Her head felt fuzzy, her eyes wouldn't focus. She knew she was burning with fever.

Suddenly, she heard the cover of the hatch

open. "Please God, no!" she whimpered. "Not again!"

Her latest ordeal was still all too clear in her muddled head. She had been clearing the rough plank table in the galley after the evening meal. The boatswain was cursing at her for being slow and clumsy. With a savage sweep of his arm, he cleared the table, threw her upon it, and ravished her while the others shouted their encouragement. One after the other they had mounted her as their shipmates offered their loud and leering approval. When they were done with her, they had knocked her to the floor and jeered obscenities and curses. Somehow she had managed to get to the hold, where she had collapsed onto a pile of dirty sacks.

A scratching sound now reached her ears. She held her breath in fear. Was that a whispered word she heard. Painfully, she inched toward the door and pressed her ear close.

"Señorita Córdez . . ." It was Caleb.

"Caleb, how did you get here?" Sirena gasped. "You must go above decks. If they find you here you'll be beaten. Go! I don't want *you* on my conscience, you can't help me."

"Listen to me," Caleb pleaded, his boy's voice urgent. "I've a few minutes. It's storming so fiercely they won't miss me. I found a medicine chest and some powders for your arm. When you serve the morning meal, I'll try and get them to you."

Surprised, she tried the door latch. It did not move. So, they had locked her in!

"It's hopeless, Caleb. My arm is so swollen and

47

festered that powders can't help me now. Go away," she muttered dejectedly. "I've a fever and my head aches so."

"Señorita Córdez, if we could find a way to get free could you manage?"

"I'm afraid not, Caleb. I don't think I can ever manage again. How could I hold my head up, after what's been done to me? I wish I could join Isabel and Tio Juan. But *you* must save yourself, Caleb. Forget about *me*."

"Never!" Caleb said in a tear-choked whisper. "I won't leave you! Your uncle shouted to me as he fell that I should watch over you and your sister. I failed once" — a sob broke his voice — "but I won't fail again!" His boy's tone was determined. "I don't know how . . . but there must be something! Perhaps when the crew is full of ale."

Sirena gave no response, and her silence inspired Caleb to ask anxiously, "Señorita, are you all right? Can you hear me?"

After a moment, she answered lifelessly. "Yes."

Caleb breathed a sigh. He knew, now, that he must do something to help her. He had never seen the señorita like this. Usually she was full of vinegar and salt and had the tongue of a viper. But now all the will and vitality was gone from her. He shook his dark brown head. What could he do? Nevertheless . . . Sirena Córdez knew her ship like the back of her hand. She knew the sea and could captain the *Rana*. If only there were some way to make her come alive again, so that if he could devise some miraculous escape she would have the stamina to follow through.

"Someone's coming," Caleb warned as he skit-

48

tered to his feet. "I'll be back if I can."

"What kind of god are you?" she screamed, raising her tormented eyes heavenward. "He's but a boy!"

Her crawl to the door and the forced scream had drained the last of her strength. Sirena lay beaten and defeated. Perhaps tomorrow she could find a way to get to the ship's rail and go over. "If you *are* my God," she gasped, "then let me die. Let me die in peace!" The fever raged within her and she slept.

Hours later, Sirena found herself being hoisted to her feet. Swaying as she determined to focus her eyes, she recognized the captain.

"On your feet, my pretty," Blackheart commanded. "Fix food and drink — and it would be best if you remember to move quickly. The men have complained about you."

His swarthy face and bushy, brown beard repelled Sirena, and the stench of his rotting teeth made her turn her face away. But he grasped her injured arm and dragged her to the ladder leading out of the hold. Sirena cried out in pain and received a sharp blow on the side of her head.

"None of your dramatics, señorita! Your cries will go unheeded. My men are not about to forget that you brought death to some of their shipmates."

Clenching her teeth, she staggered up the ladder, not caring that the filthy shirt she wore afforded the captain a spectacular view of her long, tawny legs as he followed her and pushed her into the galley.

Shaking her head in an effort to clear her clouded vision, Sirena numbly sank to her knees. "I can't," she whimpered. "I don't have the strength to stand. Let them run me through. I don't care!"

"You'll care if I tell the crew you're feeling lonely!" Blackheart growled. "They'll all come running to keep you company. Now, get to work!" he commanded, slamming the door behind him as he left the galley.

"Please don't do that . . ." Sirena sobbed, too weak to notice the captain had left. "I couldn't go through that again. Please don't!"

Caleb had quietly entered the galley and now dropped down beside the weeping girl. Quickly he withdrew the packets of powder he'd located earlier and sprinkled them liberally on the oozing wound. Next, he uncorked a small bottle and with gentle hands raised it to her lips. The smoky, amber liquid dribbled into her mouth — until she gagged.

Apprehensively, Caleb wondered if he had given her too much or too little. Whatever the case, he thought fearfully, she was so sick she would probably die no matter what he did.

"I *thought* you were up to something!" came the captain's gruff voice. "What've you got there? Answer me, damn your eyes!"

"Medicine," Caleb answered defiantly.

"Medicine, is it? And where did the likes of *you* get medicine? In my cabin, I'll wager!" His bullish face was red with anger, the cords in his thick neck swollen with rage.

"In the Señorita's cabin. It's *her* medicine —

just as this is her ship!" the boy replied as he got to his feet. "She's sick, and someone has to help her or she'll die."

Sirena, hearing their voices, struggled to attention. "Leave the boy, captain. He was only trying to help me. Please," she begged, grabbing hold of his trouser leg. "Please . . ."

Dick Blackheart looked down at the girl. How prettily she begged. Skin flushed with fever, eyes bright with tears . . . but she had cost him the services of some of his best men.

With his booted foot he kicked her away and grasped Caleb by the neck. "You'll get ten lashes, and the girl five. If she survives, you may minister to her. If you're able!" he laughed cruelly. "The señorita first. We'll lash her to the mizzenmast on deck — but you'll strip her down first!"

"I won't do it!" Caleb rebelled.

"You'll do it or go over the side. Then what would become of her? What would she do without your tender care?"

"Do as he says, Caleb. I'm ordering you. Quickly now," Sirena whispered.

Out on deck the wind was fresh and clean in a sudden break in the storm. Before the mizzenmast, Caleb shyly removed the coarse shirt and lashed Sirena to the mast, securing her tightly for he feared she would slip to the deck.

"Fear not, pretty señorita," Blackheart shouted. "I'm a well-practiced hand with the whip. I'll venture to say I won't draw blood to scar your long, exotic back."

Calling for one of his men to fetch him his whip, the pirate chief took the opportunity to study

51

Sirena's arm. The boy was right, she'd probably be dead in a day or two. He would be sorry to toss this pretty morsel over the rail.

Caleb watched as the captain brought down the whip across Sirena's back in five quick, successive strokes. Her body swayed and jerked with the force of the blows, yet she uttered not a sound.

Pray God *I* can be so brave, the boy cried silently.

Dressed again in her shirt — though the scratchy material on her back was almost more than she could bear — Sirena watched with pain-wracked eyes as Caleb's body jerked beneath the whip. But again the captain displayed his skill. Although he raised angry welts, he did not break the skin. Caleb would have no scars to mark him as a mutineer. She was puzzled by the captain's gentleness.

As the boy turned his head, ready for the eighth blow, she saw his brave, stoic expression and the quivering of his lower lip. He appeared younger than his twelve years, his round smooth cheeks crimson against the white circle of fear that was his mouth. He was manly for his years. What kind of god was it who protected only these pigs, their captors?

You're not *my* god! Sirena cried inwardly. You couldn't have been Isabel's either! Her god was merciful and kind. From this moment on, I *have* no god!

But as Blackheart laid on the tenth blow, a determination and a will to live coursed through Sirena.

Using every scrap of strength left in her, she

52

hefted herself to her feet. She stood erect and directed a pointed stare at the captain. *"There will be a time and a place,"* she said with chilling certainty, *"when l will come upon you! I will sever your manhood and force it down your throat for what you have done to this boy and to me.* You will die choking on your own blood and flesh. And if you should die before this comes to pass, I'll wreak havoc on every Dutchman from here to Capetown! There won't be one of you left alive to —"

Hearing her threat to his manhood, Blackheart brought up his hand and struck her across the face. "You're a raving lunatic," he shouted. "My men have a need for food. Crawl into the galley and see to it!"

"No!" Sirena screamed back defiantly.

"A few more lashes and well see if it's still 'no,' " the captain menaced.

"Whip me till I die. I do nothing more for you."

Grinning at the deadly calm in her voice, Blackheart turned on his heel and left the deck.

Sirena quickly unlashed Caleb from the mizzenmast. Gathering the shreds of her dignity about her, she gently led the boy back to the galley and sat him in its sole chair.

Caleb forced a smile. "Aye, but it was good to hear you speak so to him!" His dark eyes clouded with pain. "But what will happen now? What will he do?"

Sirena shrugged. "In truth, Caleb, what more could they do to us? We're beaten, aren't we? What can we do, where can we go? Though . . . we should be nearing a port soon. It's been seven days since we were captured. Does their brigantine still sail alongside the *Rana*?"

"No. When the captain noticed the approaching storm, he ordered full sail and we left the brigantine behind."

"Hmm. He wouldn't have done so if we had not been nearing his port. He would never chance sailing a small ship like the *Rana* without protection. If we're to do anything, we must decide now!"

The boy's breathing was ragged as he tried to speak. "I've wanted to tell you before, but didn't have the chance. The captain found maps in Señorita Isabel's trunks. I heard him talking to the first mate."

"In Isabel's trunks? Oh, if only I could think!" Sirena said softly, lightly touching her temples. "I can't remember any maps . . ." Caleb changed his position, wincing with pain. "Poor Caleb," Sirena crooned, "how do you feel?"

"I've been flogged before," he gulped. "Has the medicine stopped the throbbing in your arm?"

"A little," Sirena lied. "My eyesight has cleared a little also."

"Your arm must be lanced so it can drain," the boy muttered. "I think I can do it . . . if you can take the pain."

"I can take it."

Sirena, in her exhaustion, sank to the floor. Caleb secured a galley knife from the wall, and forcing his hand to be steady, with a quick motion lanced the festering wound.

"I'll have to squeeze it," he warned through tight, white lips. "It's going to hurt like the devil."

"Don't talk, do it!"

But Sirena fainted with the first pressure the boy exerted. When she revived, her arm was neatly bound in a piece of galley toweling.

"You did well, Caleb," she sighed. Then: "Listen, the storm! It will vent its wrath on us this day."

"It's not the worst I've seen. And the *Rana* rides the sea well, doesn't she, señorita?"

"If only I were at the wheel. How I love this ship, Caleb. It's all I have left. How could I have let them overtake her? It's all my fault," she wept, remembering . . .

"No, it was that drunken Captain López. But in truth your uncle didn't know what a sot the man was. Señorita, why did you curse the *Dutch* to Captain Blackheart?"

"Why? Because of the appearance of his brigantine, for one reason. She's Dutch-built, I'd stake my life on it: her lines are low and narrow. And the flintlock pistols for another — a Dutch invention!"

"These things mean nothing, señorita. Flintlock pistols are available to everyone. And the brigantine could have been a captured ship, like the *Rana*. Even Blackheart is English, not Dutch."

"I don't care what you say, Caleb. There are only two powers in the East Indies, the Dutch and the Spanish. I tell you the brigantine sails for Dutch interests! If she sailed for Spain, do you think she would have taken the *Rana*? We were sporting Spain's flag. If she'd been a Spanish pirateer, she'd at least have spared our lives — and taken only our valuables. But even though the captain is English, you and I know that means

55

nothing. Except that he may be all the more a friend to the Dutch!"

Caleb interrupted with fearful, whispered urgency: "Shh! Someone's coming. Get down on the floor and stay quiet!"

Dick Blackheart entered the galley, some of his crew of degenerates behind him.

"To show you I'm a man of mercy, I'll free you from your duties for today, girl. Toss the girl in the hold and secure her there," he instructed his first mate. "Take the boy to my cabin!"

Sirena lay undisturbed, except by the continuing storm, for the remainder of the evening. She slept. But by midnight she woke and realized her fever was gone.

Slowly, she flexed her arm; some of the pain seemed to have disappeared. Her back was stiff and painful, but she knew now that in a few days she would heal. The only scars she would bear from the lashing were the marks on her soul — and these would be small compared to the damages done to her on the day Blackheart took over her ship . . . small compared to her sorrow for the deaths of her beloved Isabel and Tio Juan.

Sometime toward dawn, Caleb swung open the door to the hold, a ring of keys clanking in his hands. "I'm to take you to the galley and we're to see to the morning meal. The crew hasn't eaten since the storm began yesterday. Hurry, Señorita."

As they mounted the ladder, Caleb murmured low, "I have a plan. I'll tell you about it in the galley."

Sirena smiled. This little sea urchin with his strange, flashing black eyes and tumble of mahogany hair had assumed the position of her protector. Little more than a baby, he displayed a sense of responsibility far beyond his years. Following him up the ladder, Sirena noticed that he, like herself, avoided extending his arms. She, who had received only five lashes, could imagine how his young back pained him from the ten.

The *Rana* rolled still, but the storm had abated and the rains ceased as Sirena cut thick yellow cheese into slices and arranged them alongside chunks of hard brown bread. Caleb was soon browning slabs of salt pork over the galley's black iron stove.

"Señorita, I was able to steal sleeping draughts from the ship's medicine chest. If we put them in the crew's ale . . ."

"And what, Caleb? Think! When they awoke, it would go worse for us. And there are no bolts for us to slide on this galley door! They would kill us! . . . Still, it may be — a good idea. Hmm. If we put the draughts into the ale — yes — and served it to them up on deck, then when they went under the drug we could easily toss them overboard . . . But I have to think," Sirena said, knowing that whatever they chose to do it would give them a chance to escape.

As they went about preparing the food, Sirena asked curiously, "What did that brute of a Blackheart want with you in his cabin?"

"I don't know . . ." Caleb said, puzzled. "He asked me where I came from and who I've sailed with. I told him the truth," Caleb said, his face downcast.

"You did exactly right, Caleb. Now tell me how you managed to get the sleeping draughts."

Caleb's eyes brightened and he enthusiastically launched into his story. "While he was asking me questions, he was swilling ale. Because he hadn't eaten, the ale worked quickly and he fell asleep. That was when I took the draughts and more medicine for your arm. I hid it out on deck. Then I lay down and slept, myself. He woke me up this morning and told me to get you and prepare breakfast."

"They're coming now, Caleb. Stay out of their way. We'll sit here in the corner and eat."

As Caleb and Sirena ate in the far corner of the galley, they listened to the conversation among the cursing crewmen, at the central table. The seamen spoke of the storm's intensity, and of how it may have driven them far off their course — which, to Sirena's surprise and delight, appeared to be Java.

"It's hard to tell, Hans," Blackheart yelled at his first mate. "We'll have to check with the stars. We may be farther to the south than you think. I'll wager we've not gone far off course!"

Later, clearing off the plank table, Sirena was smiling. "Caleb, I've been thinking. How many draughts did you steal?"

"Enough, I believe, to put the crew asleep for days."

"Good! We'll put it in their coffee and take it out on deck. Now that the sea has calmed considerably and the sun's appeared again, the men will be glad for the fresh air. They've, most of them, been confined these past two days and will willingly come on deck at our suggestion. You're sure the brigantine is nowhere near?"

"Aye. It hasn't been in sight for three days. But what happens afterward, Señorita? Neither of us is fit to handle the ship."

"We'll drift with the trade winds for a time. And we can sit on the deck and heal our wounds. It will be simple to find our course again."

Caleb watched her skeptically. Though the Señorita spoke confidently, he had noticed a fleeting, tortured expression in her jade-green eyes. Did she truly believe her physical and spiritual wounds would heal, or did she speak with such confidence only for his sake? How would she explain what had happened aboard the *Rana*? What would become of her when it was discovered that she was a used woman? Could she face the derision? And, did she really expect that the two of them could bring the ship into port alone?

The boy was shaken from these thoughts by the entrance of Captain Blackheart, who sat down at the rough table and called for more coffee. Caleb replenished his thick mug.

The pirate's voice was a low growl in the quiet galley. "We'll make port by tomorrow, at nightfall. I'll set the boy ashore, but you'll stay aboard. I'll quarter you in my cabin. The men will leave you alone from now on."

"I'm to be your whore, is that it?" Sirena demanded coldly, tossing her wealth of dark brown curls.

"And a fetching one you make!" Blackheart retorted, his voice surprisingly gentle. Though a rough man of the sea, he could appreciate Sirena's beauty. He looked at the perfect oval of her face. He had been wondering how that full, sensuous mouth would taste if offered willingly in a kiss. Her body had the slim, carved beauty of a ship's figurehead: high, full breasts and low, narrow hips. But it was her legs — tawny-skinned, slender, and supple, muscularly chiseled and far longer than a woman had a right to possess — that had fascinated him.

Sirena was sickened by the lust she saw in his face. The foul stench from his mouth carried across to where she sat, and she found the animal stink of his body vile and offensive. Furthermore, she did not think she could cope with one more attack on her bruised body.

"Finish up now. Just leave the food on the table for the midday meal. The boy will then bring you to my cabin — the first mate will see to it that you arrive safely. Now that the storm is spent, the men begin to think of other pastimes."

Sirena watched Blackheart leave the galley, and hatred was alive and running rampant in her. Dear God, not again! It was then that she remembered she had renounced her god.

Seeing the beaten expression on Caleb's face, she hastened to reassure him. "Once more, little one, then we'll follow your plan. He can't hurt me anymore. You'll place all the sleeping powders in the bucket of coffee you take to the crew. Most of them will be on deck now. Call down to the others to come up. Be sure you see them drink it. Lace the coffee with rum. That way, it won't be refused."

"Aye, you can rely on me, Señorita. I . . . I'd better take you to Captain Blackheart now. I'll lay out the meal. It'll go easier with you if he's not angry."

Sirena, dreading the ordeal, moistened her parched lips. "Caleb, you're a good friend, the best I've ever had. Do you think you can call me Sirena? It would make me happy if you would."

Caleb's young face fell into lines of sorrow. "You call me friend . . . yet I must take you to the captain."

She hesitated a moment at the anguish she read in the boy's eyes. "There are worse things in life than having someone abuse your body. I'll be all right, truly I will! Just the thought that soon we'll be free will give me strength. One day we'll find them, you and I, and it'll be a different tune they sing. I give you my word on it! The day will come for us — believe me!"

The oak-paneled cabin with its sparse furnishings was quiet and still. The captain had not yet arrived. Irresistibly, Sirena's eyes fell on a chair near the mullioned windows. In it Isabel had sat reading or reciting her prayers; it had been brought here from the sterncastle. Pulling her gaze away, Sirena swallowed bitter tears. "I won't cry! I won't!" Her brave words to Caleb seemed empty now. Instead, something her sister had said on the day of her death swelled within Sirena and resounded in her head. "I know God will intervene somehow and that this marriage will never come to pass." Isabel had been so serene, so hopeful when she'd said those words.

61

"You spoke the truth, sweet Isabel. Something did happen . . . And now you are dead. But I'll find a way to avenge you — or the Devil take my soul! After I've dealt with this animal crew I'll find the others, on the brigantine, and deal with them. But that pirate who wears a hook will receive a special fate for using you so brutally." The long red gash that had scored Isabel's body swam before Sirena's eyes and her determination to punish her sister's sadistic attacker was revitalized.

Heavy footsteps outside the cabin door announced the pirate captain's arrival. The low, narrow, oak door swung open and he ducked his shaggy black head, stepped inside, and crashed the door closed behind him. He threw the bolt.

Sirena knew that her presence was noted, yet he did not even glance in her direction. He moved to one of the narrow bunks, sat down, and began to remove his boots. His disregard of her was more shattering to her nerves than if he had immediately attacked her.

She remained standing near the windows, her heart beating rapidly, her breath ragged in anticipation of the ordeal. When at last he chose to notice her, he had discarded his shirt and belt. The sight of his muscular chest with its mat of chocolate-colored hair reminded her of the first time she had seen him, on that fateful day when the brigantine had accosted the *Rana*.

He spoke, his voice a deep basso growl. "You're frightened, Señorita. I will not hurt you, so why do you stand there cowering?"

"You ask why? After the humiliation and degradation I've suffered at your hands and those of your crew?" Her words were hot with anger, her eyes flashed like shattered emeralds.

"That's all past," he said, coming toward her. "You're mine now. The crew won't come near you again."

Sirena backed away, dreading the touch of his paw-like, callused hands. But there was no escaping his long arm, which reached out and pulled her toward him, crushing her. Savagely, he wound his fingers in her sable curls and yanked her head back until she thought her neck would snap. His thick, wet mouth burned her throat where he kissed her, nipping at her tender flesh, making her recoil.

She writhed to escape his grasp, but when she was almost free he caught her again and flung her onto the bunk. He stood over her, a lustful glitter in his eyes, his tongue moistening his viscous mouth. She cowered on the bunk, apprehensive of his next move.

Dick Blackheart appraised the woman on his bed; a temptress, enticingly seductive, full pouting lips parted, showing her straight and glistening white teeth. Her olive skin flushed pink, heightening the green of her eyes.

He threw himself on her, his weight pushing her down into the bedding. But his intimate touches to her stiff, unyielding flesh were light, seductive in their intent. His kisses to her unwilling mouth, throat, and breasts, however, were fraught with suppressed frenzy.

Sirena could not allow him to do this to her without a struggle. This attempt at arousing her was almost worse than the attacks she had suffered previously. At those times they had used her, expected nothing of her, merely demanding that she be a receptacle for their lusty cravings. But this! This blatant attempt to elicit a willing response from her. It was an admission that she was alive, real, capable of choice. That this barbarian should assume that she could be enticed by his advances was adding outrage to her already wounded dignity. She couldn't — she *wouldn't* — allow him to assume she would respond like a seductive wanton to his insidious caresses.

"Get your filthy English hands off me! Leave me alone!" she spat out, pushing him away and wriggling from under him.

The shock on his grizzly face was almost comical.

Sirena wrestled to her feet, her eyes flying to the door and its bolt. The helplessness of her situation nearly rendered her insensible. Even if she could make her escape from this animal where could she run? Over the rail into the waiting sea? Then what would become of Caleb? She could not leave him to face Blackheart's wrath! And what of their plan to regain control of the *Rana*? How could she dash the young boy's hopes, and her own?

In that moment of indecision the captain was upon her.

Well . . . if she must be raped by this animal it wouldn't be without a fight. She lashed out blindly, her nails gouging the flesh over his cheekbones. He cuffed her on the back of the head, then pinioned her arms to her sides. Her struggles were the minuscule protests of a flea biting a dog.

"So! There's spirit in you yet!" he crowed exultantly.

Forcing her to the floor, he held her wrists above her head with one powerful hand. She spit and snarled, twisting her head, trying to sink her teeth into his capturing arm. He struck her on the face, smashing her lower lip against her teeth. Her mouth was suddenly full of blood and she found it difficult to breathe because her nose had received a glance from his blow and was bleeding profusely too.

His knee was forcing her legs apart, his free hand was touching her breasts, her stomach, between her thighs. His face was directly above hers now, grinning salaciously down. She sprayed his beast's face with spittle and blood.

With that, his free hand flew to her throat and made it impossible to breathe. She choked, grappling for air till she felt her lungs would burst. Then slowly, gradually, her struggles abated and she felt herself slipping into sweet oblivion . . .

Imperceptibly, Sirena began to realize it was easier to breathe, Blackheart's pressing weight was gone. Her eyelids fluttered open slowly, as if weighted. Hazily she watched him pour himself a tankard of ale. Swallowing, he uttered a grunt of satisfaction and collapsed drowsily in a chair.

"Now, Señorita," he smiled almost benignly, "you are mine!"

"You can take me morning, noon, and night" — she spat out her words, disgust and repulsion vivid on her face — "but I'll never be yours. Never!"

Sirena emerged from the cabin raw and bruised. Hatred spilled from her like honey from a comb. If it was the last thing she ever did, she would get her revenge!

Standing outside the cabin door, she suddenly realized how calmly the *Rana* rode. The storm seemed to have run its course. Had Caleb done his work? Somehow she would have to force some of the coffee into the captain, but no — not for all the gold in the world would she ever set foot in that cabin again while he was in it. But he mustn't be allowed to come on deck and find his crew asleep. Caleb would have to do it. Soon it would be over.

Sunlight had begun to peep shyly out from the cloud cover. The storm spent, the sea was beautiful, surging gracefully beneath the ship's hull.

Raking her gaze down the length of the forward deck, she saw the crew drowsily hanging onto rigging or sprawling contentedly on the deck. Those who were still able to notice her made no move to stop her as she began to search for Caleb. Not finding him, Sirena panicked and called out his name. When he didn't answer, she ran lightly down the length of the deck. She heaved a sigh when she saw him emerge from the captain's cabin. He winked slyly as he passed her, his bucket swinging loosely at his side.

"One more cup for the lot and the *Rana* will again be yours, Sirena," he smiled.

The men swilled second cups of the steaming coffee, thankful for its warmth and the liberal lacing of rum.

"You go to the galley and rest a bit, Sirena," the boy said to her when he'd served the crew. "You'll need your strength for what we're about to do."

"I could be dying and I'd find the strength," Sirena responded grimly, her face full of hate. "Have no fear, little one, I'll do you credit." Her voice was weary and a feverish brightness was returning to her eyes.

"Sirena, your fever is returning. Have you looked at your arm?"

"No," she answered woodenly. "In truth I'm afraid to look, for I can't think of myself going through life with only one."

"Now would be a good time to dress your wound. It will be a time yet before the captain and his crew are well under the drug."

"All right, but let's hurry! The sooner the *Rana* is ours, the better I'll feel."

Caleb returned a moment later with clean dressing. When he uncovered her arm, they both gasped at the angry, swollen wound. "I'll have to lance it again," he said fearfully.

"I know. Do it!"

Sirena clenched her teeth as the knife found its mark. A whoop of pain escaped the weary girl as Caleb drained the wound. Rubbing some foul dark salve into it, and sprinkling it liberally with a healing powder, he sighed and began to wrap a clean cloth about Sirena's arm while the girl sat groaning on the foredeck.

Working diligently for over an hour, they hefted the seamen into the ship's small jolly-boat with the aid of a rope and winch. Only once had they spoken during their task. This was when, at the start, Sirena ordered him to throw the men over the side.

"But, Sirena, these are shark waters. They'll die."

"And you think I care if they're ripped to shreds, is that it? Well, I don't care! Toss them over!"

Caleb peered deeply into her burning eyes. While her voice demanded their death, her eyes were saying something else.

"Sirena, there's nothing I would not do for you, but I can't do this. It would be murder! I'll lower them in the jolly-boat and let them take their chances. You said there would be a time and a place when the reckoning would come. Please hold to that!"

"Your heart is made of jelly, young Caleb. Do what you will," she said as she swayed against the rigging.

Caleb's eyes were sick as he looked at her. As soon as the captain went over the side into the boat, Caleb released the lines, freeing the dinghy. The wind caught the sails of the *Rana* and spurred the frigate away from the drifting dinghy.

Sirena was weaving unsteadily and her eyes were glazed and feverish. Caleb was frightened, not only for himself but for Sirena. What would he do now if she died . . . ?

Chapter Three

For five days and nights Sirena lay in a delirium. She had exhausted her last reserves of strength in helping Caleb lower the crew and captain into the jolly-boat and had fallen into what was, at first, a death-like sleep. From time to time, however, she cried out in pain, and at other moments she would shout hoarsely for Isabel. In between, she cursed the Dutch and all they stood for.

Caleb wanted to cry, but there was nothing for him to do but watch her. His youth and inexperience made him angry with himself. He believed that if he were older he would know how to help her. For a time he thought the sea-water baths were helping her arm, but the next day, when he changed the bandage once more, the wound looked angrier than before. The medicinal powder was almost gone and he had nothing to use in its place. Dejectedly, he sat down next to her and continued applying cold compresses to her head. Sirena Córdez had always seemed impervious to pain — and now she was so vulnerable to it. And Caleb could do nothing but sit and watch her suffering.

Five days after the sending off of the pirates, it was time to change the dressing again. He would use the last packet of powder.

Dreading to see the wound, he closed his eyes as he untied the bandage. Merciful God! He blinked disbelievingly. The greenish-yellow pus was gone. A slight scab was forming over the gash and there was no drainage. He rolled his tearful eyes heavenward and sprinkled on the powder, replacing the soiled bandage with a clean one.

Timidly, he reached out to touch Sirena's brow, and was not surprised to find it cooler. An idea sprung into his head. Reaching the captain's quarters, he searched for the jug of rum. His feet were sure and steady on the rolling deck as he ran back to Sirena.

Holding her head in the crook of his arm, he poured some of the rum down her throat. She gagged and sputtered.

"Caleb — are you — trying to kill me?" Sirena smiled weakly.

Caleb, overjoyed to have her conscious again, burst into a fit of laughter. "Your death is exactly what I'm trying to avoid, Sirena."

Caleb didn't know if she had heard him. Sirena had closed her eyes and was falling into the first natural sleep she'd had in five days.

She slept most of the afternoon and, when she awoke, Caleb had a tray ready with hot soup and black bread.

"So, I live after all . . ." She pierced the boy with a steady eye. "Why didn't you let me die? What good am I to anyone now?"

Refusing to listen to her, he began to tell her of their situation. "The *Rana* is drifting south, I believe, and I've not seen another ship."

"That's good. Why do you look troubled?"

"You were very sick and you said many strange things." His closed face and averted eyes resisted any further questioning.

Nursing Sirena back to health, Caleb was cheerful and helpful, anticipating her every need. A few days later Sirena again questioned him about what was on his mind. He described her delirium but again refused to answer any further questions.

At length, Sirena began to tell him something of herself, and of Isabel, and why the two sisters had been on their way to Java. As she spoke, an idea was born in her mind and she began to tell it to Caleb . . .

"Caleb, Mynheer van der Rhys is expecting a bride to arrive . . . and I wouldn't want to see him disappointed. I've told you of the marriage contract concerning Isabel. What would you say . . . if I told you I intend to take her place?"

Caleb was incredulous, his black eyes sparkled quizzically.

"Don't look at me that way," Sirena laughed, liking her idea more by the moment. "Regan van der Rhys, as representative of the Dutch Crown in these isles, is doubtless responsible for the attack on the *Rana*, I'd stake my life on it! He must have a score of privateers in his employ, if only to protect his shipping. And they would not be averse to attacking Spanish and Portuguese ships — with or without his orders. I'm puzzled — but angrier than words can tell — that he gave no orders to his marauders to let pass the Spanish vessel in which his intended bride was arriving! He is, therefore, ultimately responsible for Isabel's and Tio Juan's deaths! I want to see him pay for what he did to us!"

"But how will you do *that?*" Caleb asked, not

71

liking the determined look in her eye.

"I don't know . . . yet. But as his wife I would soon find ways. The brigantine that attacked us was Dutch-built — and under the orders of the Dutch East India Company, I'd wager. Perhaps I can discover a way to undermine the Dutch hold on these waters. Destroy their business, destroy their power — and the Dutch economy will be ruined, leaving a wide perch for the Spanish to sit on!"

She smiled maliciously. "What do you think, Caleb, will it work? Will you join me in this little adventure? I'll say you're my brother, and that way we can stay together. We'll concoct some story to tell the Dutchman that will satisfy him. Now run and get me the maps and charts. I want to see if I can calculate where we are."

The young boy was delighted to have his señorita once again interested in living — even if her plans did seem wild. "I swear you my allegiance, Captain Sirena. I'll do as you say!" His round, handsome face was so serious that Sirena laughed for the first time since the brigantine had attacked her *Rana*.

Caleb brought the maps and charts to her from the deserted captain's quarters. "These are mostly Captain López's, and your uncle's. But these soiled maps, I think, are Captain Blackheart's. They were in a separate pile."

Sirena reached for the pirate's maps. "Why, they're done in great detail, and show the inlets, shoals, reefs, and straits around Java, Bali, and southern Sumatra!" she exclaimed, her knowledge of geography coming back to her as she pointed out the island to Caleb. She was grateful to Don Antonio Córdez and de Silva, his master-at-arms, for not neglecting this aspect of her education. "This is very curious. Generally, pirates have only more simple maps — and poorly drawn ones at that! These — these greatly detailed types are usually made for traders, not for marauders. And, look — these words at the sides and near the bottom! They're in Dutch, not Spanish! This makes me believe, even more surely, that Blackheart and his men were in Dutch employ. And, who controls Dutch shipping — and, doubtless, Dutch marauding on Spanish ships — in this region? Mynheer Regan van der Rhys, of course!"

She pored over the maps, and the effort made her poor head swim.

"Let's wait until this evening, when I can take a reading from the stars," she said. "I think we're not far off the south coast of Java. Perhaps another three days and we'll make port."

Caleb sighed. Sirena had had a look in her eye when she spoke of van der Rhys that boded ill for the Dutchman. Yes, Caleb would place his purse on Sirena if it came to a wager. He almost felt sorry for the Dutchman. Still, if he were responsible — even indirectly — for the attack on the *Rana* then he deserved whatever it was she would do.

Two more days had passed and Sirena was rapidly regaining her strength. The dressing had been removed and the sun was now allowed to caress the angry wound.

"It itches," she complained.

"That's good. It means it heals inside as well as

out," Caleb chided her.

"How do you know so much about medicine and doctoring?"

"I don't, but I'm learning!"

Now that Sirena felt so much better, she decided to rummage through her trunks and find something more suitable to wear than the long, tattered — and now rather filthy — shirt Caleb had tossed her immediately after her ordeal with the pirates. But her long, full-skirted gowns, with their stiffly starched crinolines, would never do — though she could use her bright crimson silk scarf to tie about her head to keep her hair from blowing into her eyes. And her mid-calf-high boots of glove-soft leather could be worn; they would permit her firmer footing than the thin, light slippers she had been wearing.

In desperation she turned to her Uncle Juan's trunk. Although some of the contents had been taken by the pirates, she did find a pair of black trousers. Don Juan Córdez y Savar had been a tall and slender man but his trousers would fit snugly over her wider, femininely rounded hips. Yet Sirena needed movement, and the wide lower parts of the trouser legs would prevent this. To remedy the situation she slashed at the material with her knife and threw the cuttings away. Slipping the shortened trousers on and pulling them up over her hips, she regretted her impatience: they were very short — barely covering her lithe, muscled haunches.

Discarding the ragged shirt in disgust, she sorted through more of Juan's wardrobe and selected a blouse of bright scarlet. Hastily, she tore away the lower parts of the sleeves and donned it, tying the shirt's tails tightly into a knot high on her ribs beneath her full breasts. Adjusting the scarf about her head and lacing the black boots, she dashed over to the shiny polished-metal mirror hanging behind the cabin door.

She studied herself with amazement. A woman long of limb and torso, dark hair haloing her proud head, then cascading from the scarlet bandana. But her expression belied the amazement. Lips parted to show fine white teeth, she exuded a brazen aura of feline grace — an animal beauty, wild and untamable.

What she saw pleased her. The costume befitted a lady pirate.

But wait! Something was missing. Swiftly, she ran and reached into the trunk and drew from it a black leather belt, then fastened it low on her hips. Slipping her knife under it, she again appraised her reflection and laughingly approved.

The *Rana* kept her course for two more days and, with the passing of each, Sirena's strength increased. She stood at the ship's wheel, exhilarated by the sun and wind and rolling sea.

Young Caleb came out on deck and Sirena was once again struck by his youthful beauty. Dark, thick, tousled hair fell over his smooth brow to accentuate the startling blackness of his eyes and his long, sooty lashes. His sturdy young body held a promise of tall, broad-shouldered manhood. His remarkable strength of character had helped Sirena through an agonizing ordeal.

Sirena smiled fondly at him. "By sunup we'll

sight Java. Have you got our story straight?"

"Aye!" He returned her smile. Caleb loved to see her this way, laughing and happy, ready to face life with the same verve with which she turned her beautiful face into the wind. "I know what to say. All hands lost at sea. Everything went overboard to lighten the ship. You are betrothed to Mynheer van der Rhys and I'm your brother. Thank the Lord I've learned some Spanish — *and* a smattering of Dutch — during my travels on the *Lord Raleigh* and with your own fleet these past months. The trunks containing my belongings were lost at sea; fortunately yours were saved. No mention of pirates or what they did to us." A touch of impatience tinged his words. Sirena had rehearsed him so many times since she first devised her plan.

"That's the straight of it, Caleb. Remember, our uncle went overboard with the crew and we're in mourning. There mustn't be any hint of Isabel, however. And give Mynheer van der Rhys no hint that we intend to discover whether it was indeed his marauders, English-speaking or not, who did us harm."

"I can remember, Sirena," Caleb assured her.

His boy's heart hardened with resolution. He would die before he let her down. Caleb's mind still held the memory of her eyes, brilliant with determination to "discover" van der Rhys, and the deadly calm with which she had said, "Power is the life's blood to men like van der Rhys! I'll *ruin him* and see him grovel — a broken man — for what he did to us!"

"Caleb" — Sirena's voice brought him back to the present — "bring the maps out here to me.

76

There's no sense struggling to read them by lamp-light in the cabin."

"Aye, Sirena." He knew she had an aversion to the cabin since Dick Blackheart had occupied it.

On the boy's return, moments later, they sat near the ship's wheel, poring over the charts. When Sirena had estimated their bearings as being just hours off the southern coast of Java, she began rerolling the maps and slipping them back into their protective leather pouches.

"I also found *this* in the cabin, Sirena." Caleb held out a long, cylindrical black leather pouch bearing the Córdez crest. "I believe Blackheart took it from your uncle's belongings."

Accepting the pouch from Caleb's outstretched hand, Sirena remembered seeing her Uncle Juan carefully place it deep between layers of his clothing. When she had asked him what it was, he had answered simply that it was a wedding gift for Mynheer van der Rhys.

Curious, she opened the leather thong draw-string and withdrew a thin, fine-grained animal skin — possibly goat skin, she thought. It had been tanned and was soft and pliant in her hands. It was a map. In the lower right-hand corner of the irregularly shaped hide was the map's legend, and from its style she deemed it to be several hundred years old, if not more. On saying so to Caleb, he asked how she could know this, and she explained to him that her uncle was a collector of ancient shipping charts and had shared his interest with her.

"It's an old map of the Indies, Caleb. Look, here's Borneo, there's New Guinea." She pointed. "Sumatra, Java . . . Although they're labeled in what looks like Arabic, or perhaps even Persian."

Caleb broke in excitedly, "In the islands they speak of Moslem kings — sultans — who sailed the seas with their navies here long ago. Legend has it that they looted the islands and killed many natives in search of gemstones and gold."

When the top of the map was unrolled completely, a delicate slip of paper slithered out and fell to the deck. Sirena picked it up and read the few short words. It was addressed to Regan van der Rhys; it was a note of congratulation on the wedding between the Córdez family and the van der Rhys. Sirena frowned.

Caleb was quite obviously fascinated with the map. Sirena explained to him what she knew of the early European explorations among these, the Spice Islands, telling him how, as early as 1525, the Dutch — blast them — followed the routes established by the Portuguese to the Indies and the Far East. When they arrived on the marshy shores of the Spice Islands, they felt almost at home among the network of waterways, which were indeed almost like a tropical "Holland." The Dutch felt they could offer the Portuguese stiff competition for the commercial conquest of the East. Just forty years before, in 1583, the burgesses of Amsterdam had founded the predecessor of the Dutch East India Company. They called it the "Company of Far Countries," and they had commissioned heavily armed ships to follow the Portuguese routes as far as possible beyond the Cape of Good Hope to the Kingdom of Spices. Because of a royal marriage, however, Spain and Portugal became in effect one kingdom and banded their forces together, the Spanish now sending out ships from their Far Eastern "capital" of Manila, in the Philippines, to aid the Portuguese in the Indies, to the south. The Dutch soon found themselves harassed at every turn. And soon the Spanish were as firmly entrenched in the Spice Islands as were the Portuguese. Only in this new century had the Dutch frequently gained the upper hand in trading.

Caleb's eyes returned to the old map, which, though it might not be as accurate as López's or Uncle Juan's or Dick Blackheart's soiled maps of the straits, inlets, and various islands of the Indies, gave interesting details of its own. "Look at these drawings of volcanos! Look, Sirena! See, here on Sumatra! I've seen them with my own eyes. And here, these on Java! I've seen some of them, too. Just sitting up out of the blue like some angry gods! But I had no idea there were so many of them!"

"What do you think these funny little drawings are next to the islands?" Sirena inquired, puzzled.

"Why, they're trees. Look. Cinnamon! Bay!" His finger darted across the unfurled skin. "Nutmeg, cloves, peppercorns . . . ginger, mace, aloes! The old map shows each area and what treasure is to be found there!"

Sirena and Caleb studied the old chart for some time and, heads spinning and eyes aching from deciphering the fine old writing, they at last began to curl the chart in order to replace it in its case. It was then that Sirena noticed a drawing of Java alone — in enlarged detail — on the back side of the skin.

Upon examination of the drawing, Caleb appeared to be surprised.

"What is it, boy?" Sirena asked.

"This river, Sirena. This river some short distance from Batavia. It must be the one that lies to the west of the town, beyond one of two volcanos that stand one on each side of its mouth . . ."

"Well?"

"You notice the drawings of ships passing up the river, and inland? I'm puzzled. You see, the natives of Java call it the River of Death, because it's impassable. The mouth of the river is wide — as it is drawn here. But there are rapids not far upstream, and the shallows at the mouth are treacherous. Only native proas enter and leave its mouth. The European merchants neither enter it or ever anchor there. Of course they've little need to use it, for the Java chieftains send down to Batavia all their spices by native carriers. And look," he continued, "there appears to be a cove, upstream some distance — and the mapmaker has drawn in two vessels, which appear to be anchored there!"

Sirena's eyes indicated that she was deeply considering something. Caleb went on.

"I've seen the River of Death when I was here aboard the *Lord Raleigh* a year ago. We bought some spices from the Dutch and Spanish in Batavia, and then traveled west, past the river and its two volcanos. Not far off, upriver, we could see a waterfall — perhaps less than three miles away, for the river is not a long one."

80

Almost with reverence Sirena picked up the skin. If what the map showed of the River of Death were true . . . perhaps, in later times, some eruption had shallowed and partly blocked the mouth of the river and earned it its cruel name. But maybe there was still a way to cross those shallows. That cove, upstream, offered possibilities . . .

Caleb noted Sirena's glittering eyes and shivered involuntarily. Nevertheless, whatever she did, he was behind her all the way; he had sworn her his allegiance and he would abide by it. He knew instinctively that the map was a wedding present Regan van der Rhys would never receive.

Chapter Four

Sirena's first sight of Java — its westernmost tip — left her breathless. Green . . . green . . . green was the only word she could find to describe the high-rising jewel that stood over the horizon at the first light of day.

Entering the Sunda Strait, which separated the island from its larger neighbor, Sumatra, the *Rana* drew in toward the shore and Sirena saw two volcanos in the near-distance, the masts of some ships and what looked like a town a bit farther east. She and Caleb managed to bring the frigate in toward Java, and approached the River of Death.

They watched the current of the river enter the sea, its frothy backwash swelling and churning.

"See, I told you" — Caleb pulled on her arm — "there's no way up that river. Even the current's against it!"

Sirena lifted her eyes to the topsail and squinted against the sun. "We're going to try it," she said in a quiet and solemn voice.

"Sirena, we can't! We'll be dashed on the rocks!" His words went unnoticed, which added to his fears. Her mouth was set in determination and she had already begun to steer the *Rana* toward the river's mouth. Then, appealing to the sailor in her: "Sirena, we've no crew. Just the two of us can't get the *Rana* up that deadly river!"

"I think we can! Look at the flag on the topsail. See the way it's blowing? Now look ahead. See? We've caught a westerly wind. There are rocks visible in its mouth there, on the right. But look to the other side, where there appears to be a clear channel. We'll sail right on up the river in that crevasse as if we were out in open water."

Caleb saw the logic behind her thinking and had to agree that it might not be a problem, but he protested again. "But even a frigate draws too much water."

"Perhaps . . ." Sirena muttered, "but I say we can do it!"

It was clear to Caleb that Sirena would not attempt it without his agreement — but she was like a dog with a bone. She would worry the subject until she wore him down and dragged a Yes out of him. Deciding to save time and nerves, Caleb shrugged his shoulders and agreed. "Let's do it, then. *I've* nothing to lose and *you've* only the *Rana* at stake. If you can bear to lose her . . ." He shrugged again.

"I won't lose her! Never! Now, please, go to the cabin and get me the chart. I want to find that cove in the river."

As the *Rana* sailed closer to the river mouth, they saw that, to the right, the fresh river waters churned over the slick, glossy-black rocks and mixed, foaming, with the blue of the sea. Under Sirena's orders, Caleb struggled to lower all but the mizzen sail. Sirena strained at the wheel, keeping to the left of the rocks in what, indeed, was a sort of channel in the river mouth.

The *Rana* rose and fell in the swell of waves, her

bow nosing valiantly, majestically out of the surf. Sirena held her breath and squeezed her eyes shut, praying she would not hear the crash and splintering of her beloved ship's hull against unseen, submerged boulders.

Minutes passed, but the wind lifted the *Rana* and drove her deftly through the channel past the rocks at the river's mouth!

Caleb shouted, "We made it! We did it!"

Daring to open her eyes, Sirena saw that they had indeed made it. The ship had skittered beyond the rocks and was now holding her own, with the aid of the prevailing westerly wind, against a swift but manageable river current.

Though rapid, the river flowed through a low, flat valley flanked on either side by the steep heights of the volcanos Sirena had seen on the ancient map — and also on one of Dick Blackheart's maps. In the distance, she spied the waterfall Caleb had described, and closer, the rapids he'd mentioned. But, suddenly, to her left — in the direction of Batavia — was a huge cove of calm deep water. Deeper water than that of the river itself, Sirena judged. And the cove was concealed behind the steep slopes of the easternmost volcano, which smoked high above them.

With Caleb's quick help, she turned the *Rana* at a ninety-degree angle and sailed into the placid waters of the cove.

The emerald-green foliage that surrounded the cove was thick with flowers. Birds called out in strange warblings that broke the eerie silence. Slowly, the *Rana* nestled into the steep cliff that formed one side of the cove.

A marvelous anchoring place! Sirena and Caleb were delighted with their victory over the River of Death, and with this haven for the *Rana*. Weighing anchor, they felt giddy with their success.

"Come, Caleb," Sirena challenged, posing bootless atop the rail of the ship. "I'll race you to the shore!" She dove into the deep waters and swam toward a miniature shoreline behind which the Javanese jungle rose steeply.

Following Caleb's direction, she could just barely see the red-tiled roof of D.E.I. Chief Pensioner Mynheer Regan van der Rhys's house. Caleb assured her it was the most splendid on the island — a sprawling two-story building built in Portuguese fashion with thick masonry walls to keep out the heat of the tropical sun. The estate was huge, encompassing thousands of acres of clove and cinnamon trees. But Sirena was unimpressed by van der Rhys's wealth and her possible share in it. With a calculating eye she measured the distance from the top of the rise where she stood to the van der Rhys mansion; just above two miles, she guessed. The cover where the *Rana* was anchored lay back through the jungle and down the opposite side of the rise, nearly equally distant from her.

"Caleb, the *Rana* needs a crew. Where are we to find one for her?"

"A crew . . . ? But why?"

"To carry out my plan against the Dutchman, of course! Now, think! Where can we get a crew? I want good men, mind you! No scurvy lot will man my ship!"

Caleb was obviously rattled by this extreme change in her mood. Only moments ago Sirena was placid, tranquil; she had allowed the green lushness of the jungle to work its spirit-healing ways. Now she was tightly strung again, boiling with determination, the fire of vengeance blazing in her thickly lashed eyes.

"Sirena, I know of some men — stout and hearty men, too — who live in a tiny fishing village, Teatoa, we passed before we sailed up the river. The village lies west of Batavia. Those men are fishers these days, but once were sailors on one of the finest ships of the Dutch East India fleet!"

"Dutchmen! Caleb, where are your wits? Dutchmen on my *Rana*? How much use do you think *they* would be to me? They would never strike a blow to their own countrymen!"

"Working for the Dutch East India Company does not make a man a Dutchman. In fact, two of the men I'm thinking of are Malayans who signed on with the company. But the others are Dutch with a very bitter taste now for the company."

"Bitter? How so?"

"Bitter because of forced retirement. The D.E.I. pays them a pitifully small pension and has declared them unfit for service. They are survivors of the plague that once riddled the ship they sailed. They were, as are all plague victims, denied readmittance to Holland — to their home and their families! Instead, they fish to feed their bellies and hate the Dutch East India Company to nourish their souls! I talked with them at length when the *Lord Raleigh* was at anchor here."

"And you think they would sign on the *Rana*

86

even if they knew I intended to sail her against the Dutch?"

"They would sign on the *Rana* just to feel like men again! To be useful and to feel the sea rolling beneath the decks."

Sirena considered Caleb's words for a moment and the risk she would be taking in revealing herself and her hiding place to these banished Dutchmen. She spoke softly, barely audibly. "Then, Caleb . . . you must bring these men to me."

While Caleb trod the long path back over the hills behind the waterfall to the fishing village, Sirena busied herself aboard the frigate. Above decks and below, she went over every inch of the ship to be certain no evidence of the pirate attack remained for her new crew to see. Perhaps later she would decide to tell them what had happened, but for the time being she preferred to keep it her secret and Caleb's.

She hesitated outside the cabin which Dick Blackheart had occupied — the scene of her final humiliating experience. Pushing thoughts of that degradation from her mind, she opened the door and stepped inside. Quickly, she crossed the distance to the wide, mullioned windows that made up the back wall of the room and threw aside the heavy draperies. Light streamed into the square cabin, illuminating millions of dancing dust motes.

Sirena wrinkled her nose at the musty smell mixed with the scent of stale sweat and sour ale, and tried not to think of Isabel.

A timid knock sounded on the cabin door. Sirena lifted her dark head from the maps she was intent upon. "Come," she called quietly.

"Sirena, this is Jan, one of the men I spoke of."

The woman straightened to her full height and authoritatively extended her hand. "I am Sirena Córdez, captain of this ship," she said quietly, looking deep into the man's eyes. He was returning her handshake with a grip as firm as her own.

"Jan Verhooch, Señorita. The boy has spoken of you and this ship you . . . captain. Forgive me, too, if I seem surprised; I thought I knew the island, but I must confess my ignorance of this cove. How did you find your way into it?"

"I found it on the advice of ancient kings," Sirena laughed lightly. She had no wish to share the secret of the Persian charts.

Seeing he would not receive a direct answer to his inquiry, Jan asked, "What is it you want of me and the men in our small village?"

"I am searching for a crew to man this ship. Reliable, honest men who will do my bidding with no questions asked."

"You ask this and will tell me nothing in return?"

"I need a crew," Sirena repeated, her tone firm.

"There is no captain — be she man *or* woman — whom I would sail for on mere blind faith. Tell me what it is you want, and I will give you my decision. It is a fair request."

"Aye, fair it is." So, she thought, I'm forced already to tell my story. Yet perhaps it's for the best. "Very well, Jan. Several weeks ago I boarded this ship — my own — with my uncle, my sister, and young Caleb. We were approaching Java, where we were bringing my sister, Isabel, to marry Mynheer van der Rhys, when we were attacked by pirates. My sister was raped and killed — gored from neck to navel by a pirate who carried a hook for a hand. I, myself, suffered at their hands . . ." Her lowered eyes conveyed her meaning. "Caleb managed to aid me and we made our escape." She explained the drugging of the captain and the ship's crew. "I carry a memento of the —" quickly, she rolled up the sleeve of her shirt to reveal the scar that ran the length of her upper arm. She smiled at the man's indrawn breath. "I see you have not seen many such wounds."

"Aye, it's true. Rarely have I seen a wound such as that."

"Regan van der Rhys was, I am certain, responsible for what happened to my sister and myself and my uncle. The brigantine was Dutch-built, English-captained, and I found Dutch trader's maps. Now he will have to pay — and pay dearly — for what he has cost me in honor and family. I plan to assume my sister's purpose and marry Mynheer van der Rhys. I will lead two lives: one, the demure wife; the other, a witch of the seas. I plan to ruin him as he ruined me. To do this I need a crew and a loyal one . . . You may keep whatever cargo you wish, when we board ship, and divide it among the men. But, also, I will pay a fair wage for all. You must swear your allegiance to me and obey me as if I were a man. Can you do this?" she demanded.

Pale blue eyes searched the depth of the green

ones opposite. "The boy tells me you command this frigate better than any man."

"Yes, Jan, I command this frigate. I think it would be safe to say that I can do it . . . *as well as* any man. I brought the ship through the mouth of the river — which, I'm told by Caleb, is called by the natives the River of Death. Perhaps that will help to convince you of my abilities."

"The boy has already told me of this. Very well . . . Capitana," he said, bowing low, "I will sign aboard this ship, as will the other men. This day I swear my loyalty and allegiance to you and you only."

"I plan to keep the *Rana* berthed in this cove. You and the crew you provide me with, since you come from a village west of the river and Batavia lies to the east, will easily be able to come aboard unseen and unsuspected by the Dutch or Spanish trading companies in the town. You will be able to prepare the ship, while awaiting my arrival, so that we shall be ready to sail. Until that time comes, however — and you will know, by a message I send with Caleb to the village — I will employ you, a bit . . . For I want the frigate painted black and her sails dyed to match. Also, her name must be obliterated," Sirena added haltingly, overcoming a catch in her throat. "As far as the world is concerned, the *Rana* lies at the ocean's bottom. Ready the ship and lay in stores soon, for I may want to set sail sooner that I now believe."

"I will take care of all this," Jan said quietly.

"One more thing, Jan. Mynheer van der Rhys will have to be informed of my arrival. Go to him, tell him you and your crew were fishing as usual

90

and happened to see the storm-tossed, invalid *Rana* off the Java coast. The seas we weathered a few days ago are common knowledge in every port of these islands. He'll believe you when you tell him the frigate was half underwater when you found her. But he may be surprised when he learns she contained no crew but me and Caleb — whom, you must explain to him, is my brother! He will doubtless be forced to conclude that one of his private marauders — knowing nothing of the expected arrival of his intended, *by his forgetting to tell them* — had murdered her Spanish crew and set her adrift with her brother. He knew, by letter, that his bride was to be en route for Java, but did not know that her sister accompanied her — so we are safe there. Nevertheless, he will expect that she had some companionship in addition to her brother; tell him of my Uncle Juan, and let him think that his privateers killed that worthy gentleman. For I must be in mourning! It is a part of my plan. Finally, tell Mynheer van der Rhys that Señorita Córdez and her brother are in your village and will be arriving at his home late this afternoon."

"It's as good as done," Jan said, smiling conspiratorially.

"Would you care for a glass of wine before you leave, Jan? We shall drink to a long, profitable relationship," Sirena said, pouring some port into elegant goblets that she withdrew from their hiding place beneath Captain López's bunk.

"To Mynheer van der Rhys's downfall," Jan shouted.

The goblets clicked against each other and

Sirena found herself smiling into the Dutch eyes of her first mate, noting ironically that this Dutchman would help her bring one of his countrymen down!

"To you, Capitana," he continued.

It was a moment before Sirena realized that Jan had coined a new word. She decided she liked it, it sat well on her. As the crew's "capitana" she would lead them on a course to destroy their common enemy, the Dutch East India Company, *and* Regan van der Rhys.

Chapter Five

Regan van der Rhys, tall and sun-gilded and with a neat white-blond thatch of hair, strode up and down his opulently appointed library, a fragrant cigar clenched between his perfect white teeth. Suddenly, and angrily, he took the slim black smoking stub from his mouth and crushed it into a pulpy mound in the glass tray on his teak desk. Hands clenched, he paced the room like a caged lion.

The last thing in this world Regan wanted was to marry again: a wife simply did not fit into his scheme of things. Now that she had actually arrived, he had learned that she brought with her a variety of problems. For one, her uncle had died and she would be in mourning.

"Damn!" Regan exclaimed. "This means that one of my privateers — those I use only to protect my traders from the Spanish — has run amuck and attacked the Señorita's ship! My warnings to those devil-may-care buccaneers should have been more explicit. Thank God they spared the lady and her brother! But for her uncle's death, I may be held responsible and rightly so. Still, the lady may not be so quick-witted as to make the connection . . ."

Regan considered himself knowledgeable on the mourning practices of Spanish ladies: heavy black gowns with high, choking collars and long, tight sleeves held aloft by dozens of horsehair crinolines; downcast features half hidden by a lace mantilla; fingers working feverishly over a chain of rosary beads.

A thought glimmered in his head. Perhaps propriety would be better served if he postponed his wedding until after the mourning period was over, but even as he thought it he negated the idea. The women on the island had wagging tongues. Merchants' wives, the agents' wives — all of them decreed the morals of the island. What they themselves did secretly behind the closed doors of their musk-scented boudoirs was another matter. But Regan knew he must marry the mournful señorita and preserve her reputation. No one would believe that Señorita Córdez could live beneath his roof and be safe from his advances.

Regan grinned wickedly as he thought of the rumors that peppered the drawing rooms of every captain, agent, and grower from the Sundra Strait to the China Sea. The men called him a rake — though they respected his expertise with his ships as well as with a woman, provided the woman wasn't one of their wives. Smiling at his reflection in the looking glass on the cedar-paneled wall, Regan decided he was flattered by the general consensus about the extent of his amours, though he knew the gossip to be greatly exaggerated.

Then his thoughts raced back to his intended. What would she look like? Probably a scarecrow of a woman, all bones and angles to prick a man in his bed. She would no doubt be as ugly as sin, and have teeth like a horse. He had personally seen the results of some of these arranged marriages. He would give the girl his name and a roof over her head. More than that he would not promise. "Damnation!" Regan roared, forcefully driving the fist of one hand into the palm of the other. He would take his pleasure where he found it and not rely on a skinny, narrow-eyed Spaniard's resentful submission to *his* lovemaking.

The van der Rhys wagon had come for Sirena and Caleb. It was driven by a small, loose-jointed man with shiny yellow skin and inquisitive, slanted eyes, who explained in halting Dutch that his name was Ling Fu and that the Mynheer had, he believed, sent the wagon to save the Juffrouw from the prying eyes of the townspeople. Although the trip through the jungles and hills was hotter and longer than traveling in a native proa, by skirting the shoreline the Juffrouw would be on display for all curious eyes in the port to see. Mynheer felt that the Juffrouw would not care to expose herself to this until she was rested from her ordeal.

His almond eyes cast downward in apology, Ling Fu shuffled his bare feet in the dust as he spoke.

To Sirena the meaning was clear: Mynheer van der Rhys did not want his bride to be seen until he himself had an opportunity to see what he was getting. Her first impulse was to feign exhaustion and demand to be taken by proa. But, although she didn't care to admit it, Sirena herself was not ready to meet those curious eyes. Yes, she and Caleb would ride to the Mynheer's estate in the wagon, skirting the town, and avoiding the possibility of meeting any of the Mynheer's friends.

Her trunks were loaded on the back of the wagon and Caleb climbed in after them. The single jounce seat in which Ling Fu sat made it necessary for Sirena to follow Caleb into the wagon and sit wearily amongst her trunks and belongings.

The heat of the day was stifling, though a gentle breeze blew in off the village quay. As the wagon bounced inland along the rutted, dusty road, the closer the air became and the more noticeable the humidity. Sirena found herself wishing for the fresh, brisk wind of the sea, the tang of the salt air, the domain of her *Rana.*

Sitting atop one of the trunks, she was able to catch a glimpse of the village, laid out along its tiny waterfront. Many of the gabled rooftops were tiled and others were just thatched, but there was a sense of permanence about it. This village — crowded between jungle and water — seemed to have been there always, unobtrusive in its surroundings. Then, the village disappeared from view, and without its diversion Sirena became more conscious of the broiling sun and red dust spewing up from the wagon's wheels. The hair on the nape of her neck stuck to her skin. Her armpits felt uncomfortably damp and her black and brown bombazine gown — one of the few of her sister Isabel's habits that the pirates had not carried off — was becoming stained with perspiration beneath her breasts and between her shoulder blades. She longed for the cool, abbreviated costume she had devised aboard the *Rana.*

Her eyes fell on Caleb, who had fallen asleep on the floor of the wagon. Poor Caleb! He had been running about all morning, first to fetch Jan to the *Rana* and, later, when he and Sirena had gone back to the village with the Dutch fisherman to help the latter brief his fellow-fishers on the care and painting and dyeing of the ship's sails. He deserved this short catnap before the ordeal of facing Mynheer van der Rhys.

"Mynheer van der Rhys" — even as she thought of his name, her spine stiffened with apprehension. She was on her way to meet the enemy!

Gretchen Lindenreich adjusted the short, sleeveless jacket that barely covered her full pink-and-white breast and left her midriff bare down to the long, brightly colored sarong skirt that rode low on her slim hips. Like so many women on the island, Gretchen had adopted the native Malayan costume to keep cool through the worst heat of the day, when any Western woman with a brain in her head stayed home and bathed her wrists in cologne. Unlike the native women's, Gretchen's brightly colored raw silk costume was cut to reveal as much of her body as she could allow in front of her servants.

Through the long gauze-covered glass doors leading to the garden, a movement caught her eye. Stepping closer for a better look, a blur of orange silk disappeared behind an ornamental persimmon bush.

"That damn Sudi!" Gretchen swore, a surly pout on her petulant mouth. "What does she care if my gowns hang in tatters!"

In the sultry damp of the tropics, the bane of every woman's existence was the preservation of her wardrobe. Mildew ate even beneath closet doors to wreak destruction in the folds of the garments, rotting and shredding the fabrics. More than once, a lady was embarrassed by the sudden tearing away of a sleeve or bodice while she was in public. Although Gretchen could afford cheap labor and inexpensive yard goods constantly to replace her Western gowns and underpinnings, she was fiercely possessive of her belongings and would not part with them either as gifts to her babo, or handmaiden, as was the custom, *or* to the ravages of the damp. Therefore it was Sudi's chore to take the long gowns and nightdresses, one by one, out of their protective paper wrappings and press them over with a warm flatiron. Hour after hour, day after day, Sudi stood at the padded board in one of the spare chambers, heating the heavy irons on the glowing brazier which, in turn, heated the closed room to a point beyond sweltering. Gretchen would not allow the doors leading to the garden to be opened, for she claimed this defeated the purpose of ironing the damp out of the garments.

Now, seeing the orange blur of Sudi's sari in the garden incensed Gretchen. She had been warned that these Hindu girls made unreliable servants unless kept under strict supervision. This was not the first time Gretchen had caught the toast-colored fifteen-year-old sneaking away from her duties to meet the young djongo or houseboy, who worked for the Daans.

Crossing the room and reaching into her closet, Gretchen groped for the familiar feel of her leather riding crop. Panting with the force of her rage, she stepped out into the heat of the day. Her small slippered feet silent on the cobblestones, she crossed the verandah, determined to find the rebellious Sudi and her lover and teach them both a stinging lesson.

Gretchen followed the path to the edge of the garden. Already a small trickle of perspiration ran between her breasts and down the small of her back. Cursing the interminable heat under her breath, she scanned the sky and noticed with some small relief the gathering of the dark clouds of the daily late-afternoon thundershower which added to the humidity yet did bring with it a dousing of the heat.

When, in her search for Sudi and her lover, she approached the tall yew hedge that separated her garden from the seldom-used country road that approached Batavia from the west, her ears caught the sound of horse hooves and wagon wheels plodding up the dusty byway. Her first thought was of Regan, who often accompanied his wagons full of nutmegs into town to supervise the loading of them aboard his ships. Her heart fluttered in her breast at the thought of seeing him again. She had not seen him for weeks, not since the night he told her of the expected arrival of his Spanish bride and had left her on a bitter note. Her eyes were hungry for the sight of him, her hands greedy to touch him, her mouth ached for his kisses.

Peering through the thick yew branches, Gretchen could see the wagon coming down the road. Her breath caught in her throat. It was Regan's wagon, yes, and there was that crafty-looking Ling Fu driving it. However, there was no sign of van der Rhys. Hope still flowered, and Gretchen remained where she stood, expecting to see Regan following the wagon at a distance, where the clouding dust would not bite into his face and sting his nostrils.

A movement in the back of the wagon attracted Gretchen's attention. There, perched atop a trunk, was a tall, black-garbed figure mopping her sweat-streaked and dust-filmed face. Dark hair tumbled from its knot down her back. The heavy black bombazine gown looked asphyxiating in the heat.

Comprehension washed over her. So this was Regan's Spanish bride! No wonder he'd sent the wagon to fetch her instead of bringing her by proa through the cool lagoons and harbor. Look at her!

Laughter bubbled up in Gretchen and burst forth in a raucous cackle.

Sirena heard the sound of laughter breaking the heavy air. How long had it been since she had heard the sound of laughter — or laughed herself? But there was a derisive note in the sound. Was it scornful and contemptuous? Was that why her skin prickled?

Boldly, Gretchen parted the thick branches of the hedge and, heedless of the scratching growth, stuck her head through the opening to laugh directly up into Sirena's face.

The women's eyes locked, and the laughter died with a gurgle in Gretchen's throat. Instead of the misery and humiliation she had expected to see in the Spaniard's face, there was a cold, chilling regality, a positive power of confidence and poise.

100

Sirena's back stiffened rigidly, her chin climbed several inches, the bright bottle-green eyes flashed in challenge. For a full moment the two women stared at each other, until Ling Fu took the wagon around the next bend, leaving Gretchen standing in a cloud of red dust.

Pulling herself back into her garden, Gretchen was silent, Sirena's expression having paralyzed her. Then slowly she moved toward the house, and the ridiculousness of the confrontation washed over her. The sight of Regan's Spanish bride covered with road dust and perspiration, rumpled and inappropriately dressed for this heat, once again amused her. Regan, she thought, it won't be long before you search out my cool blondness and white skin. If your grubby Spanish bride smells as bad as she looks, all the fragrances of the Orient won't improve her!

Slowly and surely, her laughter resumed until she was shaking under its force. Stumbling into her bedroom, she threw herself down onto the cool silk coverlet and indulged herself in howls of glee.

The echo of the blonde's derisive cackling resounded in Sirena's ears. Vainly she tried to brush away some of the clinging red dust from her skirt. The woman's laughter mingled with the remembered jeers of Blackheart's pirates and hate overwhelmed her. She had dealt with the lot aboard the *Rana* and she would somehow deal with that near-naked woman who had been cruel enough to mock her so openly.

Ling Fu drove the wagon up the cobblestone

drive leading to the van der Rhys courtyard. Seeing the European-style cobbles, Sirena recalled that because ships returning to the Indies had scant cargos they carried heavy cobbles for ballast. The enterprising settlers on Java and the surrounding islands therefore used the cobblestones to pave their drives and their streets. This helped to combat the inevitable mud that was left behind after the daily rains.

The clatter of the wagon's wheels against the cobbles woke Caleb. Drowsily, he sat up in his nest in the wagon, face flushed from the heat, eyes bright. Sirena reached out a gentle hand to smooth his dark-chocolate hair. With a pang, she realized how infrequently over the past weeks she had thought of Caleb as a child, for with her he had witnessed things no child should witness. He had been her only friend in a time of need and she relied on his good common sense and his strength of character. What's more, Caleb had proved he possessed the heart of a lion. When she referred to him as "little brother" in rehearsing the plot they were executing against van der Rhys, Sirena realized how meaningful the words were, after all. She loved the boy and to her mind he could not have been more her brother than if they had shared the same parentage.

Within her breast welled a fierce protectiveness toward him, the likes of which she had not felt since Caleb had suffered the lashing at the hands of Dick Blackheart aboard the *Rana*. Caleb's young back had been lashed because of his determination to help her, to tend her wounds, and to revive in her a will to live. And to repay him for his devotion to her, she was involving him in a plot against Mynheer van der Rhys — a plot that could place him in a dangerous position. Perhaps it would be better to admit her true identity, go to Mynheer van der Rhys and tell him of Isabel's fate and her uncle's and beg his assistance in helping her to return to Spain. Caleb would then be safe. She could take him back with her and give him all the advantages a young man could desire.

An audible gasp escaped her. What was she thinking? Go to Regan van der Rhys and beg his assistance? For a moment she had forgotten that it was Regan who was responsible for the pirate attack on the *Rana* and for the subsequent deaths of Isabel and Tio Juan.

Regan van der Rhys might even have engineered the attack on her ship. He might have decided he wouldn't care to marry a Spaniard and while Isabel lived he was honor-bound to do so. The thought of the dowry, too, those chests of gold coins had been too tempting. So he had ordered them accosted at sea, all aboard murdered, and the gold and the ship gained for himself.

How he must have felt thwarted when he realized that Señorita Córdez and her brother had been found — alive! — aboard the fast-sinking Rana. Sirena smiled as she guessed at the Mynheer's puzzlement. He would be wondering what had happened to Blackheart and his crew. How had the English pirate failed in his mission? Where was Blackheart now? How had the two Córdezes manages to escape death?

She would enjoy seeing the surprise on his pasty-white ferret features — as she imagined all

Dutchmen must have.

The wagon slowed as it neared the front entrance of the two-story, white-pillared verandah and the massive, intricately carved mahogany double doors. The grounds about the house were meticulously kept. Even now several gardeners went about their chores of pruning and weeding along the brightly colored flower beds. The scent of spices and flowers permeated the air, and exotic wild birds called raucously to one another. The house, the grounds — everything — showed evidence of pride of ownership. Many years and much labor had gone into the acquisition of the van der Rhys mansion. The deep red stone from which the front steps were chiseled she recognized as the precious "pink marble" from the foothills of the China mountains. In Europe jewelry was carved from it and statues of great beauty. Here on Java, a wily agent for the Dutch East India Company used it for his front steps!

Caleb and Ling Fu assisted her descent from the wagon. When the Chinese turned to unload the trunks and baggage, Caleb made a move to assist him, but Sirena placed a restraining hand on his arm. "No, little brother," she whispered, "you are no longer a paid cabin boy. You are Caleb Córdez of the shipbuilding Córdezes. Remember to leave the servants to their own duties."

Caleb flushed slightly. Not even inside the van der Rhys house and he had almost made his first mistake! He would have to be more alert, he promised himself, but he still felt uneasy about the role he was to play. How does the son of a wealthy shipbuilder behave? he questioned himself silently.

With a sigh and a shrug, he stepped closer to Sirena as they waited in the comparative cool shade of the verandah for someone to answer the Senorita's calculatedly timid knock on the impressive door.

Although Sirena did not let Caleb know it by either word or action, she felt indignant at this apparently intentional inauspicious welcome. It was as if she were a peddler begging for a sale! At any moment now, these ostentatious doors would swing open and an imperious servant would look down her long nose at her and insist that all beggars and peddlers were received at the back entrance.

She extended her arm, about to knock a second time, when the door swung wide. A young, harried-looking girl of about seventeen stood glancing back and forth from Sirena to Caleb with a frightened, shocked look on her face. The loose printed smock which hung from her shoulders fluttered from the force of the girl's trembling. Then, seeming to regain her senses, she turned on her heel and ran down the hall, calling, "Juffrouw, Juffrouw is here!" Caleb and Sirena heard a great commotion in the room at the end of the hall and, lastly, the sound of a sharp slap and a choked sob.

A tall and stately woman with a coronet of salt-and-pepper braids wrapped about her head stepped into the hall and moved swiftly toward them, a look of consternation about her tightly pinched mouth.

"Welcome, welcome, Juffrouw," she smiled, her florid complexion offsetting strong white teeth and a square jaw. "Come in out of the heat, please. Come in! I am Frau Holtz, Mynheer's housekeeper. Come in!" she repeated in a thick German accent.

Sirena and Caleb stepped into the cool hallway. Frau Holtz quickly stepped behind them and quietly closed the heavy doors. "We wish to keep out the heat," she stated simply, as if Sirena and Caleb were ignorant schoolchildren who didn't know enough to keep the doors closed against the elements.

An assemblage of servants now appeared in the wide, stone-floored hall, including the tearful young girl who had answered the door.

Frau Holtz explained, in clipped tones, "This stupid girl will be dismissed, Juffrouw. It is because of her that you rode all the way from the village in the baggage wagon. She is incapable of delivering a message correctly! As if the new lady of the house would be made to ride in a baggage wagon! There was a proa at the Batavia quay sent to meet you purposely. This idiot," she said, pointing a finger at the trembling girl, "mixed everything up. Even now Mynheer is at the landing, where he was ready to greet you. Ach! These lazy servants! Be sure, Juffrouw, this girl will be dismissed as soon as the Mynheer learns what trouble she has caused."

Sirena glanced at the young honey-colored servant and experienced a pang of pity for her. Besides, she didn't care for Frau Holtz's imperious attitude. It was clear that the van der Rhys house was the woman's domain. She had probably managed the household for years and years and secretly resented the intrusion of a new "Mevrouw" to answer to. More to be perverse than to assert her rights, Sirena said, "I do not want the girl dismissed. The message concerning my arrival should never have been entrusted to a child to begin with, Frau Holtz. You should have seen to it yourself."

The housekeeper's jaw slackened and she stammered for words, but Sirena spoke before the woman could answer:

"I'd like to be taken to my rooms now. Also, my brother will need quarters and a fresh change of clothing until a new wardrobe can be made for him."

"*Ja,* Juffrouw, I shall see to it myself." Frau Holtz motioned toward the wide, gracefully curving stairway.

"That won't be necessary, Frau Holtz," Sirena said coolly. "The girl whom you find so offensive will do very nicely. I believe I will even have her for my personal maid. I should think she'd be easy to train, once she is given kinder treatment!"

Frau Holtz stepped back from the staircase to allow Sirena and Caleb to pass in front of her. As they mounted the stairs, they heard the housekeeper's voice. She spoke coldly to the girl. "Do not stand there, Juli, the Juffrouw wants you for her servant. Now, show her to her rooms — and the young señor also. Pieter will be up in a moment to see to his needs."

Frau Holtz's tone was so clipped and cold that Sirena regretted overruling the housekeeper's authority. Juli, as she had heard Frau Holtz call her, had made a terrible bungle in delivering the message incorrectly and justly deserved the housekeeper's scorn. Now that Sirena had come to the girl's defense, it would go very hard with her.

Just as Juli lifted the hem of her long, colorful, sack-like garment to climb the stairs, Frau Holtz spoke again; this time her tone was softer and not unkind. "Juli, the Juffrouw has found the kindness to forgive your blunder, which must have caused her great discomfort. You are to serve her well and be helpful and loyal."

Turning to look at Frau Holtz, Sirena was surprised to see that the expression in the woman's eye matched the softness in her tone. Juli's expression brightened, her ink-dark eyes glistened with happiness as she smiled at the woman. Sirena felt instantly contrite for her misjudgment of Frau Holtz. In spite of the woman's overbearing manner, it was evident that she was fair and just to the servants. Frau Holtz would consider herself above petty grievances, and Juli and the other servants apparently knew this and respected her for it.

Sirena turned to climb the stairs.

"Juffrouw, it is much cooler in here," Juli said as they entered the suite of rooms set aside for Sirena.

The room was draped, all around, in silk gauze embroidered with gold threads depicting pomegranates and birds with glorious plumage. Fresh pale blues deepening to indigo were woven into the thick carpeting. The window hangings were sheer, of a pale blue silk, and the light streaming through them gave Sirena the impression that the whole room was a soft, pale blue cloud.

"Would you like a bath?" Juli asked as she stood behind Sirena undoing the buttons of the black bombazine gown.

"Yes, Juli, a bath is just what I need. But before you go to prepare it, tell me where my brother's room is to be."

"Down the hall, I believe, Juffrouw, to the left. But I'll see to the bath now. Mynheer will want to see you soon." Juli's eyes dropped. "I have shamed Mynheer before his wife-to-be, he will be most angry with me."

"And well he should be!" Sirena chastised her, reinforcing Frau Holtz's position in the matter. "But I'm sure that if you promise to serve me well, he will deal fairly with you. Now hurry my bath water!"

"Yes, I will get the water. Then you can rest. Mynheer will want to have dinner with the Juffrouw. I heard him order a very special dinner!"

Sirena paled visibly as a knock sounded on the door. What if it was Mynheer van der Rhys! She couldn't possibly meet him now! Not in this condition!

Juli opened the door cautiously to admit Frau Holtz.

"I came to see if you needed . . ." Sirena's blanched face alarmed Frau Holtz. She bustled into the room and immediately took command. "Juli! A cool cloth for the Juffrouw's brow! There, there, sit here, my lady. Hurry with the cloth, Juli!"

By Frau Holtz and Juli's ministerings, Sirena's normal color resumed.

"Frau Holtz, when Mynheer returns to the house, you are to go to him and explain that I can't see anyone in my condition. Not for several days at least. I am prostrate with grief, and only my brother is to be admitted." Although Sirena's voice was quiet and soft, there was a ring of iron to her words.

The Frau stayed with Sirena and saw to the placement of the trunks that the djongo had brought up from the verandah. Juli now returned once more, leading two djongos, who toted large pewter urns of steaming water and poured it into a gilt hip bath which Juli revealed by the removal of a lacquered Chinese screen. Several urns of cool water were added to the steaming wetness to bring it to a comfortable tepid temperature.

After the djongos had gone, Sirena addressed Frau Holtz. "I wish to have a bolt on my door! Please arrange to have this done as soon as possible. No one is to enter my room without my permission! I am in mourning. I hope I am understood?"

"Yes, Juffrouw," Juli and Frau Holtz chorused.

The housekeeper considered Sirena's instructions peculiar but said nothing. God only knew what strange ways these olive-skinned Spaniards practiced!

Frau Holtz impatiently bided her time until Regan returned to the house. Marching to the library, on his instructions, to answer his inquiries concerning the señorita, she closed the teak doors discreetly behind her and promptly explained the mix-up concerning his bride's arrival.

"She is not . . . receiving anyone," the housekeeper said, lifting her eyebrows. "She knows you expect her for dinner, but she claims she is prostrate with grief. She also requests a bolt to be put on her door and that no one — no one," she repeated — "was to enter unless she admitted him!"

Regan suppressed a grin. It was so rare that Frau Holtz felt displaced, and he was enjoying it. The elderly and imperious housekeeper prided herself on her proprietorial rights due to long years of service first to his father and now to himself.

Acquiescing to the anger he knew Frau Holtz expected of him, he raised a shaggy brow. With what he hoped was an angry tone, he said, "I'll go and speak to the Juffrouw immediately." He wanted to meet this woman who could so effectively rattle the unflappable Frau Holtz!

The Frau smiled her satisfaction and dismissed herself. As she left, Regan noticed the thick salt-and-pepper hair at the back of her head creeping out from its heavy coronet of braids. Now Regan was even *more* eager to meet his Spanish bride, for the last time he had seen a mussed hair on the housekeeper's head was when, as a boy, he gave the dictatorial lady a few healthy shocks.

Regan strode down the hall and up the stairs and stopped at the door of his intended. He grasped the ornate door handle and hesitated, but only for a second, before he swung open the door.

Sirena, bathed, with her thick dark hair in a tight, discreet knot on the nape of her neck, and dressed in a loose-flowing blue wrapper, turned with a gasp as he burst into her room. Maddened by the sudden intrusion that was precisely against her request, her first impulse was to vent her anger; but she held herself in check, conforming to the pattern of a well-bred Spanish lady in bereavement — which after all, was true.

"I told Frau Holtz I was not receiving anyone. I am in mourning," she choked out, lowering 'her lids over dangerously glittering eyes.

Angered by her abrupt statement, Regan explained hotly, "I came to wish you welcome to your new home and to apologize for the confusion which caused you to ride in the baggage wagon." A vision of this aristocratic Spanish lady riding along the hot, dusty roads in the back of the wagon floated before his eyes and he fought to suppress a smile. He continued, striving for a note of sympathy in his voice: "Ever since Jan Verhooch told me how he and his crew rescued you and your young brother from the sinking frigate and brought you here to Batavia . . ."

"Your apology is well offered, Mynheer," Sirena interrupted as she turned away from him to look out over the gardens.

Regan noticed that she had not really accepted his stumbling apology, but he decided not to press the issue. He was momentarily stunned by the picture she created standing before the long windows through which the late-afternoon sun filtered — outlining her slim, softly rounded body. Pulling his eyes away from the shadowy outline of her full, round breasts to her exquisitely molded oval-shaped face, he was conscious of his good fortune. Other men could have searched a lifetime for a bride of such beauty. Her gleaming dark hair off-set the slight ocher tint of her flawless skin; her features were delicate: high cheekbones, wide-set eyes fringed with thick, lush, black lashes . . . When she had spoken to him, he had seen a flash of straight white teeth behind her full, promising lips. She was exquisite!

Regan van der Rhys was a man accustomed to culling an unintentional envy among his associates. Immediately, he recognized the advantage of having a beautiful woman to grace his table and drawing room. He owned the most opulent home, the most productive groves, held the highest position with the Dutch East India Company in the islands — and now he would have the most stunning wife on Java. A white wife, who was not a "company daughter": one of that heartlessly exploited group of girls, instruments of one of the company's schemes to keep their agents contented and useful, and sent out East for the purpose of ensuring the continuance of the white race in the East Indies. "Company daughters" were mostly girls of poor or unknown beginnings, some of them rescued from the gutters and alleyways of Holland's port cities; they were given some formal education, a bit of the social graces, and then were exported like any other product — to marry any planter, agent, merchant, or clerk who had failed to secure a white wife for himself. Since not many "proper" girls cared to leave behind family and homeland for the uncertainty of a tropical island and a never-before-seen husband, the company's scheme worked exceedingly well and initiated many happy marriages.

If the *only* criterion for a wife was being white, Gretchen Lindenreich would have been a logical choice. But Gretchen's reputation certainly would not have enhanced Regan's prestige on the island.

Regan was still not reconciled to marrying *any-one*, but since he should marry, this Spanish señorita held both a promise of delight and auspicious possibilities . . .

The jolt of his good fortune registered on Regan's handsome features, and Sirena took his expression to mean he was surprised to find she had escaped the ravages of his pirates apparently unscathed. Her gaze flicked over him steadily now for the first time, and as she took him in her shamrock-green eyes widened with the impact of his appearance. Instead of an aging, fat, milk-skinned barbarian, there stood before her this tall, muscular sun god whose rugged features were offset by a crop of hair as pale as the moonlight shining on a still, black sea.

Raising her ire with an amused twinkle in his agate-blue eyes, he spoke softly in thickly accented Spanish: "We will settle this matter now, so you may be left to your mourning," he scoffed. "Our marriage was arranged by our fathers — an agreement which we will fulfill as soon as it can be done."

Sirena lowered her eyes, her thoughts racing. She had not been prepared for this handsome, virile man — one who would never allow his wife to play a chaste, prayer-filled "nun." Not this man! Heart thumping wildly, Sirena looked up, forcing her face into lines of placidity.

"I beg of you, Mynheer, to respect my year of mourning. I have many prayers to be said. And I must see to my small brother . . ."

"Our marriage will take place one month from today. That should give you ample tune to recover from your ordeal. You'll find that although Java is far removed from the courts of Europe, propriety must be served."

Regan assumed that the wild ray of disbelief that lit her eyes was because he was insisting upon an early wedding date. In fact, Sirena was finding it almost impossible to keep from lashing out at him and demanding to know exactly what part he had played in the "ordeal" of which he spoke so lightly.

Regan, hoping to smooth the lines of dismay from her lovely, cameo-like features, amended his previous dictum: "Señorita, it is only to protect you that our marriage must take place in what seems such a short length of time. I will not expect you to share my bed until your mourning period is over."

How magnanimous of him, Sirena thought spitefully, but she quietly murmured, "Thank you, Mynheer," and clasped her hands before her to prevent their trembling.

What had come over her? No man had ever made her tremble, except her father — and then only when she was guilty of something and knew she deserved his wrath. Not even the pirate captain, as he wielded the lash against her naked back, had had this effect on her.

Regan stepped closer, his height intimidating her. "Señorita . . ." he began, then hesitated, "I cannot always refer to you as *Señorita* Córdez, can I?"

"No, Mynheer. In view of our relationship it

115

would be absurd." Lifting her eyes and challenging him with her voice, she blurted out, "You must call me Sirena."

"Sirena. Your name suits you. Quiet, poised . . ." he continued with his gallant flattery.

All the while Sirena's mind screamed: You cur! You son of a viper! Hijo de puta — son of a whore! Not to realize that the girl you were to marry was named Isabel and that *she* was, in truth, all you are saying of *me!*

Regan saw her lower her lids and sensed her withdrawal, and he was angered by it. "Look at me!" he commanded softly.

Sirena raised her eyes to meet his and was once again impressed by his height. There were few men she had to look up to, for, tall herself, she met most men at eye level. Standing close to Regan, she realized she only stood as tall as his shoulder and noted he was deeply tanned from the sun. Did he also love the freedom of the seas, the tangy salt spray stinging his face? Sirena looked at his hands. Yes, she answered her own question: he would know how to hoist a sail, and captain a ship. There were rough calluses on the palms of his capable angular hands. She wondered what it would be like to have those hands stroke her . . . Blushing, she again lowered her eyes.

Noticing the riot of color that now stained her cheeks, Regan smiled. There was something about the girl. Was it in the eyes? He couldn't be sure, she seemed so timid and generally avoided looking directly at him. Was it possible that he somehow offended her delicate sensibilities? Rot! He preferred women with spirit and vivacity. A woman who would answer his caresses in bed. Bah! This frightened girl would lay like a newborn calf, mewing for homeland and mother. He would have to find his pleasures elsewhere. The Spaniard could grace his table and he would give her the considerations due a wife. He would feed and clothe her and her brother, and in her spare time she could pray for his soul!

Suddenly, he reached out and grasped her face in his callused hands. His grasp was firm, yet gentle. Cool green eyes returned his mocking stare. Regan was perplexed for a moment. Was he mistaken? Something stirred in him as Sirena continued her now-bold scrutiny. Regan was the first to look away in confusion.

"I will expect you to keep your word, Mynheer, that I won't be expected to consummate the marriage until my mourning is over."

Once again her emerald eyes sparkled dangerously. Regan drew in his breath. Perhaps he had been hasty. A *spirited* newborn calf, perhaps. With the proper . . . Stunned, he found himself a moment later in the dim, cool hallway, and not quite sure how he got there.

Sirena collapsed on the edge of the blue-and-white bed, consciously attempting to control her quaking and trembling. Regan van der Rhys would be a formidable opponent. She realized that he was not a man who could be easily fooled. His keen intelligence was mirrored in his cold, agate-blue eyes. His stubbornness was evident in his lean, square jaw. With great accuracy of thought, however, she also realized it was not his strength as an adversary that troubled her — it was the man

117

himself, his animal magnetism.

Would he keep his word and not demand his rights as a husband? And did she want him to?

Chapter Six

Dappled sunshine wove a lacy pattern on the cobbled walk beneath Sirena's feet as she strolled the paths through the lush tropical gardens surrounding the van der Rhys house. Her eyes were sharp and alert as she gauged the distance from where she stood at the rear of the mansion to the cove where the *Rana* was secretly berthed. Regan's property lay on the western edge of the town of Batavia, rather isolated from other houses and mansions — as befitted the position of the D.E.I. Chief Pensioner. Then her attention was drawn away from the ship to the splendid array of brilliant, multicolored flowers. From her window she had seen Oriental gardeners painstakingly weeding and pruning the lush flower beds. They had transformed the wild jungle into a paradise of scents, color, and landscaping. Stooping near a row of particularly bright blooms, her fingers picked a crimson blossom from its stem. Sniffing experimentally, Sirena was disappointed to find it without scent.

"That particular bloom, Sirena, has no scent, although it does possess other interesting properties," Regan said quietly, startling her as he approached. She wondered how long he had been observing her.

"I'd arrange to have a bouquet of them sent to your room, but I'm afraid it would never do. It wouldn't be wise to arouse speculation among the servants," he said snidely.

Ignoring his attitude, Sirena inquired, curious, "But why *can't* I have them in my room? How could this gorgeous blossom offend anyone?" she asked quietly and modestly. She must remain the mourning Spanish lady!

"Offensive isn't exactly the word I would use. Actually, in many parts of the world they're very much in demand," he explained guardedly.

"It looks very much like a poppy," she said, bewilderment sharpening her tone. "I think it's beautiful, and I . . . would like to have some in my room. I'll get one of the gardeners to cut them for me," she said coolly and stubbornly with averted eyes.

Regan looked aghast and Sirena enjoyed this. Now he would probably tell her some trite superstition that made the flowers unlucky.

"Since you persist, I'll see to it myself. In fact, I shall have your room festooned with them. I'll have your balcony hung with garlands of them. I'll drop their petals in your wine. Everywhere you go their bright color will greet you — along with the quizzical expressions on the faces of the islanders." By this time Regan had worked himself into a subtle rage.

Delighting in his anger, Sirena said, with great control, "Do that, Mynheer. Immediately will not be too soon." Her fingers caressed the blossom langourously.

Regan's eyes narrowed, "Your wish is my command." He bristled. "But first there's something you should know. This particular variety of blossom has a unique usage among the natives. To be more specific, its stamens and seeds are ground into a fine powder which amorous lovers apply to a particular part of their anatomy. Upon the penetration of their partner, the powder causes the sex organs to enlarge and swell. I've heard of couples being locked together for hours and —"

Sirena blanched. "I see, Mynheer . . ." she said as her gaze perused the thick, lush beds of the infamous flowers. "And you keep yourself well supplied." As she spoke, she casually let the petals slip through her fingers; then, walking away, her foot ground the blossom to a dark, bloody pulp.

Regan was stunned by her quick recovery. He hadn't meant to tell her the history of the flower, but when she became so coolly imperious he could not help himself. "I'll be damned!" he muttered, feeling like a little boy caught with his fingers in the jam pot.

"I think you've taxed your poor head enough today, Caleb," Sirena grinned. Seeing the lost look on the boy's face, she widened her smile. "You did well today, little brother. Don't be in such a hurry. It took me years to learn what I'm teaching you. Navigation is an art. You must learn it thoroughly. A mistake could be deadly. But I don't want you to despair," she said, rolling up the charts and sliding them under the bed.

"Let's pray that Frau Holtz doesn't take it into her head to clean this room. I'll have to find a better hiding place for your charts." His tone was light but his eyes revealed some secret disappointment.

"What's troubling you, Caleb?"

121

The boy stood scuffing his feet on the thickly carpeted floor. "You promised to teach me to fence," he blurted out.

"So I did — and I will. Tomorrow I shall give you your first fencing lesson. I've noticed a secluded area in the garden. But I tell you, the navigation lessons must come first. Patience, Caleb," she sighed.

Since their arrival in Batavia, Sirena's mode of living and behavior had conformed not only to her mourning pose and to her position in the van der Rhys household as mistress-to-be, but also to the weather — and she and Caleb were both restless. During the cool mornings, she busied herself with seeing to the completion of Caleb's wardrobe. The heat of the afternoons and the daily thunderstorms — which lasted sometimes an hour — forced her to take life slowly then, either napping or giving Caleb lessons on navigation. The evenings were sultry, but the nights cool for sleeping. To all outward appearances, Sirena seemed reserved and contented. Inwardly, she constantly battled to control her energies and her impatience to learn enough about the van der Rhys trading business to implement her revenge plot.

"Aye, Sirena, you're right as usual," Caleb was saying. "It's just that I want to learn to protect you. Perhaps the time will come when you'll need my help."

"Little brother, why don't you go outside or down to the quay. The rains are over for the day. Possibly you can pick up some information useful to us."

"I'll do my best, Sirena."

"I myself have an appointment with Frau Holtz to go over some of my wedding plans," Sirena said bitterly. For she had not been able to convince Regan to postpone the wedding. "I fear she'll find me sadly lacking in enthusiasm. Despite her politeness, the woman resents me, Caleb. She jealously guards the position she has established for herself over the years, and is fearful that her authority will all too soon be usurped by me. As for my feelings toward her . . ." Sirena continued, "I find her overbearing. '*Ja!* You may have your breakfast now, Juffrouw!' " Sirena mimicked Frau Holtz, making Caleb laugh. "Really! She acts as though the courtesies and luxuries of this house flowed merely from her beneficence!"

"But she means well, Sirena. It's perhaps just the way the German language sounds."

"And that's another thing! When we first arrived here, I couldn't bear the way she stumbled over the Spanish language. So I told her I'd been schooled in several languages and that German was one of them. So now she speaks to me in German and I answer her in kind . . ."

"I know, I know," Caleb giggled uncontrollably, "and now *she* rolls up her eyes at *your* terrible *German!*"

"Not only that" — Sirena joined his laughter — "but now she speaks so loudly, enunciating so distinctly, as though I were hard of hearing! I think she feels me an idiot child and she's going to teach me correct German. I've a confession to make, Caleb," Sirena said, her eyes sparkling with devilment. "Sometimes I purposely mispronounce the words or misuse them — just to get her back up!"

123

As Sirena finished speaking, a knock sounded on the bedroom door. Putting a finger to her lips as a signal for quiet, she said, "Open the door, Caleb. It must be Frau Holtz."

Caleb ran to the door and, with a flourish, bowed extravagantly low — only to look upon shiny, booted male feet. Flushing, he straightened himself and glanced from Sirena to Regan.

"I've come for Caleb," Regan said in a stilted voice. Then he mused: Could these two somber faces have been responsible for the rollicking laughter I heard coming from behind this door . . . ?

Sirena lowered her eyes, her hands busy in her pocket searching for her rosary. Finding the round beads, she drew them forth and held them in her clenched hand.

"Why is it, Sirena, that every time I see you, you immediately seek your beads? Do I frighten you so much? Enough to make you seek solace in prayer?" Regan's tone was lightly sarcastic, but a muscle in his cheek jumped with suppressed rage.

"Hardly," Sirena said softly, her head half turned. "But I must continue with my prayers, so if you'll excuse me . . ."

"Of course," Regan answered gallantly, taking Caleb by the arm. "But as I've told you before, your period of mourning may be practiced in private and as frequently as you wish. Nevertheless, it is not to interfere with our small social life here on the island."

"Have you no respect for the dead?" Her soft voice rose a trifle as she swung to face the tall man opposite her.

"Very little, I'm afraid," Regan said coldly.

"These things are overdone. The dead are dead. What good does all this praying do them? The world is meant to live in. And, tonight you shall live in *my* world. I am arranging a small dinner party, several of my friends are to attend. I insist on presenting you to them. I expect you and Caleb to join me at the table."

"But my mourning —"

"You will carry on your mourning in this room only!" Regan cast his eyes to the window and then lowered his lazy blue gaze on Sirena. "You have *five hours* yet to mourn. I suggest you get on with it and save your strength for this evening's entertainment. Caleb and I will be home before dark."

Sirena narrowed her eyes to slits and glared at him. Caleb noticed the dangerous glitter and hoped that Regan did not.

For a moment Regan was startled by Sirena's stare. Was he mistaken? Was that anger in those cat-green eyes? In his cool, composed Sirena? Not likely, it must have been a trick of the light. Then, having delivered his order, he motioned for Caleb to follow him. At the sound of the door closing behind them, Sirena tossed the prayer beads on the silken coverlet and swore. "How dare he! Who does he think he is? He has actually ordered me to attend his dinner! How dare he?" Anger rose to the surface as she paced the room. Yes, she would have to do as he ordered — but she didn't have to like it!

Once more a knock sounded on her door.

It was probably Frau Holtz, she thought. Quickly dropping to her knees at the side of her bed, she held the rosary beads loosely in her fingers and lowered her eyes. "Come in!" she called.

The housekeeeper took in the picture Sirena created, and grimaced. Did the Spanish have nothing to do but pray? A belief in God was commendable, but this obsessive, continual praying made her want to shake the quiet, secretive girl who kneeled stiff-backed near the bed. Boldly, Frau Holtz strode to the windows and folded her heavy arms across her buxom chest. "I have come to discuss some of the last details concerning your wedding, my lady."

Sirena looked up at the housekeeper. "I think, Frau Holtz, that I can trust you to handle my wedding. Whatever you and Mynheer decide will be acceptable to me."

"Juffrouw, it is not as simple as that . . ."

"And may I ask why not?" Sirena said, raising one perfectly arched brow. Frau Holtz stepped back as she noted the shimmering green eyes. "Mynheer seems to be so authoritative, so discerning, and so in command, one would have thought he had this wedding all arranged."

"For the most part it is. He did handle all the arrangements concerning the guests and those who will stay overnight because they live on the out-islands. But there are hundreds of smaller details —" Frau Holtz stammered, "Mynheer thought —"

"Mynheer thought wrong," Sirena said flatly. "Do what you will. I won't object to anything you decide. I will do as my intended orders. But," she said, holding up a long, slender finger, "I will not help. I am in mourning. Is that understood?"

"Perfectly, Juffrouw," Frau Holtz answered

coldly, turning to leave.

"Frau Holtz, there is . . . something else. When I first arrived, I requested a bolt for my door. As yet, I have received none. I am also requesting, now, a new lock with a key only for myself. As I told you before, I don't want any of the servants in this room. Except when I ask them in to tidy and clean. Even Juli knows she is not to disturb me unless I call for her. I wish to be alone, *alone!* There may be times when you will not see me for days. On these occasions, I go into retreat here. My brother, Caleb, joins me on these longer occasions."

"And your meals, Juffrouw?"

"You may leave food outside the door. If we have a need for it, we will eat it. Under no circumstances are you to try to enter this room when I am in retreat here. Even ordinarily when I am in the room, I would like the least disturbance possible. Attend to the bolt and key for the door this afternoon. Oh, and also for my brother's door!"

"This is unheard of! There *are* no rooms locked in this house!"

"You have heard of it now. A bolt and a new lock by sundown! Leave me now. Go and prepare lavishly for my wedding. And don't stint, for I understand Mynheer is quite wealthy. I wouldn't want my wedding to be considered lacking." Sirena suppressed a smile as she watched the horror dance across the housekeeper's face. "Go now!" She said imperiously as she fluttered the prayer beads in the air. "I must get back to my prayers, you have put me behind in my schedule. We Spanish must say many prayers each day —

127

otherwise, how shall we ever get to Heaven? You Protestants may not see the logic, the reason. And I fear for you. We shall surely not see you in Heaven." Quickly, she lowered her head onto prayer-clasped hands. A rich bubble of laughter threatened to erupt from her mouth.

With the sound of the closing door, Sirena doubled over, laughing silently. With Frau Holtz at the helm, she could hardly wait to see what shape her wedding would take.

Regan stood on the quay and considered the youth who was soon to be his brother-in-law. Caleb was shy and quiet, and he could understand the boy's timidity: he'd come to a new land, was living with strange people . . . But there was more to Caleb than met the eye. Regan had not failed to notice the hard, rough calluses on the boy's hands. They were, in fact, like the hands of a seaman; and he wondered what had made them that way. Curiously, too, though both were dark-haired, Caleb and Sirena had little resemblance one to the other. Caleb, indeed, did not look Spanish. But to question the boy would be unfair at this point; Regan wanted to be friends with him.

"How do you like my new ship?" Regan asked quietly.

"She's a beauty!" Caleb said, a light dancing in his eyes. "I'd like to sail her someday."

Regan looked questioningly at the youth. Most young men of noble birth would have said "sail *on* her someday." Caleb sounded like a well-salted old seaman the way he'd spoken.

"It can be arranged," Regan answered. "She

makes her first voyage back to Holland carrying a precious cargo of spices and silks on the day after my wedding. Why don't you think of a name for her?"

"I'd like to do that, Mynheer," Caleb said shyly. "I'll think well."

"Why not call me Regan? Soon you'll be my brother-in-law. There's no need for formality. I call you Caleb, and I think it would help if we were to be more informal. We'll be living together until you choose to return to Spain."

The boy seemed flustered and confused. Sensing his discomfort, Regan spoke gently: "If the name Regan doesn't come easily, then continue as before. Whenever you're ready and feel more at ease with me, it will come to you."

Caleb smiled his relief. Caleb liked Regan and at times it was difficult to think of him as the enemy. Somehow to call the man by his first name would denote a friendship and Caleb wasn't exactly sure whether or not Sirena would feel betrayed by this.

"Come up to the offices with me, Caleb. I want to change out of this damp shirt. There's a meeting of clerks which I must attend this afternoon. And, in my office, I have models of my fleet — and some of my father's. One of the natives carved them for me and I assure you they're works of art!"

In the hot, airless offices of the Dutch East India Company Caleb ran his hands lovingly over the small models. "They *are* beautiful! The man who carved them must have a gentle hand," Caleb marveled.

Regan, naked to the waist, walked over to the boy and held one of the tiny ships in his hand. "This was one of my father's ships: the *Tita*, named for my wife. We sailed on her, my wife and young son. We were going to Europe. She was a native princess, daughter of a Siva high priest, and it would have been her first time away from Java. As we were about to round the Cape of Good Hope into the Atlantic, the *Tita* was attacked by pirates." Regan's eyes clouded. "I saw my wife killed, and my son . . ."

Caleb's eyes were mirrors of compassion. "I was put aboard a jolly-boat. Given food and water, too. I'll never know why. Two or three days later, a Spanish brigantine discovered me and took me aboard. But the captain refused to believe that I and my father owned the ravaged *Tita* — and I knew not whether the *Tita* still floated. When I insisted that we search for her, he informed me that he'd seen the ship sinking into the sea. Then he falsely accused me of being a member of the crew of a Dutch pirate ship that had been preying, at that time, on Spanish and Portuguese vessels near the Cape.

"I never saw my son again," Regan went on with his story. "I don't know if he's alive or dead. The last I saw of the child, he was crying in terror and holding fast to the ship's wheel."

A long moment passed before Regan seemed in sufficient control to complete his story. "I was taken to Spain as a criminal and thrown into prison, where I rotted for six long years. My father eventually secured my release at a great financial cost. *Your* father, Caleb, was of great assistance to me. He exerted his influence where it did the most good. And I am grateful."

As Regan turned away, Caleb gasped in horror at the deep ridged scars that ran across Regan's muscular back. Regan turned at the sound that escaped the boy.

"A momento of the Spanish prison I resided in for six years," he said cruelly. "And they say the *Dutch* are barbarians!"

"All . . . all Spaniards aren't barbarians," Caleb said hesitantly.

"True," Regan answered coldly. "And all Dutch and Germans are not barbarians, either. Perhaps you could explain that fact to your sister."

His fresh lawn shirt buttoned, Regan lit a cigar and perched on the edge of his massive desk, his leg swinging lightly. "So, young man, what do you think of the East India Company?"

"It's impressive! I respect you, Mynheer, for making it the success it is!"

If Regan noted the formal address he gave no hint as he replied: "It's a devil of a job. Leaves little time for leisure, and now that I'm to marry your sister there'll be even less time. Work, work, work!" he joked.

"Are you wealthy, Mynheer?"

"By some standards, I suppose so. But several ransackings of my own ships at sea by pirates would clean me out. Nearly all my holdings are tied up in my private fleet. Even the plantation would be almost useless to me without the ships to carry my nutmegs back to Holland — I would have to use other Dutch carriers, and the

131

cost would be high!"

"Do you have much trouble with pirates?"

"Not if I can help it. I've spent a small fortune for weapons to outfit the fleet." Regan did not mention the pirateers he sometimes employed to protect not only his own fleet but any D.E.I. ships against the Spanish.

"You spent a fortune? But I thought the ships belonged to the company, why didn't they spend the money?"

"They do, Caleb. But now I'm speaking of my own ships! I had to provide my fleet with cannons, the newest, largest guns now being made. Shipping becomes more precarious by the day. If one doesn't have an advantage over scourges of the sea, one would find himself out of business!" Regan looked out the window and saw the sun low on the horizon. "I think it's time for you to head back to your sister. By now she should have finished with her prayers. She may be concerned for you," he said cynically.

Caleb obediently made a move to leave.

Regan detained him, his tone softened. "I've told you how your father was instrumental in gaining my release from prison. I've always felt myself in his debt although I've never met the man. Nothing gives me greater pleasure than knowing you, his son." Regan touched the boy's shoulder. "Do you think you can find your way back to the house alone? If not I'll have one of the clerks take you . . ."

"Yes, I can find my way back. I know you have a meeting you must attend."

Regan crushed Caleb's hand in his own. "I en-

132

joyed our time together this afternoon. We'll do it again very soon. Go now so your sister doesn't worry needlessly. I'll see you at dinner."

When Caleb returned to the house, he stopped by Sirena's room before going to his own to prepare for dinner. His young boy's heart was a kettle of boiling emotion and confusion. On one occasion aboard the *Rana*, he professed his doubt that Mynheer van der Rhys was responsible for the attack of Dick Blackheart and his men. Now again he was finding it difficult to believe that Regan was the power behind that attack. How could a man who had suffered so crushing a blow as seeing his wife murdered and losing his only son perpetrate a similar attack on innocent people? Caleb was lost in these thoughts when he heard Sirena bid him enter.

"How did your outing go, little brother? Did you enjoy yourself?"

"Yes, I did. Mynheer showed me his new ship and asked me to name her. He also asked me to call him Regan. He said there's no need for formality. But I didn't call him by name," he hastily volunteered, fearing he would gain her disapproval. He had pledged his allegiance to her and he would keep his word, regardless of his doubts about Regan's guilt.

Quickly, he recounted the afternoon's events. "Did you know he was married before, Sirena, and had a son?"

Sirena's face masked her surprise. "Yes. It was one of the things father told Isabel and me. You like the Mynheer, don't you, Caleb?"

133

"Yes, I do," he hesitantly admitted. "But don't worry, I didn't tell him anything. He says I don't talk much and he likes that in a man. He says actions speak louder than words."

Caleb related the story of Regan's imprisonment in a hushed voice, though Sirena knew something of this. "You should see his back, Sirena. It's a mass of scars and welts. They're old and healed but nonetheless they're ferocious."

"Held and beaten in a Spanish prison and yet he agreed to marry a Spaniard — or at least agreed to follow his father's instructions . . ." Sirena pursed her mouth in a round of surprise. "If what he told you is true, then he must hold a vengeance for the Spanish. Just as I do for the Dutch because of what happened."

"Mynheer praised your father, Sirena, for helping secure his release from prison."

"And the Mynheer repaid his gratitude by having his scurvy lot of pirates plunder the *Rana* and kill my sister and uncle!" Sirena spat bitterly.

Sirena turned her back on Caleb and went to the long, low windows that led out into the gardens. For a long time she stood there and Caleb suspected she might be crying. But when she once again turned to face him she was dry-eyed.

"It would be wise to bathe and dress now. I have the feeling promptness at the dinner table would be to our advantage. I hate grand entrances!"

"How many guests are expected?" Caleb asked.

"In truth, I don't know and at this point I don't care. I only hope Mynheer will discuss the sailing of his new ship. The one which is to sail on the day after the wedding."

Pulling herself from her thoughts, she realized Caleb was showing signs of apprehension. Thinking it was because of the dinner that night, she said, "I know this is a big step for you, Caleb, your first formal dinner. Everything will be fine. Just watch me at the table and do as I do. You possess a keen sense of courtesy, you can't go wrong. If for some reason you become confused, plead a poor appetite. The Dutch are nothing but barbarians, I doubt they know what good manners are. Just relax and enjoy the meal. We've been confined too long, I'm rapidly tiring of this exile I've placed us in." The look of vexation on her face made Caleb laugh. "All this praying is becoming tiresome!"

Caleb laughed again, tears brightening his dark eyes.

"Why do you laugh at me, Caleb. I know this is all my own doing, but" — she held up a warning finger — "once I put our plan into effect there will be no room for boredom. Only fear that we'll be caught."

"We won't be caught, Sirena, you've planned it well. The plan can't fail." The boy's dark, sultry eyes glistened in anticipation. Returning to the sea, where he felt he belonged, was his wish.

Distant rumblings forced a halt to their conversation. At first it sounded like the very distant roar of a great cannon. The roar grew louder, more persistent, and Sirena and Caleb hurried to her window to study the horizon for the black smudges left by exploded cannonballs. Was it possible that Batavia was under attack from the sea by enterprising pirates? They stood at her balcony, their eyes straining into the distance. Behind them

135

the crystal globes of the lamps on Sirena's dressing table began to vibrate, emitting a tinkling tune. Caleb turned abruptly, relief and understanding smoothing the concerned furrows on his brow.

"It's only the fire mountain," he sighed, "one of the volcanos is just voicing an objection to being ignored." Almost before he finished speaking the tinkling crystal gave up its song and the rumbling in the distance subsided.

Sirena was clearly disconcerted; her fingers were coiled about each other in agitation and her lips were drawn into a thin, nervous line.

"If you're to remain here on Java, Sirena, you must become used to the whims of the fire mountains. Rarely do their rumblings amount to anything. Sometimes rockfalls are caused by the trembling . . ." Immediately Caleb and Sirena had the same thought: the two volcanos guarding the entrance to the cove where the *Rana* was hidden. If enough rocks and boulders fell into the River of Death the *Rana* would be landlocked — or buried! Beads of moisture broke out on Caleb's upper lip.

"Tomorrow, before the rains, after Mynheer leaves for his offices, take a ride over the hills and see how near completion the *Rana* is," Sirena said, hoping to distract Caleb from his apprehension. "Then ride as far as you can down the river and see if the channel is still open to the sea, although I've no doubt that it is." Thinking of the *Rana* was just what the boy needed. His face brightened. If Sirena said the narrow channel was still open then it was. Youthful trust shone brightly in his face.

"Yes, Sirena, I will! It'll be good to see her again!"

It was more evident than ever that Caleb felt out of his element here in this richly appointed house wearing fine cambric shirts and glossy, stiff new boots. It was the open sea and a rolling deck for which he longed.

Sirena prayed that she would be proven correct. If the *Rana* was landlocked it would mean the end of her plans for revenge. If that should happen she would rather be dead.

It was just past sundown and no bolt had been installed. Sirena was furious. Who was at fault, the housekeeper or Regan van der Rhys? If she were to place a wager, the odds would be against Regan. The Frau merely carried out orders after they were issued. Evidently Sirena's order was not sufficient.

Rapping sharply on the stout teak door, Sirena waited patiently. Regan himself opened the door, a goblet in one hand, a fragant cigar in the other. He smiled wickedly at the suppressed fury in Sirena's face.

"You see," he said expansively and a bit drunkenly, "I knew we could be friends. How . . . thoughtful of you to pay me a visit — and without prayer beads." He waved his cigar airily.

Sirena's heart hammered in her chest. Never had she gazed on such a virile man. He exuded a presence, a forcefulness, a maleness that she found eminently exciting and enticing. Forcefully, she brought her mind back to the matter at hand.

"I wish a bolt for my door," she demanded. "A strong heavy bolt made from iron," she said slowly, enunciating clearly to be sure the man opposite her understood her meaning.

The agate eyes narrowed slightly. Regan brought the silver goblet to his lips; he drank slowly, never taking his eyes from Sirena's flushed face. Then, deliberately, he lowered the goblet and brought the cigar to his mouth. An aromatic puff of smoke swam before Sirena.

"It would take more than a bolt made from iron to keep me out of your room — assuming first of course that I wished to enter. Which I don't. Not yet. I want that clearly understood," he said mockingly.

Sirena flinched inwardly, as if she had been slapped. Fighting for control, her unfathomable green eyes darkened till they resembled pools of murky water.

"If," Sirena said quietly, "there were someone in this house who chose to enter my room uninvited, I would be obliged —"

Regan interrupted, his eyes laughing, his voice cool and mocking. "You would be forced to bring out your beads and pray that some magic force would open up the heavens and swallow the . . . intruder. My dear Señorita, let me repeat: Neither iron bolts nor magic prayers said on circles of beads will keep me from a room I wish to enter." The blue eyes fell to the goblet in his hand, as did the emerald ones. Transfixed, Sirena watched Regan's bronzed hand slowly crush the goblet until both sides met.

She wanted to lash out — scratch, spit, snarl at

this man. She wanted to make him feel her real presence, feel her nails raking the length of his handsome face. How dare he think he could intimidate her by a display of strength!

"I find it amusing that you would smash down a door locked against you. I would have thought a man of your character and breeding would be above such an insult. In any case, Mynheer, the bolt and lock would not imply any denial of your marital privileges, but would maintain my solitude from *any* intrusion — yours, or the servants', or Frau Holtz's — when I am praying or in retreat. But this discussion gets us nowhere. Secure the bolt and change the lock by the noon hour tomorrow," Sirena said coolly as she turned to leave, her breath coming in quick, hard gasps. God in Heaven, what was there about the man to make her feel this way?

Her hand on the door pull, Sirena felt herself abruptly being lifted and turned around. Once again she found herself locked in a stare with the Mynheer's hard eyes. Without warning, she felt hard, bruising lips crush her own. Her head reeled with the man's passion, her body trembled from his male nearness. His body scent, clean and masculine, assailed her as she parted her lips automatically in response. Then she felt herself being roughly thrust aside. Regan's eyes were laughing at her bewildered, abashed countenance.

"I always win, Señorita," he said coolly. "Remember that."

Sirena fought to control her humiliation and fury. She matched his tone. "What happens, Mynheer, if the prize you win is worth nothing?"

"Then, Señorita, I shall have won nothing. There are times, such as now, when nothing is better than something." With a slight inclination of his head, he dismissed her. "You shall have your bolt and lock by the noon hour tomorrow. Perhaps we should both pray that it serves your purposes."

Chapter Seven

Once again, Sirena tossed the prayer beads on the bed and flung open the door to the clothes press. She was trying to dispel a vision of the teak door lying in splinters, herself standing at bay in the closet, clutching her beads while Regan advanced on her. Finally the thought fled, and she returned to her perusal of the gowns there.

Frau Holtz had, at Regan's request, obtained Sirena's measurements and bought several new gowns from a dressmaker in the town who had willingly obliged to make them quickly, but these she preferred not to wear. Furthermore, she must wear something long-sleeved in order to hide the unsightly scar on her upper arm — which might arouse questions she was not yet prepared to answer.

Oh, what to wear to this travesty she must attend . . . ?

And then she saw the gown she had salvaged untorn and intact, from what Dick Blackheart's men had left, when they'd gone through Isabel's and her belongings. It was her mourning gown, the one she had worn following her father's death a year before. The wide, low-cut neckline trimmed with jet beads offset her long, slender neck and highlighted her skin to a paler tone of amber. A close, dropped waistline displayed her high, full breasts and accented her flat stomach and low-slung, full hips. She would have Juli dress her dark, gleaming hair in the style she had assumed just before she came to the house of Regan van der Rhys, a sleek, heavy knot tightly drawn back from her face and arranged at the nape of her neck. For the final accessory she would wear a high comb studded with moonstones that peeked through the delicate lace of a black mantilla.

In a flight of fancy she toyed with the idea of wearing her rosary around her neck. She knew she would never do such a thing but thinking about it amused her. She could see herself in the flattering black silk, the rosary about her throat, the cross falling upon her bosom. Every time Regan would glance at her he couldn't help but be reminded that she preferred her solitary prayers to him.

In her imaginings she could almost see Regan set his jaw, gnash his teeth, narrow his eyes, and rip it from her neck. His hands, when he ripped the beads from her, would they . . . ?

She remembered the scene between herself and Regan. "I always win . . ." he had said confidently, his cool, unruffled tone sending icy fingers dancing up her spine. Was it his words or his unbridled passion that she feared? Were those icy fingers of fear she felt, or was it something else? The awakening of an answering response; the tender, teasing touches of her own sensuality.

Shaking her head to clear it of the carnal notions that threatened to invade her, she sat down at the window and directed her thoughts back to young Caleb. Caleb liked Regan, he had made it quite apparent. Sirena had seen Regan look at Caleb in much the same way she herself looked at the boy, with fondness. He had sought Caleb out on two occasions already, to take him riding over the plantation and down to the quay.

Caleb called through the door. Juli, who was putting the final touches to Sirena's hair, set down the silver-backed hairbrush and went to open the door. Sirena had to smile at Caleb, who was struggling with his cravat. "Let me help. There, that's better. You look incredibly handsome. I'll be proud of you this evening."

"All these clothes, all these underthings! How often do I have to dress this way?" he complained.

"You'll become used to them, they look well on you. Mynheer will be impressed."

"You look beautiful, Sirena," Caleb blurted out. "Mynheer will be impressed with you, not me!"

Regan, standing at the foot of the staircase, prepared to light another of his exotic cigars. Sirena followed Caleb down the wide, curving stairs, holding her voluminous skirts up from the toes of her slippers, and affording Regan a glimpse of her slim ankles.

The effect her appearance had on Regan was visible. His hand poised in midair, the flaring taper just touching the end of the cigar. His glance was appreciative, so much so Sirena thought his cigar would drop from his mouth

Regaining his composure, Regan blew out the taper just as its flare was about to singe his fingertips. Moving to the bottom step, with his arm outstretched, he reached for her hand which she extended toward him.

"You're breathtaking, Señorita."

"You are most gracious, Mynheer," she answered, lowering her eyes modestly. His hands slipped over hers, making her aware of their hard strength. The little game she had played in her room pierced her and she knew her cheeks were burning. His strong, capable hands would find it easy to rip beads from her neck or do anything they wished with her.

"You must call me Regan. Our guests mustn't think we stand on ceremony." His expression of scornful amusement rankled her. Sirena's nails itched to rake the smile from his face.

Instead she smiled sweetly. "Thank you . . . Regan." Her eyes mocked him in return, the light of the lamps bringing them alive. "Who are our guests?"

Her reference to "our guests" did not escape his notice. Her voice was sweet, her smile saintly, but beneath the black, heavy fringe of her lashes there was a glint of something he had seen in Gretchen's eyes. He must be mistaken, it couldn't be triumph!

"Tonight we'll be entertaining Captain Anton Kloss and his wife, Helga; Señor Chaezar Alvarez, the principal authority for the Spanish government in the East Indies; and Frau Lindenreich, the widow of a company captain — a German lady. It is only a small, intimate party, but I'm sure you'll find it enjoyable."

"I'm sure of it, Myn— Regan," Sirena smiled demurely, leaving him standing at the foot of the stairs as she walked into the drawing room.

Perplexed by her indifference, he floundered for something to say. Caleb's presence provided him with a remark: "And you, young man. How smartly you're dressed! I'm afraid you'll have to suffer through a dull dinner, but I want my guests to see what a fine little brother I'm gaining as well as a beautiful wife! I'll look into some young friendships for you tomorrow. I want you to be happy here in your new home."

Sirena heard Regan speaking to Caleb. If she wasn't careful he'd woo the boy from her.

"Perhaps later, Mynheer. Right now I prefer my sister's company. At least until she's recovered from her grief."

Good work, little brother, Sirena thought to herself.

"Very well, if it's what you prefer," Regan said, "I won't force you into anything."

A djongo dressed in loose-fitting white pants and a collarless white shirt shuffled in on bare feet. He ushered in a tall, heavyset man with a round, rosy-cheeked woman, both in their late middle years. They wore light clothing and seemed comfortable and at home in the van der Rhys house. It was obvious they were frequent visitors. Regan made the necessary introductions and Sirena murmured graceful replies.

"Señorita, you must call me Helga," the ebullient lady laughed. "Regan, you sly dog, you never said how beautiful your intended was. The island will be in an uproar! Rarely have I seen such clear, glowing skin! Now we have two beauties on Java. Frau Lindenreich will have to watch her rival here, thus far she's held the crown for beauty!"

Helga winked slyly in Sirena's direction. "I don't think Gretchen is going to like having someone as lovely as you on the same island with her."

Sirena smiled, liking Mevrouw Kloss. "If I were to put my mind to it I could appear quite ugly."

Regan frowned as the buxom Helga laughed happily at Sirena's joke. Sirena was lovely and Helga was correct. Gretchen wasn't going to like it one bit. He should have waited for Gretchen and Sirena to meet *after* the wedding. It was too late now to reconsider, for the voluptuous, hazel-eyed widow was advancing into the room, the houseboy shuffling at a furious pace to keep up with her.

"Regan, how handsome you look this evening! You quite take my breath away." She smiled sensuously as she raised her luscious mouth for his kiss. Regan silently cursed her and dutifully touched his lips on her pink cheek.

Still smiling, Gretchen slid her arm about Regan's waist. "Captain Kloss and Helga, how nice to see you," she said softly. "And this little creature curled in the chair, don't tell me," she winked roguishly at Captain Kloss, "this must be Regan's bride . . . to-be, that is. What a shy little thing, Regan. Introduce me," she said, jabbing Regan playfully in the ribs.

"Señorita Córdez, Frau Lindenreich." Regan's tone betrayed his misery. Sirena stood and, recognizing Gretchen as the woman who had laughed up at her through the hedge, acknowledged the introduction.

"Does she speak, Regan? Or have you cut out her tongue already?" Gretchen saw the glint of recognition in Sirena's face and silently challenged her to mention it.

Regan glanced from Sirena to Gretchen and then his agate-blue eyes swept to Captain Kloss. The air was charged with conflict.

The captain's watery blue eyes clearly stated that Regan could handle his own affairs. Two beautiful women in one room! A mistake. The evening had hardly begun and he wished he were at sea, basking in the comforting company of the only female he could depend on, his ship! Women! Bah! They meant nothing but trouble and Regan was soon going to find out he had one, large, troublesome handful.

"Well," Gretchen persisted, "does she speak or not?"

Sirena faced Gretchen, the filmy black-lace mantilla casting mysterious shadows on her creamy skin. "I speak when I'm spoken to," she said slowly and carefully, as if she were speaking to a dimwit. "Thus far you have talked around me, as if I weren't here. Address me and I'll answer you like the civilized person I am." Her tone clearly indicated she didn't think Gretchen civilized.

The hazel eyes sparkled dangerously and Regan laughed loudly. Caleb fidgeted nervously and Helga smiled openly. Sirena remained cool, her lovely eyes on the furious Gretchen.

Recovering her composure, Gretchen forced her facial muscles to smile. "My dear, I meant it as a joke. Of course I knew you could speak. How else could you have accepted Regan's proposal of marriage? You did tell him Yes, didn't you?"

"Regan would not accept No for an answer."

That should settle her, Sirena thought nastily. She must be Regan's whore. Why else would he tolerate such ill manners? Gretchen's proprietary ways were obvious to anyone with half an eye. Well, she can have him! But I'll make her sweat first!

Gretchen seemed as if she'd been slapped, but before she could retort Captain Kloss prodded his wife. Mevrouw Kloss was annoyed. Life could sometimes be very dull on Java — she would have liked to see the Spaniard dress Gretchen down. When Helga saw the pleading in her husband's expression she stepped between the two women. Honestly! she thought to herself. It never ceased to amaze her that men who could show bravery and valor in battle could be reduced to squirming cowards if they witnessed a little showing of claws among women.

"Señorita Córdez, Anton and I have been remiss," Helga stated. "Please accept our sympathies. Regan told us of your recent loss."

"You're very kind, Mevrouw, both of you." Sirena's sad smile encompassed the captain and his wife. Her beauty was not lost on Captain Kloss who, in the early days of his career, had made countless voyages to Spain and had always considered Spanish women intriguing, their reserved manner a foil for their sultry, passionate temperament.

Regan's a lucky man, he thought, beauty and breeding. The girl has the face of a madonna and a nature to match.

"Poor Señorita," Gretchen said, clicking her

tongue in sympathy. "I didn't know."

Quickly, Regan related Sirena's story for Gretchen. As he spoke his eyes trailed over her familiarly. She was stunning this evening. She had outdone herself in her choice of gowns, a bright yellow the color of daffodils which offset her pink-and-white skin and silver-blond hair.

"That explains it!" Gretchen cooed.

"Explains what?" Helga asked, and was immediately sorry when she saw Gretchen's eyes change from hazel to deep green.

"It explains why she's dressed like a crow, of course!"

Sirena had to hold herself forcibly in her place. To be insulted by Regan's whore was intolerable. Ooh, she seethed inwardly, wouldn't I just love to snatch her bald-headed!

Regan was speaking: "I find Sirena's dress most refreshing. On a tropical island even the birds wear bright hues, and when women attempt to compete with nature's colors it can be very glaring on a man's eye."

The djongo shuffled into the room again and announced Don Chaezar Alvarez. In his own subservient way, he pointedly looked at the softly ticking clock on the mantelpiece. Sirena could imagine Frau Holtz's storming and bustling back and forth from the kitchens to the dining room, pushing servants out of her way. The last guest, Alvarez, was late in arriving and the Frau's specially prepared dinner was spoiling.

Alvarez entered the room, resplendent in deep-wine knee breeches and rose-colored brocade frock coat which was cut away at the front to reveal a silver-threaded waistcoat and shimmering white ruffles at his throat. His colorful apparel paled Regan's dove-gray costume. Don Alvarez was tall, though not as tall as Regan, and he was well built. His flamboyant clothing might have made another man appear feminine, but his carriage was decidedly masculine. He was obviously a dandy, not a mere fop.

Regan quickly made the introductions. Sirena was puzzled by the sudden coolness in Regan's voice. If he didn't care for the Spaniard why had he invited him to this quiet, little dinner?

"You must call me Chaezar, Señorita, society on this godforsaken island is too small to stand on ceremony." He bowed low over Sirena's hand and smiled at her. The effect was startling, lighting his face with a flash of strong, white teeth amid a close-cropped forest of thick black beard trimmed into a point at his chin. His eyes were dark and there were fascinating lights in their depths as he looked at her from beneath thick, steeply arched brows.

Sirena was charmed and very aware of his handsomeness. In Spanish she said to him, "And you may call me Sirena. How comforting to meet a fellow countryman."

"It must be unbearable for you, it took me quite a long time to adjust to these 'Nederlanders' who garble our mellifluous language with their hard, guttural accent. It was so painful to my ears that I returned the compliment and learned to speak Dutch. Now it is their ears which suffer, not mine."

Sirena laughed mirthfully, drawing an annoyed

150

look from Regan. What did she care? Chaezar was witty and handsome and her countryman. Also, it was somewhat comforting when he referred to the Dutch as "they" and included Sirena in "our."

"For tonight, Sirena," Chaezar said, bringing her fingers to his lips, "we will speak Spanish between us." Feeling Regan's contemptuous glance on him, he turned to face his host. "Regan, you've won yourself a prize. The Señorita is quite beautiful, you don't deserve her."

"I see that you're impressed with my intended, Chaezar," Regan answered coldly.

Gretchen seethed as the two men sniped at one another. Like two dogs snapping over a bone, she thought disdainfully, raking a glance over Sirena, and so little meat on the bone! "Behave yourself, Regan, you have other guests who demand your attention!"

Chaezar was amazed by Gretchen's rebuke. The cat was jealous! "Gretchen is correct, Regan. Entertain Captain and Mevrouw Kloss and, of course, Gretchen. I myself want to become acquainted with my lovely compatriot and her little brother."

"Perhaps later, Chaezar. We've kept dinner waiting too long." Stepping nearer Sirena, he offered her his elbow. "Ladies, gentlemen, shall we go into dinner?"

Sirena's fingers barely touched Regan's sleeve yet she could feel a tension in his arm that matched the tautness of his set mouth. So, the Mynheer had a strong sense of what was his and jealously guarded his rights! I wonder how far he can be pushed? This may be an interesting evening, after all.

A servant opened the double teak doors to the dining room and Regan led Sirena to her seat at the candlelit table.

Regan carried on a low-voice conversation with Captain Kloss while Gretchen was left to talk with Helga, a chore she abhorred. Gretchen's full mouth pouted sulkily and her glances went from Regan to Sirena and Chaezar. I could have stayed home this evening for all the attention I'm getting, she thought. Why in the name of God did Regan invite me? To show me off or to make the Spaniard uncomfortable? He's behaving as if he regretted his decision, whatever the reason.

"You and your young brother, Caleb, must grace my *casa* for lunch and I will have Spanish dishes prepared for you which are fit for the gods."

"I'd like that," Sirena smiled wickedly. "Will you invite me before or after I am married?"

"Before. Then perhaps I can entice you to change your mind. You have no objections, do you, Regan? There are so many things we can discuss about our homeland." Sirena was keenly aware of Chaezar's conspiratorial "our" again. "I haven't had a stimulating conversation in months. All we ever do is discuss trade and our ships. Isn't that right, Regan?" he said, piercing Regan with a fiery gaze.

"True," Regan said coldly and brusquely. What had made him invite the Spanish devil? He must have been out of his mind! Why couldn't Chaezar have paired off with Gretchen? No matter how much Regan blamed his lack of judgment, he still could not have expected the prayer-filled Sirena to be such a scintillating dinner partner.

Sirena perked up her ears as she heard Captain Kloss discuss the *Batavia Queen,* one of Regan's ships. "I keep telling you, Regan, you must travel with a full hold of cargo. Otherwise, the venture is not worthwhile. We spend too long at sea to make it profitable!"

"If you would only hear me out then perhaps you would agree," Regan said authoritatively. "I agree you must travel with a full cargo to port, but that's on your forward journey. On your return I want an empty cargo hold on every second voyage. This will cut your sailing time in half. By my best calculations this would enable you to make four extra trips a year. Besides, we export much more than we import. Why won't you agree? Chaezar has already put the plan to use and it has worked successfully."

"Bah! Empty cargo space! It's a sin! Your father would turn in his grave if he heard you speak like this, Regan."

"My father would have been the first to agree and you know it. You have to move with the times! The Dutch East India Company will sanction my plan."

"Why don't you do something with the pirates and let us sea captains sail our ships!"

"What would you have me do?" Regan demanded. "I've installed extra guns and new heavy weapons with which we'll be better able to defend ourselves." Regan took a breath and modulated his angry tone. "Anton, you force me to say something. I would rather not, but you leave me no other choice. If you don't agree to my plan I'll have to relieve you of your ship. I would hate to do it but the choice is yours."

"Bah! You're infuriating, Regan. I think what you're trying to tell me is I'm too old to captain your ships. If that's what's behind this then just come out and say it!"

"That's not what I'm saying at all and you know it! I merely want an empty hold on every second return voyage."

"Very well," the pompous sea captain agreed. "But you're wrong."

"Wrong! Why, Captain Kloss, Regan is never wrong! He told me himself on more than one occasion," Gretchen broke in. That the occasions were intimate was obvious from the tender look Gretchen bestowed on Regan. Regan scowled at her and she pouted prettily.

Sirena had to bite back her words, so eager was she to voice her opinion on Regan's plan. Inwardly she smiled. If they only knew. Soon the *Rana* would be ready and she would see how great the Dutch expertise was on the sea.

As the evening progressed, Chaezar became more and more openly attentive to Sirena. Caleb watched the dark Spaniard as he amused Sirena with his anecdotes and boastful stories of which he was always the hero. Sirena laughed at his jokes and listened rapturously to his tales of derring-do. During them, her eyes furtively slid across the room to Regan who was smoldering quietly with jealous rancor.

Gretchen made several attempts at conversation with Regan, all unsuccessful. His face a storm cloud of fury, Regan centered his attention on the coquettish Sirena.

Helga Kloss was clearly enjoying herself. Chaezar's discourse on his adventures while in the Spanish Navy was exciting and Sirena's clever repartee was thoroughly entertaining. Helga, too, was aware of Regan's barely suppressed fury, and she secretly applauded the entrancing Spanish señorita who could ignite the tiny flame of misgiving in the self-assured Regan.

Captain Kloss huffed and puffed like an overstuffed walrus. His manner clearly indicated the whole affair was not only in poor taste but spelled trouble.

Once, during a particularly charged lull in the conversation, Helga Kloss addressed Gretchen: "Frau Lindenreich, the little mission is in need of contributions again. If you have any clothing or dress material you no longer want, I can assure you they would be greatly appreciated. Several of the older girls are ready to step out and make their own way by going into service. They can use almost anything you care to give. Shoes, dresses. . . ."

"Never!" Gretchen exclaimed with such vehemence all eyes turned to look at her. "I can see it now, one of your little sniveling orphans going into service wearing one of my gowns, cavorting about the island dressed better than the ladies who employ them. You must be daft, Helga, to even entertain the thought that *I* would have anything in my wardrobe befitting a serving girl!"

"I didn't mean to suggest . . ." Helga sputtered. "It's only that the need is so great. Other women on Java are most happy to contribute . . ."

Gretchen was clearly enjoying herself at Helga's distress. Her upper lip curled in what was to pass for a smile. "I was thinking of taking another girl into my household to help Sudi with the laundry and such. Why don't you have one of your little orphans come to see me. I'll look her over."

Helga's lip quivered in agitation. The *last* thing she would ever do was place one of the mission girls with Gretchen. The German's reputation for cruelty toward her bonded servants was notorious. *And* her morals . . . Helga had devoted herself to the little mission on the outskirts of Batavia and the children had captured her heart. Life had been hard enough on most of them without placing them under Gretchen's heavy hand. "I'm sorry, Gretchen . . . but all the girls are placed. Perhaps next year . . ."

"Yes, of course. And perhaps next year I'll have something to donate to your little charity," Gretchen smirked. She knew full well Helga's reasons for not wanting to place one of the girls with her. Sliding her gaze to Sirena, she said in a mock-soothing tone, "Poor, poor Helga. She just wears herself out with those smelly, little native children. It's a wonder she isn't all skin and bones!" Her glinting eyes swept over Helga's ample girth. "Well, I suppose that's the way of it when a woman is past the hope of having a child of her own. Not that you haven't tried, isn't that right, dear Helga? If they had all lived, how many children *would* you have now, dear?"

Sirena gasped. This German bitch was insufferable! Perverse! Helga was white-faced and at a total loss for words. Out of pity, Sirena said, "Mevrouw Kloss, I consider your obvious interest in this mission most worthy. I'm certain Frau Holtz and myself can contribute to the cause. I'll discuss it with her at the first possible moment."

Helga threw Sirena a look of gratitude and enthusiastically answered the questions Sirena asked concerning the mission and its little inhabitants. All the while both women pointedly excluded Gretchen from their conversation.

As the guests were departing, Gretchen stretched to whisper to Regan. Her face wore a doubtful look as she pressed her luscious mouth to his ear, then assumed an expression of triumph. Throwing Sirena one last scornful look, Gretchen bid her good nights.

With Regan's slight, almost imperceptible nod, Sirena judged he had agreed to meet Gretchen later. She was humiliated as Chaezar smiled knowingly, and his words stung although she gave no hint of her feelings.

"Perhaps Regan's whoring ways will change when you are married. Sometimes it pays to close one's eye to unpleasant things," Chaezar commiserated as he bent to kiss her hand. Sirena's eyes blazed as she returned Regan's cold stare.

Chaezar clapped his host on the back lightly. "A delightful dinner. We must repeat the occasion at my house after you're married. Your intended is charming, I envy you." His dark eyes smoldered as he noticed his host's frost-tipped glare. "Señorita," he said, bowing low and taking his leave.

Sirena's eyes bored into Regan's back as he

157

closed the door. As though her burning eyes were scorching his back, Regan turned and said curtly, "Caleb will take you to your room. It was most generous of you to devote your evening to entertaining Señor Alvarez."

"Yes, Mynheer, the courtesy of my homeland is difficult to abandon. I found Señor Alvarez . . . intoxicating. You must tell me, Mynheer, do you Dutch always make rendezvous with your whores at social functions before the notice of your intended? I only ask so I will know how to act in the future." Her soft voice was an ominous purr and Caleb, standing to the side, gulped as he watched Regan control the fury that boiled within him.

"Somehow I thought you oblivious to my doings this evening. You were so openly . . . intoxicated with one of our guests."

"The word you search for, Mynheer, is polite. I was merely being polite to one of your guests." Her purring tone was fast losing its caress as her eyes bore into the tall, quietly raging man. "You should hurry, Mynheer, it's not polite to keep a lady waiting!" Swiveling abruptly, she took Caleb by the arm and they mounted the stairs.

"Perhaps you misunderstood, Sirena . . ." Regan called, groping for an explanation for his actions. Perhaps Sirena *was* being polite to Chaezar, merely as a compatriot.

"I did not misunderstand. Please, don't insult me further by insinuating I am a fool!"

At the top of the stairs, out of Regan's earshot, Caleb said in a voice that was puzzled and tinged with accusation, "You were occupied with Señor Alvarez all evening. You paid him your complete attention. I noticed the Mynheer didn't like it, he cast murderous glances on the Spaniard. Weren't you doing almost the same thing you accused the Mynheer of doing?" Caleb asked, his face fiery red with embarrassment.

Caleb's spine tingled with the low musical sound of Sirena's strange laughter. "Ah, little brother, it would seem I left something out of your education. There is more to life than charts and maps and fencing. I should have warned you of 'wily women.' True, I was occupied with Señor Alvarez, but for a reason. I was trying to secure information which would help us. In order to accomplish this, I had to make myself attentive. It's not the same as what Regan was doing. He made an appointment with his whore beneath my nose. I find it unforgivable!"

"Did you hear him make the appointment?" Caleb said, defending Regan.

"I didn't have to hear it, it was obvious to everyone. Even Señor Alvarez mentioned it, something a lady should never abide, but I'm sure he only meant to warn me. It's over, we'll forget it for now. You have to trust me, I know what I'm doing. Go to bed now, little brother, tomorrow you must see how our *Rana* progresses."

"Good night, Sirena." Dejectedly, Caleb walked down the carpeted hallway to his room. Wily women! Regan doing that to Sirena! Señor Alvarez kissing Sirena's hand every chance he got! Shaking his head wearily, Caleb quickly shed his constrictive clothes. He liked Regan. He didn't like Señor Alvarez. The woman Gretchen made him feel strange things when he looked at her.

159

Was Sirena right? He had never heard of a "wily woman." Sirena would have to teach him. I like Regan, he muttered to himself. I'd like to be like him when I'm a man. Regan said he would teach me. Would he teach me about men? Was there such a thing as a 'wily man'? What name would they give to Señor Alvarez?

Juli tended Sirena, sleepily brushing her long, thick hair free of its pins. "Don't bother about hanging my gown away, Juli. The morning is soon enough."

Hours later, Sirena found herself lying awake in the low, wide bed, listening for Regan's footsteps. She swallowed a bitter taste that kept rising in her mouth when she didn't hear him. She refused to admit, even to herself, that the bitter taste was unshed tears.

Regan's mood was savage as he mounted his horse in the cobbled yard. His heels dug into the animal's flanks and it shied before taking off in a mad gallop. The temperate breezes were a stimulus to murderous thoughts. Chaezar should see him now, he thought. Riding the beast as if the devils of Hell were on his heels, thinking of that Spanish bitch he had to marry, making cow eyes at the Spaniard all evening!

He rode along the country road that led up into the mountains, then turned back and galloped toward Batavia, reining in at the cobblestones that flanked the steps to Gretchen's front door. Rapping forcefully, he stepped back and waited for the heavy mahogany portal to open.

160

Her eyes widened in mock-delight, Gretchen herself opened the door. "How nice of you to call, Regan," she said impishly. "To what do I owe the pleasure of this late-evening visit, as if I didn't know."

Regan laughed openly, seeing the humor in the situation. "What would you say if I said I found myself in the vicinity and decided to pay my respects?"

"I'd say I was delighted," Gretchen gurgled. "Sit down, Regan, I'll get some wine to toast your visit."

"It's not wine I have in mind," Regan said harshly.

"No, I didn't think it was. Would you like to talk?"

"That's not what I had in mind, either. On second thought, I will have a glass of wine."

Her eyes dancing with merriment, Gretchen handed him a crystal decanter. She waited as he poured himself a drink.

"So, I'm not a guest, is that what you're trying to tell me?" he asked.

"Anyone who comes to visit me after midnight could hardly consider himself here on a formal basis," Gretchen said. "What is it, Regan; why are you here?"

"No reason. Every reason. Perhaps the horse had a mind of its own. Somehow I found myself on your doorstep," he said, draining the goblet and refilling it. He drained the second glass of wine and immediately poured himself another.

Whenever Gretchen saw Regan like this she knew his thoughts were on the events aboard the

Tita. Usually a temperate man, Regan only drank heavily when he was wishing he had been killed, too, that day off Africa. Now he was drowning himself in memories and Gretchen's sweet wine, but Gretchen had other plans.

Taking another long drink, Regan eyed the woman over the rim of his goblet. Suddenly, he stood up and lurched to the side, forcing Gretchen to grasp his arm. "I think," he said slowly and distinctly, "I should go outside. Perhaps the night air will restore my wits."

Gretchen smiled to herself; it had been far too long since she had made love under the stars. She stepped with him through the parlor and dining room, and out into the jasmine-scented gardens behind the house. "I think that's a wise decision," she said, helping him to the door. "Your being here will be our little secret," Gretchen said slyly. "We'll lie on the cool grass and make love. That's why you came, isn't it?"

Regan's eyes narrowed and he peered at Gretchen in the bright moonlight. "Yes, that's why I came. Unfortunately," he laughed, "I didn't bring Sirena's prayer beads with me as you instructed."

"I'm forced to forgive you . . . this time," Gretchen laughed. "I don't think either of us needs any beads tonight. Come to me, Regan, let me make love to you as I would have done had you asked *me* to be your wife." Gently, she removed the wine decanter from his grip and tossed it into the shrubbery.

Slowly, she opened the buttons on his shirt and pulled it down over his arms. Loosening his trousers, she instructed him to remove his boots. With one fluid motion, her own garment slid to the ground. Regan reached out to bring her close to him but she nimbly sidestepped him. Cupping her breasts in both hands, she swayed to some unheard music, her movements seductive and tantalizing. Her skin, wet and shimmering with perspiration, gleamed in the moonlight. Her sultry eyes beckoned and teased the mesmerized man who groped for her.

Regan lurched and this time grasped her shoulder, forcing her to him. His feverish mouth sought for and found hers as they tumbled to the ground. She parted her lips and clutched him to her as if to make them one. Their passion was a seething volcano teetering on the brink of eruption.

Spent, Gretchen lay cupping his head to her breast. Why can't you love me as I love you? she questioned silently.

Regan stirred, his head nuzzling the soft suppleness of her breasts. Gently, he brought his mouth to one rosy tip and crushed her body to his. Gretchen writhed beneath him as he aroused her again. Moaning with pleasure, she rolled from beneath him and crouched on her knees, her breathing ragged. She gazed down into his eyes and with a feline movement was atop him. Regan groaned with pleasure and sought her breasts with his groping hands. Wildly rocking, she brought him once again to the heights of passion.

Regan woke to the shrill cries of exotic birds as they fought their way through the lush, tropical foliage. For a brief moment he felt at a loss to explain to himself why he was lying here at dawn on the cool green moss, naked as the day he was born. His eyes searched the locale and came to rest on Gretchen's house. Memories of lust rushed through his body as he recalled his midnight activities. So, this was where he had spent the night! A vision of Sirena in a frilly black nightdress, cap on her head and the beads in her hands danced unbidden into his mind, and suddenly he laughed.

Chapter Eight

Sirena ignored the light, whispery breeze that stirred the gauze draperies as she paced her large, opulently furnished room. She had opened the shutters, allowing the sun to drench her quarters with its light and heat.

Tomorrow was her wedding day, she would marry Regan van der Rhys and there would be no turning back.

Since the first dinner party with Chaezar and Gretchen there had been several others. She had been introduced to the most prominent people on Java and the other islands. Their faces passed before her and they remained nameless. She knew she was considered quite beautiful by the men and charming by their wives. "Regan is a fortunate man, indeed," they had repeated time and again. And why not? she questioned. Hadn't she made herself pleasing to look at, yet with a restraining hand so as not to be the cause for jealousy among the older, more plain women? Hadn't she sat meekly by, leaving all consequential conversation to the men while her ear was bent with meaningless trifles?

Even Regan seemed approving of her. He was attentive and flattering although once or twice she caught a glimmer of his dismay when he eyed the unrelieved black gowns she wore and her black mantilla. He would have liked to see her wear gay colors and perhaps dress her hair more elegantly, but nevertheless he would allow his gaze to fall on her quite frequently during dinners and afterward when the guests would pair off for card games.

Even when her back was to him she would often feel his eyes on her. The effect was disconcerting, arousing in her contradictory feelings. Mevrouw Kloss, who was a frequent guest, would glance from Regan to Sirena and release a deep romantic sigh. It was evident Helga had formed an opinion that Regan and Sirena were deeply in love. On several occasions Helga tittered excitedly to another of the women and together they looked at Sirena with bright eyes and flushed cheeks.

At times like these Sirena was glad Caleb was excused immediately after dinner to go to his room or walk in the garden. Sirena knew the boy took the opportunity to scale the low foothills on his way to where the *Rana* was hidden and that sometimes he spent nights in the company of the crew. But Caleb was spending far too much time in Regan's company and was coming to respect the man more and more. They had a rapport, a kind of instant understanding. The relationship between them would have been complete if Caleb wasn't always on his guard not to reveal the secret of the *Rana* or Sirena's plan.

Sirena was not offended by Caleb's admiration for Regan. She could understand the boy's feelings. Regan was attentive, sensitive to the moods of others, and he could be very charming. Many times, during the month she had been on Java, she found herself enjoying Regan's company. Waiting expectantly for the end of one of his amusing stories, walking beside him and looking into shops on the busy, planked walkways of Batavia, bumping into Regan's friends and joining them for sherry and tea in their homes.

At first the only way she could bear his company was to push back thoughts of Isabel. Now, and much to her chagrin, there were moments when the *Rana*, Isabel and Uncle Juan seemed to belong to a past life. But it had not happened in a past life, it had happened not long ago! She had seen suffering and she had suffered. The sound of Isabel's screams echoed in her ears, the vision of Uncle Juan's last valiant efforts to defend the ship and his two nieces blurred with the onset of tears. The memory of Caleb's degrading lashing, the spoiling of her innocence never failed to stun her.

No one would make her suffer again! Gone was the girl she had been when she began the journey from Spain. Now she was a woman and she thought as a woman thinks! She had a voice and she would be heard. If they refused to listen, then they would feel the wrath of her actions!

Why should men have all the say? — even the inept, the uninformed, the least of them was put above a world of women! Women must sit meekly by and bend to the wills of men. But not *this* woman! she thought, her blood stirring with the injustice. She had no doubt that, before long, news of a female taking to the seas, captaining her own ship, playing a man's game by men's rules, would create an unbelievable stir. In society's drawing rooms the Capitana would be discussed, condemned. Ladies would raise their eyes heavenward and click their tongues, but every woman who had suffered at the hands of a man merely because she was a woman, and ineffectual in the face of male brutality, would cheer her, applaud her, and whisper silent accolades. She had vowed revenge and she was determined to prove that muscle does not a warrior make!

Her pacing had taken her back and forth before the windows and her last steps left her standing in front of the open clothes press. Sirena's eyes fell on the white gown hanging on the wardrobe door. Wearily, she closed her eyes as her fingers felt the layers of sheer delicate silk. God in Heaven, no woman had less right to wear white! Opening her eyes, forcing herself to scrutinize the blue-white purity of the gown which until now she had avoided looking at, she wailed aloud, "Mother of God, where are the sleeves?"

In a frenzy she turned the gown, examining the bodice. No sleeves! Why hadn't she noticed before? She raced for the door, fumbling with the bolt. "Frau Holtz, Frau Holtz!" she called shrilly, all her frustration and anxiety coming to the surface.

The network of servants brought word to the housekeeper that the Juffrouw was upstairs shouting for her. Frau Holtz mumbled beneath her breath and climbed the stairs, her back held stiffly. Stepping into the hallway and hearing Sirena's frantic call sent chills through her, but the torment in the Señorita's voice twisted her heart. Puffing from the exertion of running up the stairs she flew into the blue-and-white bedroom.

"What's happened, Señorita?"

"Where are the sleeves on the wedding dress? I

168

told you when my measurements were taken that I must have sleeves!"

Relieved her mistress wasn't bitten by a poisonous snake or bug, Frau Holtz was irritated by Sirena's abrasive tone. "Señorita, the climate doesn't call for sleeves . . ."

Sirena whirled on the housekeeper. Her voice was low and dangerous: "I want sleeves on this gown by tomorrow or there will be no wedding. Is that clear? Mynheer van der Rhys will be embarrassed when he stands at the altar *alone!*"

Frau Holtz raised her head haughtily and stared into the glittering green eyes. "The seamstress cannot be recalled. She has left the island."

"Fetch her back," Sirena ordered.

"I'm afraid it's too late. She was going to one of the inner islands. I didn't think to ask which one."

"Then Frau Holtz, it would be wise if you produced a needle and thread and took this gown with you."

"But Señorita, there is no material left. The seamstress did not bring anything but the gown."

"You'll think of something," Sirena said, pulling the gown from its hook on the door and thrusting it into the unwilling arms of the housekeeper.

"Very well, Señorita. What will Mynheer van der Rhys think when he hears of all this commotion?"

"Who knows?"

Who cares? she muttered under her breath.

Frau Holtz heard, and gaped, her eyes protruding from her head in amazement.

Caleb sat hunched in Regan's chair in the

169

D.E.I. offices. Tomorrow was Sirena's wedding. If only he didn't have to appear at the ceremony. After tomorrow everything would be different . . .

If there was only something he could do. What could he, a boy, do? Nothing. He slouched deeper in the chair and started to doze. Voices startled him to awareness and he listened.

"Where did you come by this information?" It was Regan's voice.

"By way of Michel Rijsen's brother, Jacob, first mate aboard the *Jewel of China*. I spoke with Jacob on Sumbawa; he'd just arrived with his ship, and I was ready to leave with mine, bound back to Batavia. Jacob says that Michel, whose ship is loading sandalwood at Sumba, just east of Sumbawa, has seen the *Tita* in Sumba harbor. She did not plan to stay long. Michel was, you remember, to be first mate aboard the *Tita*, but was taken with the pox the day before the . . . fatal trip you made, and could not go with you."

"The *Java Queen* is being loaded this day for its journey to Capetown the day after my wedding. She'll carry a full cargo. Order the men to unload the ship. I'll take the *Java Queen* myself and recapture the *Tita*. I've long thought her sunk — these past eight years. That lying Spanish son of a whore! Does she carry cargo?"

"Aye, Regan, her hold is full. Spices, rice, and silk."

"Michel is sure it's the *Tita*? He should be surprised — he thought the *Tita* sunk!"

"Aye, it's the *Tita*. Michel told his brother your son's initials are still carved in the quarterdeck. You see, he pretended to be wanting to sign on,

170

and went aboard the *Tita* to speak with its captain. He wanted to be absolutely certain she was the ship he remembered. He said he remembered how you and the boy were laughing when you did it and you told the boy one day the ship would be his and the initials would prove it was. Michel said the boy laughed and started to call it his ship."

"True, Fredrik," Regan said, his eyes glazed with memory of that long-ago happy day. "Who captains the ship and what flag does she fly?"

The man Regan called Fredrik said he didn't know. "Michel told Jacob she's named the *Wanderer.* She sails for Capetown in, let's see . . . three days. Can you overtake her and recapture her? Perhaps," Fredrik said kindly, "you'll find some news of what happened that last, terrible day — though the men aboard cannot be the old crew. All perished, you have told us."

"Finally . . . after all these years . . ." Regan said, his voice husky and low. "Thank you for coming and telling me this, Captain Daan."

"We're friends, Regan. But remember, the *Tita* is only a ship. The . . . boy won't be aboard."

"*Ja,* I know!" To Caleb the words sounded tortured.

Regan paced the room, never raising his eyes from the floor. Caleb watched him as he paced up and then down, one large fist smacking into the other. Unable to stand it a moment longer, the boy got up from the chair and left the room. Regan didn't raise his eyes, nor did he hear the boy leave.

Returning home, Caleb raced to Sirena's room

on trembling legs. Quickly he told her of the conversation he had overheard. "What do you think?" he asked.

"I think we take to the sea as soon as Regan does. I'll study the maps of the eastern isles. Even if we're unlucky enough to be chased when we reach the mouth of the river, we'll disappear around the west tip of Java — as if the sea swallowed us." Sirena looked at the anguish in the boy's eyes. "It's an eye for an eye, Caleb. Yes, I'll take the *Tita*, and yes I know what you say the ship means to him. I remember what Isabel meant to me. *She* was alive! *She* was flesh and blood! The *Tita* is only wood. She's a thing, not a person."

"What will you do to her?"

Sirena eyed the boy across from her. "Ask me when the time comes, not now."

Regan chewed thoughtfully on the butt of a cigar. The initial shock of hearing the *Tita* was still afloat had subsided. There was no action he could take. He would have to bide his time until he could sail the *Java Queen*.

Regan became reflective, his thoughts jumping back over the space of time to the good years with his honey-skinned wife and infant son. Hope sprang anew in his heart. Might there be, perhaps, one member of the crew — one of his Dutch sailors who'd not perished, or even one of the cursed Spanish pirateers who took the ship — who knew of the whereabouts of his son?

Though she undoubtedly knew something of his past from her late father, it was typical of Sirena not to have asked him questions concerning his first marriage and his child. More and more, over the past weeks, he had come to admire the cool, poised Spanish woman with skin the color of ivory and the texture of Chinese silk. How well she fit into his social circle! The men found her beautiful and desirable, constantly called Regan a lucky man. The women seemed to find her sincere and interesting, her beauty admirable yet not a source of envy because Sirena was careful not to flaunt it or use it as a tool to attract their husbands' attention. She was intelligent, fiery when her anger was aroused, and every inch a lady.

When Regan thought of Sirena he could still taste her full, moist, petulant lips. He could almost feel her smooth, warm flesh beneath his hand. Could he wait a year, until her mourning was over, to possess her! Whatever, he told himself, provided he could enjoy her company, see her daily, delight in her friendship, he would wait. In fact Regan was fearful to make an advance toward her. In doing so he might alienate her friendship and possibly destroy any chance of making her completely his.

Suddenly he jumped to his feet and called his manservant. Quickly, Regan scribbled a note to Sirena requesting that she leave her rooms tonight for a quiet, intimate, dinner . . . for two.

Sirena had dressed carefully for dinner. She had never dined alone with Regan, and in spite of herself the idea excited her as she descended the wide, curving staircase and walked to the dining room door.

Regan waited in the richly furnished room busying himself by pouring a sherry at the Chinese red lacquered cabinet decorated with black-and-gold firebreathing dragons. At a sound behind him he turned.

"May I join you, Regan?" Sirena found herself admiring his cat-like grace as he stepped toward her.

"You are beautiful, as always," he said, kissing her hand.

"And you're a flatterer, as always," she murmured, disconcerted by the warmth of his lips.

Regan had ordered a table set for them on the verandah outside the dining room. The area was hung with netting to ward off mosquitos and the carefully kept gardens just beyond were lit with lamps that created a fantasy scene.

"It's almost like peeking out from a cloud. Thank you, Regan, it's lovely." Her voice was low and sultry, her eyes gleamed brighter than the candlelight.

Through the dinner which was served by a silent djongo, Regan and Sirena were quiet, almost constrained. Each seemed to be lost in private thoughts. When the table was cleared and the claret was served, Regan asked Sirena if he might smoke. Their silence became companionable and Sirena emitted a deep sigh.

Regan enjoyed seeing her like this. He was contented, knowing that in some way he was responsible for her mood. Her head was turned, looking out into the garden, and the night breezes lifted the mantilla from her cheeks to reveal her delicate bone structure and exquisite profile.

Gently, he reached across the small table and touched her fingertips. "Sirena, I'd like to talk to you." Slowly and in detail, he told her the complete story of the *Tita*. She listened, attentively, aware of his carefully held-in-check anguish. She noticed he skirted mention of the Spanish prison, possibly because he didn't want her to think he was criticizing her homeland. He concluded by explaining the visit of Captain Fredrik Daan and the man's information concerning the *Tita*.

"Our wedding is tomorrow, Sirena. I've told you all this so you can understand why I must leave day after tomorrow. I've got to see the *Wanderer* for myself and determine if she's really the *Tita*."

Sirena lifted her eyes to face him, but the thick black fringe of her lashes obscured the triumph glittering in their depths. "I understand, Regan. Of course you must go." Victory fluttered in her breast and brought a slow smile to her lips. Her plan was succeeding! Her display of affectionate friendship and gentle manner were winning him. If he could tell her this — something so close to his heart — he would tell her anything: his shipping routes, the time of departure of his ships laden with precious cargo . . . He would confide in her and she would execute her revenge!

"Regan, what will you do when you find this ship?"

His face hardened into chiseled lines, his eyes smoldered with determination. "I realize that when I find her my son won't be aboard, but I pray the bastard son of a pig The Hook is!"

The hatred that distorted his features practically took her breath away. "Who is this man you hate with such fervor? What has he done?"

Bitterness twisted his mouth, and through clenched teeth he said, "The man is a brutal killer. My wife suffered greatly at his hands, or should I say hook!"

Even by the light of the candles Regan saw Sirena blanch when he mentioned The Hook. The girl had a vivid imagination! He should have kept his own counsel and refrained from upsetting her.

When Regan mentioned the man with the hook and how his wife had suffered, it brought back that misty night on the *Rana* and Isabel's screams. Now she knew she *must* go after the *Wanderer* herself.

"Regan, surely you don't imagine you can comb the seas, stop every ship, to look for this beast with a hook. Why, the man you seek might even be in your own employ!"

"That could well be, Sirena. Seamen are a closed-mouthed lot and there's no way I can be certain. But I will tell you this: If he's out there, I'll find him!" Sirena experienced an emotion close to pity for him. She understood his determination, could sympathize with his bitterness and even share his thirst for revenge. But satisfaction would be denied Regan; his search for The Hook would bear no fruit. If anyone would capture the beast with the hook it would be Sirena Córdez! Her vengeance would be sated — and she would do it without the help of the man responsible for her sister's death. She would best them all!

Chapter Nine

Sirena stood before the long, smoky mirror. Her reflection was that of a tall, white specter in the distortion of the glass. Frau Holtz had done a fair job of setting sleeves into the gown's bodice. Actually they were only elbow-length, but their fullness and modest double layer of silk organdy disguised the wound on the upper arm which had healed leaving a raw, red angry-looking scar she hoped would fade in time.

Carriages had been dropping off their passengers for more than an hour. Many of the wedding guests had arrived by native proas, drifting up the lagoon that bordered the van der Rhys' property a quarter mile to the north. From the private quay, natives from the plantation compound carried those ladies who did not care to walk the distance to the house along the cobbled path, in tandoes, Javanese sedan chairs.

The hum of conversation had become louder and Juli had breathlessly announced to Sirena that the musicians were tuning their instruments. Caleb appeared shyly at Sirena's door, looking as uncomfortable as could be in his starched white shirtfront and stiff new boots.

A meaningful look passed between the young boy and the girl in her white wedding dress. A look that said there would be no turning back, they were entrapped by vengeance as surely as if they

177

were caught in a whirlpool. The dice were thrown, the deck was dealt, and Sirena and Caleb knew there would be no real winner in the game they played.

The musicians struck a chord below, in the drawing room, and Sirena's spine froze. The moment had come. Solemnly she lifted the translucent veil over her face and stepped forward, taking Caleb's arm.

"Here we go, little brother. Are you with me?"

"Until death, Sirena." His black eyes looked up adoringly although his mouth was ringed with white betraying his fear.

Down the wide stairs they stepped, the strains of music a dirge in Sirena's ears. Seen through the veil, everything about her seemed distant and unreal. There was an expectant hush from the guests who flanked the long, tiled hallway and spacious drawing room, now empty of furniture save the benches seating the ladies in their full, gaily colored gowns. The perimeters of the room were decked with flowers whose lush blooms lent an exotic scent to the air.

Standing before the glass-paned doors leading to the garden, Regan awaited her. A tightness about his mouth and a furrow between his brows betrayed his nervousness. He turned to watch Sirena's progress on Caleb's arm with that infuriating expression of amusement laying about the corners of his flashing blue eyes.

He's actually enjoying all this! Sirena thought, anger flushing her cheeks. He's won! He insisted we be married as soon as possible, regardless of my protests, and he's delighted with his victory.

Enjoy it while you may, Mynheer van der Rhys, your victory will be short-lived!

Father Miguel, religious leader of Batavia's Catholic community and missionary, stood before the garden doors, his tall, stately form outlined against the late afternoon sun. He looked out of place away from his church, but the ornate wooden structure had burned to the ground a month before. A worried look creased the Father's forehead, for although Regan had promised that the children — when they were born — would be raised Catholic, the Portuguese priest was well informed about Regan's lack of religion. Even as a Protestant, van der Rhys was not a true believer. Father Miguel feared for the young devout Señorita who was to marry the strong godless man.

Regan took his place next to the priest and turned to watch Sirena's slow, steady approach. She was dazzling; the white of her gown emphasized the rich golden tones of her skin and the black of her hair. Beneath the fine veil, Regan thought he perceived a glimmer of tears in her wide, heavily fringed eyes. She's beautiful, he thought, any man would be proud to take her to wife.

Sirena stood beside Regan, her right hand in his. As Father Miguel commenced the ceremony in his deep, resonant Portuguese-accented Latin, Sirena chanced a glimpse at Regan. Standing beside him this way, she felt so small and vulnerable. As tall as she was, he towered over her. His sheaf of winter-wheat hair reflected the sun rays filtering through the glass. His expression was serious, his blue eyes penetrating, his clean, square jaw set.

Suddenly Sirena felt her knees weaken and the hand resting so lightly in Regan's began to tremble. The enormity of the situation struck her full force. Could she carry it off? Could she actually marry this tall, handsome man next to her? Marry him and swear before God to honor him, to love him, and then wreak havoc upon him? Was this actually necessary — couldn't she have found another way to avenge Isabel and Tio Juan?

It was too late for thoughts such as these, she reminded herself. It was because of this man she could never marry anyone else, for no one would want a ruined, soiled woman. There was no turning back, she had made her decision and now she must live up to it! For Isabel, for Tio Juan and, she admitted, herself!

The trembling of her hand ceased, her back stiffened with renewed determination as she became aware of Father Miguel's rich tones announcing: ". . . before God and these witnesses, I now pronounce you man and wife."

Through the long, exhausting hours of the evening, Regan remained attentively at Sirena's side. Considerate of her needs, introducing her to guests she had not met before, he was the picture of a delighted groom.

Sirena's nerves were strung as tautly as the violin strings on which the musicians played. She felt herself passing through the celebration of her wedding as if through a dream. Nothing seemed real or to have substance. The food was tasteless, the wine flat, the conversation meaningless. During one of the dances she glanced up at the mirror over the mantel and saw herself on Regan's arm. Her cheeks were flushed, her eyes were bright, a becoming smile was on her lips. For a moment she hadn't recognized herself and she found herself thinking, What a pretty girl and she seems so happy, I wonder if she's in love with her dance partner? Startled to realize the glowing girl dancing in the mirror was herself, she missed a step. Regan held her arm and steadied her. "You must be exhausted, Sirena. Come sit here." He led her to a chair. "I'll get you a cool drink."

As she waited for him to return with the punch, once again her eyes gravitated to the mirror. Her image seemed one-dimensional, flat and lifeless. Where was that spark, that fragile thread-like flicker of animation that made her unique unto herself? Had it evaporated, become absorbed into the atmosphere like the puddles on the cobblestones after the rain? Looking across the room, she saw Regan — her husband now — quipping with several guests. He was lively, vital, throwing his head back in laughter. He had stolen her spark and crushed it in his powerful hands by forcing her to play out this farce pretending to be someone she was not. That he was unaware of this travesty was of little consequence to her. It was enough that *because* of him her personality was buried in a sham. Her eyes accused him and found him guilty.

Alone in her room, Sirena prepared for bed. The windows overlooking the gardens were open, allowing the night breezes to carry the sweet, aromatic scents of flowers and spices into the room. She had slipped away from the last lingering guests an hour ago to seek the peace of solitude. Climbing the stairs, she had looked back and her eyes were drawn to Regan. As if her glance were a physical touch, he turned from his conversation and looked up at her and their eyes locked. After a long moment she lifted her chin, turned her back, and proceeded up the stairs.

By the time she reached her room her heart was beating wildly, her pulses throbbing savagely. His one brief glance desired her, coveted her, and was regretting his promise to free her from sharing his bed. She remembered the smile which had played about his lips and in the corners of his eyes. Could it be he had no intention of honoring his promise?

In spite of herself, Sirena took elaborate pains with her toilette. For a final touch, she placed a few precious drops of civet musk on her pulse spots; its heady scent enveloped her in a cloud of sensuality.

Sirena arranged a soft, loose knot atop her proud head, with curly, wispy ringlets feathering her brow and the nape of her neck. Satisfied that she created an alluring picture, she waited.

Over and over she rehearsed the scene in her mind. Regan would tap on the door, seeking entrance. Hesitantly, shyly, she would admit him. His eyes would cover her hotly, their searing passion and need burnishing her soft flesh. She would stand with her back to the dim lamplight, allowing him to discern the voluptuous outline of her body through her thin, lavender nightdress.

He would stand close to her, the musk intoxicating him with desire. His hand would reach out and touch the soft ringlets falling against her cheek, then caress the smooth, silky skin of her neck. Roughly, desperately, he would pull her against his muscular body, his breath would come in light, wine-scented pants. His mouth would seek hers in a long passionate kiss. Drawing away, his eyes would burn into hers, pleading, begging her to release him from his promise.

Sirena smiled wickedly as she imagined his desperation when she allowed him to see that he had aroused her and yet continued to demand that he hold firm to his word. He would concede to her wishes grudgingly, and being the proud man she knew him to be, would never beg his rights as her husband.

Finally, in a modest manner, she would insist he leave. And he would, his head held high, his back straight and tall. And Sirena would know he didn't take her gentle rejection gracefully. His pride would prick him and he would spend a long sleepless night tossing amongst his bed covers . . . alone.

The scene she imagined was so vivid, so real, Sirena felt her first, faint stirrings of desire for a man. That the man was Regan, who she blamed for the tragedy aboard the *Rana*, was a ludicrous affront to her reason. Yet she found it difficult to still this sudden awareness of her sexuality and berated herself for her wanton cravings. The picture of Regan, tall, muscular, sun-gilded, silvery-gold hair dipping low over his broad, intelligent brow, flashed before her, almost taking her breath away. It was only when she remembered his powerful ca-

183

pable hands and cold, agate-blue eyes that her resolution returned.

Back and forth she paced the room, straining to hear his knock on her door. She heard the departure of the last guests and sounds of Frau Holtz and the djongos securing the house for the night. Still she waited . . .

The long, exhausting day was taking its toll. Sirena eyed her bed longingly. Leaving her lamp burning so Regan would see the light beneath her door and know she was still awake, Sirena removed her slippers and crept beneath the silken coverlet. Deliberately opening the button of her nightdress and posing alluringly, she waited . . .

Once or twice she felt herself drift off into a doze and she shook herself awake. She waited . . .

Suddenly the sound of Regan's boots coming down the hall toward her room shocked her to full attention. Expectantly, she listened as the footsteps came closer and stopped outside her door. Her pulses pounding, her breasts heaving with anticipation, she drew in her breath sharply.

A footfall, then another and another!

He was going right past her room. He hadn't knocked and sought entrance! There would be no gentle touch, no burning kiss, no sweet rejection!

A few minutes later, still awake, she heard his steps pass her door once more, then the sound of his boots on the staircase, and finally the front door open and slam shut. Moments later, hoofbeats sounded their tattoo on the drive and she knew it was Regan. He was leaving, galloping down the country road toward town — the same road that passed Gretchen Lindenreich's house!

Grasping at straws, Sirena willed herself to reason that Regan was making an early start for the *Java Queen.* He had explained to her during their intimate dinner that he would be leaving the morning after the wedding to search for the *Tita.*

That's what he had said, yet no power on earth would convince Sirena that Regan wasn't going to stop at Gretchen's first. Sirena could imagine the Teutonic bitch's triumph to know Regan had left his nuptial bed to fly to his Valkyrie's arms and die a little in the throes of passion as she transported him to Valhalla.

Shamefaced, Sirena buried her head beneath the cover, pummeling her pillows with tightly clenched fists. In place of sweet rejection, she was being raked by the sharp talons of scorn. She had waited and he never came! He had left her for his German whore, denying Sirena even so little as the right of refusal!

She would make him pay, somehow! Unbidden, a plan began to take form in her mind. Regan had deprived her of the satisfaction of turning him away. Now, without a doubt, she would deprive him of something he wanted . . . the *Tita!*

Regan spurred the beast beneath him. He had to get away before he did something he would regret.

The cool fragrant breeze was a balm to his tortured body. Never in his life had he wanted a woman as much as he wanted Sirena. He had seen the light under her door and for one brief moment his step had faltered, but he hadn't stopped. The hour was late, she should have been asleep hours

185

before. Quickly, he reined in the horse. He could go back, he could take what was his, but was that what he wanted? No, his mind rebelled. The unbidden memory of Sirena demanding a bolt and new lock for her door sprang into his mind. A door bolted against him in his own house! She had been beautiful, desirable, exciting him to lose his composure. He had seen the fright in her eyes when he had crushed the silver goblet. What a fool he had been. Instead of intimidating her with a display of strength, he had alienated her further. He had almost felt the sting of her nails across his face. And to make a bad situation worse, he realized he'd made a fool of himself and instead of backing off and allowing her the dubious victory, he had forced himself on her. He had demanded she acknowledge him the victor by surrendering to his embrace. He had been aware of the faint response stirring in her and he had also realized that if that response were allowed to blossom, she, not he, would have become the vanquished. "I always win," he had told her with false bravado to disguise the passion she had roused in him. The taste of her lips, the feel of her lush body crushed against his were as fresh in his memory as if he'd thrust her from him the second before. With a composure which was beyond his belief, she had asked, "What happens if the prize you win is worth nothing?" Regan's instincts became thoughts and he knew that if he had insisted on his marital rights he would have won the battle and lost the war; her words would have become reality. He would have won nothing: her body without her spirit would be meaningless.

What was this sultry Spaniard doing to him? Why did she make him feel this way? Why, after all his experience with women, should he suddenly care about her spirit, her soul, instead of just the delights and desires of her body? Would she come willingly to his bed?

He needed a drink, needed it badly. With a flick of the reins he spurred the horse down the hard-packed, dusty road toward the D.E.I. offices. There was a bottle of rum waiting there to keep him company through the long, lonely night.

The bend in the road took him past Gretchen's house. A yellow light winked behind gauze draperies. A drink was much closer than the D.E.I. offices and Regan turned his mount into Gretchen's drive.

Not bothering to knock on the heavy door, he thrust it open and stared into the brightly lit room. Gretchen stood before him, a goblet in each hand. "You're late, Regan. I expected you an hour ago."

Regan laughed harshly as he downed the wine in a gulp and his free hand drew her to him. He flung his goblet against the wall, as did Gretchen. His mouth crushed hers, his hands ripped the gown from her body. Her creamy breasts became taut as Regan's hands cupped their suppleness. Moaning with desire, Gretchen pressed her body to his as she loosened first his shirt and then his trousers. Locking her arms around his broad back, she undulated against his nakedness.

Regan brought his arms around her and pushed her onto the bed. A fierce cry of pain escaped her as Regan entered. Frantically, low moans shaking her, her body moving, writhing against him, she

187

clawed his scarred back, her mouth burning beneath his. Tearing her mouth from his she pleaded, "Love me, Regan, love me." With a sudden thrust from Regan the words died in her throat as his lips ground into hers.

Consumed, she relaxed in Regan's arms. Gently she nibbled on his ear lobes. "Sleep," she crooned. Regan sighed heavily and was asleep in seconds.

Gretchen lay with her head on his massive chest. He had come to her on his wedding night. It must mean something, it had to mean something. Did the Spaniard reject him? What had made him come to her? Did he love her? He must, otherwise why would he be lying next to her. "Oh Regan, I love you so," she whispered. "This should have been our wedding night, yours and mine, our unforgettable wedding night." Regan stirred restlessly beneath her and she whispered softly in his ear. Well, it wasn't her wedding night . . . but she could make it unforgettable. She had the power to make it unforgettable. Gently, she moved away from his naked body and padded over to the chest in the corner of the room. She glanced over her shoulder as she withdrew a small pouch.

Quietly, on tiptoe, she peered down at Regan; he was sleeping soundly, his face was relaxed.

Stealthily, she padded away to the kitchen and sprinkled a little of the powder into a small wooden bowl. She added a few drops of water to the finely ground powder and stirred it with her index finger. She crept back to the bed and knelt down at the side of the bed and gently spread the mixture on Regan's manhood. Touching a bit of the mixture to her own, most intimate parts, she then washed her hands and discarded the bowl.

Gracefully she slid into the bed and lay next to Regan. She pulled the gauze-like coverlet over her legs and lay still a few minutes measuring Regan's quiet breathing, trying to relax her own tortured gasps. What would he say when it was all over? Would he hate her? She stifled a laugh. He'll be so drunk with passion one of the houseboys will have to take him home, she mused.

When she decided enough time had elapsed she began to stroke his body, and dart her tongue over his hard mouth. She moved so that she lay atop him, with her breasts crushing his chest. Bringing her face close to his she forced her passion-seared lips against his. His lips parted and her tongue explored his.

Regan opened his eyes, every muscle in his body twanging to be released as he wrapped his arms around her. His back arched as his legs spread, forcing Gretchen's body to move against him. "You bitch," he groaned, "why did you do it?"

Gretchen, held like a vise in his grasp, sought to elude him, to heighten his desire. With a vicious thrust he pierced her, locking her to him. Animal lust burst forth as both bodies arched and plunged again and again. Gasping, his body glistening with perspiration, Regan flung Gretchen on her back.

"Ride me, Regan," Gretchen screamed. "More, more."

Unable to control himself, Regan plunged again. Wave upon wave of passion ripped through him. His heart hammered in his chest as he sought release, only to find himself once more on the crest of desire.

Gretchen, eyes glazed, body gleaming beneath the titan astride her, rocked her body to meet each wave of passion and cry out demanding still more.

An eternity later, Regan lay, his breathing harsh and ragged to the point of a death rattle, his body limp, his loins raw and burning. "Bitch," he gasped. He wanted to kill her with his bare hands but he couldn't move.

Gretchen, her breathing normal, smiled wickedly. "Regan, I didn't know . . . I swear . . . I thought . . . I just assumed —"

"Damn your soul to Hell, were you trying to kill me?"

"Only with love," she cooed. "Wasn't it magnificent, Regan?"

"What time is it?" Regan croaked.

"An hour before dawn," Gretchen laughed. He gasped in awe. Gretchen laughed again. "A memorable night, wouldn't you say?"

Clenching his teeth in agony, Regan rose from the bed and was forced to grab the bedpost for support.

"How manly you look," Gretchen gurgled as Regan began to dress himself.

His trousers secure, he looked at Gretchen and said quietly, "I'll kill you for this. Not today, not tomorrow, but one day soon — do you understand?"

"But darling Regan, you came to me, and on your wedding night. I only wanted you to have a night you could remember," she said fearfully.

"I'll remember," Regan said, opening the door. "I'll remember."

His ominous words sent a chill over Gretchen's perspiring body. Well, no matter what he said, he enjoyed it, she pouted. What a performance! she sighed sleepily. A night to remember . . .

Chapter Ten

Caleb and Sirena lowered themselves quietly down the trellis beneath Sirena's window. As their feet touched the ground, she breathed deeply with relief. They had been unobserved. What was more, Juli could be trusted to set the food inside her bedroom door, should she and Caleb not return within a day. The handmaid had been puzzled when Sirena first gave her her instructions — and had looked quizzically at the key given over to her. But the girl now loved Sirena, and would certainly not question her mistress. Yes, she would unlock the door, set the food inside — not even opening the door wide enough to see into the room — then reclose and lock it; no, Frau Holtz would not see the key, and yes, she would return it to Sirena on the Mevrouw's return . . .

"Mevrouw"! What strange words the Dutch had, Sirena mused, as she and Caleb made their way across the vast gardens behind the estate. First I was "Juffrouw" — "Miss" or "Señorita." Now I am — and how ugly the term is! — "Mevrouw," or "Mistress." A graduation to true mistress of the household. Let Frau Holtz beware!

Jan Verhooch met them, with horses, at the westernmost end of the gardens, and smiled encouragingly at his "capitana."

"Good evening, Jan," Sirena whispered.

"You've not waited long?"

"I would wait much longer for a chance to be back at sea again, Capitana!" he chuckled.

Caleb, who had secretly carried the message to Jan two hours before, now helped Sirena mount the placid roan steed. It and two others had been pastured near the *Rana*'s cove several days before, to be ready whenever they were needed to convey Sirena and Caleb to the ship.

Painting the ship black had been an ingenious idea. Even this close it was difficult to see the ship against the dark night.

Jan leading, for this was the first time Sirena had followed the jungled slope down to the cove at night, they made their way at last to the tiny beach that cupped the cliff-framed cove, and approached the ship. Only one light burned on deck.

"Jan," Sirena whispered as they climbed up the ship's ladder, "tell the night watchman to go below — and any other of the crew who may be on deck. When I call to you and the men, after passing through the channel at the river's mouth, then — and only then — are they to come up on deck. I want them to see how I skirt the rocks at the ocean's edge and triumph over this River of Death!"

In her cabin, Sirena shed her clothing and rummaged in the large battered sea chest for her abbreviated costume. Gleefully, she donned the tight shorts with the tattered bottoms. She buttoned the shirt over her jutting breasts and pulled the tails high on her midriff. The first several buttons refused to remain closed. No matter that the buttons popped open to reveal a deep, full cleavage. She shrugged as she pulled on shiny leather knee boots and folded the tops to above her knee. Her creamy, tawny skin glowed in the dim lamplight. Next she tied a multi-colored striped scarf around her head, its ends hanging loosely over one ear. Suddenly she laughed aloud as she pictured herself standing on the rolling, pitching deck. Perhaps the enemy would die of shock when they saw who captained the frigate.

Carefully, she unrolled the charts that rested next to her bunk and scrutinized them. Satisfied, she dug beneath her bunk and withdrew a cutlass which she fastened to her side. Confident with the weapon next to her, she left the room to meet the crew.

Her hands gripping the wheel, Sirena felt at peace for the first time in weeks. She threw back her head, the warm salt sir like a balm to her body. She felt as free as the air.

The frigate had skimmed out of the cove and down the winding river, over the white-capped breakers and — into open water. The sea was rough and Sirena found it took all her strength to hold the frigate steady.

There'll be a storm before the day is over, she muttered to herself, the wind is from the west and it's wild and to be reckoned with. Excitement made her heart beat fast as she pictured herself winning the battle against the elements. But she would always be the victor. The sea would never beat her.

Less than five minutes out to sea, she called for Jan to take the wheel. "Do as I tell you and there will be no problem," Sirena said loudly over the crashing waves as the frigate precariously topped one swell to challenge another. "Remember, at the wheel you are its master."

Picking up the horn that lay next to the wheel, she spoke loudly, her voice carrying over the wildly thundering swell. "All hands to the quarterdeck. Heave to!"

Sirena climbed down from her perch and strode to the deck as the men came out of the ship's hold; she was greeted with loud exclamations of surprise. Instinctively, Sirena reached for the cutlass at her side. Her hand on the hilt, she stood and gazed from one to the other of her crew.

"What say you, men? Speak up now. I'm your captain. Look back ashore. We've passed the rocks at the mouth of the River of Death. Do you not now trust my skill? For Jan has doubtless told you of my sex, and you may not have placed full trust in me. From this moment on you owe allegiance to no one save me and this ship. If there's one of you who refuses to obey, then over the side you go for the sharks. I'll play fair with you. I ask the same in return. You'll be given good food and ale. Any booty we secure you may divide among yourselves. Is there any man jack of you that doesn't agree to my terms?"

Sirena stood facing them, legs slightly parted, hands low on her hips, her wild and night-dark hair streaming behind her.

"Aye, Capitana," came the reply from one and all. Then, from Jan: "We give you our allegiance and our lives while aboard this ship." The others nodded agreement as their eyes met her boldly.

"Very good," Sirena said curtly. "There's one more thing. I'm a woman, and I wish to be respected as a woman first and your captain second. The first of you who makes a move in my direction will find himself cleaning his guts from the deck!" With the agility of a cat, Sirena had the cutlass free of its sheath, advanced a step, and nicked the button from the shirt of the man closest to her. He lowered his eyes to see his naked chest and lifted his head, a surly look on his face.

Sirena backed off a step and narrowed her eyes. "Your name, seaman," she said harshly.

"Wouter . . . Capitana." The surly look was now openly insolent and suggestive. Sirena drew in her breath and brought the tip of the cutlass to the man's throat. Gently, she pressed the tip of the blade against his flesh and smiled. Her words were cold and clipped as she tilted her head to the side to observe the man's bulging eyes.

"A moment ago I read lust in your eyes, your countenance carried hostility and insolence. If I ever," she said slowly and deliberately, "see such a look again, I'll burn your eyes from their sockets. Understand?"

Saliva drooled from the seaman's mouth. If he swallowed the tip of the blade would draw blood. He tried to make a sound only to feel warm wetness drip on his chest. Sirena laughed as she withdrew the blade and carelessly wiped it on the man's trouser leg.

"It's well you fear me, seaman. For a moment I thought your brains were in your loins. Don't ever make that mistake again." The seaman gulped and backed against the quarter rail, the eyes of the crew boring into him.

His dark eyes were thoughtful and crafty as he muttered, "Aye, Capitana."

" 'The matter is ended. One warning is all I ever give. Who's to serve as cook aboard this ship?"

"Tis me, Capitana," replied a wizened old man with not a tooth in his mouth. "I know me way about the galley."

Sirena smiled. "And your name, cook?"

"Jacobus, Capitana."

"You're the only man besides Jan, my first mate, who has access to my cabin. To anyone else I will consider it an act of mutiny. Is that clear?" she asked, her eyes on Wouter.

"Aye, Capitana," came the chorus of replies. Sirena noticed that Wouter's lips remained compressed. Her eyes narrowed. She would kill him if she had to. His blood on the *Rana*'s deck wouldn't bother her at all.

"Remember, I told you a ship will make better time with the hold empty. Speed is of the essence."

"Aye, Capitana, I remember," said Jan.

"Now I want to study these charts and I have entries to make in the log. This log is for your eyes and mine alone — and Caleb's."

Sirena unrolled the charts and studied them carefully. Her father had taught her well, just as she had been teaching Caleb, who was a promising seaman. If she shortened sail and kept to windward she should be able to outmanuever Regan and reach the rendezvous ahead of him with time to spare, even though she was following a course

197

along the southern shore of Java whereas Regan would doubtless take the northern shore to reach Sumba. She hoped the *Tita*, or *Wanderer*, had not left the sandalwood island yet, for if it had, she knew not which route it would follow. She had one important advantage over Regan. His larger ship wouldn't sail too well in heavy weather. The *Java Queen* wouldn't heave to in a gale under a reefed main topsail.

Sirena looked toward the skies; there would be heavy weather shortly. Her heartbeat quickened at the thought of meeting Regan commanding his ship — perhaps after Bali, the beautiful island off Java's eastern tip, where Regan too would take a southern route. What would he think when he saw her aboard her ship. Would he know she was his wife? Not likely. What could a man know of a woman if he wasn't interested enough in her to sleep with her?

His rejection stung again. How she would love to have reminded him that night of his promise to respect her period of mourning and leave her to her prayers! But her cheeks burned with shame as she remembered her careful toilette, how she had waited for him, even rehearsed what she would say. And then he had denied her the pleasure of the argument, of seeing his desire in those hard eyes. At times, she almost hoped he *would* recognize her! She'd rather have him learn her secret than think of her waiting alone in her room, crying with her need for him. Anything was better than being the object of his ridicule. Still she might not see him at all. If she was clever she could overtake the *Wanderer* and get away quickly. A few moments in some instances could be an eternity. Speed was the answer, it always came down to speed. Once again she studied the charts — and laughed.

Two days now, the *Rana* had been urged on by a strong westerly. She had passed the eastern tip of Java, and Bali, and could see Sumbawa — Sumba's northern, sister isle — off the larboard bow.

"Sail ho!" came the shout from the rigging.

So, we made it after all — I was right, Sirena thought gleefully. I outraced him and I'll outsmart him too! "What flag does she fly, Caleb?"

"None. And she's tightened sail!"

"Good! Caleb, come here! All hands on deck!" Sirena shouted. "Four men to mount the shrouds, four men to the yardarms — they'll slice the *Wanderer*'s rigging. I'll steer her directly astern at full speed and our ram will puncture her stern. Look lively now and tighten sail. When I give the order, fire from the bow as I ram the stern. She won't have time to turn her sail. Heave to, men!" Sirena yelled as she gripped the wheel. "Caleb," Sirena ordered, "raise the red flag on the foretopmast. Speed, Caleb, quickly now. Surprise is our best ally. We cannot lose a minute!"

Caleb climbed into the shrouds with the other men and hung onto the rigging. She was actually going to ram the *Wanderer*. He didn't think she'd have the nerve to try it. From the looks on the crewmen's faces they hadn't thought so either. But if Sirena said she would do it, she would. She handled a ship better than any captain he had served under.

199

The quarry was dead ahead and Sirena could see the *Wanderer*'s men scrambling on the deck. "Fire on the count of three!" Sirena ordered. "One! . . . Two! . . . Three!"

A loud deafening crash sounded as the cannon-ball made contact with the renamed *Tita*, splitting a hole in her deck. As the ram punctured her stern large splinters of wood flew in the air. Men toppled overboard as other seamen ran to check the rolling cannon, which was no longer stationary. The crackling and rending of broken wood was deafening.

Sirena shouted the order to board the ship. "Quickly, she'll sink within the hour."

"Lower the flag," Jan ordered one of the men as he swung with his cutlass.

Sirena stood on the bow of the *Rana* and watched as her men fought tooth and nail to over-take the galleon. But the *Wanderer* was old and rotted with teredo worm; the crew was just as rotten.

"Secure the ship!" Sirena shouted from the bow. "Let no man escape!" With an agile move Sirena grasped the rope Caleb swung to her from the rigging and leapt aboard the galleon, her cut-lass clanking on the deck as she landed. "How many men, Caleb?" she asked breathlessly.

"Two score if that many and they've no stom-ach for fighting. Already we've won!"

"Lower the jolly-boats so that we may toss these men into them and let them wait to be rescued. But first," she called out, "is there a man on this ship with a hook for a hand?"

The men stood before her gawking, their

mouths hanging open because of her dress and the authority she held over her crew. There was no answer to her inquiry.

"Hold out your hands, the lot of you!" Sirena unsheathed the cutlass and held it in front of her. Angrily she sliced the air as she watched first one man and then the next hold out his hands.

"It is well for the lot of you there's no such man aboard," she said coldly and cruelly. One of the men, the first mate, shivered slightly at her words.

Suddenly Sirena laughed a gay musical tinkling laugh that raised the hackles on Caleb's neck. Sirena paced threateningly before the *Wanderer*'s crew. The men were lined up against the rail, their complexions oily yellow in the light from the smoky lamp pots. She strode down the line, the heels of her boots clicking a staccato on the wooden deck, and stopped before a tall, heavy man who stood apart from the crew. From his dress and feathered cocked hat she assumed he was the captain. They locked stares. Sirena's upper lip curled in distaste. The man was sweating profusely, his chest heaved, his thick lips trembled with fear.

"You're the captain, aren't you?" she demanded. "Answer me!" she challenged his silence. The man could only shake his head in the affirmative.

"Who does this ship sail for? Who's your superior?" Sirena asked, her tone almost light and conversational; but deep within her she burned with shame, for the enemy crew by and large spoke Spanish. The captain, his eyes riveted on the cutlass she brandished, was quaking in his boots.

"Answer me, swine! Who owns this ship?"

Her green eyes glittering dangerously, she advanced on him, and he backed away from her, gasping with fright. Before her disbelieving eyes he toppled over the rail, disappearing into the swells below. The wind was rising, howling about her head, but the captain's scream resounded in her ears. The crew looked down into the turbulent sea muttering: "He's done for . . ." "Never was any good in the water . . ." "Serves 'im right . . . the coward."

Sirena had no stomach to pursue her questioning. Caleb's call came to her over the howl of the wind.

"All cargo is aboard . . ."

"Into the jolly-boats, the lot of you!" The *Wanderer*'s crew were lowered in the ship's jolly-boats, for their galleon was sinking fast. "All hands, back to our ship!" She jumped the widening gap between the two ships with agility. "That's it, Jan, hove away from this scurvy marauder! She'll not last long. Steer before the wind, quickly now!"

The frigate true now on a westward course, Sirena stood at the bow, one hand on the rigging and the other on the hilt of her cutlass, measuring the sea. For the wind, increasing steadily all that day, had now churned up the waves into a fury. It would be a stiff fight to best the wind to westward, where her course now lay, and she might have to veer off the south or north until the gale changed somewhat.

She saw the sail before the cry came from the rigging.

"Sail ho!"

Quickly she turned to Caleb, who stood not far from her. "Go below, little brother. If it is Mynheer van der Rhys, he mustn't see you. And, I pray, he will not recognize his timid señorita!" She had added lip and cheek rouge to her face, and hoped that the new look, plus her costume, would utterly confound him.

Unwillingly, Caleb obeyed.

"Man the guns, but fire only if I give the order," Sirena called back to Jan. "Steer straight on. She's coming to accost us, and if she doesn't veer off we'll ram her as we did the *Wanderer!*"

Hair billowing behind her, Sirena stood, a smile on her lips as she spied the man who commanded the ship that was bearing down on her frigate.

"Have no fear," she shouted to the sweating Jan, "she'll bow to us. If not, the order to ram stands. She's loosening sail, I can see the men in the shrouds. They're furling the sail. She's a brig and she looks top-heavy. In a few minutes we'll be almost broadside. Fire only when ordered!"

"Aye, Capitana," came the chorus of shouts from her crew who now trusted her judgment and were exhilarated over their conquest of the galleon.

"Her master stands on the bow, Capitana."

The ships were almost directly broadside. Regan van der Rhys looked with shock at the figure of a woman standing on the bow of the specter-black frigate, her hand on the hilt of a cutlass, wild black hair streaming behind her, a smile of victory on her lips. His eyes went past her to the broken, tilting ship fast sinking some distance behind her. Cold blue eyes narrowed to slits as he watched the nearly naked woman who now made

203

a mocking bow, her cutlass still grasped in her hand.

Regan stared, not seeing her as an adversary but as a woman. She had incredibly long legs, planted slightly apart; her hold on the rigging was secure, as was her grasp on the cutlass as sure as his own. He glimpsed an angry red scar which ran the length of her upper arm. Her sensuous, reddened lips formed a smile, showing white teeth in her sensuous face. Mesmerized with the sight of her, Regan could only stare in surprise.

"To the victor go the spoils, Captain!" Sirena shouted over the wind.

"Only because I allow it," he returned her shout.

Sirena laughed, the gay musical tinkle that usually raised hackles on Caleb's neck.

"Till we meet again, sultry tigress!"

"And we'll meet again — and again and again," Sirena called in answer. Lithely she swung around to stare at the man as his ship plowed past toward the sinking *Wanderer*.

"A woman pirate!" Regan's crew said in awe.

"She's overtaken the *Tita* and dismantled her."

"Took her booty, no doubt."

Aye, Regan smiled, still thinking of her magnificent limbs, and temptress's face. Like a devil angel! There was no doubt in his mind he could have run her frigate broadside and drilled her with a cannon shot, laying her low and killing every hand aboard. But he was in a charitable mood.

The face of an angel! The tightening in his thighs relaxed and his nether regions again relaxed.

"Shorten sail," Regan called as the *Java Queen* quickly approached the fast-sinking vessel. "And man the rigging! All hands to secure the *Queen*, as we approach. We're in for a real blow!" he yelled to his first mate, who stood at the wheel.

Both ships rose and fell in the heavy waters, and boarding the *Tita* would be dangerous, Regan knew. But, quickly throwing out ropes to secure her even while she pulled his own ship dangerously atilt, he leaped aboard the galleon and ran to the quarterdeck — where, sure as he knew it must be, were the initials of his lost son. The memory of their carving, and the boy's laughter, clouded his eyes with tears.

But even without the initials, Regan needed no further proof than seeing the familiar old galleon's lines — his father's design — and the arrangement of her rigging. She was like a lost friend — and a dying one now. Remaining no longer, he raced to regain the *Java Queen* and ordered his men to loose the *Tita* . . .

Now she was surely dead and gone; at least she soon would be. He wished the memories she aroused were equally dead.

Sirena took the wheel from Jan's sweating hands. He relinquished his hold on the hard wooden wheel gratefully. Where was she to get the strength to take this ship through the storm? he questioned himself. She was only a woman.

Caleb came to stand at Sirena's side as the Dutchman withdrew to the hold.

"Caleb, help the men secure the ship. Then come back here to relieve me when I tire. Tell the

205

men to go below, I don't want anyone going overboard when I'm in command. Tell them," she smiled slightly, "that I personally guarantee they'll reach port alive and in one piece."

"Aye, Sirena, I'll tell them," Caleb shouted above the mounting storm.

The wind howled in the rigging as Sirena steered the frigate under her close-reefed sails. She kept her bow pointed as near into the wind as possible, but never dead into the eye of the storm. Gigantic waves, whipped by the gale into curly white combers, rolled continuously from the west. Spindrift flew in flakes, stinging Sirena's face as she fought the wheel.

The holocaust demanded her full concentration. Hands gripping the stout wheel, which was almost as tall as she, Sirena stood erect and brazened the storm. Lightning flashed, illuminating the dark, spectral shapes of clouds scudding across the sky. Rain had not yet begun to pelt the decks, but it was out there before her, waiting for her. Sirena knew the rain was as much her enemy as its sister, the howling wind. She'd heard tales of helmsmen drowning while at the wheel in the teeming, pouring wet — even though not a single breaker had dashed the decks. The rain could beat the strength out of a man, wearing and draining his vitality bit by bit, sip by sip, like a vampire draining the life's blood. It could choke off a man's air by driving in solid sheets, whipping up the nostrils and down the throat. The rain could pound a helmsman from the wheel and the wind could lure the ship onto a certain course of destruction.

Fearing the worst, Sirena grappled with a long length of sailcloth and lashed herself to the wheel with it. Now if she died, she would die at her post and her crew would know she had done all she could to save them.

Minutes seemed hours and hours seemed eternities. The storm was raging in full fury. Lashed to the wheel, Sirena, blinded by the savage downpour, kept her ship to its heading by instinct. Her body was battered by the elements, her hair beat against her face and twisted about her neck like insistent strangling fingers. When physical strength began to fail, an iron determination to survive became her mainstay.

Suddenly Sirena had a sense of her own magnificence: A woman alone, battling the elements which thundered about her, seeking her destruction. And in that moment of awareness she knew she would win. She was "conquistadora" — the conqueress, the winner, mistress of the seas. She knew herself to be unbeatable. She would survive, no matter what. Nothing, no one, could topple her. Not the rain, nor the storm, nor the sea. Not Dick Blackheart, not The Hook.

A renewed vigor seeped through her as she thought of Blackheart and his men. The sounds of thunder became the roar of the harquebusiers the pirates had fired from the rigging. The dashes of lightning became the quick sparks of rapier against rapier as they boarded the *Rana*. The tenacious pelting of the rain bruising her flesh became the rough, wounding hands of the pirates as they ripped her clothes from her and handled her body intimately. Groping, hurting fingers prodded her, searched her, tearing her flesh as they tore away her dignity. Her legs, her breasts, her most private parts laid bare to leering eyes and persistent fingers. The mournful howl of the wind became Isabel's shrieks of terror. The black hovering clouds were the dark hulking forms of those animals who had violated her, forcing themselves between her thighs as they sweated and grunted, straining for satisfaction.

Sirena bit her lip with remembered agony and tasted the rusty tincture of blood. She thought of other blood she had shed here on the deck of the *Rana*: the blood of her virginity.

The decks heaved with the force of the surf, the masts groaned with the weight of the saturated rigging. Rhythmically, like the rutting movements of her rapists, the *Rana* rose and fell as it rode the angry, swelling sea. Sirena's tears mingled with the rain, but hers were not the tears of the defeated. These were purging tears born of a renewed sense of indomitability. She rode the frigate from the trough to the crest of each swell. For moments she would ride dizzily on the crest, then rode down it steeply into the next trough. Each time she rode up to the next crest she felt buoyant and invincible.

Caleb crept out onto the deck to see how Sirena was faring. The men, experienced sailors all, were voicing their doubts as to how a mere woman, though she be their "capitana," could have the strength needed to ride out such a storm as this. Of the complainers, Wouter was the loudest. Only

208

toothless old Jacobus exhibited complete faith in the Capitana, saying, "She's no mere woman, *that* one! She's driven by the Devil himself. She said she would get us to port, and she will or I'll be a landlubber's mother."

The wind buffeted Caleb against the quarter-deck rail, and only by taking a fast hold on the rigging was he able to pull himself laboriously across the deck to the ship's wheel. He saw Sirena lashed to the wheel. She was drenched, her raven hair hung in thick slices.

"I came to help," Caleb shouted.

Sirena acknowledged him with a nod of her head, but never took her eyes from the sea swells. Inching his way between Sirena and the wheel, he braced himself against her and placed his hands on the laterals next to hers.

"Take the wheel, Caleb, head her steady onto the seas. An error on your part, allowing her to lay broadside on and broach to, will be the end of her." Tons of water suddenly crashed onto the frigate's decks from abeam, threatening to stove in her hatches. "Steady on, Caleb. Can you do it?"

"Aye, Sirena," he muttered through clenched teeth. He would do it if it killed him. How in God's name had she, a woman, rode this ship with no rest for three hours. Only minutes at the wheel and his arms ached fiercely.

For an hour Caleb steered the frigate with encouragement from Sirena who remained lashed to the wheel supplying him with needed support.

"It's over, calm waters ahead," Sirena shouted happily. "Didn't I tell you there was nothing to fear." Caleb massaged his aching arms and made a valiant attempt to smile. "You did well, little brother," Sirena laughed. "You did well."

Basking in her praise, Caleb went below to tell the men of Sirena's daring run with the ship. The men listened in awe as the boy spoke. Their pride swelled in their Capitana. All save Wouter, who remained silent, his mind racing with furious thoughts of bedding the near-naked witch he served under.

One day later, Sirena ran the frigate before the wind to northeast into the mouth of the Sunda Strait and an hour later between the looming volcanos.

Wearily, Sirena contemplated her first sea voyage as captain. She had done well. There was no doubt of that. The men would have no qualms about sailing with her again. Tired as she was, her thoughts flew to her husband as she remembered him standing on the bow of the ship as she herself had done. He had looked magnificent, all rippling, corded muscle. And when he smiled, her heart had fluttered madly. She had felt strange from the moment she laid eyes on him. He was so sun-bronzed his hair stood out like pure gold and his blue eyes had turned dark and . . . There had been a certain look about him, as if he desired her and wanted her right that very moment. She reveled in the thought and then instantly sobered. What would he think if he knew that she had been ravaged by Dick Blackheart's pirates and that the woman he had really contracted to marry was her dead sister?

Wouter stood on the foredeck and watched Sirena, below, mount the horse the boy held steady for her. The sailor's large, filthy hands caressed his loins as he stared intently till all three horses — the Capitana's, Caleb's and Jan's — were out of sight in the jungle.

Old Jacobus, who stood watching Wouter, remembered Jan's words that first day aboard: "Keep that leering Dutch bastard in sight at all times. He must not get near the Capitana!"

Nor *would* he! the old man vowed.

Chapter Eleven

Tired, yet still exhilarated, Sirena and Caleb dismounted and gave their two horses into the care of Jan Verhooch, who bid them a quiet goodnight in a clump of nutmeg bushes and rode westward, toward the rise, with orders for the men to return to their village and await her further word. They'd best stow away in the jungle — or leave on the ship, temporarily — some of the cargo they'd taken from the *Wanderer*; the villagers might suspect . . . and she wanted no word to leak back to Batavia of her activities. Not yet, at any rate.

She and Caleb walked the remaining distance through the fields of nutmeg and slowly crossed the lush gardens at the back of the mansion. It was a dark night; no one would spot them, she was sure. In minutes, both she and her "brother" had climbed the trellis and were standing in her room. Plates with the remains of food nearly five days old sat just inside the door.

I must tell Juli to unlock the door to retrieve the plates from time to time, Sirena told herself. But she had done well . . . and can be trusted. "Frau Holtz will be surprised to see us, after our long 're-treat'!" she laughed.

Abruptly, she reached and squeezed the boy to her breast. "We made it, Caleb!"

The boy joined in her laughter. "I — I wonder where your crew think you come from? Only

Jan knows for sure."

"They'll know when I want them to. Though they may one day learn — for I've many trips to sea to make, until I ruin Regan van der Rhys and find the man who ravaged poor Isabel with his hook *and* his body. When I come face to face with him . . . !"

Caleb walked tiredly to the door of his room — which adjoined Sirena's suite. "Good night, Sirena," he called back. "Rest well, my sister!"

Before retiring for the night, Sirena collected the dishes and food and hid them in her closet — Juli could dispose of the spoiled food and take the dishes down to the kitchen in the morning.

It seemed only minutes before the sunlight streamed through the windows of the bedroom to awaken her. She had forgotten to draw the shades! A moment later, a knock came at the door. It was to remind her that, outside, her breakfast awaited her — if she wanted it.

Leaping from the bed, refreshed and happy, Sirena surprised Frau Holtz by loudly unbolting and unlocking the door!

The woman stared, unbelieving. These Spanish — who could stay five days in retreat for somebody long since dead and buried!

With the breakfast tray, the housekeeper handed Sirena a note folded and sealed with the emblem of the Spanish Crown. The Señorita tore it apart as she walked back to her bed, the Frau following her with her morning meal. Sirena turned abruptly, nearly upsetting the tray in the housekeeper's hands.

213

"I'm having luncheon with Señor Alvarez," Sirena announced.

The housekeeper, surprised, left the tray on a bedside table and left the room.

"Caleb! Caleb, come here!" Sirena called, and a moment later the door to the adjoining room opened and a sleepy-eyed boy appeared in nightclothes. "I'll be out much of the day, and I want you to study these maps of the reefs and shoals at the entrance to the River of Death." She pulled them from the back of the closet, where she'd placed them the night before, on her return from the *Rana*. "You should one day be able to navigate the channel as well as I. Also, study this chart of Java's western tip and the Sunda Strait." Then, suddenly, Sirena changed the subject. "Caleb . . . what do you think of Don Chaezar Alvarez? You've seen him frequently here at dinner or luncheon."

The boy opened his mouth to speak, but Sirena continued: "I find him most charming and gallant. But then all Spaniards are gentlemen. Not like these uncouth Dutch. He carries himself so regally . . . He doesn't stomp and clatter when he walks, and he smokes a most fragrant cigar. Not like Re— I find the Señor charming," Sirena repeated.

"Aye, Sirena, charming." Not for anything would Caleb say he much preferred Regan over the Spaniard. It was true, the Dutchman's words sounded rough and guttural to the boy's ear. But Chaezar Alvarez reminded him of a devil, with that pointed, manicured beard and mustache. Caleb preferred to see all of a man's face. What was

214

the Spaniard hiding behind all that hair? A weak chin perhaps, something that would make him appear less a man?

Sirena gathered up the rolled charts and handed them to Caleb. "Take these to your own room and be careful no one sees you with them. Remember, Caleb, that perhaps your knowledge of navigation will one day save our lives." At this ominous declaration Caleb left the room and Sirena continued with her toilette.

Sirena sat comfortably in Chaezar Alvarez's library, a glass of wine in her hand.

"May I say how lovely you look, my dear Sirena?"

"You may," Sirena said quietly but impishly.

Black eyes laughing at her reply, Chaezar stroked his pointed beard. Sirena looked at the man's dress. Elegant was hardly the word. He carried his height so regally. Sirena drew in her breath. He was so . . . so masculine.

"I find it . . . amusing that I can see my reflection in your boots," Sirena remarked.

Chaezar smiled, aware of her beauty and appreciating his effect on her. She really was a stunning woman, with remarkable bearing. Ah, he thought, these Teutonic barbarians didn't know how to begin to appreciate a woman like Sirena. They were only stirred by their lusty, Nordic cows with their pale coloring and white skin like the underbelly of a fish. But a woman like Sirena with her dark hair and dark nature could entice a man's imagination, stir him to new heights of passion. He had observed her, studied her, and he was positive that

215

behind that cool, composed mask of good breeding and manners lurked a passionate, fiery nature capable of masterful cruelty. It was her suspected capacity for cruelty that aroused his lust.

"How is Regan these days? Busy as ever, I'll wager."

"To be quite truthful, I really don't know," Sirena replied as she sipped her wine daintily. "He has been away these past five days . . . where, I don't know. But why do you ask, Don Chaezar?"

Sirena listened to his voice which seemed to come from the depths of the man's broad chest. But while deep, it had a soft and crooning, almost soothing quality. Even after so short a time she felt at home in the Spaniard's house. The easy elegance, the soft tone of her native tongue spoken so easily, loosened her taut nerves.

"Yours is such a beautiful name, Sirena. It reminds me of soft, exotic things, rare flower petals, the tip of a bird's wing, a pinch of a cloud."

"How gallant, sir! But . . . you must remember that I am in mourning. My father, my uncle . . . And, I am now Mevrouw van der Rhys," she said softly. But she could just picture the mighty Regan trying to describe her name. He would probably say it was like the name someone would give a stray rooster. Ah, well, Regan wasn't here and Chaezar was.

"Sirena, I asked you here for a reason. And I mean to get right to the point. Where does your allegiance lie? I know that's a foolish question, — once a Spaniard, always a Spaniard — but I must hear it from you. There was no more loyal Spaniard than your father. Because you've married a

216

Dutchman doesn't alter anything, does it?"

"Why . . . no," Sirena stammered. What did the man mean?

"I want to enlist your aid. As . . . allies . . . I feel that we could perhaps strike up a suitable bargain that would benefit both of us."

"Go on . . . Don Chaezar . . ."

"Before I do, let me tell you that I would never have invited you here and would not attempt to ask this alliance with you if I didn't know of the situation at your house — What I mean," he hastened to explain, "is I am aware that yours and Regan's is an arranged marriage. A marriage that he dislikes as much as you must. I am told you each have separate quarters. Regan has his . . . well, affairs . . . servants do talk," he said glibly, "I would assume, and correctly so I hope, that you have little love for the man. If you did, he wouldn't be running with every whore from Java to Sumatra."

"God in Heaven," Sirena murmured to herself. Did the man know what he was saying? Next thing he will offer to partake of my assumed virginity. The thought was so ludicrous that Sirena smiled. Chaezar, taking the smile to mean he should continue, did so.

"Right now, my dear, I find myself in a slightly precarious situation. As you know I direct the inter-island shipping for Spain. Just as Regan does for the Dutch. For the past several years, the Dutch have attained the major foothold. I must outdo the Dutch, for then I will be able to return to Spain in honor. I would like to return a hero. For I do intend to return in the near future. This island life begins to fatigue me; I yearn for the

217

court at Madrid. And, unfortunately, my life — that is to say, my accomplishments — has gained me thus far little prestige, it has been without *éclat*, if you will . . ." he said suavely.

"Regan and I have our little . . . rivalries. I take a little from him and he takes a little from me. I wound him a little and he wounds me a little. What can I say" — he shrugged his shoulders elegantly — "except that . . . if you could perhaps glean bits of information from him, such as departing ships, alternate routes . . ."

Sirena leaned back in the comfortable chaise and listened to his soft, crooning voice. She was hearing something she did not like. Not that Alvarez's competition with Regan surprised her, nor their schemings against one another. No. It was something else that angered her . . . and she was hard put to contain herself.

Slipping on a dressing gown, Sirena hastened to Caleb's room. She watched him for a moment as he made marks on his slate. His concentration was so great he didn't hear her enter the room. She called his name twice before he lifted his head.

"Caleb, I want you to go to the wharves and find out when Señor Alvarez sends out his next ship. Listen for any information that will be valuable to us. I've decided," she said coldly, "that we will take to the sea and ruin *him*, as well as the Dutchman."

"But — I — What happened to make you decide this?" Caleb asked hesitantly.

"Several things that don't concern you at the moment, little brother. Perhaps some of the fishermen or some of the little children will tell you things that we couldn't find out otherwise. It's close to the dinner hour, so you'll have to hurry."

Caleb looked into the green eyes and a chill ran up his spine. He hadn't seen that look on Sirena's face since those days on the *Rana* — the days she had forbidden him to speak of. He wondered what had happened to bring that look into them.

"Aye, Sirena. What if I should meet Mynheer van der Rhys? How shall I explain what I am doing asking questions about the Spaniard?"

"You'll tell him that since you have noticed how . . . interested I've become in the Spaniard you want to know more of him and his ship. Let the Mynheer believe you are on his side and mean to deter any friendship that might develop between Don Chaezar and myself!" she laughed.

Her recent conversation with Chaezar had both embarrassed and infuriated her. Had Regan actually made it common knowledge that he disliked their marriage? Regardless, Chaezar was assuming too much to repeat it to her! And all his talk about allegiance to home, mother country, forming an alliance . . . this had been only his method to win her over as a conspirator, a spy! He only wanted to use her! Sirena vowed she would never be used again, never put herself in the hands of a man whose only motive was to exploit her, either her body *or* her brain. Chaezar would have her be his instrument to attain his ends. Well, one day soon, he would discover that her sweet smile and gentle compliance were merely a sham.

"Does this," Caleb asked, "is this . . . something to do with . . . 'wily women'?"

219

Sirena's eyes lighted and she nodded curtly. She tossed Caleb a small bag of coins. "If you have to, give these to the men to loosen their tongues. I'll take the maps and the charts now. Tomorrow we shall again go over them together. Caleb, have you spoken to Regan since he returned today?"

"I passed him in the corridor and he was in such a black mood he did nothing more than nod. I spent time in the library hoping to overhear something, but no one has come near the house. I heard him shout to Frau Holtz not long ago. She appeared to be telling him something he did not want to hear. I couldn't make out the words but I could tell he was terribly angry."

Sirena's green eyes darkened as she stared at some invisible object above the boy's head. She knew well what angered Regan. Suddenly she smiled, much to the boy's discomfort.

He didn't like the look on her face nor did he like her smile. Suddenly he felt sorry for the Spaniard. What had he done to make Sirena turn on him? Whatever it was she wasn't going to confide in him. It was just as well. He already had so many things on his mind his head felt like a beehive. He had difficulty in remembering what he was to say and what he wasn't to say. If only he could go to sea and forget all this — what was the word Sirena had taught him — "intrigue." Intrigue and "wily women". . .

"Hurry, Caleb. When you return, join me in my room for dinner. I intend a ferocious headache and won't be able to bear the thought of dining downstairs with Regan. Report to me as soon as you return."

220

Back in her room, Sirena pulled a bell cord to summon Juli. She told the girl to serve them dinner in her room. Sirena saw Juli's curious look.

"I feel the ailment coming upon me," Sirena explained. "The one we Spaniards are so susceptible to. I wouldn't want to infect anyone. Once it takes hold, it rages unmercifully. It will be best if perhaps you knock and leave the meals outside the door, as you did these past days. But set them inside the door after a time has passed, and relock the door with your key. The next day, if I'm still not well, and the food is untouched, take the plates back down to the kitchen. Do not let them pile up as you did before. Do you understand, Juli?" The native girl nodded. Sirena raised a slim hand to her face and said wanly: "I feel very ill. You'd better hurry!"

Caleb returned to Sirena's room shortly before the dinnertime in a state of near-hysteria.

"What is it? Has something happened?" Sirena questioned anxiously.

Caleb was finding it difficult to get the words out. "Aye, Sirena, at the wharf they speak of nothing but the woman who sank the *Wanderer* galleon. Everyone knows Regan wanted her for himself. They say the witch that captained the ship was barely interested in the cargo. All she wanted was to destroy the ship. Regan is in a fit of anger. The Spaniard smiles and says the Dutch are going to have a run of bad luck. The old fishermen say the black ship with the black sails was mystical. Regan's sailors are telling everyone how that, once he picked up the crew of the galleon, he

221

pursued the black ship through the storm. It seems that they had just glimpsed the top of our sails when we disappeared off the face of the earth. They say you're an avenging angel."

"Disappeared off the face of the earth, did we?" Sirena cried jubilantly. "That must have been when we entered the mouth of the river!"

"Captain Kloss was boasting that Regan could have run you through and dismantled you in minutes if he had so desired. They say that he was in a charitable mood and smitten by your beauty."

"Never!" Sirena snorted. "Regan only said that to save face. What else was mentioned?"

"The Spaniard has sent two ships out to sea. They left less than an hour ago for Capetown. Both travel with a full cargo. The second galleon is escorted."

"What does she carry?"

"Silk and cloves. Very costly at this time of year."

"And Regan, what of . . . *him* — Regan?"

"The *Java Queen* leaves at dawn tomorrow. She'll be loaded to the top of the hold. She carries cinnamon, nutmegs, and cloves."

"To which port?"

"Straight through to Amsterdam, except for stopping at Enggano, off Sumatra, where Regan will disembark and return home in a fishing sloop. His plan is to see the *Java Queen* out of the waters where the female pirate lurks. And I heard Regan say the *Queen* comes back with an empty hold."

Quickly Sirena pulled the charts from the back of the closet. "If the tides are right we can leave the cove and river less than two hours from now.

222

The *Rana* is light — and swift. We'll catch up with the Spaniard's ships, heavy as they are, not far beyond the Sunda Strait. This time we sail west, little brother! And after we attack and dismantle his ships, we can reverse course, and attack the Dutchman on our way home. It will be a tight schedule, but if the winds are in our favor it should work out well."

A knock sounded on the door and Sirena quickly thrust the charts and maps beneath the bed. "Who is it?" she called.

"It's your dinner," Frau Holtz called through the door.

"Very well, leave it. If I get hungry I'll bring it in. Leave me now, please, for I feel rather ill."

"Very well, Mevrouw."

There followed a loud clatter and much muttering. Sirena smiled at Caleb who was grinning openly. Just the thought of going out to sea again was enough to make him happy.

Suddenly Sirena unlocked and pulled open the door. "Frau Holtz," she said, holding her hand to her forehead in a weary gesture.

"*Ja,* Mevrouw," the housekeeper acknowledged, straightening her back from placing the heavily loaded tray on the floor outside the door.

"I have just spoken to my brother and he has agreed that we shall go into another retreat starting immediately. We've also decided to fast so there will be no need for you or Juli to bring food as often. The fasting will break this devilish ailment that has overtaken me. Don't concern yourself over my health. It's happened before and a few days of light fasting has always cured it. My brother will see to my needs. I also want to thank you for this sturdy bolt that was placed on my door. Remember, if you should knock there will be no answer. When we are in retreat we do not speak. It would defeat the purpose of the prayers. Do you understand me, Frau Holtz?"

"*Ja*, Mevrouw," Frau Holtz answered, her expression stating she didn't and never would.

"We'll eat now. This meal will sustain us till the end of the retreat. God go with you," Sirena sighed lanquidly.

Frau Holtz turned and left abruptly. "Heathen ways," she muttered on her way down to the kitchen. But, then, what did she care? For all she cared the Mevrouw could retreat till the moon was again full. Her room could gather dust and mildew till it was rank with it. If Mynheer didn't care, why should she? Such a marriage! Never in her life had she heard of such a thing! She stomped her way into the kitchen and bit her tongue to keep from offering her complaints to the cook. Frau Holtz was not given to gossip concerning her employers.

I must inform the master, Frau Holtz thought, unable to keep still any longer. God knows what he'll say when he hears!

The housekeeper entered the offices occupied by Regan on the first floor of the house and spoke hesitantly: "The Mevrouw . . . has gone into a . . . retreat. She wants no food and she's bolted the door. Mevrouw said she will not answer any knock. Is she allowed to do this?"

"Is she allowed to do this?" Regan parroted her. "Of course she is allowed to do this! The Spanish do things differently. If Mevrouw wants to stay locked in her room to pray, then allow her to do so. What seems to be the problem, Frau Holtz?"

"Why — I — I — just thought that you should —"

"Know what is going on? My dear lady," Regan said coolly, "this will mean less work for the servants. You will obey my wife's wishes and leave her and her brother to their prayers. Just because we do not believe as they do doesn't mean we can't respect their wishes. I wish to hear no more about the matter."

"But, Mynheer, I worry about the bolt on the door."

"Perhaps she is afraid of you, Frau Holtz. And this is her way of keeping you out of her eyesight. Have you thought of that?" he teased.

"Why — I —"

"You are not to concern yourself with my wife's activities, is that clear," Regan said, his voice firm and controlled.

"Yes, I understand perfectly. Thank you, Mynheer."

Regan watched the housekeeper's retreating back, a smile on his face. She was disturbed. Perhaps it would do her good. Too long she had reigned over his domain like a dowager queen.

But a thought occurred to him. Who was Sirena keeping out of her room — Frau Holtz or himself? She need not fear him, he had other fish in the ocean. He would be charitable and leave her to her prayers. With luck she would pray for his soul. And perhaps for a safe journey.

His heart quickened momentarily — would he

see the sea witch again? What would he do if she attacked his ship? He had never seen a more beautiful woman. The memory of those long, tawny legs haunted him. He drew in his breath at the thought of how she would bed. And there was no doubt in his mind that he would bed her!

Chapter Twelve

Caleb's eyes were apprehensive as he watched Sirena steer the frigate along the river. "At the most, you have a few minutes and the tide will ebb. Can you do it?" he asked anxiously.

"Have no fear, little brother, the *Rana* will make open water — and safely." Then her eyes turned from the wheel to look to the right of the ship — as did those of the men on deck. "One thing worries me, however. Sister Red, as you call her, there to the east. It is she against whose sides the *Rana* nestles, in our cove. Did you notice the warmness of the water surrounding the ship . . . and the red mist that hovers there, near her top, and around the mouth of the river?"

"Aye, the men have been speaking of it. It will make your passing through the channel doubly hazardous, Sirena."

Sirena laughed, the sound bouncing off the jagged rocks of the red volcano's slopes. "I can see, have no fear. The mist is high."

The boy clenched and unclenched his fists as he watched Sirena, her stance sure on the slow-moving *Rana*. The men in the rigging had as much fear of passing the rocks as he did. But confidence returned as he watched Sirena's face. If she said they would reach the open waters safely, then they would. She had never been wrong before.

Sirena glanced down at the frightened boy beside her. And immediately the feeling returned — the feeling that she'd seen Caleb before, sometime in her past, further back than the time he'd signed on to her merchant fleet in Cádiz. Even his walk, she realized, was familiar, and the sultry eyes haunted her.

"Caleb," she said impulsively, "have you ever traveled in Spain?"

"I've only been in Cádiz, Sirena. Why?"

"It's . . . just that you seem so familiar to me — like someone I'd met before, not in Cádiz, for Father's house was not there but in Seville."

"The only time I've been in Spain is when your uncle so kindly rescued me from the *Lord Raleigh*, when he saw me being whipped aboard the English ship, and encouraged me to sign on with your fleet. I'd never visited your country before that time — though I'd learned enough Spanish through Carlos, the *Raleigh*'s cook."

Caleb threw back his head and laughed. "You seem puzzled, Sirena. I have never seen you in this mood. What is it about me that you don't understand?"

Sirena shuddered. The laugh! She had never heard Caleb laugh in quite that way. The way he threw back his head, and the sound of the laughter itself, was so reminiscent of someone . . . She wanted to reach out and touch the boy, thinking it would come to her. She forced herself to concentrate on the water and the slowly lowering thick reddish mist. "Open water ahead!" she shouted to the men on deck. "And not a minute to spare! Tighten sail."

Caleb breathed a heavy sigh of relief, as did Sirena, when they had passed through the narrow channel at the rocky mouth of the river.

A shout of pleasure, and admiration, rose from the crew, and Jan came up to speak with her.

"Does the crew fare well?" she asked.

"Aye, Sirena. The booty from the last trip was quite enough for them. They have enough to last them the rest of their lives. As it is they lead a simple life, all their needs are for food and a little ale from time to time! They only want to be regarded as men again, save . . . Wouter," Jan said softly. "The man worries me — and he's ever been something of an outsider, Dutch though he is, and dismissed like all of your crew, from the same ship we once sailed. I would discharge him but I fear his tongue."

"He's not content with his share of the booty?"

"Those are his *words,* but Martin says his eyes say the meaning of the word 'booty' is not . . . 'goods'. He wants *you,* Capitana," Jan said bluntly. Sirena flinched. "Every seaman aboard keeps him within eye range. But he grows more hostile as the days go on."

"I've noticed, Jan. My gut does strange things when I'm forced to look at him. One of these days . . ."

Caleb's face drained as he imagined what "one of these days" might bring.

"But enough! I told them I'd play fair with them. I want no ill feelings among the men."

"Aye, Capitana. That would never happen. They say that you're the best captain they ever sailed under. The fact that you manage the straits almost makes you a sorceress in their eyes!"

Sirena acknowledged the compliment humbly, her eyes straining ahead of her. She turned to Caleb. "Get some rest, little brother. Soon you'll need all of your strength."

Sirena gripped the wheel as Jan left her, with the boy. Her hands were moist and clammy. On coming through the straits she had moments of misgiving. She would never again cut it so close. And of course all the expertise she possessed could not get a ship through those narrow waterways if the tide was low. One day, if in retreat from Regan or Chaezar, she found the river mouth shallow . . . She pushed the thought from her mind. Now the question was: Would she be able to attack and ravage both of the Spaniard's ships? The ship riding as escort with heavy cannon troubled her. She prayed that night would soon fall.

Clouds covered the night sky.

Excellent! Sirena thought. A black ship. The black night. If only we'd been able to depart sooner . . . Where are the Spanish ships?

"Sail ho!" came a muted cry from the rigging of the *Rana.*

Sirena picked up the spyglass and squinted into it. In the dim moonlight that filtered through a sudden break in the cloud cover, she saw them. Dead ahead at five knots, she estimated quickly. She lowered the glass in time to see Caleb poke his head around the wheel.

"Softly, little brother. Remember, your voice will carry across the water as clear as a bell. The brig sails in the second galleon's wake. I do not spy the first galleon, but who cares? We'll cripple the two behind and lower Alvarez's prestige as we lower their sails! But we must fire simultaneously. One shot broadside into each of them and they'll buckle. We'll have time for only the one shot so it must be true on its mark. We'll get no second chance. Pray God that the moon does not decide to peep out before the shots are fired. Now . . . silent as the dead, little brother."

Caleb nodded as he scampered off to give her orders. He was back in moments. "On your count of five we fire," he said softly. "Have no fear, Sirena, the shots will be true on their mark. All hands are on the quarterdeck."

Moments later, whispered orders passed from Sirena to Caleb, and down to Jan and his gunners. On the count of five a double roar split the night as the cannon shots found their mark. Sirena held the glass to her eye and watched men spill into the sea as others ran over the two ships' decks. Hoarse shouts of fear and alarm raged in the night. The first rays of the moon lighted the night as the *Rana* ran broadside of the broken galleon. The brig was listing to starboard as its men leaned on the rail, not sure yet what had happened. "Take the wheel, Caleb. Steady as she goes."

Sirena raced to the bow, her cutlass hanging loosely in her hand. "Surrender!" she called, her voice high and clear, "and there will be no bloodshed. Shout for quarter and you can take to the jolly-boats!"

"It's the pirate witch," someone shouted. "We give no quarter! We sail with silks to Spain, our mother country."

231

"Your country's people need food in their bellies, not silks," Sirena shouted. "Silks are only to make fat merchants fatter. I'll count three and if you still call no quarter, you go into the sea. We fire on the count of three."

The heavy cannon fired on Sirena's count of three.

"Fools!" Sirena shouted. "Why didn't you listen? I don't speak to myself and to the open sea. You had your chance!"

The galleon was fast sinking. Sirena ordered her gunners to blast its jolly-boats with shot. Those proud merchantmen would feed the sharks! The men on the brig sent to escort the merchant ship, warriors that they might be, were now shouting, "Quarter! Quarter!"

"Move quickly, you have but minutes," Sirena yelled to the brig's crew as she swung down from the ship's wheel with the aid of the rigging. She raced to the *Rana*'s quarterdeck and leaned over, calling: "Is there a man among you who carries a hook for a hand? Think before you answer or a shot will go into your jolly-boats too, and you'll all be fodder for the sharks!"

"There's no man aboard the brig with a hook for a hand. And none that we know of on the galleon," came the captain's fearful reply.

"You lie!" Sirena hissed. "Show me your hands. I'll cut out your tongues if you're lying to me!"

"There's no hook among us," the man said bravely. "I give me word there's no man with a hook!"

"Tell me, have you ever heard of such a man? But remember your tongue! A gaping hole in a man's face is nothing to be proud of!"

"I have heard of such a man. They say he killed the Dutchman's wife and may have stolen his son. That was the story years ago. Since that time, I myself have never heard of him." Confident now that his tongue would remain intact, the man boldly asked why she was seeking him out.

"That is *my* business, seaman! If you're fortunate enough to find yourself in a port, tell the story that I look for such a man, as does van der Rhys. I'll sink every ship I meet on the seas till I find the man. He'll be like the teredo worm. He'll emerge or his fellow seamen will kill him and send me his body."

"What if the Dutchman finds him first?" the man asked boldly.

Sirena laughed, the sound tinkling over the water like musical chimes. "Then I'll kill the Dutchman and take the man with the hook from him. The man with the hook belongs to me."

The sudden hush was proof that the men on the brig believed every word the woman said.

"I'm in a charitable mood, so cast off before I change my mind — as we women have a tendency to do!"

The seamen needed no second warning; they set the brig's jolly-boats adrift, pulling frantically at the oars and never looking back.

"Tighten sail and heave to," Caleb called from his stance at the wheel.

A smile played about Sirena's lips, amusement sparkled in her eyes. "Somehow those jolly-boats will get to port and I can imagine the stories that'll be told. No doubt they'll say how well they fought and how a quirk of fate gave me the advantage."

Caleb questioned her with his eyes as she returned to the wheel.

"I've no doubt their tale will fall on Regan's ears and he'll know my plan to comb these waters and sink every ship until I find The Hook! And Señor Alvarez," she grimaced, "when he learns about the sinking of one of the Spanish galleons — and the brig sent to protect her — I can imagine him pulling out his lovely, well-trimmed beard!"

A picture of Chaezar's naked face with a weak, trembling chin made Caleb laugh to the point of tears. After a few moments he asked, "The Mynheer . . . do you plan to attack him, too?"

"Of course!" She noticed the rueful smile Caleb gave her, and remembered his growing affection for Regan. "The Dutchman is expecting us, is he not? We wouldn't want to disappoint him! But we may already have passed Enggano — it is impossible to see in this gloomy night. So we must reverse course, to meet him before he reaches that isle. I want to attack the *Java Queen* while Grand Pensioner van der Rhys is aboard her. And that she's his own ship, rather than simply another Dutch vessel bound for home, will give me double pleasure in sinking her!"

Sirena turned, her eyes seeking her first mate. "Jan!" she called out, "you will come and take the wheel." Then, to Caleb: "You must remain out of sight, should we approach the *Java Queen* suddenly. As for me, I will rest a while out here on deck. The cabin is far too stuffy!

"How do you fare, Jacobus?"

234

"Well, Capitana. I compliment you on your sea-manship."

Sirena laughed. "And I compliment you on the food."

The toothless old Netherlander grinned at her praise. "Capitana, a few years ago I served aboard a ship with a man with a hook instead of a hand. He was a villain and a cutthroat. But there is something you should know. He finally had a 'hand' carved for himself by a Chinese artisan. The hook fits into a sheath in the center of the 'hand.' When he wears a glove, as most seamen do to protect their hands from the rigging, you'd never know it was a wooden hand. I know this, Capitana, I've seen it with my own eyes when I served with him. I tell you this because it seems to be very important to you. When you search for the man with the hook, be certain you see a *bare* hand, not a gloved one."

Sirena gazed at the toothless old man. "Thank you, Jacobus, for telling me this. Someday I shall return the favor."

"There's no need. You already gave me my dearest wish, to feel useful again — and to be at sea. I couldn't ask for more."

"Would you . . . happen to know if the Dutch-man knows of the false hand?"

"Mynheer van der Rhys probably does not know of the 'hand.' The attack on the *Tita* came eight years ago, before the villain had the 'hand' made. Though once it was fitted, he seldom showed his hook again. Unless he keeps *pirate* company these days, as he kept merchant com-pany before!"

Sirena winced at the man's words, as memories flooded over her.

"I'm glad you told me this, Jacobus."

"Aye, Capitana."

Dawn showed in the eastern sky.

"Feed the men lightly this morning. No full bellies for what we have to do today," Sirena told the old man.

Once more Sirena lay back on the deck dozing. The rising sun soon caressed her body and a brisk breeze lulled her into a state of calm she hadn't felt for days.

"It is day," Caleb said, shaking her gently. "I gave the order to tighten sail and full speed. If your calculations are right, we'll make our contact with the *Java Queen* before noon."

Sirena was instantly awake and on her feet. "If we're successful, her cargo goes into the sea, remember that. I'll take the wheel from Jan now, till we spot their sail. Stay out of sight, Caleb, that's an order."

"Aye, Sirena."

A feeling of pity washed over him for the unsuspecting Dutchman. Surely she wouldn't kill him. Suddenly it was important to him that she not harm Regan. He wanted to run to her and beg her to show Regan mercy. Instead he remained quiet and fought the anguish that threatened to overtake him. The frigate sailed dead ahead in the rippling water, the ship secure beneath the woman's hands. When the cry of "Sail ho" came, it startled him so that his hands fell to his sides.

Sirena picked up the spyglass. It was the *Java*

Queen and Sirena was looking at her broadside, dead ahead.

"She's sighted us. Fire into her stern and her bow. Hurry!"

A deafening roar thundered into the air. The *Rana* rocked and Sirena was thrown off balance. "Fire at once!" she ordered.

"We did, Capitana. See, she flounders. But she got off a shot and hit our bow."

"How much damage have we?" Sirena screamed, outraged that the Dutchman should have hit his mark.

"She can be shored up, Capitana. We take on little water but our progress home will be slow."

"We can't be held up, shore her up now. We're approaching the Sunda Strait, and if we lose time, the tides will shift. We'll not be able to enter the river mouth after our fight with the *Queen* and will be open prey for any ship on the sea. Heave to!" she called out.

Sirena squinted into the glass. Bright orange-red flames danced their way from the Dutch ship's bow to stern.

"There's no way the *Java Queen* can save herself, Capitana," Jan grinned, approaching the wheel. "She'll go into the sea with her cargo. Look! The men go into the jolly-boats!"

"I see . . ." Sirena said softly.

Where was her Regan? Yes, there he was, with the ship's captain, the last to go over the side. And just as he lighted into the ship's second jolly-boat an earsplitting noise and a great billowing of smoke and flames above him made him look upward. A cannonball from the attacker had hit his ship's powder room! He stood in the small boat, his hands to his eyes — and murderous eyes they must have been, Sirena judged, for she could not see them clearly. This was his new ship's first voyage to Amsterdam and what bitter gall it must be for him to swallow, that she'd been sunk by the sea witch!

Then, all at once, she recalled her own ship's damage. "Bring us broadside," she shouted to Jan, who now took the wheel. With a lithe movement, Sirena ran to the bow of the *Rana* and surveyed the damage to the side of her ship.

"You'll pay for this, Dutchman!" she shouted hoarsely to be heard over the deafening roar of flames from the *Java Queen*. "You'll never again be so fortunate as to land a shot in my direction. I'll hunt you down and sink every vessel you send to sea. My patience is sorely tried at this moment, so answer me quickly: Is there any man aboard your jolly-boats that wears a hook for a hand?"

"If there were," Regan answered, "I'd have run him through long ago. I myself seek The Hook!"

"Which of us will succeed, Captain?" Sirena asked mockingly as she nicked the air with the tip of her cutlass. "I think," she said, driving the point of the cutlass into the deck, "that it will be me! It's said you've searched for three long years and as yet have no clue to his whereabouts. True or false, Dutchman?"

"True!" Regan snarled.

"Then you'd better give up. He's mine! Have your men show me their hands. Quickly now, or I'll order a shot fired into your jolly."

"Obey the 'lady,' " Regan ordered the captain

and crew members mockingly. The men held out their hands, looks of fear on their faces.

"You — you — and you!" Sirena roared, pointing the tip of her cutlass at three of the men in the tiny boat below her. "Remove your gloves and roll up your sleeves."

"What's this?" Regan demanded, his eyes narrowed into slits.

"I feel sorry for you, Captain, so I'll tell you a little secret. The man with the hook wears a false hand. He wears a glove to cover his deformity. What say you now, Dutchman? You'll have a long time to think about that on your sail across to Sumatra in the jolly-boat!"

Regan's eyes roved the crew sitting in the jollys. All the faces were fearful yet none uttered a word.

Sirena chuckled. "Let me be the first to console you on the *Java Queen*. It's a pity she didn't reach port. But don't feel badly. This morning at dawn I sunk two Spanish ships, a galleon and a brig. The brig's men are in the same position as you. Perhaps you'll meet them on the way to the island. You'll have much to discuss. Until we meet again, Captain," she said, giving him a low, mocking bow. Her cutlass found its way into the belt at her waist as she grasped the rigging and swung herself to the quarterdeck. "Heave to, men!" she called, "tighten sail and full speed dead ahead. Have a safe journey, Captain!" Her tinkling laugh raced across the waves and came back to grate against Regan's ears.

"Bitch!" he shouted hoarsely, his eyes fiery.

" 'Bitch' am I? Several moments ago you called me 'lady.' Are Dutchmen always so vacillating?

239

Before I'm finished with you you'll have exhausted your vocabulary to aptly describe me." She added strength to her words with a sweeping gesture of her arm that widened the gap of her loosely buttoned shirt and exposed even more of the dark cleft between her full breasts.

Noticing Regan's attention shift from her face to her bosom, Sirena smiled wickedly. Men, she thought disgustedly, could be diverted by the sight of heaving breasts and a shapely thigh, even in the face of losing an empire.

Regan recovered himself and feigned hatred at the lovely sea witch. He had lost his ship at the hands of a woman but his masculine ego shielded him from the full impact of her victory. It was even possible for him to feel a faint amusement. "We'll meet again, and next time *I'll* have *you!*" he boasted.

Sirena's laugh rippled over the water and reached him.

Unconsciously, he stiffened, suppressed rage roaring in his ears.

"Have me, will you? And if you *could* have me, even now, this minute, what would you do, Dutchman! Whisper sweet endearments, caress me with your sea-callused hands" — she shuddered delicately, her eyes sultry, her red lips teasing. "And your mouth, Dutchman, what would you do with your mouth? Swear obscenities at me or kiss me and tantalize me. Would you kiss me here?" She pointed to her neck. "Or here?" Her finger moved to her breasts. "Or here?" Her hand touched her mouth lightly.

Regan turned abruptly to escape her teasing —

240

hating her, wanting her, and wanting to kill her, yet knowing every word she spoke was true. The hackles rose on the back of his neck; she was laughing again, laughing at *him!*

As the *Rana* pulled away from the sinking *Java Queen*, Sirena felt a bit queasy in her heart. The Sumatra shore, sixty or seventy miles away, was visible only by virtue of the immense mountains that fringed its southwestern shore. She hoped, despite herself, that Regan and his small company would reach the shore in their two craft. Nevertheless, she mused, the sea is calm . . .

"Shore up this bow and heave to, men!" she called out abruptly, leaving her thoughts behind her. "We've taken on too much water as it is. Bastard!" she yelled back at the tiny figure in the jolly-boat, "how did you manage to get off a shot at me?" Then: "Caleb, and Jan, were our gunners at their stations?"

"Aye, Capitana," Jan Verhooch answered. "The *Queen* had time for only one shot and I think it was blind. She didn't have time to do more than merely sight us. It was a lucky shot, I'd say, Capitana."

"I want no more lucky shots!" she growled, then asked soberly, "How much time do you think we have to make it through the strait and to the mouth of our river before the tide turns?"

"We'll have an hour to spare, Capitana," the Dutch first mate replied, cheerful and smiling.

Sirena's mood softened. "Well . . . our men did themselves well, this day. When the ship is secure and we're berthed in the cove, have Jacobus bring the ale on deck. A celebration is in order!"

Sirena left Caleb at the wheel and the crew to their work of shoring up the bow of the *Rana*. She went to her cabin to quell the trembling which was threatening to overtake her. She threw herself on her bunk and tried to renew the feelings of jubilance over her victory. Instead a dread seeped into her bones, the dread of discovery. She had met Regan twice on the seas and twice she had cost him dearly. Neither time had he shown any recognition of her identity. But in this last meeting he had had a closer look at her, and they had argued. Had she given herself away? Or would recognition dawn on him the next time he met with her as his shy, introspective bride? If he did comprehend her identity what would he do? A vision of strong, capable sun-darkened hands flashed before her. She gagged, so vivid was the illusion of those hands closing about her throat.

Chapter Thirteen

Safe in her room late that same morning, the charts in their hiding place beneath the bed, Sirena breathed a sigh of relief. "Go to your room, Caleb. Our retreat and fasting is over."

The boy walked to the door, his shoulders slumped. "What is it, Caleb? Something is bothering you. Tell me now so I can relieve your mind."

"Regan in the jolly-boat. What if a storm comes up? What will happen to him?"

"There will be no storm. What kind of seaman are you that you couldn't tell by the winds."

"Perhaps a squall?"

"The jolly-boat could ride out a squall and you know it. Rest easy, little brother, Regan will be home by this time tomorrow. He was on a well-traveled route."

"There'll be no living with him when he returns," Caleb muttered.

"You speak the truth. Are you worried?"

"For myself, no. What if he should take his vengeance upon you?"

"Why me? I have been locked safely in my room. Rest, little brother, you're as tired as I am. Tomorrow is another day."

Sirena bolted the door, lay down on the bed, and was instantly asleep. She dreamed of a sun god smiling at her mockingly.

She awoke to a knock at the door. "Who is it?" she called.

"Frau Holtz, I have your breakfast tray." The housekeeper was surprised to receive an answer to her knock.

Sirena remembered the condition of her hair and the spray of the spindrift on her skin. "Leave it, please. I wish to bathe first. Have one of the girls bring water. Then I will breakfast."

"Very well, Mevrouw." Frau Holtz hastened below to order Juli to carry water to the Mevrouw's chambers.

The little maid soon trudged down the corridor, the pails grasped tightly in her hand. Once inside the room, she glanced at her mistress. Juli was shocked at Sirena's condition. The wild unruly hair cascaded down her back and white flecks glistened on her face. Was this the ailment? To Juli it looked like the spindrift that settled on one's skin when one was out at sea. How could the Mevrouw's hair have become so matted and straggly just sitting in her room? What kind of ailment was it? Fearfully she backed from the room, the pails knocking against each other.

"Bring more water! Have someone help you. You're much too small to be carrying those heavy pails. I need at least six more. I wish to wash my hair."

"Six?" bleated the little maid.

"Six," Sirena said firmly. "The ailment has to be washed away so I do not get reinfected."

Juli was skeptical as she scurried off. Back in the kitchen, she repeated the happenings and the Mevrouw's orders to a fellow servant. Unknown to her, Frau Holtz stood quietly listening.

". . . It looked like the spray of spindrift. Her hair was matted and tangled. It must be a fearsome ailment. Who'll help me with the water? She says I am too little," Juli prattled on to the alert cook.

The housekeeper now stepped from behind the door that led to the dining room, where she had hidden to overhear anything Juli might say.

"Get a djongo to carry the rest of the water! You stay here in the kitchen. You can start by peeling the potatoes and then slice cabbage," Frau Holtz ordered, interrupting the intolerable gossip.

Frau Holtz stood outside the door of Sirena's room when the djongo left with his empty pails. She waited till he closed the door before she spoke.

"Is it true the Mevrouw's skin is covered with a substance much like spindrift?" she asked craftily.

The houseboy shook his head. "I heard it said below that she suffers from some rare Spanish ailment," the boy replied, eager to please the stern housekeeper.

"And is her hair in disarray?"

The boy nodded.

Frau Holtz was in deep thought. She must speak to the doctor when he next visited the house. Surely he would know of this strange ailment. *If* it was an ailment!

The days dragged on and Regan had not yet returned. Caleb went to the quay every day to see if there was news of him. The wharves buzzed, for many knew that Mynheer van der Rhys had intended to leave his ship at Enggano and soon return home to Batavia. The crews, especially those loading and unloading the Dutch ships, were alive with worry. Each day Caleb would return to Sirena, dark questions in his eyes.

Sirena found it hard to comfort the boy. "And the Spanish crew, has there been news of them?"

"No, and I couldn't ask questions for fear I would give us away. What do *you* think happened?"

"I have no idea. But rest assured, little brother, Regan would never let the sea get the better of him. I would imagine he washed up in some cove or inlet on Sumatra and is waiting there for a ship of rescue."

The boy seemed dissatisfied with her obvious confidence and lack of concern.

"I see by the look in your eye that your next question is: Why don't I take the *Rana* to sea and pick him up." Sirena laughed.

"Don't tease me, Sirena. I would have never thought to ask you that."

"Then I won't have to refuse you. Regan will return, have no fear."

Two days later at the noon meal, Sirena heard the furious pounding of horse hooves. She looked out the wide windows in time to see Regan dismount from his horse. Turning, she smiled at the expression on Caleb's face. The boy's relief was unrestrained. He rushed out of her room and down the wide staircase, Sirena fast on his heels.

Regan stood framed in the doorway. He had a

week's growth of beard and his blue eyes stood out starkly in his coppery face. His clothing was tattered, his shirt hanging in strips from his titan shoulders. The golden hair on his broad chest matched the stubble on his chin. A magnificent figure of a man, a very angry man, Sirena thought.

"Frau Holtz!" he thundered.

The housekeeper emerged into the front hallway, a look of fright and awe on her face.

"Bring water up to my quarters and food. Caleb," he said, piercing the boy with a steady stare, "follow me. I have an errand for you. With your permission, Sirena," he said, disregarding her shocked expression.

Sirena nodded and the boy followed Regan without a backward glance.

"What — what happened that you look like this, Mynheer?" Caleb questioned in a quivering voice.

"If I told you I doubt if you would believe me. Remember the promise I made you that I would let you sail on the *Java Queen*?"

"Yes."

"I must break that promise to you. The *Queen* was sunk, by . . . she was sunk! I won't bore you with the details, they aren't pretty. I want you to go to town and leave messages for those that I tell you. You'll tell them they are to come here for dinner this evening. We shall have a party to celebrate the loss of the *Java Queen* and her cargo," he said bitterly, once in his room, as he ripped the rags from his back. "I have a feeling in my gut that this is only the first of many ships that I'll lose."

"Who . . . was it a pirate ship or just some wild marauder?"

"It was a pirate all right, the likes of which I've never seen," Regan said grimly. "I don't understand why it happened. The *Java Queen* was destroyed, her cargo lost into the seas. There was no reason for it. Not only did I lose the *Queen*, Don Chaezar Alvarez, I . . . learned, lost two ships also by the same . . . pirate!" A knock sounded on the door, interrupting him.

A maid and one of the boys carried steaming pails of water and carefully poured them into a large tub in the corner. "Fetch twice as much," Regan ordered. "It will take hours to wash away the filth and the stench.

"Caleb, go to my offices. On the desk is a list. You will go to each of the persons inscribed on the list and ask them to come here for dinner. Tell them I will not take no for an answer. Before you do that tell Frau Holtz that there will be sixteen at table. Tell Sirena I wish her, of course, to attend and to act as my hostess. Speak to me when you return."

Caleb scampered away to do Regan's bidding. He found Sirena and quickly explained his errand. A chill ran up his spine at the smile she gave him.

"Then go now and do the master's bidding. I will tell Frau Holtz about the dinner. *I* wish a full report, too, on your return," she said in a voice ringing with steel.

"You'll have it, Sirena," the boy said, taking his leave.

Sirena found the housekeeper in the pantry.

"There will be sixteen guests for dinner, Frau Holtz. Have the cook prepare a full-course dinner." And she said ominously, "I want no sour cabbage served at the table. I think perhaps . . . some rice, properly spiced of course, and . . . a whitefish baked in cream sauce. I'll leave the choice of vegetables to you. For a sweet, I think perhaps some dates and figs in a thick syrup with some heavy cream."

"But . . . Mynheer . . . prefers the sour —"

"I have just told you what to prepare. You'll see to it immediately. And from now on if you cook your sour cabbage for my husband, do *not* make a portion for my brother and myself. In Spain we feed it only to the swine. In a while, I myself will come into the kitchens to inspect the cook's progress. I would hate to see any last-minute disasters. One other thing: you will have the cook serve a fruit-flavored wine."

When Sirena left her, Frau Holtz's face was a purplish red. The housekeeper made her way to the kitchen and, in a voice choked with venom, she gave the cook the order to prepare the food Mevrouw had ordered. Grimacing, the cook accepted the change in menu and ordered a sack of rice to be brought upstairs from the pantry.

"The . . . Mevrouw . . . wants spices and herbs in the rice."

"Then she shall have spices and herbs," the cook said calmly, and Frau Holtz was aware of the woman's satisfaction. For years Mella, a Malayan, had rebelled against the bland German food she was made to prepare. Tonight, thanks to the Mevrouw, she would have an opportunity to dis-

249

play her true creativity.

Sirena returned to her room, where she patiently waited for Caleb. When, hours later, Caleb burst into her room, his face was wreathed in smiles.

"I did just what Mynheer said. Every person is coming to dinner. Even Frau Lindenreich is attending — with Señor Alvarez. She was at his house when I went there and she pouted so that the Señor said he would bring her."

"Is there any talk at the wharf?"

"I don't know. I heard nothing myself. There was no time for me to stand around and ask questions."

"Did you come to me first or have you reported to Regan?" Sirena asked, her voice nonchalant.

"I came to you first, Sirena. I must go now and tell Regan what I accomplished."

"You did well! Go to Regan so I can go to the kitchens and see how my evening meal is progressing. I have a surprise for you tonight."

"What?" Caleb asked, his eyes lighting inquisitively.

"There will be no sour cabbage tonight."

The boy sighed. "I am glad! Boiled meat, boiled vegetables, boiled cabbage! Ugh! As bad as the food aboard the *Lord Raleigh*!"

Sirena followed the boy's departure and descended to the kitchen. Her entrance caused a stir and the servants stopped what they were doing, looking at her in awe.

"Continue as before, I merely wish to see how the meal progresses." She sniffed delicately as the cook stirred first one pot and then another. Sirena nodded her approval as she walked around the kitchen. "And the fish, have you boned it?"

"Yes, Mevrouw. I myself boned the filets," Mella answered. "I added a few herbs and some butter — along with a touch of lemon."

"My mouth waters. I wish to thank you for following my directions."

"Mevrouw, you've only to ask and I'll prepare anything you wish. I added some cloves and cinnamon to the dates and figs." Sirena smiled her thanks at the cook.

"You seem pleased with yourself, Mella. Something tells me you'd rather cook like this than boiled cabbage." The roly-poly Malayan cook smiled brightly, white teeth sparkling in her nut-brown face. "Perhaps you'd like to cook especially for my brother and myself every night. If you've the time . . . we'd greatly appreciate it."

The cook's delight was evident in the way she went about her business, a watchful, victorious eye out for the door — and Frau Holtz.

"I'll make you anything! In the morning have Frau Holtz send Juli with your breakfast orders, and I will prepare it for you."

Sirena nodded and left the kitchens. The cook looked up to see Frau Holtz standing in the doorway.

"You have enough work cooking for the Mynheer," the grim housekeeper said. "Where do you expect to gain the time to prepare another set of meals. You will forget what she has just said and do as I tell you."

"But — the — Mevrouw —"

251

"*I* give the orders in this kitchen! You will do as I say, and only as I say. Is that understood?"

Sirena, her back against the wall outside the kitchen door, quietly opened the door and stood, her hands on her hips, her green eyes glittering angrily.

"You take it upon yourself to countermand an order that I have given? How dare you? *I'm* mistress of this house! You will do as *I* say. And I say you will follow me to my husband's quarters and we shall straighten this matter out immediately. You too, Mella, I want you to hear what my husband has to say."

No sooner were the words out of her mouth than she regretted them. This certainly wasn't the time to confront Regan, when his mind was no doubt occupied with the pirate woman! Especially after their last meeting at sea! Pulling the lacy mantilla closer about her cheeks, Sirena made a conscious effort to control her anger against Frau Holtz. Regan must not see any resemblance between his saintly wife and the bold, fire-breathing piratess.

Down the hall they marched, three women at odds. Standing outside his study door, Sirena gulped a deep breath and willed her voice to a sedate tone free of the anger knotted in her breast. Then, before she could change her mind, she rapped sharply on the door and was told to enter.

"I have a problem," Sirena said coolly, "I'm afraid only you can solve it, Mynheer. Am I mistress of this house or is Frau Holtz mistress?" Her voice was softly modulated, her eyes lowered in humility.

Regan stood up from his seat next to the window, his eye narrowed. "You're mistress, of course. What is the problem?"

"I issued orders to the cook and Frau Holtz countermanded my orders."

"What sort of orders?" Regan asked testily.

"I asked the cook to prepare separate meals for Caleb and myself. But," she added, "only if she had the time to do it. Cook answered that she would be glad to prepare such meals for us."

Regan's eyes clearly stated he wished himself elsewhere. "Cook has agreed, then why do you come to me?"

Sirena's heart fluttered madly. Regan was looking straight at her, a glimmer of admiration behind his penetrating, blue stare. To her relief there was no hint of recognition.

Confidence restored, Sirena went on, more boldly. "We came to you because . . . Frau Holtz told the cook not to prepare our meals. She told Mella there was enough to do without cooking for my brother and myself. Please settle the matter for us, Mynheer," she said softly, her voice controlled.

"You defied the Mevrouw," Regan said to the German housekeeper, his face a mask of fury. "Why," he shouted angrily, "why in God's name does this have to come up now, when I've other things on my mind? . . . Well, are you going to answer me?"

"I did not think, I — It seemed to me the cook had plenty to do with three meals a day without making extra work for her."

Regan pierced the Malayan with a cool eye.

"And what do *you* have to say? Do you mind the extra work? Will this cause you any problem in the kitchen?"

The cook shook her round head, her lips betraying a smile. "Mynheer, I told the Mevrouw I'd be glad to cook for her. She asked me first if it would be too much trouble. I told her no."

"The matter is settled then. You will prepare whatever my wife wants."

The cook and the housekeeper left the room, Sirena in their wake. She was almost at the door when Regan spoke: "I've heard it said that the Spanish are effusive in their thanks when a favor is granted them." Sirena watched him, her eyes cool and aloof. She said nothing. "Well?" he continued, prodding.

"That was a favor . . ." Sirena raised an eyebrow, making the statement a question. "I don't consider it a favor, Mynheer. Frau Holtz should have been told, much earlier, that I was mistress and she was to obey me. You did me no 'favor.' Had you denied my claim, however, I would have found ways to have myself and my brother invited to Don Chaezar Alvarez's house to dine."

"You would have done that?"

"Of course. I wish no tension in this house. Since you're the master I would think you would control the servants — not the other way around."

"What is that supposed to mean?" Regan shouted.

"I apologize. In Spain we do things differently," Sirena said softly, bowing her head so that the mantilla hid her face in a shadow. "I must constantly remind myself where I am." She couldn't resist adding impishly as she turned, "I wonder how it feels to have a paid servant issue orders and have them obeyed by the master."

"No such thing happens in my house," Regan said briskly as Sirena closed the door.

Or does it? he raged within himself. His last encounter with Frau Holtz vivid in his mind, he flushed as he rang the bell to summon her once more to him.

Regan stood at the woman's entrance. "Listen to me carefully, Frau Holtz, for I shall not repeat this again. You will do as the Mevrouw says. She is mistress of this house. I told you once before that you take much upon yourself. Things are different now that I'm married. I don't wish to be bothered with the household management. If there are any problems you will go to the Mevrouw. I want none of this backbiting and tattling. If this should happen again I will have to discharge you. I wouldn't like to do that as you have given my family loyal and efficient service over the years. The matter is ended."

"Very well, Mynheer."

Sirena dressed carefully for the dinner party, choosing a new — and sedate — black gown.

Caleb knocked and entered, his face a big smile. "I can hardly wait to eat!"

"Tell me, what sort of mood was Regan in when you returned to him."

"Angry, I've never seen an angrier man. He wouldn't tell me who sunk the *Java Queen*, he just said it was jettisoned along with her cargo. But I know he can't make any sense of it! He also said he

255

had a feeling in his gut that this is only the first of many ships that he'll lose. Then he said the Spaniard, Alvarez, lost *two* ships. What do you suppose will happen at dinner? Why this last-minute party?"

"There will be only one topic of conversation this night. I actually feel sorry for Frau Lindenreich and the other ladies! They won't get much attention. The men will be preoccupied with the fortunes they've lost and those they might lose in the future. It will be hard to keep a straight face." Sirena laughed. "Be sure you don't correct any mistakes they may make."

Sirena came downstairs just as the first guests arrived.

In the drawing room, moments later, glasses of wine were served and small sweets. Sirena declined both and settled herself next to the loquacious Helga. They spoke of the good lady's charges at the mission and the warm, balmy weather.

Sirena leaned closer to Helga after a few minutes and asked softly, "Why are the men in such a state this evening? My husband tells me nothing of business affairs. I assume it is business they discuss."

"I don't know. The invitation, or should I say 'summons,' " Helga amended, "came this afternoon. It must be serious — whatever it is. Regan rarely invites anyone at the last minute like this. But I see that Frau Lindenreich is here. Perhaps I'm wrong and this is just a social gathering after all."

"She's the guest of Don Chaezar Alvarez. Since the Señor is unmarried he supplies his own partner."

"Quite, quite," Helga replied as she marveled at the deep cleavage exposed by Gretchen's shimmering red gown. The vast expanses of creamy skin drew more than one man's eyes in her direction.

Sirena's hot, Latin temper raised her temperature several degrees and Gretchen's chameleon-like eyes swept over toward her several times, the corners of her mouth curved into a smirk. Sirena knew Gretchen felt she surpassed the Spaniard in the drab, black gown. When Gretchen clawed at Sirena with her glance, the blonde's eyes would afterward sweep over Regan in a caress. Only the memory of the flaming desire burning in Regan's eyes for the long-legged scantily clad piratess kept Sirena from slapping the smirk from Gretchen's too-red mouth. Furthermore, the handsome widow was receiving too much attention as it was. And if the wanton German moved too suddenly the shimmering red gown would slip even lower and reveal *all* of the cow's udders!

Dinner was announced. In the dining room Sirena was pleased to note large silver bowls of flowers at each end of the table, the candlelight reflected in the mirror surface of the metal. There was much scraping of chairs and appreciative low-voiced comments as the djongos began to serve the meal.

Sirena looked at Caleb, who was holding his breath in eager anticipation as a servant filled his plate. It was all Sirena could do to contain her mirth at the hunger in the boy's eyes. After the first course of consommé the tempting rice and baked fish were served. The vegetable was to be served next. What had Frau Holtz decided upon? The emerald eyes were pinpoints of flame as they sought out the housekeeper standing aloof in the corner, her eyes on the servants. Cabbage! How dare she?

Sirena spoke softly to the servant ladling out the cabbage. "There has been a mistake in the kitchen," she apologized to the guests. "Remove the cabbage and bring the other vegetable."

Regan watched Sirena's eyes seek out those of Frau Holtz. He was amazed to see the anger emanate from the housekeeper and from his wife as well.

The cook must have been intuitive, for within minutes a large steaming bowl of peas with onions was being served.

"An excellent dinner, Señora." Chaezar smiled. He looked around at the assembled guests and they added their approval. Even Regan had emptied his plate and seemed satisfied.

The meal over, the ladies settled themselves in one corner of the drawing room and the men in the other. At a signal from Sirena, Caleb joined the group of men.

Sirena tried to keep up her end of the conversation but found it difficult as she strained with one ear to hear the men's discussion. Her eyes traveled from time to time to the voluptuous Gretchen. She was a beautiful woman and was fully aware of her effect on the men as well as the women. Feeling Sirena's eyes on her, she turned and spoke. "How do you like our island by now?"

"I find it quite beautiful, Frau Lindenreich," Sirena replied graciously, her voice low and controlled.

"And our men, Mevrouw, what do you think of these tall virile Dutchmen?" Her eyes fell possessively on Regan.

Sirena pondered the question a moment as all the ladies' eyes swung in her direction.

"I really haven't had time to meet any of these . . . virile men you speak of save my . . . husband. I do however find Señor Alvarez enchanting." Her voice was a rich purr as Sirena met Gretchen's glare.

Helga raised merry eyes to Sirena and laughed. "I understand that Señor Alvarez plans a ball in a few weeks' time. Every one on the island will be invited. Even those merchants from the inner islands."

"I doubt Chaezar will hold the ball now," Gretchen said coolly.

"Why is that?" Helga asked.

"Don't tell me you're not aware of what's happened! Chaezar told me on the drive here that there's a woman pirate who has been robbing and plundering his ships. Regan's, too! I hardly think anyone will be in a festive mood for a time. Nor will Chaezar be able to afford a lavish party, considering the loss of his cargo."

"What else has he said, Gretchen?" Helga demanded, her eyes dancing.

"Chaezar lost two ships. A galleon and a brig which rode as escort. He himself wasn't aboard, but Regan *was* on his *Java Queen*. This devil of a woman blasted his ships fore and aft and left the cargo to sink into the sea. She told Regan she searches every ship she meets till she finds someone she is searching for. A man with a hook for a hand."

Sirena lowered her gaze to her folded hands. "And the men, Frau Lindenreich, why didn't the men fight back? I find it a mystery that a woman could prevail against our formidable seamen."

"Chaezar says his men said they hadn't a chance. She captains a ship whose hull and sails are as black as the night. She attacked under cover of darkness. And," Gretchen said, her voice rising, "this female buccaneer disappeared as if the ocean swallowed her up near the Sisters of Fire."

"The Sisters of Fire?" Sirena asked, lowering her lids to hide the excitement dancing in her eyes.

"That's what the natives call them. Actually they're two volcanos. Surely you've seen them from the garden. Their purple peaks are as bleak and ominous as shrouds."

A few of the ladies gave involuntary shudders, their complexions paling perceptibly. Earth tremor had increased in the past weeks and there were reports of sulphurous gases. Volcanos were a very unpopular topic on Java.

"Don't pay any attention to them, Sirena," Helga clucked. "Not in anyone's memory have the Sisters erupted. It's just a lot of silly prattle the natives drum up. Though it seems" — she scolded her neighbors — "that many otherwise sensible colonists' wives believe it!" She cast a scornful glance in the direction of the frightened ladies.

260

"And, I'll admit, mention of the volcanos is enough to shock even some of our brave men into silence. The most the Sisters have ever given us, however, is some earth tremor and a hearty pelting of hot stones. We've never suffered the devastation and the spewing of lava that Krakatoa wreaks, out there on the southern tip of Sumatra where she sits like some angry god! . . . Well, we Netherlanders — as well as you Spanish — are a stubborn lot! No sooner have the Sisters sighed their last angry rumble, than the debris and stones are cleared away and whatever was damaged or burned is restored. But enough about the fiery Sisters! Gretchen, what else do you know of this adventuress?"

Gretchen, annoyed with Helga's interruption, was glad to be the center of attention again. "Regan said she headed for the straits after she came upon his ship and sank it. But she allowed him and his captain and men to go into the jolly-boats. Regan said he got off a shot into her bow, first, but her seamen shored the frigate up and she made her getaway. Regan said she's like no other woman he's ever seen, and," Gretchen lowered her voice conspiratorially, "the piratess captains her ship nearly naked. She wears rags and her breasts are nearly exposed and her legs are part bare! One of Chaezar's men says she has a wicked scar that runs along her arm. A scar, vicious-looking and cruel!"

"Don't you . . . exaggerate, Frau Lindenreich?" Sirena asked skeptically.

"When the men join us, ask for yourself. Listen: It's all they can speak of. Chaezar said Regan is

261

mesmerized by the woman and has given her a name. He calls her the Sea Siren!" Gretchen's tone was malicious as she pierced Sirena with a cold, haughty look.

"I've never heard of such a thing! A woman! How can a woman captain a ship and do all these things without being caught?" Helga argued.

"She's like a devil. She attacks at night and, as I said, her ship and sails are as black as midnight."

"Does anyone know why she searches out this man with a hook?" Helga asked.

Gretchen shook her head. "Regan, himself, searches for such a man. *As* we all know . . ." she said, her eyes dark and fathomless. "He holds the swine responsible for his wife's death." Thoughts of The Hook brought the *Tita* to mind, and Gretchen hastened to continue. "You all know the story of the *Tita*, and Regan's feelings for the vessel, and how little more than a week ago she was sighted in harbor at Sumba. Regan set out with the *Java Queen* to find the old ship and met the Sea Siren instead! She'd beat him there and sank the *Tita* before his eyes! What do you say to that?"

The ladies had heard much of the tale before, but the telling of it once more added enjoyment — and a certain fear — to their evening at the van der Rhys home. They shook their heads, clucking their tongues. However, their eyes revealed their satisfaction that a woman, a mere woman, could wreak such havoc.

"I wonder why this . . . Sea Siren, as you call her, would seek a man with a hook? It must be very important to her if it provokes her to attack innocent men," Sirena said, her voice just above a whisper.

"Who knows? But she'll never find him! Regan has searched for him for three long years," Gretchen said confidently.

Sirena spoke again. "It would seem to me that Regan and Chaezar should redouble their efforts to find this man, perhaps put bounty on his head to increase the effort. This way, once the man is caught the . . . Sea Siren might cease and desist."

"That makes sense!" Helga said excitedly. "If the men haven't thought of it, then perhaps we should mention it. Sometimes we women come up with an answer that completely eludes them. We're stronger than men give us credit for being. The Sea Siren has only proved my point: the piratess wants something — and fights like a man among men to get it. I'd like to ride her ship!" the loquacious Helga bubbled.

"And I . . . I too would like to join her," Sirena smiled. "I find it admirable that a woman can do these things." The other ladies nodded their agreement with some hesitation. Not so, Gretchen.

"I don't believe what I hear," Gretchen sniffed. "You! Ride the seas like a wild wanton!"

"What makes you think she's . . . wanton?" Sirena queried.

Gretchen snipped, "If she's not a slut now she'll arrive at it eventually. How can a woman with any respect for herself carry on like that?"

"You're only . . . well, speculating, Frau Lindenreich," Sirena said softly. "Personally, I applaud her aggressiveness."

The hazel eyes sparkled dangerously. "Would you favor her valor if your husband bedded the slut?"

Sirena pulled her mantilla modestly across her face, and spoke delicately. "I . . . I should imagine that, here alone these past three years, Mynheer van der Rhys will have . . . will have patronized many 'sluts.' Don't you think so, Frau Lindenreich?" she asked sweetly.

Gretchen's shocked face boded ill for Sirena, but the beautiful widow's comeback was cut off by Regan's crossing the room.

"I think we're ready for our coffee now," he said, the pleasant host.

"All this talk of a Sea Siren has made my mouth dry," Anton Kloss said from across the room.

"Dear, is all the talk of a Sea Siren true?" Helga questioned her husband.

"Unfortunately, yes. She appears bent on destroying the Dutch fleet — along with the Spanish. Any ship! It is not a laughing matter!" Captain Kloss admonished his smiling wife.

"Sirena has said something I think you should hear," Helga announced to him and the other men, stifling an even wider grin.

"What is that, Helga?" Captain Kloss cast her a stern eye.

"Sirena said you should all band together to seek out the man with the hook and put a bounty on his head. That may be all the Sea Siren wants. If she's successful in capturing that man, she'll stop her plundering and then all our ships will be safe."

Anton Kloss looked at Sirena with admiration.

264

"We've already decided this matter. Regan, as you know, seeks the same man. We've agreed to send out word about him, perhaps even some of our smaller ships — to go out among the nearer islands — beginning at dawn tomorrow."

Sirena sought Caleb's eyes and was amused by the twinkle in them.

"What will happen when you find him?" Gretchen asked hesitantly. "Will you run him through or will you turn him over to this . . . Sea Siren?"

"I will run him through," Regan said brutally.

"But, Regan," Helga interrupted, "the Sea Siren . . . *wants* him. If *you* succeed in finding him and she hears of it she may seek revenge."

"Yes, Mynheer, what if that happens?" Chaezar asked, as he stroked his beard thoughtfully. "That in itself could pose even more problems. I think we should decide now that if we do find him we hand him over to the piratess."

"Never!" Regan shouted. "I bear him too great a personal grudge."

"But, Mynheer, what we do has to be what is best for *all!* Forget your vengeance, my friend. How many more ships do you think you can afford to lose?"

"She is only a woman! You all talk like scared rabbits. I shall refuse to turn him over to her if my men or myself capture him."

Sirena saw the fear mount in Gretchen's eyes yet the woman's voice was calm when she spoke: "It's a mistake, Regan. Let the Siren run him through, it will be less blood on your conscience. For that matter, the man could be dead, washed

265

overboard in a storm or run through by some other cutthroat. Do you plan to spend the rest of your days tracking down a ghost!"

"Quite simply, I'll never allow a woman to dictate to me," Regan said harshly. "I am not speaking of you, Mevrouw, but of this female buccaneer!"

Anton Kloss broke in: "Even at the cost of your fleet? From what I hear, the woman has as much . . . well, expertise as any of our captains. And," Kloss added ominously, "I fear that if it is put to a vote, Regan, you will lose. Change your mind, old friend."

"Never!" Regan thundered.

"You're a fool, Regan." Don Chaezar Alvarez's voice was arrogant in his disdain. "It's not just a question of *your* survival, it's all of us. How can you be so blind?"

"You have my answer. I'll not change it. Do what you will, but if I come across the man first I'll run him through!"

"And let the rest of us lose our ships!"

"If it comes to that, yes. It's every man for himself."

"Bravo," Sirena murmured to herself. Almost shyly, she spoke: "Regan, what will you do if this . . . Sea Siren learns what you've decided? What if she takes a double vengeance?"

"Such as?"

"It is said she doesn't kill unless necessary, that she . . . lets the men go into the jolly-boats. What if she decides to retaliate and starts to run men through? From what's been said, that would seem to be her vengeance. Speaking from a woman's point of view, I would say that if she's gone this far, nothing on this earth will deter her from her mission in finding . . . The Hook." She shivered delicately. "Perhaps you had better give it some thought?"

"I agree," Helga Kloss said, her eyes snapping. "A woman who has gone to these lengths to do what she's done will never bend to you."

"Nor will I bend either!" Regan stated, as adamant as before.

"You sound so determined, Regan. Almost as if you hate the Sea Siren," Don Chaezar said softly. "It's difficult to believe you commissioned a figurehead in her likeness!"

It was as if a shockwave had passed through the room, almost as if the Sisters of Fire had grumbled and sent tremors through the group assembled in the van der Rhys drawing room. Sirena's eyes expressed pure shock — and then delight — and she pulled the mantilla close around her face. Gretchen's face turned beet-red with fury, though she dared not speak. Helga and the other ladies in the room lowered their eyes to the kerchiefs they held in their hands.

Regan strode, somewhat embarrassed despite his determination not to lose face, toward the wide window that looked out on the verandah.

After a momentary silence among the men, they began talking once more as the houseboys entered to serve them coffee. Was Regan enamored of the Sea Siren? they wondered. Did he really *want* to see her again?

"Let me put it to you another way!" Don Chaezar said quietly. "Let's just suppose for a mo-

267

ment that what Mevrouw van der Rhys has said comes to pass and the Sea Siren begins to show no quarter. Will you then agree?"

Regan let his eyes travel the length of the room. He did not like the look of hostility on his guests' faces. "Very well," he acquiesced.

Sirena's eyes sought those of Gretchen and she was surprised to see them full of relief. What had Gretchen been afraid of?

Chapter Fourteen

The next morning Gretchen rode over to the estate of Don Chaezar. She found him sipping his morning coffee in his study. Always the gentleman, he rose to greet her and promptly offered to order her some breakfast. Gretchen refused his offer and dropped wearily onto the settee opposite the windows overlooking the garden.

It was obvious to Chaezar that Gretchen had come to his home for a specific reason and he hoped she would get to the point quickly. Women on the edge of hysteria — which certainly described Gretchen this morning — bored him.

"How did you find the dinner last evening?" he asked the pensive blonde next to him.

"It gave me much to think about, Chaezar. What — do you think will — happen now?" A hint of fear made her voice quaver.

"God only knows. Regan is like a madman! I shudder to think what will happen if and when he finds our friend with the hook. If Regan merely kills him I'd have no complaints. However, if he gives him a chance to talk, then it will be another matter. If that gruesome thought should come to pass I intend to be reclining under a Spanish sky. And you, Gretchen, where will you be?"

"You make it sound as if it's already a fact. If Regan has not succeeded in three long years, what makes you think he can find our friend now?

Be realistic, Chaezar!"

"I *am* being realistic, Gretchen. When Regan searched before, there was no bounty on The Hook's head. And, too, there was no Sea Siren on his trail!"

"The money we paid him should have made him content for the rest of his life," Gretchen pouted. "He promised to go to one of the inner islands — Borneo — or Celebes — and retire. What in the name of God could have gone wrong? Why did he take to sailing again?"

"It won't do either of us any good to question it now. We have to find him ourselves and turn him over to the Sea Siren. If it comes right down to it and Regan somehow manages to find him, his hate will never allow him to hand the man over to the pirate woman! If I were in his position I wouldn't either."

"There must be some way to find him! A word here and there. Offer your own reward. You have to do something!" Gretchen screeched, panic disfiguring her beautiful face.

"Why do *I* have to do something? I'm sorry I ever allowed you to talk me into the affair in the beginning. You convinced me that Regan would marry you if Tita was done away with. You've had three long years now to capture him!"

"I would have had *eight,* and he'd surely be mine by now, if Pedro Gomez — instead of your own ship — hadn't picked Regan up in his dinghy and carted him off to Spain to rot in a Spanish prison. A fine outcome our schemes had for me!"

"I deeply regret the scheme now. It was a mistake," Chaezar said wistfully.

"A mistake? You got an unexpected benefit out of it — if the benefit *was* unexpected. When Vincent van der Rhys heard, later, of his son's imprisonment, he paid you well and aided Spain to regain some of the trade privileges she'd lost to the Dutch those past years. But, Chaezar," Gretchen sputtered, "you helped me once, and you must help me again! I should say 'help *us*'! For if Regan van der Rhys learns from The Hook what happened to his son and our part in it — he'll kill us both! Both, do you hear me?"

"That's where you are wrong, my dear. Regan could never prove a thing against me. Now you," he said thoughtfully, "are another matter. He'll believe the story — the true one — that you wanted Tita killed so he could marry you. I think he could understand your kind of jealousy and hatred — although he would never forgive you. What he won't understand is the boy! I told you *that* was a mistake. But you said you wanted 'no reminders of his marriage' and that the boy had to go, too! Where did you send him, Gretchen, when The Hook returned from Capetown with the boy? I'd washed my hands of the affair by then, and let you have your way. If you want my help, you'll have to tell me where —"

"To Mindanao, in the Philippines — Spanish territory, where the Dutch do not trade." Gretchen hesitated, as if thinking. Finally, she said, "I've been thinking, Chaezar. Since last night. Do you suppose if we went there, or sent a ship up, we could somehow manage to reclaim the boy and get him back here? Tell Regan we'd heard rumors of his whereabouts and sent out to find the

271

boy? Out of pleasure at his son's return, Regan might forget his anger against The Hook — and let the Sea Siren have the man, if and when he's found . . ."

"How would you prevent Reagan from suspecting we'd had some part in the boy's abduction — *and* his mother's murder —"

"We could have one of your marauders 'discover' the boy — at our command — and play no part in his return at all."

"And on his return, it would be interesting to see whether or not the boy tells some interesting details about his capture and his being sent away — by you, no less, for he saw you here when The Hook brought him back — to Mindanao. He's no doubt about twelve years old now, but he was an alert four-year-old at the time of his mother's death."

Gretchen was speechless for a moment, and trembling visibly. "Or perhaps a letter could be posted to Regan telling him where we think the boy is, but not giving our names . . . anonymous." She pursed her tremulous lips.

"For the first time I see you're truly afraid. Do you love Regan as much as all that? And fear for his life at the Siren's hands?"

"Love has nothing to do with it," Gretchen sobbed.

"Regan is married now. And I would wager before long Sirena will make him happy, and they'll begin to raise healthy, happy babies."

"Then she'll grow fat and ugly!" Gretchen spat.

"What difference will that make? She'll still be married to him!"

"Please Chaezar . . . you must help me."

"And if I do? What will be my reward?" the Spaniard asked softly, his dark glance falling on her sulky mouth and coming to rest on her bosom.

"Name it, and it's yours," Gretchen whispered.

This would be easier than she thought. She'd known that his assistance would require some sort of payment and she had been momentarily fearful that he would demand several pieces of her jewelry. Most of her jewels were merely costume baubles, but several gentlemen admirers had gifted her with exquisite and valuable pieces. Gretchen was both amused and relieved that Chaezar obviously would be satisfied with an hour's dalliance.

From the fervid gleam in his eye she knew that his appetites ran to the exotic today. Chaezar gripped her wrist with a feverish hand and led her to his chamber. She followed him willingly, eager to meet his demands so that she could leave early enough to keep an appointment with her dressmaker.

Chaezar, on the other hand, attributed Gretchen's willingness to eager anticipation and, as was his way, he stripped off his clothes without a word. He preferred not to engage in any conversation at these times — as Gretchen well knew; she supposed it was because he wanted nothing to divert his concentration on his role.

Gretchen knew the rules by which Chaezar insisted this game be played. She stood coolly in the center of the room and waited.

Each time Chaezar played this exotic game that was about to begin, Gretchen was amazed at the transfiguration of the man. She knew, from other experience with him, that the Spaniard could be a dynamic, vigorous lover, completely at ease and fully masculine. But this was one of those "other" times. Gone now was the forceful yet urbane gentleman sure of his every move. Before her stood a simpering, mincing, cowering minion — it was a fantasy, of course, or so she hoped — intent on pleasing a cruel, flint-hearted mistress . . . and trembling with the knowledge that she would be impossible to please. The Mistress was a role Gretchen herself had no trouble playing.

Reverently his hands went to the buttons at the back of her gown. Carefully, he undid them one by one, his fingers barely grazing the silky flesh beneath her gown. Layers of clothing were removed until all she wore was her satin corset, frilly lace drawers, black silk stockings, and high-heeled slippers. Deliberately, yet feverishly, he snapped her garter and immediately recoiled in terror.

Gretchen knew her cue. "Clumsy oaf!" she said sternly. "See how you've bruised your ladyship's thigh!" She extended her silky limb, pointing to where the garter had snapped against her creamy leg. "Kiss it!" she ordered him harshly.

Chaezar dropped to his knees before her and pressed ardent lips to the imaginary wound. Gretchen was pleased to notice how aroused he was: a little while longer and she would be free to leave.

"You realize you must be punished for your clumsiness," she said with great authority.

Chaezar's answer was to grovel pitifully at her feet, kissing her insteps, her ankles; his whole attitude was that of a panic-stricken animal.

"Get the whip!" she ordered. Chaezar cowered close to her legs, whimpering. "Get the whip, I tell you! Now!"

Chaezar hesitantly pulled away from her and dragged himself to his feet. His eyes were black pools of anguish, his lips quivered with fear. From his face and posture anyone would have believed him to be the badly used servant of a monstrously brutal master. Only his loins betrayed his pose. Alive and erect, his phallus betrayed the true object of his desires.

From the top of his clothes press, he withdrew a long, evil-looking whip. The handle was heavy carved wood, ornate in design. At one end of the handle were large, round opalines, and when one looked closely one could see that the shaft of the handle and the placement of the opalines represented the male sex organ. The tails of the whip, while cruel-looking, black, and knotted, were actually braided silk, designed to sting the flesh yet not cut or tear it or even raise a welt.

Humbly, Chaezar offered the instrument to Gretchen. Chaezar worshipped the whip in a way he could never adore a woman's body. While fascinated by its uniqueness, she therefore abhorred its significance to him. In some twisted way the whip represented a rival to her. To know that Chaezar could be sexually satisfied by three long cords of braided silk was an affront to her self-esteem. That she cared nothing for the man — in fact didn't even like him, only used him as a means to an end — mattered not at all. She was a woman who recognized her own desirability

275

and she demanded that a man, any man, appreciate her qualities.

Gretchen accepted the heavy-handled whip noting the slavish, fanatical light in Chaezar's eyes. He was ready. He had goaded himself to fever pitch. The muscles in his back and thighs quivered in anticipation. The dark curling hairs on his chest and belly were practically standing on end. His breathing was ragged; small flecks of saliva danced on his beard.

Gretchen brought up the whip and spun the long, trailing braids in wide circles about her head. Chaezar held his breath and watched, mesmerized, waiting for the curling ends to strike his flesh. His eyes never left the whirling braids. At last, Gretchen brought down the adored instrument of torture. Again and again she lashed him about the back and chest. Again and again the long, trailing tails would glance off his buttocks and thighs. Chaezar moaned in ecstasy, his body trembling with paroxysms of passion.

At last he fell to his knees gasping for air, until his convulsive excitement abated. He crawled across the floor until he reached her, tears of gratitude shining in his eyes. Like a dog at his master's knee, he pressed his dark head against her thigh, small sobs catching in his throat.

Now was the time for the cruel mistress to become the magnanimous benefactor. She petted his head and held him against her, soothing his pain and humiliation. Mutely moving closer, Chaezar began to kiss her hand, her thigh, begged her forgiveness. His face was moist with saliva and tears, staining her skin with silvery wetness.

He kissed her fervently and she cradled him in her arms and led him to the bed. Soothing him with soft tones and maternal gestures, she dried his tears and held him close. With narrowed eyes she estimated the length of time she must stay with him until, still sobbing heartbrokenly, he would fall asleep.

This was the part of Chaezar's little play that really repelled her. She didn't mind beating him with the whip — she enjoyed seeing him pay her homage and groveling at her feet. It was when she was obliged to forgive him that he disgusted her by crying all over her, his wet mouth and cheeks pressed against her skin.

Chaezar's grip on her was slackening now. Soon he would be asleep and she could leave and the events of the past hour would never be mentioned by either of them.

She *must* have a bath before she went to the dressmaker's!

Chapter Fifteen

"Sirena," Caleb fretted, "Regan and Don Chaezar Alvarez are gone looking for The Hook! Why aren't we chasing them?"

"Remember what I told you about 'wily women?' Regan and Chaezar *expect* the Sea Siren to be out there. Never do the expected. Have no fear, little brother. The Hook will have gone into hiding as soon as word spreads he's being hunted. He'll wait, as we do. You must always be one league ahead of your adversary. This time we'll let the men chase themselves. What they're doing is sailing blind. Before long they'll all be frustrated and losing money, for nearly all Dutch and Spanish shipping will have ceased for the time being."

"How do you know this?"

"Because, if you'll forgive me, little brother, men think with their loins. If they used their brains they'd never act so foolishly. I tell you, they sail blind. At best they'd find some wild marauder and get their ships damaged — perhaps get themselves killed for their effort! I'll give them ten days and they'll be home, half-crazed with rage. Just in time for Chaezar's party." Sirena's tone was light, her expression amused.

"Perhaps there won't be a party."

"There'll be a party. The invitation came today from Chaezar."

"It should prove interesting?" Caleb smiled.

"*Very* interesting," Sirena agreed.

One day ran into the next as Sirena and Caleb awaited Regan's return. Every day the boy went to the wharf, but there was no news. On the ninth day he was sitting on the edge of the quay when he spotted the first sail. Waving excitedly, he raced to the end of the quay and waited.

The minutes seemed like hours to Caleb, as the ship approached. Then, finally it was at anchor.

Regan was the first to disembark. His face was a mask of cold fury. "No sight of the long-legged bitch *or* of the man with the hook, Caleb. The scurve must have his ear to the wind and is hiding out. Either that or he is on a lengthy voyage. We came upon one small pirate ship, smaller than our own vessel, that would have run from us. But I signaled that we had peaceful intentions toward the tiny, flagless frigate, and they approached. They said they'd come across him in recent months, but none of them knew now of his whereabouts. One cutthroat is much like another — but I'm sure they told the truth. The bounty on the bastard's head is too attractive. And we inquired among the ports of Borneo, Celebes, Bali, with no luck. We'd have gone farther — to the Moluccas and New Guinea — but have left such long trips till later."

"Perhaps the Sea Siren has given up too!" Caleb said hesitantly.

Regan clapped his arm around the boy's shoulders as they walked into the D.E.I. offices. "I think not. I believe, however, she learned of our voyage. She's probably, right now, this very minute, laughing her head off at our stupidity. I admit it was ridiculous going to sea like that. When a man's fortunes are at stake he is apt to do many foolish things. She's won again."

"How could she 'win' if she didn't go after you?" Caleb asked, puzzled.

"She made fools of the lot of us!" Regan closed the door to his office and sat down on his leather-backed chair. "Fetch me a cigar, will you, boy?"

Caleb looked around the small office then went to the heavy-laden shelves. He let his eyes wander over the array of objects on the many tiers and finally bent down and reached for a square leather humidor; but he hesitated and reached instead for a small wooden box. He grasped it in both hands and handed it to Regan.

Regan's eyes blazed and the skin pulled back over his teeth suddenly like a snarling dog. "How did you know what was in that box?" he demanded harshly.

Frightened by the man's intensity, Caleb drew back, clutching the box to his chest. "But — you — said — to fetch you a — cigar."

"I know what I said. How is it you knew where they were?"

"I . . . I don't know. I must have seen you get them the the last time I was here with you. Did I do something wrong? Is something in this box that you don't care to have me see? I'm sorry, Mynheer!"

Regan perceived Caleb's fright and his tone calmed immediately. "I'm sorry, Caleb, it's just that my own son used to get my cigars for me. I used to keep them in the big leather humidor, but, being less than five years old, he couldn't lift it. I

280

moved them to the box you're holding now. When you bent over like that, it just reminded me of those long-ago days. I'm sorry if I upset you — I guess I've been out to sea too long. Sometimes I get caught up in the past and can't forget."

"You must have loved your son very much," Caleb said hesitantly.

"Very much," Regan said gently. "But you'd better get home now. I'll see you at dinner. Tell your sister I've arrived, safe and sound — if she should inquire, that is."

"I'll deliver the message, Mynheer," Caleb said as he closed the door behind him.

Regan paced the small room, his mind in a turmoil. He was positive he had never taken a cigar from the wooden box when Caleb was in the office. As a matter of fact, Regan preferred the brand of cheroot he kept at home and always carried several in his shirtfront. Lately, he'd kept the cigars in the office only for visiting merchants. His heart pounded wildly in his chest at the thoughts that invaded his mind.

Chinese paper lanterns swayed lazily in the timid breeze that floated in from Batavia's harbor. From the distance they resembled hundreds of fireflies dancing among the tropical shrubbery surrounding Don Alvarez's palatial home. Situated on the elite Avenue of the Lion, within the walls of the city, Don Chaezar's home surpassed any of the city's dwellings in its charm and grace.

Music spilled out the verandah doors into the dark garden. The lavish ball was a huge success. His guests tipped their fragile, long-stemmed wine glasses to smiling lips, toasting his generosity. Everyone on his long guest list had come — Spanish, Dutch, and Portuguese alike. Even some English and French merchants were here.

Sirena and Regan had arrived nearly an hour late, owing to last-minute business Regan was forced to conduct in his office on the wharf. Whatever business it was that detained Regan, Sirena noted that it had left him in a black humor. His heavy brows were drawn together in a scowl, the muscles in his jaw were knotted beneath his lean, clean-shaven flesh. His eyes were bright, the black pupils narrowed to pinpoints glowering with barely suppressed menace.

Prior to their arrival at Chaezar's, Sirena had timidly asked Regan what was wrong. She had even gone so far as to suggest that perhaps he didn't care to attend Chaezar's ball. If that were the case, she would understand and stay home with him. His answer had been to laugh. A great, booming, angry sound of derision. "Stay home?" he had exclaimed "Never! I'm going, even if I have to crawl!" Perplexed, Sirena had stepped into the carriage and held her skirts to make room for Regan on the seat next to her. They drove to Chaezar's in silence, the Mynheer puffing angrily on the cheroot he held between tightly clenched teeth.

Now, standing at the entrance to the ballroom, the blazing candlelight turning his pale blond hair to silver, Regan's eyes raked the room in more than just a curious perusal of the party. Sirena knew he was looking for something . . . or someone.

Sirena noticed Gretchen's approach before Regan. As the blonde moved across the room, all heads turned to watch her. And why? Gretchen's gown was infamous! Sirena saw. Made of incandescent blue silk studded with crystals across the bosom and pelvis, it clung seductively to her figure, revealing the fact that she wore absolutely nothing beneath it. As formfitting as a snake's skin, the dress molded itself to her every curve, revealing quite plainly the separation between her buttocks and the sensuous indentation of her navel. Nevertheless, while her scantiness of clothing was shocking, she carried herself with dignity and grace, giving the effect of a mythical goddess instead of a brazen whore. The women were scandalized, the men delighted.

A mocking smile spread slowly across Regan's face. Sirena knew from the appreciative way he appraised Gretchen that the hillocks and valleys of her body were familiar territory.

Sirena felt dowdy and outmoded alongside the German temptress. The blue of the scanty silk gown turned Gretchen's hair to a pale shade of silver which almost matched Regan's. Sparkling gems glimmered from her curls, their brilliance matching the sparkle in the widow's eyes.

It was Don Chaezar who rescued Sirena from the embarrassing spectacle of the charged glances between Regan and Gretchen. Bowing low over Sirena's hand to plant a delicate kiss on her fingertips, he swept her away to introduce her to several guests from outlying islands. Faces swayed before her and names became garbled in her mind. The jealousy she had felt at the gleam in Regan's eyes

283

when he looked at Gretchen left her seething with rage. It was only with a concentrated effort that she was able to prevent herself from turning around to follow their movements.

Alvarez, the perfect gentleman, never left her unattended. He was a genial host and had planned his party with consideration for his guests' enjoyment. The music was gay, the wines superb, the tables laden with tempting food of every variety. Once, when Chaezar left her for a moment to instruct his servants on the serving of the wine, Helga Kloss hurriedly approached Sirena.

"You must share the secret with me, Sirena," she gasped breathlessly. Her little, round eyes shone with excitement. "Surely Don Chaezar has told you what the surprise is! You *must* tell me! I shall faint with suspense if you don't!"

"I've no idea what surprise you speak of, Mevrouw," Sirena laughed. "Unless, of course, you meant Frau Lindenreich's surprising attire."

Helga Kloss's face went blank for a moment before understanding flushed her round, pink cheeks. "Oh yes, did you see her? Of course, you must have," she tittered. "Captain Kloss is simply scandalized! Whenever she's within sight, the poor man doesn't know where to look. But no, Gretchen is not what Don Chaezar has planned for this evening. It's something else. He's been hinting at it for most of the evening, hadn't you noticed?"

Helga cast Sirena a quizzical eye. What was wrong with the girl? Helga had always considered her quite clever. What was Sirena thinking of all evening if she hadn't heard mention of Don

Chaezar's secret "spectacular"!

After Helga ran out of gossip to impart to Sirena and she had secured a promise to "come to tea very soon," she departed in search of her husband, leaving Sirena blessedly alone. The number of people, the music, and the sight of brightly colored, bobbing and dipping skirts had become a trifle overwhelming. Sirena looked for an opportunity to be alone with her thoughts and saw the perfect answer: the doors leading onto the verandah.

The cool night air felt fresh against her cheeks, the strains of the music seemed sweeter out here in the moonlight.

After a few quiet moments, Sirena became aware that she was not alone. From behind some large shrubs near the verandah the sound of a woman's light laughter was wafted by the evening breeze. She was about to go inside when something about the pitch of the woman's voice struck her as familiar. The slight intonation of derision, the lilting quality — husky yet girlish. Gretchen!

Suddenly Sirena remembered riding on the back of the baggage wagon along a hot dusty road, the sun baking the black bombazine dress into the flesh of her back, heavy black hair falling awry, sticking to her damp, perspiring neck. And the sound of the laughter — taunting and scornful. Followed by the sight of a beautifully coiffed head peeking out through the hedge, a laughing face looking up into hers, enjoying Sirena's misery.

Sharp stabs of hatred shot through her, an icy resolve to slap that snickering mouth until its full ripe lips were swollen and bloody.

Without further thought, Sirena pushed her way through the shrubs and found just what she had expected: Gretchen and Regan holding each other in a tight embrace.

For a full moment she went unnoticed as her rage mounted and all reason was swept from her. She only half saw Regan's lips pressed against Gretchen's, one arm around her back, his hand caressing the firm, round flesh of her buttocks, the other hand pushed down into the wide deep neckline of the iridescent blue gown.

In one sweeping motion, Sirena was upon them, tearing them from each other's arms. Like a spitting, snarling cat, she turned on Gretchen in unleashed violence. "Since you seem bent on exposing yourself, Frau Lindenreich," she hissed, "why allow a slip of dress fabric to stand between you and my husband!" With a claw-like hand Sirena reached out, grasped the neckline of Gretchen's gown, and ripped it nearly to the hem.

Gretchen rose to Sirena's attack with surprise but with bared teeth and a show of sharp nails. Cursing with rage, she reached for Sirena's hair, but Sirena dodged her flailing arm. Like two spitting cats the women faced each other, each seeking the destruction of the other.

"I've wanted to slap that snickering smile from your face for some time," Sirena continued. "Now I intend to scratch your eyes out, too!"

Her tone was low, yet held such menace that Regan was taken aback. He'd have never thought his composed Sirena capable of such violent speech. More to get a closer look at Sirena than to protect Gretchen, he stepped between them. Immediately, his action was misinterpreted by both women.

"Stand aside, Regan. *You've* had *your* lark with this German whore! Now I intend to have mine!" Her eyes flashed with venom; she poised, lithe as a cat, to resume her attack on the German. "If you insist on protecting her, be warned: I'll cut you down to get to her!"

Fear now began to take hold of Gretchen. Sirena had said she would scratch out her eyes and Gretchen had no doubt whatsoever that the Spanish cat meant to do it. So, when Regan placed himself between the women, Gretchen allowed herself the luxury of hysterics. Her mind now ran to the actual damage done to her. "My gown!" she wailed. "Look what she's done to it! It can never be repaired!" She took a step closer to Regan's back, enjoying its protection. Something crunched beneath her foot.

"The crystals! They've been torn off! Regan, help me find them, they cost a fortune!" Crawling about on her hands and knees, she sought out the tiny beads which had been sewn onto her gown.

Sirena glanced down at Gretchen crawling about searching for the lost beads and saw Frau Lindenreich's breasts fall unbecomingly out of the shredded bodice. The woman's hair had come undone and was falling in an untidy mass down her back.

Regan, too, glanced down and saw the ridiculousness of Gretchen's position. He burst into a great peal of laughter. Then, seeing the murderous looks the woman cast him, his mirthful sounds froze in his throat.

A shuffle of feet and the appearance of Don Chaezar standing just outside the verandah immediately cooled the charged atmosphere.

"Chaezar!" Gretchen sobbed, jumping to her feet, "see what she's done to me!"

"I see . . . Gretchen," the Spaniard soothed her. "And how magnificently she's done it!"

Gretchen, stupefied by his remark and wide-eyed with surprise, was about to return the insult, when she noticed Chaezar's eyes fall on Sirena. Gretchen thought she saw a light of admiration in his black gaze.

Turning to Gretchen, however, he said, "You may go around the verandah to my chambers. Take one of my dressing gowns to wear home. I'll have my coachman bring the trap around to the back. You can leave from there and no one will see you. I assume you don't want to be seen in the state you're in."

"I don't give a damn who sees me!" Gretchen spat.

"But *I* do," Chaezar said threateningly. "I won't allow you to make an even greater spectacle of yourself in my house, and before my guests."

Regan and Sirena were amazed at how quickly Gretchen's temper quelled in the face of Don Chaezar's authority. They watched her sulk around to the back of the house, silently prepared to follow Chaezar's orders.

Both Regan and Chaezar now viewed Sirena with bewildered expressions. They were clearly wondering how she could have been a seething spitfire only a moment before and now appear to

288

be in complete control of herself, composed and unruffled.

In a courtly and solicitous manner, the Spaniard flashed Sirena a dazzling smile and offered her his arm. "You must put all this behind you, *querida*. Don't let anything spoil your evening." His eyes were quick to note, however, that rather than spoiling his countrywoman's evening, Sirena's fray with Gretchen had been the highlight of it. "Now, you must both come back into the ballroom. I am ready to unveil my little surprise — my 'spectacular,' as everyone prefers to call it."

Sirena saw that Regan was scowling at the easy manner Don Chaezar had with her. And, her eyes glued on her husband, she had noticed the sudden alertness about Regan when Chaezar mentioned to them his "surprise."

"Yes, Alvarez," Regan was saying, a biting edge to his voice, "I'm most interested in this little 'surprise' of yours. Let's go with him, Sirena. We wouldn't want him to keep us guessing any longer than necessary." Muscles knotted in Regan's jaw, the thick column of his neck was corded with fury.

So this is what Regan was angry about on our way here, Sirena thought with amusement. Whatever Chaezar's little surprise is, Regan knows — and doesn't like it. She was curious to see what was going to happen.

As the three entered the ballroom, all eyes turned to watch them expectantly. The musicians had stopped their playing and all the guests milled about a tall, shrouded shape which stood in the center of the ballroom. As Sirena and the two men stepped into the center of the throng, she heard

289

Helga Kloss call out, "Hurry, Chaezar! The suspense is making me feel faint. But I can guess what it is, you rake. You've imported one of those statues from Greece, haven't you? The ones that hardly have anything on . . ." Helga's voice ended in a muffled giggle.

A small titter of laughter broke out from around the Dutch captain's wife. Smiling, Sirena guessed that Anton Kloss had put an end to his wife's speculations.

Chaezar left Sirena and Regan standing on the inside perimeter of the circle of guests. With great aplomb he stepped up to the tall shrouded object. Clearing his throat importantly, he began to speak: "As is well known by all of you, the islands of the East Indies are recently under siege by the most ruthless marauder of the seas that we have ever known. There are those among us who have been fortunate enough to have glimpsed this notorious piratess on her own domain, the sea. There is even one among us who, having confronted this sea witch, has become so infatuated with her that he commissioned the construction of her likeness."

Standing next to Regan, Sirena felt him stiffen. His hand, which had been resting lightly on her arm, gripped her flesh painfully.

"Without further ado, my honored guests, I give you the Sea Siren!"

Chaezar pulled lightly on a silken cord, and the draperies fell away. There on a podium which had been especially constructed was Regan's figurehead.

Gasps and oohs of delight filled the ballroom. It

was magnificent. Carved with loving hands, the figure was nearly life-sized. What Sirena saw when she looked at it was a startlingly close resemblance to herself, her flowing hair sculpted to appear as though the wind were sweeping it back from its beautifully molded face. The arms were fashioned close to the body; the breasts were high and full, and accurately displayed beneath the illusion of a short body-hugging blouse tied high over the ribs. The long satiny torso was smooth and rounded into the swells of its hips. The figure was astoundingly correct — even to the dramatic headband tied about the forehead of its finely chiseled face.

Fearfully, Sirena looked about the room to see if anyone had noticed the astonishing resemblance to herself. Finally having the courage to glance at Regan, she watched him as he studied the work he had commissioned. She wondered nervously how he had remembered the Sea Siren so . . . so accurately? As Regan gazed upon the figurehead of the Sea Siren she saw in his eyes the same hunger and desire she had seen when he looked at her as she stood defiantly on the deck of the *Rana.*

As the guests gathered around the figurehead — some to stare, others to touch the satiny teak — Sirena backed off, her stomach muscles knotted in apprehension. She accepted a glass of wine, keeping her face in profile to the guests as she sipped the crimson liquid.

Turning back toward the crowd of guests a moment later, for she dared not be too obvious in her lack of interest in the figurehead, she saw something in the Spaniard's eyes she'd dreaded since she had first heard of the construction of the image of the Sea Siren: recognition.

Don Chaezar watched Sirena bring the fragile wineglass to her lips once more; then an expression of consternation, of infinite surprise, stole across his features.

Regan turned away, finally, from the figurehead. As he did so, he saw the look on the Spaniard's face. Quickly he glanced back at the representation of the Sea Siren; then he shifted his gaze to his wife — he too as intent as Don Chaezar.

Then Regan's piercing blue eyes met Chaezar's black ones. "If," said the Dutchman, "your purpose was to embarrass me this evening, you've fallen short of your victory, Don Chaezar Alvarez. The figurehead's beauty far outshines its scandalousness! And, we shall see who is so cocky when you yourself mount my figurehead on my ship tomorrow — at the end of my sword-point!"

The tip of Chaezar's tongue wet his dry lips. The Dutchman's rapier was a thing not to be taken lightly.

Chapter Sixteen

Shortly after eleven o'clock on a cool, balmy night several days after the ball, Sirena crept into Caleb's room and shook him awake. The entire household had retired earlier than usual, and Sirena was certain that all were asleep.

"Dress, little brother, we take to the sea," she whispered.

Caleb was instantly awake and reaching for his trousers.

"I'll wait for you in my room. It's down again, by way of the trellis, for both of us. Hurry now! After dinner as I passed the kitchen door, I heard Frau Holtz say that one of the Mynheer's ships was to set sail late tonight. She's doubtless gone by now, but we may be able to overtake her. Quickly now!"

"But the men! The crew! I've taken Jan no message to have them aboard ship."

"I sent Ling Fu to Teatoa with a sealed message. You needed some sleep. The old Chinaman's not one to puzzle out the whys and wherefores, he'll suspect nothing, and he's probably asleep in the servants' quarters once more by now. It's been nigh on two hours; the men should long since have left the village and reached the *Rana.*

A few hours later, the first hints of dawn

293

streaked the sky. Sirena, Caleb, and Jan stood near the wheel, the Señorita's hands clasping it professionally.

"It won't be long now," Sirena purred. "Order all hands on deck, Jan."

"Aye, Capitana."

"You'll take the wheel, as usual, when I speak to the enemy. And, Caleb, you'll go below as soon as we've approached them. I want none of our Dutch traders to recognize you. You're too well known in Batavia now, little brother!"

"Sirena," Caleb asked softly, "will you . . . send the enemy into the sea this time without the jolly-boats?"

"No. Not as I did with the Spanish trader's men. But, remember, even then I gave them fair warning."

Only minutes later came the cry: "Sail ho!"

Sirena called down the deck, to Jan: "Get her in your sights and fire when ready. Blow her stern first, then her bow!"

"She's too far away, Capitana," Jan called back.

"True, Jan. And only one of our shots may make its mark. But by surprising them, we may get in another shot before they've readied themselves."

"Why do you gamble like this?" Caleb asked anxiously.

"Because we don't have the cover of darkness."

The *Rana's* deck rocked with the blast of two of her cannons.

"Good!" Sirena called to her men, lifting the spyglass. "Yes, one of our shots has hit the Dutchman's bow. I told Mynheer van der Rhys that no

294

Dutch ship — his or any of the Dutch East India Company's — would strike mine again!"

A cannonball from the Dutch trader exploded from her port side but fell far short of the black-rigged *Rana*.

"She fires, you see, Caleb — but in blind panic! Now, boy, out of sight below!"

Jan Verhooch ran up to take the wheel from Sirena as the ship approached the burning Dutch brig.

"Call for quarter and I'll allow you to go into the jolly-boats," Sirena shouted in order to be heard over the melee.

"Quarter!" came the high-pitched shout.

"Do you see the heavy cannon she carries?" Sirena yelled up to Jan.

"Aye, Capitana. For all the good it did her," he grinned.

"If her shot *had* found its mark, we wouldn't be standing here now. She might have hit us straight on if she hadn't panicked."

A hiss of steam pierced the air as the brig now listed sharply to starboard. Before long she would settle into her new home fathoms deep.

"All hands on the Dutchman!" Sirena shouted. "Do you carry a man aboard who has a hook for a hand?"

"No, there's no such man aboard!" came the reply.

"Hold out your hands and remove your gloves." Her order was instantly obeyed and Sirena lifted the glass to her eyes. Satisfied, she nodded. "On your return to Batavia — *when* you get there —" she laughed, "give Mynheer van der Rhys a message for me. Tell him I've heard he refuses to turn The Hook over to me if he finds the man first. I give only one warning and this is it: The next time I capture a Dutch ship, woe be it to the man who tells me the Grand Pensioner hasn't gone back on his plan to keep The Hook from me!" She dug the point of her cutlass into the *Rana*'s rail and stood peering down at the brig's crew. "What was it you carried in your hold today?" she asked.

"Cloves and nutmeg and peppercorns."

"The price of spices in Europe will soar," Sirena laughed, her voice high and melodious.

The captain, a brash and outspoken man in well-pressed, perfectly tailored clothes, stood up in one of the jolly-boats as it was being lowered and shook his fist menacingly at Sirena. "If the Dutch East India Company is hurt by this loss, you won't take all the credit, Sea Siren! You'll owe some Spaniard your thanks for doing his damnedest to help you!"

"How is that?" Sirena shouted her question.

"Native gossip has it that unlimed nutmegs have been cached somewhere on the island of Java. The slaves who lime the nutmeg seeds have loose mouths — thank God for that! — and report that bushels of the seeds often fail to reach them. No Dutchman would do a thing like that. Only a Spaniard! To break the hold we Netherlanders have on the majority of the trade! The cursed Iberian will be wanting to start a plantation near the shores of Europe, that's what!"

The Dutchman's complaints were cut short.

"Sail ho," came a cry from the *Rana*'s rigging.

"What's that? Another ship?" Sirena called

up to her man aloft.

"A mile or two to starboard, Capitana. By the shape of her, she's Spanish or Portuguese."

"Loosen sail!" Sirena ordered her crew. "I want to be behind her stern."

A quarter-hour later, the Dutch brig in her watery grave and her jolly-boats bobbing in the distance, Sirena's frigate approached a Spanish brigantine lately out of Batavia.

Behind Jan at the *Rana*'s wheel, Sirena spoke calmly: "Don't fire unless I give the order. We won't touch this ship. She goes free."

At the first mate's puzzled expression, Sirena smiled; Jan, she remembered, was a Dutchman after all.

"What if she fires at us, Capitana?" he asked his commander.

"In that case, we ram her. But only on my order. You see, Jan, she's Spanish, and if I let her go free — after sinking the Dutch ship — well, Mynheer van der Rhys will be at Don Chaezar's throat at once, for he'll suspect I've made a bargain with the Spaniard. For a time, then, the Mynheer will be too busy watching the Spaniard to give much thought to The Hook.

"Here, Jan, take the wheel. And give me the glass." Sirena raised the glass to her eyes and read the name of the Spanish brigantine. It was the *Crimson Fire*.

Picking up the ship's horn, for the two vessels were still at some distance from one another, she called out: "Hear me well, *Crimson Fire*! I see that your men are at their guns, so be aware of who I am — the Sea Siren! One shot and all aboard are dead men. However . . . I will be kind," she laughed through the horn. "Captain," she said, addressing the blackbearded figure near the *Crimson Fire*'s wheel, "remove your men from their positions at the guns and lay down all arms, and I will allow you to sail on." She waited for a moment. "Well," she shouted through the horn, "do I have an answer?"

As a response, a cannonball exploded from the *Crimson Fire*'s flanks and cut through *Rana*'s foremast sail. But no other shot followed. Raising her spyglass, Sirena quickly sent her men to their gunner's positions.

Through the glass she saw that the Spanish captain was smiling — his shot was a challenge to battle, he thought he could quickly best the black frigate, ill-captained as he deemed she was.

The *Rana*'s guns burst in rapid succession and raked the brigantine's decks and rigging. Turning about, to provide only a narrow profile to the Spaniard's guns, the *Rana* continued to fire and, under Sirena's keen direction, was preparing to ram the larger vessel.

As the two ships neared one another, the captain of the *Crimson Fire* raised his ship's horn and called out in haste: "Quarter! We ask quarter!" Then, throwing his cutlass to the deck, he called out, "We surrender! We surrender!"

Few of the Spaniard's missiles had struck the *Rana*, and those had caused little damage. Nevertheless, Sirena was not of a mind to spare the crew of the offending trader until Jan reminded her that since she had not been able to let the Spanish ship sail on — and bring the D.E.I. Chief Pensioner to

suspect her allegiance to the Spanish Crown —
she ought, at least, to spare the *Crimson Fire*'s
crew as she had the Dutch brig's. "Why stir up
Alvarez's suspicions of a Dutch alliance?" he said.

"You're right, Jan," the Capitana replied.
"We'll take her cargo this time, however — to
share among the men." Sirena laughed heartily.
"We'll get the Spaniards into their jolly-boats,
check their hands for any sign of The Hook — and
off they may go, paddling away, home to Java! Unless they want to try for Spain!" she roared. "Two
ships in one day!" Sirena smiled. "And I only
sought one!"

A cheer rang out from her men for the gallant
Capitana.

Sirena stood on the captured trader's decks,
musing, and grinning as she did. In the distance
she could see the *Crimson Fire*'s jolly-boats rowing
wearily back toward the Sunda Strait — on the
heels of the Dutch trader's two tiny craft. What a
sight the four would make, limping into Batavia
harbor late that night or the next morning!

Her crew, ransacking the brigantine's hold, had
brought up silks and other Javanese handicrafts
and left the nutmegs, peppercorns, and other
spices below. What need had they of *those*? They
lived in the Spice Islands! But their wives, back in
Teatoa, would put the other cargo to good use.
And the Spaniards had, they discovered, also carried kegs of a type of Javanese whiskey that could
be transferred to the *Rana*'s stores.

"Make haste, men!" Sirena cried out finally.
"We've the tide with us yet, and we want to reach
the river by midday. We'll want to pass those four

cursed dinghies long before they see us turn into the River of Death!"

She turned on her heel as she heard a heavy puffing behind her. It was Jacobus, the *Rana*'s cook.

"What have you there, old man?"

"An interesting chest, Capitana — which I found in the captain's cabin . . . and," he chuckled wickedly, "which I just happened to open with my handy blade." Dramatically lifting the lid of the chest, he displayed to Sirena myriad shining pieces of eight, as well as a rainbow of gemstones.

Sirena toyed with the gems, and pocketed a few. Then she called to her men. "Here, my hearties, a pleasant booty Jacobus has discovered for you! But fast, men, we must away. And we still must gut this proud brig!"

The sleek black frigate skimmed the calm sea, several miles away now from the slowly sinking *Crimson Fire*. Caleb stood, once more, next to Sirena as she held the ship's wheel.

"What do you think will happen when the four jolly-boats get back to Batavia?" he asked.

"Don Chaezar Alvarez will throw a beastly fit — and Mynheer van der Rhys will charge around his office like a bull!"

Caleb laughed, but Sirena's expression turned thoughtful. Mention of Chaezar had brought to mind the startling information the Dutch captain had passed on earlier . . . "Unlimed nutmegs" — what were they? What did the expression mean?

Her musings were interrupted a moment later. Jacobus, the toothless old cook, came out on deck carrying a mug of strong, fragrant coffee for his "capitana."

Accepting the mug from him, she asked, "Jacobus, you were on the deck, were you not, when we took the Dutchman's ship?" He nodded. "What did he mean when he spoke of 'unlimed nutmegs' and how some Spaniard, he thought, might be intending to start a nutmeg plantation nearer Europe?"

From his surprised look, it was evident to Sirena that Jacobus was amazed to find she was ignorant of the most stringent rule of the Indies — and the single most important precaution upon which the Indies trade, both Dutch *and* Spanish, was based. "Capitana, no fertile nutmegs are allowed to be shipped out of the islands. All the merchants — Dutch and Spanish alike, as well as any incoming ships of other nations — abide by the rule. For only if the Indies holds the monopoly for the spice trade are the Dutch and Spanish fortunes secure. We want no other plantations established in, say, the Caribbees or Africa by, say, the French or English or Austrians, or anyone else."

Sirena noticed that Caleb was evidently embarrassed at her ignorance. The boy must know the rule, too, and had obviously thought she was aware of it . . .

Jacobus continued speaking: "Every planter has his slaves pick the ripe nuts, and then certain of the slaves immediately steep the nuts in a bath of lime — which makes them infertile, though when they're cleaned they can of course be used without fear." A sharp gleam burned in Jacobus's watery, pale-colored eyes. "As for the common seaman like me — well, he'd never be able to get his hands on the fertile nuts, but" — the old cook shook a warning finger — "our persons and gear are frequently checked anyway. And, Capitana, anyone caught smuggling fertile nutmegs out of the Indies can expect the death penalty!"

Later, alone at the rail of the frigate, Sirena thought over Jacobus's words. And the Dutch captain's, whose ship she had gutted. Who among the Spanish — if indeed it was the Spanish — could be foreswearing the agreement made between the two nations and stealing great hordes of fertile nutmeg seeds? It would have to be a person of some power. And . . . only with difficulty and a great deal of bribing could it be a merchant or trader, for he would have only tenuous contact with the plantations. The most likely suspect would be a plantation owner, or someone who dealt directly with the island chieftains whose people grew the nutmegs. Someone like Regan . . . or — Don Chaezar Alvarez! The man's vainglorious personality, his desire for luxuries, his wish to return to Spain an honored and wealthy man . . . all these things came immediately to mind, though Sirena cursed herself that she should accuse, even mentally, a proud Iberian, a man of her own race. But . . . *could* Don Chaezar be removing the nutmegs from the island — hiding them somewhere beyond the seas, or even on a neighboring island? Or perhaps simply secreting them somewhere on Java, ready to abscond with them to his beloved Spain when the opportunity presented itself? But, then, where would he grow them in the homeland? Spain was far too dry, too rainless . . .

The wind blew Sirena's hair back from her face, the salt spray misted her eyes. Her heart lay heavy in her chest. Mournfully she remembered Jacobus's words: "Anyone caught smuggling fertile nutmegs out of the Indies can expect the death penalty." She was so mesmerized by her own thoughts that she failed to hear the soft, padding footsteps behind her. And then, suddenly, an uneasy feeling settled between her shoulders. The ship was too quiet. Where were all the men? Oh, yes, she remembered, she had told them to go below for ale. Perhaps she should join them — she had been "distant" for far too long.

She swung around from the rail —

And stared into the lustful eyes of the seaman Wouter.

She stood as if rooted to the deck, her mind spinning back in time to the moment when she stood like a trapped animal, staring into Dick Blackheart's eyes. Panic stunned her, but she willed her body into movement. Stumbling, she backed off one step, then two steps, her eyes glazed with fear. Step for step, Wouter stalked her — till he had her backed into the doorway of her cabin. Sirena knew she had to do something, but the fear coursing through her veins rendered her immobile. Her cutlass! She had to get her cutlass. Where was it? God in heaven! It was resting on a coil of rigging, where she had stood at the rail. But she had to do something. Anything! Her indecision cost her dearly, for Wouter forced her into the room and slammed the door shut.

No words were spoken as the seaman forced her backwards . . . backwards . . . till she collapsed on the narrow bunk, her eyes dilated with fear. Merciful God, not again! Not ever again!

A blood-curdling, high-pitched scream ripped from her throat just as Caleb burst into the room. Fearlessly, the boy brandished his rapier, and his voice was high and shrill as he demanded Sirena's release.

"Get out of here before I kill you, you whelp," Wouter shouted. "That puny blade is no threat to me. Now get your carcass out of here!" the seaman said, bringing up his cutlass.

Caleb, beside himself with fury at the torment in Sirena's eyes, shouted, "En garde!" and advanced a step aiming the rapier low and bringing it up with a lightning-quick movement. He noted the surprise in the hooded eyes of the seaman — for Caleb brought his blade straight up and then down with such force that the man's trousers ripped from groin to ankle. Clumsily, the seaman swung the heavy cutlass, missing the boy and slicing the air, and agile and quick-footed as a cat, Caleb leaped and parried with expertise.

Sirena knew that she must summon aid: the boy was not yet fully trained in the art of swordsmanship. And he would soon tire. On trembling legs she sidled out the door and shouted, with all her strength, "Jan! Jacobus! Anyone!"

The two men, accompanied by another seaman, Willem, and quickly followed by several more, arrived on the run, their cutlasses drawn.

"Nothing must happen to the boy! Nothing must happen to my brother!" Sirena screamed, gripping Jan's arm.

"He appears to have the battle in hand," Jan

grinned. "That scurve Wouter is so full of ale he can barely see straight! The boy will finish him off in another minute."

"No, no, Jan, Caleb mustn't kill! Somehow you must intervene. The boy is too young to have blood on his hands!"

Jan looked with compassion at the Capitana. He nodded, waiting for an opportune moment. Caleb parried each thrust of the seaman's cutlass with wide purposeful lunges. Twice he drew blood from the drunken sailor. And both times he seemed to regain his stamina at the sight of his opponent's spouting blood.

"End it!" Jan shouted. "Let him go, Caleb, or kill him!"

The youth turned at the sound of the first mate's words and lost his advantage. Quickly Jan sliced the air between the seaman and Caleb, thrusting the boy out of harm's way.

"Open your drunken eyes now and fight like a man," Jan said brutally as he sliced at the man's legs. "No man on this ship swears his allegiance to the Capitana and then turns mutineer. You deserve to die like the vermin you are!"

"Bah," Wouter spat. "She's a piece of flesh, just like all women! She has one use and I claim her as mine!"

Wouter's hooded eyes were those of a vulture as he swung his cutlass, missing Jan's head by a wide margin. The first mate thrust again and again, forcing Wouter against the wall and knocking the cutlass from his hand. Then Jan drew back and swept the cutlass between the rebel seaman's ribs.

A fountain of blood gushed from Wouter's

chest; his eyes went wide and disbelieving as he fell forward, his hand grasping for Sirena's booted foot. "You're — just a — piece — of flesh," he managed to gasp out in a froth of blood as his body slumped to the plank floor.

Chapter Seventeen

Sirena bided her time with short strolls around the vast van der Rhys gardens and frequent excursions into the kitchen to talk with Mella about the tasty new dishes the cook was now preparing for her mistress and young Caleb. Sirena had a growing affection for the kindly Malayan woman, who was enjoying her work immensely now.

At the back of Sirena's mind, however, the question still nagged: Was it truly Don Chaezar Alvarez who was hiding vast quantities of unlimed nutmegs somewhere on the island, or sending them off to a cache in Africa, India, or some Caribbean isle? She hoped, out of pride for her country's honor, that it was not he — not a Spaniard. But, she told herself, I must discover whether or not he is the offender. And discover it I will! If only to clear the name of the Spanish Crown!!

Today Sirena had been sewing in the shade of a luxuriant, wide-leaved shrub in the corner of the gardens farthest from the house. Abruptly laying aside her needlework, she stretched her arms wide and gazed around at the beautiful flowers that met the eye on all sides. Graceful breadfruit trees swayed and dipped in the light easterly breeze. Soon it would rain and then she would have to go indoors. With an anxious eye to the light fluffy clouds that were rapidly changing color, she noticed Caleb catapulting himself over the garden gate.

"Sirena!" he gasped, out of breath. "What a story I have to tell you! I had taken a walk — to the east side — of Batavia harbor," he stammered.

"Slow down, Caleb, or I won't be able to understand a word you say," Sirena ordered him, breathless in anticipation herself. Somehow she knew that what he had to tell her had something to do with the mystery of the unlimed nutmegs.

"Well, I was lying, out of the sun, in a clump of mangroves near the edge of the water. There are only a few small fishing boats at that end of the harbor, and almost nobody goes there. I was falling asleep when — when I heard him, and another man!"

"Heard who, little brother?"

"Señor Alvarez!"

Caleb took a deep breath and sank to his knees at her side. His breathing more normal, he hastened to explain: "I heard the Señor tell a man — and a cutthroat he was from the tone of his voice — that he was to help him tomorrow at dawn to move some nutmegs to a safer hiding place. That's what he said, Sirena, a safer hiding place. The other man was angry and called the Señor a 'worrying old woman.' And he said he had no intention of breaking his back a *fourth* time! He said he'd moved the nutmegs in their heavy casks three times already. He called Señor Alvarez many names and told him all the money in the Indies wouldn't make him move them again."

"What was Chaezar's answer to this?"

"The Señor told the man this was the last time they would be moved. He said one more trip and

308

he would be ready to go to his 'kingdom' — whatever that means. And I know where he's going to move them, Sirena!"

"Where?" Sirena asked excitedly. This was what she'd been waiting for!

Caleb frowned. "To the southwestern tip of the island, fairly far from where he has them stored now. Now they are not far from Teatoa, where our crew live. "I think," he said, continuing to frown, "that if . . . if *we* were to go there, however" — his eyes sought Sirena's and she nodded to go on — "it would be best to go by land, and on horseback. The Señor intends mainly to go by sea and the lagoons, in a small launch with his man."

"You are right, Caleb. We could not risk attacking his tiny boat with the *Rana*, for we would be too close to shore, and would be seen."

Caleb continued: "I remember from my study of the maps, Sirena, that the cove where the Señor must berth his ship is small and narrow — and is the only suitable landing place on that part of the island; the other coves nearby are full of coral reefs. It is logical that he must take the nutmegs by boat, for carrying them overland would take more time and would be dangerous. Natives, or even white traders, might see him and his man. But you and I, and perhaps Jan and some of the crew, could go overland without too much suspicion."

"It certainly would be a novelty to have the Sea Siren attack by horseback. Yes, little brother, horseback it is." He smiled as she continued: "Did the Señor say, more specifically, where near the cove he plans to store the nutmegs?"

Caleb laughed. "He was most explicit when he

told his man where to place them. He said he wouldn't have to carry the casks far inland and that he had no need to worry about a strained back. Actually they are to be placed in a cave in plain view of the cove. Mangroves are to be cut and thrown over the entrance when the casks will be secured."

"You did well, little brother. When does he sail, did he say?"

"At mid-evening, Sirena."

"Do you think it would be wise for us to travel tonight by horseback and wait near the cove, or let them secure the nutmegs and set out tomorrow night?"

Caleb's eyes danced with excitement. "Speaking for myself, I'd rather go tonight. I'm tired of sitting about with nothing to do. I'd best set off immediately to alert Jan, and maybe Willem, to meet us as usual with the horses." Then, as was his custom when he became bored, he harked back to his favorite subject "When are we going to have another fencing lesson, Sirena?"

Ever since the day he had confronted Wouter and had failed to finish the job himself, Caleb had insisted on doubling his fencing lessons. More than once Sirena had been tempted to tell him that Jan had only intervened on her orders. The boy had taken a wide leap toward manhood when he challenged Wouter to defend Sirena, and his expertise with the rapier had been formidable. Indeed, he could have finished off the lustful seaman. But Sirena had not wanted the youth's hands to be tainted with blood — not yet. And, she had told herself several times since the encounter aboard the *Rana,* too much confidence — if he had in fact killed Wouter — might be the death of the boy.

Nevertheless, Caleb believed that Jan had intervened because he had not had the skill to fight Wouter to the death. And this belief nagged at him, hurt him.

"We could practice tonight, Sirena. After my return from the village, and before we follow Señor Alvarez and his man."

"On our return from the cove, little brother. On our return. You've enough to test your strength before our departure! Now — off you go to Teatoa!"

Caleb's eyes swung overhead to the daily gathering of dark clouds as Sirena picked up her needlework and headed for the house.

Because of a dense fog that hid him and Willem, Jan Verhooch brought the horses from their jungle pasture and stable near the river directly to the edge of the van der Rhys gardens. Sirena put her finger to her lips in a gesture to be silent as she and Caleb approached the two seamen. And only when the four were at a safe distance from the house, crossing the vast plantation and headed up into the foothills that lay inland, to the south of Batavia, did she speak a word.

"Caleb has studied the maps carefully, Jan. But we'll all have to be alert if we're to cross the island and not lose ourselves in these forested foothills or in the jungle we're sure to meet as we descend toward the sea on the south side of the island." Turning to Caleb, she asked, "What would be your guess as to when the Spaniard and his accomplice will arrive?"

At the word "accomplice," Jan's and Willem's faces became grim masks: as Dutchmen they realized fully the treachery in which Don Chaezar Alvarez was engaged.

"The Señor travels with a full hold. But the breeze is fresh. If he sails the launch with a half-furled sail he should arrive at Rara Cove — that's what it's called on the maps — within three hours. He had, of course, perhaps an hour or two's start on us. However . . . if the fog moves out to sea before long, he may be delayed."

"Aye," said Willem, turning to look back down toward the plantation and the town. "See how it curls like wisps of smoke and how it moves toward the sea's edge."

On reaching the highest hills in the spine of low mountains that separated Batavia and the island's north shore from the less populated southern coast, Sirena ordered the two men and Caleb to a halt.

"I've brought some fruit and cheese and wine. We'll rest now, and eat!"

As they tethered their horses, Caleb asked Sirena, "Will you attack the Spaniard, once he's beached the launch? And will you destroy the nutmegs?"

Jan and Willem were all ears.

"Too many questions at once, little brother. I'll do neither. Though we've Jan and Willem with us, there's no need to attack Don Chaezar. And as for the nutmegs, I have what I believe is an interesting plan. We'll move the nutmegs to another hiding place! And leave evidence that will let him know he's been robbed of them! What a surprise for our elegant representative of the Spanish Crown when he next looks in the cave!" Then, turning to the men: "We'll rest a while, Jan. We've the time. Will either you or Willem keep watch, and let us not sleep too long?"

Willem responded, "I'll do the duty, Capitana, if you and Jan agree. He's had a busy day today, what with the fishing. Busier than mine, I'll wager — for I caught none!"

Chuckling, Sirena finished a small slab of cheese and wrapped her heavy cloak about her, for here in the highlands the temperature was chill. The thick fog swirling about her gave her a lonely feeling despite the company she had with her. She dozed from time to time, and woke an hour later at Willem's nudging.

The small party descended the slopes toward Java's southern coast.

Sirena, Caleb, Jan, and Willem crouched in a clump of palms and mangrove bushes some fifty feet from the eastern bank of narrow Rara Cove. Caleb's map study had brought them to their goal half an hour before.

All four came suddenly to alert attention at the sound of oars hitting against the sides of a small boat. They had not seen the launch approach!

Within minutes, they saw a bobbing light through the fog and heard the scrape of the boat's hull on the sand at the end of the cove. Soon the sound of voices — two men's, they judged —

reached them. They heard muttering, labored breathing, cursing, as well as what was evidently Don Chaezar's voice peremptorily ordering his man to more speed. "More foot power —" and curses. From time to time there was a thump, as of a wooden cask being let fall from the edge of the launch onto the sand below; then followed the heaving breathing of a man who must be lifting it to his shoulders. This last sound was repeated, Sirena noted, twenty-five times.

"Traitor!" Sirena murmured half to herself. "That traitor Alvarez — who would break his country's word to gain wealth for himself alone!"

Abruptly now, words reached the four clearly for the first time.

"Well . . . that's the last of them. An easy night's work, wouldn't you say?" The elegant tones of Don Chaezar Alvarez rankled Sirena.

"If all I'd had to do was hoist the casks to the launch's rail and drop them to the sand — yes! But lugging them to the cave — some forty yards away — that's a different story! My back will be bent out of shape tomorrow. And, I tell ye, I want double the amount you promised me!"

"I'm paying you precisely what the work was worth. Greed," Alvarez sneered, "is not an admirable trait."

His accomplice's answer was a harsh and guttural cry — and Sirena heard the man spit. "I'll have twice the amount or —"

Chaezar broke in: "You leave me no other choice, José." Then, in a softer tone: "Sooner or later I knew it would come to this."

"But — I didn't mean — No! No!" And then

they heard a gurgling sound, and no more words.

Sirena placed a restraining arm on Jan's as he began to rise.

The sound of oars reached their ears once more, and through the fog the yellow launch light bobbed as the boat moved away, out of the cove, toward the lagoons it would follow back around the island's western tip on its return to Batavia.

When she was certain the launch had raised its sail and was safely out of the cove, Sirena rose and, followed by the men, crossed down the sand to the spot from whence the voices had come.

As she stumbled on something soft and unmoving, she fell to her knees. "Here he is, Jan!" She put her ear close to the man's chest. "No signs of life. Will you — Jan and Willem — do what you can to bury him?"

Caleb touched Sirena's arm. "Sirena," he said, "the fog is still thick here — but inland it will not be so. Shall I search out a new hiding place for the nutmegs?"

"Yes, little brother. But first let me light this oil lamp. By it, you'll see where we stand."

As her two seamen dragged the unfortunate José's body back into the bushes, Sirena, another lamp in her hand, made her way toward where she thought the cave must be. Caleb disappeared into the jungle.

Through the lifting fog, Sirena spied Caleb, clambering through some mangroves and onto the beach.

"I found another cave — and it's not far from here!" he cried exultantly.

"Good lad!" shouted Jan.

"Aye, aye!" Willem yelled.

"We have our work cut out for us, men!" Sirena sighed. "But I want to scatter the contents of one cask in his cave, for I want him to think he's been robbed."

"You'll not lift a cask, Capitana!" Jan smiled. "Not if I have anything to say about it!"

"But you don't." And Sirena pitched in to help.

Within minutes, the first of the twenty-five casks had been transported up a slope behind the cave to what appeared to be a screen of impenetrable bamboo. Behind the stalks of thick bamboo, however, lay the low and narrow entrance to a tiny cave. So low was the cave roof that only Caleb could stand inside. It was he who, for the next hour and a half, rolled the casks as they arrived — sometimes carried by Jan and Willem, sometimes by Jan and Sirena, sometimes by Willem and the Capitana — back into the depths of this lucky hole he had found.

"Now let Señor Alvarez wonder what has become of his treasure!" Sirena exclaimed, somewhat breathless, as the last of the kegs was pushed by Caleb to the dark extremities of the cave. "He'll have to begin again, if he wants nutmegs for his 'kingdom'! And, what's more, I doubt that there's another man on Java whom he'll trust with his secret from this day on!"

Riding slowly upward through the foothills, through the forests which the sun barely penetrated, Sirena's horse — as well as the mounts of the other three — began to shy nervously.

"There, there . . ." she soothed the roan, "what's troubling you, my beauty?" Petting the horse's sweat-slick neck, she continued to coo to him, persuading him to keep steady in his pace.

Caleb, his mount in control after a moment of fright, scanned upward toward the highest slopes for some sign of what had made the horses skittish. Exchanging glances with Jan and Willem, he rode on watchfully, leading the small party.

As they entered a clearing at the top of the final slope, the group halted, alarmed. The sunlight, not an hour old, for they'd wanted to reach Batavia before the day was much spent, appeared suddenly to dissolve behind a gray, ashen sky that was ominous with pale yellow streaks darting toward the horizon. A noxious odor of sulphur struck their nostrils and made them smart. Then, without further warning, the earth beneath them volleyed and trembled, and the trees about them swayed as if pummeled by a silent wind.

The horses neighed and whinnied now in panic, pawing the air with their forelegs and nearly throwing the four riders from their backs.

Jumping down from his saddle, Jan warned, "It's the Sisters of Fire!" A white ring of fear circled his mouth, his eyes were bright with anxiety.

Quickly following his example, the others dismounted and attempted to calm their frightened horses. The sky had now almost completely darkened, and was peppered with a glowing red ash that began to rain down on them, though the Sisters were many miles away.

Pulling the horses behind them, the four ran for cover beneath a dense clump of breadfruit trees.

There, safe from most of the singeing and stinging ash, they soothed the nervous beasts. Gratefully, Sirena's roan nuzzled his velvety nose against her, nickering softly.

Then, abruptly, the still trees were shaken by a second tremor and another gush of sulphurous gasses reached the noses of the four hidden among the trees.

"Capitana, have you heard the legend about the Sisters?" Willem asked Sirena.

She shook her head.

"Native stories have it that the Sisters are angry at some proud and sinful woman, and that one day they will destroy her."

" 'Tis true, Capitana, what Willem says," Jan put in. "All the Javanese who trade with our fishing village — so near one of the Sisters — confirm the legend. Lately, though the Sisters have been quiet, a story has gone about that they are nearly ready to render judgment on the woman." Jan laughed softly, as if he disbelieved what the natives thought true.

But Sirena was wondering who the "proud and sinful woman" might be . . .

Chapter Eighteen

"Are you ready, Sirena? Regan is waiting for us downstairs," Caleb exclaimed breathlessly as he burst into Sirena's room.

She was seated before the silver-framed mirror that hung over her dressing table. "Let him wait!" she grumbled as she impatiently tugged at a tendril of hair that had escaped the sleek knot at the nape of her neck. She had adjusted her black lace mantilla for the fourth time and was still dissatisfied with the effect.

Caleb watched her, questioning her disgruntled mood. Sirena read his expression in the reflection of her looking glass. "I didn't mean to snap at you, Caleb. It's just that I'm so sick and tired of wearing the same black gowns and hiding behind this lace curtain. I always look the same!" She was thinking of Gretchen and the myriad of colors she wore. "And now I can't get this comb to stay where I put it! Go tell Regan I'm not going to the wedding. Tell him I've got a headache! Tell him anything — but I'm not going!"

"Sirena, you must go. The bride is the daughter of a Javanese chieftain, a very important man. Regan's the head of the Dutch East India Company, and as his wife you'd insult the man if you didn't go. This could stir up trouble: insult the chief and you insult every Javanese on the island. All the native servants would refuse to work, the sailors, the fishermen . . ."

"You've made your point, Caleb. I've stirred up enough trouble, is that it?" When he didn't answer she turned around and gave him a sharp look. "The least you could do, little brother, is *pretend* that isn't what you meant!" Still, when no excuse or answer was forthcoming, Sirena conceded: "Very well, go tell Regan I'll be a few moments yet. There's no help for it, I'll have to go to the wedding dressed like a nun!" She turned back to the mirror and picked up the mantilla.

"No you don't! Wait a minute, Sirena, don't do anything, I'll be right back!" Caleb ran out of the room as quickly as he had entered it. Within minutes he was back again, holding several camellia-like blooms in his hand. "Try these instead of your comb."

"Caleb! They're — they're just the thing!"

Sirena arranged three of the waxy-white flowers on the crown of her head, their paleness making a striking contrast with her raven hair. She arranged the mantilla over them, allowing the flowers to peek through the fine web of scalloped lace. For effect, she placed an unopened bud in the bodice of her gown between her breasts.

"There, how do you like it?"

She needed no answer. Caleb was wearing an expression of admiration on his boy's face.

"You're a genius, Caleb. Well, don't just stand there. Do you want to make us late?" She picked up her skirts and breezed out of the room.

Sirena rode between Regan and Caleb in the carriage on the way to the Javanese village. Sirena remembered it was called Djatumi, a village in the mountains southeast of Batavia. Regan's eyes kept sliding covertly to the bud Sirena had placed between her breasts. The delicate white of the flower perfectly offset the silky texture and the buffed ivory tone of her skin.

Feeling Regan's eyes on her, Sirena was annoyed that it should excite her so. She almost wanted to tear the flowers from her hair and rip the bud from her gown. Then she thought of the almost-dressed Gretchen at Don Chaezar's ball and the way Regan's eyes drank her in. Let him look, she thought, a smile of mischief playing about her lips. Looking wasn't touching.

From her seat in the carriage she could hear their baggage thump behind them each time the wheels hit a rut in the road. The actual wedding ceremony would not take place until the next day. But Caleb had explained to her that he'd learned that the day before the wedding was, to the Javanese, almost as important as the actual ceremony. There were rituals to which every bride must conform, and Sirena — as Regan's wife and therefore a most honored guest — would be privileged to witness these solemn preparations. She and Regan would sleep in the village compound tonight as a further honor to the bride and groom.

Until this moment Sirena had not realized the implications of staying away for the night with Regan. She chanced a worried look at her husband.

As if reading her thoughts, Regan said, "Don't worry, Sirena, you'll be left to your prayers." His eyes then lighted with a mocking look. "It's against local custom for men and their wives to cohabit until after the bride and groom are married. The men and women will occupy separate quarters. Kalava, the chief, will have had separate huts prepared for us."

Regan laughed aloud when he saw he had been correct in guessing her thoughts, for the tiny frown between Sirena's finely arched brows faded. "As a matter of fact, once we get to the village the women will sweep you away and Caleb and I will go on to the groom's house."

For more than an hour they rode through the lush, green foothills. Then, in a clearing just below the cliff-like slopes of the first full-sized mountain they had encountered on their trip thus far, sat the tiny town of Djatumi. The village was festooned with flowers and garlands. In its center, over a wide open pit, several old women were roasting a wild boar and baking little round loaves of bread on flat rocks near the fire. There were no men in the town, Sirena saw at a glance.

When the women saw Regan's carriage drive into the clearing, they dropped what they were doing and ran to greet their guests, calling to other women inside the huts. Regan jumped down from the trap and courteously helped Sirena from the high carriage step to the dusty ground. From over Regan's shoulder Sirena now saw a lovely young brown-skinned girl come running out of a large hut. Several women were chasing after her in squealing protest. As Regan turned, the girl threw herself into his arms in joyous greeting.

"Telaga! How you've grown!" he roared.

The women who had been chasing the maiden

had caught up with her, but stood a respectful distance away from Regan and Sirena. The Mynheer continued his conversation with the young girl in Javanese dialect. A moment later, he greeted an older woman who was looking sternfaced at the impetuous girl. It must be some joke, Sirena guessed, for the woman covered her mouth with her hand, tittering in delight. Sirena speculated the woman must be the girl's mother — who was very perturbed that her daughter should break custom and show herself — before her wedding — to a man. But Regan, with his charming ways, had cajoled her into a better temper.

With great ceremony, Regan now introduced Sirena and Caleb. Several of the native women hurried forth and picked up Sirena's trunk which Ling Fu had lifted out of the baggage compartment. Others crowded around Sirena and she was glad to hear one of them address her in Spanish.

"I am Nalu, Mevrouw," she said, her voice high and delicate-sounding. "The bride is my cousin, Telaga. Please forgive the naughty girl, but she could not help herself — Mynheer van der Rhys has been a family friend for many years. He knows Telaga since she was only a little girl. I speak Spanish very good, *si?* I will stay with you, Mevrouw — or would you rather have me call you Señora?" Sirena nodded; she so detested the awful-sounding "Mevrouw." "You will please come with me?"

Just as Sirena was about to follow Nalu and the other women, Regan stepped up to her and made a courtly bow. "Until tomorrow, my dear."

Taking advantage of her inability to protest

without making a fool of herself, he put his arms around her and kissed her tenderly on the mouth. Before he released her, he plucked the bud from between her breasts, looked mockingly into her eyes, and kissed its pearly petals.

The Javanese women nearly swooned with the implied sexuality of his gesture. Sirena felt her cheeks grow warm and her temper flare. How dare he do this to her when she was a helpless prisoner of propriety? How she would love to scratch that smile from his face!

Regaining her composure, she turned to say good-bye to Caleb, whose reddened cheeks betrayed that he had witnessed Regan's intimate gesture.

It was then that she felt something else, as though a spear of ice had been thrust into her back, chilling her to the bone. Her glance fell on Telaga, whose black eyes were staring into her, through her, with shocking hatred! Telaga's mother also noted her daughter's distorted features and hurried the girl away, making a hasty good-bye to Regan and Caleb.

Nalu, who had also seen the undisguised hatred in Telaga's eyes, led Sirena toward the huts. "Please, do not pay attention to my ungrateful cousin. She is a spoiled and willful creature. Mynheer van der Rhys has been almost an . . . uncle to her since she was only a child. She always had grand ideas and imagined that someday she would be his wife. Not that the Mynheer ever gave her reason to hope for such an unlikely event," Nalu hastened to add, her embarrassment suffusing her brown cheeks with pink. "Mynheer has been like an . . . uncle."

Sirena followed Nalu into one of two new-looking huts that were separate from the other buildings in the village. "Our chieftain, my uncle, had these huts erected especially for the Mevrouw and Mynheer," Nalu explained. "As you know, all husbands and wives in the village must remain apart until after the wedding ceremony. I know this is a great hardship on the Mynheer. Everyone in the village could see how much he loves his Mevrouw."

Nalu giggled and Sirena knew she was referring to that tender kiss Regan had given her before he left her in the woman's hands.

When Sirena made no comment, Nalu was afraid she had spoken out of turn. These Europeans had such strange attitudes concerning love and passion . . . They were so tight-lipped about love, easily embarrassed and secretive. So unlike the easy free-living Javanese.

"Has the Señora ever attended a Javanese kawin — that is to say, wedding?" Sirena shook her head. "Not to worry, Señora, Nalu will explain everything to you and you will do everything exactly correct." The plump, smiling native beamed at Sirena confidently. Her smile was so infectious and friendly that Sirena found she was liking Nalu more each minute.

"We will have to hurry, Señora. You must change into this humble garment. All women attending the pre-nuptial pageant must wear them."

Nalu held up a kaftan of sheer, cool, gauze-like material richly embroidered around the neck and sleeves with the most exquisite handwork Sirena had ever seen. Humble indeed! Quickly Nalu helped her make the change. Her dark, heavy, and unsuitable gown was exchanged for the cool kaftan. By suddenly calling Nalu's attention to the lace mantilla's proper storage, Sirena was able to conceal her scarred arm. When the native woman had returned to her side, Sirena's hair was unloosed and allowed to fall in a heavy cascade down her back. A circlet of flowers was placed on her head. On her feet she wore the soft, calfskin sandals common to the natives.

"It is a disgrace for the Señora to dress like a Javanese servant," Nalu sighed, fingering the rich material of Sirena's black gown. "But it is the custom that all the women be dressed alike."

Sirena noted that although the style of her costume was similar to what the others wore, great pains had been taken with its embroidery to make it worthy of the honored Chief Pensioner's wife.

"Come, Señora, it is time for the dilalar and Telaga is a bad-humored girl when kept waiting."

Sirena followed Nalu out of the hut into the sunshine of the village clearing. Across the space, in the shade of the trees, all the women were gathered expectantly. Apparently they had been waiting for Sirena, for when they saw her approach they all welcomed her in light, musical voices and turned their attentions at once to the pageant.

Telaga was sitting on a grass mat in the middle of the circle formed by the women. Sirena was not expected to sit cross-legged on the little cushions strewn over the ground; Nalu led her instead to a comfortable-looking little chair upholstered in soft, shimmering satin.

Telaga cast Sirena a momentary stinging look and then turned her attentions back to the ongoing events. Immediately several village matrons stepped out of the circle and went to the girl. They stripped her of her clothing, leaving her body bare to the afternoon sun now filtering through the trees. Sirena saw that Telaga was breathtakingly beautiful! Her heavy jet-black hair was tied in a knot atop her head, lending grace to her long, slim neck. Her body was slim and delicate. Small but full breasts rested high on her torso. Her legs were long, and gracefully tapered to tiny, narrow feet. Her skin was the color of honey — tan with rich golden depths that heightened the whiteness of her teeth and the blackness of her eyes.

With great dignity, Telaga now lay face down on the mat. Three village matrons dipped their hands into pots of a coarse-looking powder and began to massage Telaga's body with it until the honey skin turned pink. While the massage was taking place the other women in the circle clapped their hands and sang songs. Telaga's mother bit her lips and held back tears of pride and sympathy at this, the first step toward her only daughter's marriage.

"The powder they use is called lalar, Señora," Nalu explained. "It is made of temoe and ketan leaves ground together."

Whatever it was, Sirena noticed that it seemed to be quite abrasive. Telaga's skin was now a deep and angry shade of red. When the matrons turned the girl onto her back, Sirena could see she was biting her lips to control tears of pain. But with seemingly no pity, the women continued to rub her with the coarse powder from head to toe — until not an inch of her body was left undone. Then they helped her to her feet and sat her in a large tub of water, washing away the dull gray powder and cooling her stinging flesh. After they had dried her off, they led her back to the grass mat.

Over the voices of the chanting women, Nalu explained: "Now they will rub her with bedak wida. This is not so bad, Señora. It is ground very fine and smells good." Nalu also explained that the recipes for the lalar and bedak wida are strictly adhered to and that every Javanese girl must submit to the massage according to custom. Working diligently, not an inch of flesh escaping their notice, the women rubbed Telaga with a mixture of the bedak wida and rendered fat. It had indeed a pungent smell, filling the air with a scent of herbs and leaves reminiscent, to Sirena, of spice and woodlands. Telaga's body glowed pink and fresh.

Moments later, Telaga was bathed again in fresh water and returned once more to the mat.

"Now, Señora, now is the time Telaga must show great courage. You will see. If she utters one sound during this ceremony her mother will be obliged to beat her. To cry now would be proof that Telaga is not a virgin."

With great pomp and circumstance six matrons surrounded Telaga's supine form. The bride's mother stood just outside the circle of crouching women, holding a long switch cut from a tree. Her expression was solemn. The singing halted abruptly and the air was still with expectation.

The six matrons immediately attacked the

bride's body from the neck down, plucking the hairs from her! Telaga displayed her virtue by not uttering a sound.

When the women had plucked every hair from her arms and legs, a woven, circular grass screen was placed between Telaga and the audience to protect her modesty. Only Telaga's mother was allowed to witness the completion of the depilation ceremony.

When at last the screen was removed, Telaga was standing on the grass mat, her body completely denuded of hair, her expression triumphant. She had undergone the Test of the Virgin with tremendous success! The mother of the bride beamed with pride.

Another bath, another massage with soothing oil . . . and Telaga's body shone with a soft, supple glow. Her hair was now loosened from its topknot and her mother washed it and rinsed it with coconut milk; it was then smoked over a fire of sweet-scented wood to give it a pleasant odor. The ritual was at last ended by Telaga's being anointed with exotic oils called tapel.

Nalu's eyes were misted with tears. "How beautiful she is! I remember when *I* was prepared for my husband . . ." she sighed wistfully.

The singing began again, but instead of the cheerful, high-spirited songs of before, the new tunes were sensual and almost mournful. Several of the older women, who Nalu told Sirena were Telaga's aunts, began keening and wailing. They were crying for the lost flower of Telaga's youth. They had seen her through the ritual of readying herself for her husband and were joyful for the exciting night of love Telaga would experience, but they were mourning for the loss of her carefree youth. Soon would come the pain of childbirth, the responsibilities of maturity, the sadness of growing older . . .

Telaga's mother finally stepped forward and draped her daughter with a fine kaftan edged with pale blue flowers. Telaga stood tall, her slim and graceful body held erect, her demeanor prideful and even haughty, for she was certain of her beauty. A crown of flowers was placed on her head and smaller garlands were fitted to her wrists and ankles. The girl had been prepared for her groom, her skin shone like sleek satin, she was the essence of femininity and desirability, pampered and petted for a night of erotic love.

Telaga's dark, insolent gaze met Sirena's. In that one glance Sirena understood with infallible womanly intuition that it was Regan, however, for whom Telaga yearned. She wanted Regan alone to enjoy the delights of her body, to smell her sweet, wood-scented hair, to caress her silky, anointed skin. Sirena wondered if Regan's first wife, Tita, had undergone this difficult ritual and if it had, indeed, made her more desirable to the Mynheer.

The women now swarmed about Telaga to congratulate her, and the girl glowed with pride. Huge platters of food were quickly brought forth and the women ate with gusto. As did Sirena, who had seldom tasted more delicious fare.

When the last of the rich, spicy food was eaten and everyone was sated, the platters were cleared away and a stirring of excitement ran through the gathering. Night had come with its velvety softness. In a few hours the men of the village would be returning and the women's festivities must come to an end. Nalu told Sirena that the time had now come for the women to present their gifts to the bride.

Sirena hurried back to her hut and brought out her gift, which was wrapped in rice paper. Regan had given it to her to present to Telaga, but Sirena had seen the present and admired it. It was a length of fine Chinese silk dyed a jewel-toned emerald.

When Telaga opened the rice paper and withdrew the length of silk, gasps of appreciation escaped the retinue of onlookers. Telaga, too, was seemingly impressed with the gift, for she smiled at Sirena and thanked her. Then, with a graceful flourish, she wrapped the silk about herself, looking quite smug and satisfied.

The gifts that followed Sirena's overwhelmed her by their diversity — and practicality: household items of every sort . . . grass mats . . . lengths of cloth . . . the necessary carven images of Javanese gods. Then, after what had seemed, to Sirena, like hours, the village women once again surrounded the bride-to-be. With native-crafted knives they snipped an inch or so from Telaga's luxuriant length of hair; the snippings were divided among the girl's relatives.

Once again Nalu came to Sirena and explained the custom. "Her relatives are each to place their lock of hair into the shell of a young coconut and toss it into the sea. This is to insure that Telaga will bear many healthy children."

Telaga was finally led to a hut constructed of palm leaves and thatch, which she entered alone. Before her daughter could step inside, Telaga's mother hurried up to her to embrace her solemnly and issue directions for her behavior during the night to come. Huge tears stained the cheeks of the woman as they walked away, leaving Telaga in the palm hut.

"She's to spend the night in contemplation," said Nalu. "She is to think seriously of the life before her as a married woman. All night she will sit, among pots of flowers, with nothing but the Klapagading to keep her company. Oh, this is a bowl of bananas, betel-nut, and two yellow coconuts on one of which is a drawing of the god Ardjoeno and on the other of Soembadja, his wife."

From the forest nearby, masculine shouts of revelry abruptly broke the solemn silence and Nalu cautioned Sirena, "Hurry, Señora, to your hut! It is unlucky for the bride if the men gaze upon even one of us. Hurry, my lady!"

Sirena dashed into the hut with Nalu close behind. As the noisy men marched into the village Nalu peeked out from behind the palm leaves which made up the walls of the hut.

"Nalu, I thought it was unlucky for Telaga if one of the men sees the women!" Sirena called to her.

"Yes, surely, Señora, the most horrible things will befall the marriage! Telaga's hair will fall out, she will be unable to bear children, her husband will take a lover and bring the woman to Telaga's house for Telaga to tend her and wait on her . . .

Terrible things! Bad luck, Señora!"

"Then why are you peeking out at the men?" Sirena demanded.

"It is not bad luck for the women to see the men, Señora," Nalu said with incomprehensible native logic. "You can believe me that each woman here looks out to see how much rum her husband has drunk so she can plague the poor man and make his life miserable if it was more than to his wife's liking."

Sirena heard Regan's booming voice singing loudly above the other men's. It came closer and closer and Nalu noticed Sirena stiffen with apprehension. "Do not worry, Señora, the Mynheer will not come in here. He knows the custom, he would not want to bring bad luck on Telaga," Nalu whispered. "His hut is next to this one, he goes there. The Señora's brother will sleep with the other village boys tonight."

Regan's roaring voice could be heard clearly as he entered the hut that had been erected not ten feet away from Sirena's. His singing continued for a moment or so, then stopped.

"The Mynheer will sleep well tonight — as will all the men. So much rum drowns their need for a woman. Good night, Señora, until the morning."

"Good night, Nalu," Sirena answered politely. But her thoughts were on the man in the next hut.

Having changed from her kaftan to a night-dress, Sirena lay on the low mat bed, taking care to drop the fine mosquito netting into place around her. She closed her eyes, ready for sleep. Her last waking thoughts were of Telaga sitting alone in the darkened hut, with pots of flowers,

333

fruits, nuts, and two coconuts for company.

The night was hot, the humidity oppressive.
Sirena awoke with her nightdress clinging uncomfortably to her perspiring body. She was aware of
the sound of wind blowing through the treetops,
though no air stirred within the hut's palm-leaved
walls. She sat up, pulled the wispy mosquito netting away impatiently, and slipped her feet into
the calfskin sandals Nalu had given her.

Stepping outside her door, she saw a faint glimmer of light in the eastern sky; it must be near
dawn, she mused. Sirena stretched out her arms
to the breeze, which caught her damp nightdress,
cooling and refreshing her. Then suddenly a
sound fell on her ears and quickly she stepped
back into the doorway of her hut, realizing that according to village custom she should not have
been out, beyond the enclosure of her hut. If one
of the men had seen her, she would be accused of
wishing to bring bad luck on Telaga. The sound
was closer now, the sound of stealthy footsteps!

A cloud crossed the waning moon and, from her
hiding place just inside the doorway, Sirena could
see little. Then, peering out cautiously, she saw a
figure nearing the hut next to hers. As the steps
halted, she heard a scratching noise. A moment
later, the door to Regan van der Rhys's hut
opened, the light from a candle outlining the man
in its flickering yellow light —

And casting a golden glow on the girl Telaga!

She wore a sarong made of the emerald-colored
silk Sirena had given her as a wedding gift!

Sirena gasped and involuntarily took a step outside her own hut. The two — caught at their moment of meeting — turned to see her. Telaga's eyes gleamed triumphantly and a wicked smile distorted her pretty mouth. After an instant's surprise, Regan's full mouth opened wide in a mocking grin; his eyelids, reflecting the golden light of the candle, were heavy with the effects of rum.

Sirena froze immediately in her tracks as her husband stepped gallantly aside, allowing Telaga entrance to his lodging. Red-faced with embarrassment, yet quaking with fury, Sirena rushed inside her stifling, airless hut and flung herself down on the mat bed.

Minutes passed as she lay listening, imagining her husband caressing the Javanese girl — only a few feet away — though not a sound from the neighboring hut reached her ears. Only the wind, rising now as morning dawned over the village, blotted out the sound of her tormented sobs.

Chapter Nineteen

Days raced into months as the Sea Siren plundered the Java seas at sporadic intervals, generally sparing neither Dutch nor Spanish ships in her search for The Hook. Her laugh rang across the water following each victory, making the men in their bobbing jolly-boats tremble with fear not only of the sea they faced in such small vessels but of the "sea witch" herself! Some now called her the "devil witch," too. Many were her names. Her own crew were more and more proud to serve under her — not only because of her expertise but because she refused to gut any ship that asked for quarter, letting it pass by unharmed after inspecting the hands of its seamen.

One particular star-filled evening, when Sirena and Caleb stole out of the house to ride with Jan to the secret cove where the *Rana* was berthed, she was welcomed with cheers from the crew. Old Jacobus, the cook, seemed especially glad and excited to see her.

"Capitana! Capitana! Come see what we've done!"

Solemnly the crew led her to the bow of the black frigate. Willem held high a lantern. There on the frigate tip, painted in bold white letters, was the name *Sea Siren.* Once, Caleb had explained to her that the superstitious crew were uneasy about serving on a now-nameless ship, for when the ship had been repainted black the name *Rana* had been oblitered.

Sirena was touched, the crew proud. Jan cracked a keg of ale, Jacobus opened a wheel of cheese, and the crew and their capitana spent the evening telling tales of derring-do — all the while singing seafaring songs. Sirena played the guitar she always kept in her cabin, and sang love ballads. Some of the older men, remembering their youth — in Amsterdam, Rotterdam, The Hague, Delft, and other cities of the Low Countries, so far away — cried shamelessly at the sound of her lovely voice and the sad music.

Riding home, near dawn, after finding no quarry that night, Sirena was quiet and thoughtful. "What's worrying you, Sirena?" Caleb asked.

Jan merely rode along silently.

"Our many absences from the house. Have you noticed how Frau Holtz watches us?"

"Aye, she makes me nervous. She almost seems to play cat-and-mouse."

"Not cat-and-mouse. Rat-and-mouse! I think our story of taking these frequent retreats is becoming weak. Soon she will go to Regan and then there will be trouble. I have a feeling she suspects, now, that we leave the house."

"Perhaps she should be given a pension and retired to a tiny house somewhere in Batavia," Caleb volunteered.

"She's done nothing to warrant her dismissal, little brother. I would find that difficult to justify to Regan."

"Then if that is the case, the days the *Sea Siren* is being refitted with new riggings will be to our advantage. They will keep us at home!"

"It will help. But we'll think of something, have no fear."

Caleb smiled, and Jan too. "When I'm with you, Sirena, I never quail. I know that you will find the solution, however hard that may be to do."

Sirena stood, her legs slightly parted, hands on her hips, looking toward the upstairs window. Sighing wearily, she lamented, "I don't seem to recall the window being so high, do you?"

"In truth, no. Every time we return it grows higher to my eye, and the trellis longer. You first, big sister. I'll be close behind."

Boy and woman were midway up the stout vines when a shadow crossed the garden beneath them. The figure stood in the darkness of the lush foliage and watched the ascent of the duo as they made their slow progress upward. When a faint, murky glow appeared in the window, indicating that a lamp was lit, the figure crossed the garden and re-entered the house.

Caleb made daily journeys to the cove where the *Sea Siren* was berthed and came home each afternoon with a report on the progress the men were making.

"Enough of this lazing about," Sirena muttered to herself as she got to her feet one afternoon. "What sort of life is this?" she questioned herself. "If it weren't for the fact that I take to the sea I'd be a babbling idiot by now! I think I'll pay Don Chaezar Alvarez a visit. I long for some conversation and a little flattery . . . The bastard! Perhaps I can find out, too, what he's up to."

She was descending the wide staircase when Regan emerged from his office. He looked at her coolly and she raised her eyes to meet his. "And where is it you go, Sirena?"

At sight of him, Sirena's eyes narrowed, but she pulled her mantilla modestly across her face. "I . . . I thought, my husband, that I would lunch with your friend Don Chaezar Alvarez. But . . . would you care to join me?" Regan's face made no answer. "No? Well, then, I'll leave you to your duties or pleasures —"

"One moment, Sirena!" His voice had grown stern. "I can't allow this. You are my wife, you are yet in mourning for your uncle, *and* this is not your first luncheon with Don Chaezar!" Regan strode up and down on the hall rug. "You are — well, making me look a fool. There is talk . . . in town . . . that I cannot control my wife."

Sirena ventured a challenge: "Your wife, if I may say so, in name only. As yet." Despite her calm tones, Sirena felt a churning in her stomach when she thought back to the humiliation of her wedding night.

Regan stood rooted to the spot and gazed, curious, at this odd Spanish woman. Why did she bring up the fact that their marriage was one in name only when that was exactly what she herself had wanted! Or was it? The woman was passionate, perhaps, after all?

"Ah, my dear husband," Sirena went on, seeing his bewilderment, "do these same people . . . who say that I am making a fool of you . . . know of our agreement that I shall live a separate life until my year of mourning is over?"

"The matter is ended. If you wish to go for a ride I'll have one of the servants accompany you."

"I need no servant to play nursemaid, Mynheer. I shall, of course, be discreet. I shall not stay long. I need no duenna."

"*I* say you do," Regan replied coldly. "Which is it to be? I have a great deal of work that demands my attention. Decide now, before I lose my patience."

"Very well, send for Juli. I must obey my husband's orders." Though her voice seemed cool, Regan detected the heat in it.

Sirena rode in the open trap next to her handmaid. She smiled upon hearing Juli's indrawn breath when she ordered the trap into Don Chaezar Alvarez's tree-lined drive. "You will wait here," Sirena said to the girl.

"Mevrouw, Mynheer said —"

"And I have said for you to wait here. You may report that to Mynheer upon our return. Amuse yourself with the magnificent view of the wharf."

Chaezar himself opened the door. Grasping her hand and bowing low, he brought it to his lips, his eyes searching hers.

"You're truly a gallant, Chaezar. I want you to know that I have come here at great personal risk to myself. Regan has practically forbidden me to visit you."

The Spaniard shrugged his elegant shoulders. "I see that you are here — and that's all that matters, is it not?"

"Tell me, Chaezar . . . do you miss Spain?" she asked, settling herself in a deep, comfortable chair.

"There are no words to describe the agony my absence from my homeland causes me. One day soon I shall return."

"Then we are compatriots, are we not? I don't think I will ever be able to adjust to this godforsaken island." Then: "Chaezar," Sirena said carefully as she accepted a glass of wine, "why don't you like . . . Regan?"

"Why *should* I like him? I detest him!" Chaezar spat. "At one time Spain and Portugal were supreme in these islands. Now the Spice Islands are referred to as the 'Dutch East Indies'! Regan's father was largely responsible for that. Then, following Regan's imprisonment several years back, it appeared the power might be changing hands again. But Regan returned . . ." Chaezar remembered the important part he himself had played in the young Dutchman's return to the islands, and the resultant losses for Spain as Regan and Vincent van der Rhys managed to steal back their dominance in the spice trade from the Spanish and Portuguese. "Our country plays second fiddle to the barbaric blond Netherlanders — and their greedy efficiency!" Then he recalled, too, the small fortune he had milked out of Vincent van der Rhys for Regan's release, and he smiled. He, at least, was rich himself — and had plans to become richer. If not Spain, then Don Chaezar Alvarez would win in this struggle with the Dutchman!

Sirena saw the smile on Chaezar's lips, and knew he thought of his nutmegs and his plans to establish a "kingdom," as he called it, where he might grow them. And, the proud Spaniard was not poor — indeed, his fine mansion gave adequate proof of that! No doubt he was more interested in his own fortunes than in those of his fatherland.

"What . . . can I do to help you . . . against the Dutch?" she asked.

If he was surprised at her complete willingness to work against her husband, Don Chaezar did not show it. Instead, he surprised Sirena.

"Do? Nothing! Just promise me that when the time is right for me to leave the Indies, you will come with me!" There was a sense of urgency about him as he left his chair and dropped to his knee beside her. "Sirena, *querida,* say you'll come with me and I'll put the world at your feet! Say you agree!"

For answer Sirena allowed him to press his lips to hers in a warm but brief kiss. Chaezar's eyes were soft at what he took for her affirmative answer. Mentally Sirena compared the sultry dark orbs to Regan's blue slits of steel.

"You must give me time . . . to think on the matter. I much prefer to make up my mind in my own surroundings!" Her laugh tinkled in the richly furnished room.

Chaezar stroked his lush beard. Regan was blind. There was no other excuse for it. Couldn't he see past the cool, poised exterior to the fiery she-demon that breathed within this woman? How he longed to make her his mistress.

"What do you know of the . . . Sea Siren?" he asked lightly while watching her face very closely.

"Very little. I've . . . heard of her, naturally,"

Sirena lied. "It's said that she is the most unbelievable captain. They say she rides the seas like a goddess. She plunders and robs, I'm told — and she must be neither Dutch nor Spanish, for she robs and kills both. Is it true that cargos the ships carry are seldom of interest to her, and that she throws them overboard? And laughs? Her laugh must carry over the water, making the crews — which she is said to send into their jolly-boats — even more frightened of her. I know she has Regan bewitched. The figurehead is proof of his obsession with the 'water witch.' I also understand, from Helga, that you and Regan have both set trap after trap for her and that she manages to elude you each time."

"Everything you say is true," Chaezar said grimly. "I envy the Mynheer his figurehead. It makes a stunning addition to his newest ship," he added slyly, watching for her reaction.

"Does it *really?*" Sirena smiled. "Does he think perhaps the Sea Siren will spare his ship if she sees her likeness on the bow?"

Chaezar laughed. "Perhaps. No man knows what *Regan* thinks! But I know he's obsessed with the piratess. I see it in his eyes, as have other men. But . . . I hope, my dear, that I haven't offended you."

"Not in the least," Sirena said, smiling. "Let us both hope it is a good-luck charm for him. I would not want my husband to be disappointed . . . But tell me more, Don Chaezar, about the Sea Siren. Why does she ride the seas?"

"God only knows. All I can say is I wish she was in *my* employ."

343

"Have you seen her yourself?"

"No," Chaezar replied, tugging at his beard. "But it is said that she is what every man would want in his bed. She is what every woman would secretly like to be — wild and untamed. Speaking from a man's point of view," Chaezar murmured softly, "I wager we would all like to be the one to capture her and tame her. But," he continued carefully, "she is not a wench to be tamed. She is as wild as the sea she rides. The man who could tame her would, indeed, be a man."

Sirena laughed inwardly. "I find this so . . . thrilling — though" — and Sirena lowered her eyes in false modesty — "of course I should not!" she breathed.

"Another glass of wine, dear Sirena?"

"No, thank you. I must be getting back before Regan turns into a bull and tramples the house because of my disobedience. Today I felt the need of a small outing and a little conversation in our mother tongue. The way Regan desecrates our language makes my blood boil."

"It was my pleasure! You must come here, my dear, whenever the pressures of your home become too much for you. My house will always be a sanctuary for you. I — I would defend you with my life if need be," he said gallantly. "Till our next meeting," he finished, bringing her hand to his lips.

On arriving in the van der Rhys courtyard, Sirena instructed Juli: "Hurry now, dear, to the Mynheer. Tell him precisely what we did. Do not worry. If he is angry, it will be at me, not you!"

The native girl hesitated on the doorstep, "Hurry in, now. Obey me!"

At the foot of the wide staircase, Sirena turned once more to see Juli knock at the study door. "Oh, and tell the Mynheer not to disturb me for the rest of the day. I have much to pray for this day!" she said, smiling wickedly behind her mantilla.

Pursing her mouth as she climbed to her room, Sirena wondered how long it would take the "bull" to trample his way upstairs. Not long, she surmised, so she had best position herself by the bed, with her rosary, and keep her head bowed. Less than a minute after she had sunk to her knees, Regan burst through the bedroom door, fuming.

"You defied me!" he shouted. "You deliberately defied me!" Sirena said nothing, her fingers moving over the beads, her head bent. "What did you do, alone inside the Spaniard's house? Answer me, damn you!"

"You are a . . . bull, Mynheer. When you address me, you will use a civil tongue. This is not the twelfth century — when a woman was a slave to the man she married. In the future you will *ask* me to do something, you will not *tell* me. Nor will you ever again order me to do as you say. If you do, I shall only be forced to . . . ignore you. Now, please leave me to my prayers."

All this in a calm, almost emotionless voice, soft yet demanding attention.

Uncertainty flickered across Regan's face. Who in the name of God did she think she was speaking to? Some saint, perhaps?

"Did you . . . wish to say something else, Mynheer?" Sirena asked, raising her eyes.

"There is nothing else I need say. You are aware of my deman— wishes in regard to Don Chaezar Alvarez. It would be wise if you obeyed them in the future. Otherwise I *may* have a chance to show what a bull I really can be — by locking you in your room!"

"I would not do that if I were you, Mynheer van der Rhys." The green eyes sparkled and glittered with something Regan could not define. "For, if you do, then you will force me to seek sanctuary in Señor Alvarez's house. I will not be treated like one of the whores who do your bidding in order to win your favor. Leave me to my prayers, as I've asked, and perhaps . . . if I have time . . . I'll pray for your soul."

With a savage gesture Regan reached out and grasped the beads from her hand, snapped the chain in two. He looked at the ruined rosary a moment and tossed it onto the floor.

"You behave, Mynheer, like a schoolboy who doesn't get his way," Sirena shot back vehemently for the first time. She had had enough of this! "Remove yourself from my presence! You offend me!"

Regan stood, the furies of Hell engulfing him as he gazed down into her emerald eyes. Suddenly he wanted to rip the clothes from her body and press her into the softness of the bed on which she rested her arms.

"Your lust sickens me," Sirena said as she read the expression in his eyes. "Go to your whore! Leave me!"

Stunned at her fury — something he had not yet witnessed — Regan could only stalk from the room, his booted feet making harsh sounds on the marble floor.

Chapter Twenty

"Sirena! Sirena!" Caleb shouted as he burst into her room without knocking a few days later. "Listen to me! I just came from the anteroom outside Regan's library. He has cloistered himself there with Señor Alvarez. Regan looked extremely angry when he received the Señor in the entranceway a few minutes ago!"

Sirena gathered up her heavy skirts and followed Caleb downstairs at a near-run. "Station yourself in the corridor and ward off any of the servants who might come this way," she hissed as she leaned against the stout library door.

"Aye, Sirena," Caleb replied, his eyes bright with the excitement of conspiracy.

Her hands clasped tightly to her breast, Sirena pressed her ear to the wood. Smiling wickedly, she pictured both men staring into each other's eyes. Chaezar was speaking, his warm, rich voice carrying through the thick door paneling.

"So . . . now you have come to the point. Mynheer, what could you and I have to discuss other than business, however?"

"Quite simply, the matter of my wife. I know you, Don Chaezar, for the libertine you are. I want you to stay away from her. She is vulnerable at this time in her life, she wishes only to lead a life of prayer. You are making me the laughingstock of Batavia in your pursuit of her." Regan cleared his throat somberly. "She is . . . of course . . . too much of a lady to tell you directly that you offend her. I must do that. So . . . whether you are her countryman or not, I warn you to stay away from her from this day forward!"

Chaezar took a moment to speak. "Sirena . . . has said this to you — that I 'pursue' her?" he asked suavely. "I think not. And, indeed, on the other hand, she has been most sympathetic to my . . . attentions."

"Are you intimating that you have bedded my wife?" Regan shouted hoarsely.

"Mynheer, I beg of you! We . . . we Spaniards are not a breed like you Dutch. No Hispanic would besmirch a lady's good name — especially a married one's. And no Spaniard would . . . tell of it . . . if he did. However, I can assure you that my attentions have not gone so far with your fair Sirena." Then, quickly: "Though you, Regan, with your whoring ways, what should my feelings toward your wife matter to *you?* You — who have cut a swath from Sumatra to Guinea a mile wide. I'll wager," Chaezar laughed quietly, "you've bedded every female who's able to walk without the aid of a cane! But you'd best be careful, Regan," the Spaniard warned. "These Javanese beauties are well versed in the art of poisoning their lovers when something doesn't go their way!"

"You speak of my 'cutting a swath from Sumatra to Guinea.' By God, Chaezar, you have always been right behind me to pick up where I left off!"

Don Chaezar Alvarez chuckled loud enough for Sirena to hear. "What you say is true — but there's a difference between us: I use discretion; I don't tread like a bull elephant and leave my mark wherever I go. We Spanish would never darken a woman's good name — be she a lady of quality or a whore."

"Bah!" Regan said brusquely.

Sirena heard a chair scrape the floor and judged that her husband had risen. Chaezar would be grinning at the sun-bronzed Dutchman as he paced the richly carpeted room.

"But enough of this talk!" Regan finally resumed. "I reiterate what I asked you here to tell you: Leave my wife to her prayers!"

"And I'm telling you, Regan, the decision must be hers. And besides, the lovely lady cannot sit by her bed during every waking hour! If she chooses to visit me . . . But, I agree — enough of this prattle! You must settle your own marital problems with your wife. What's more, I find it in exceedingly poor taste to discuss a man's spouse with him."

A chair moaned and Sirena knew that Don Chaezar had risen. Dare she stay a moment longer?

"There is, however, one thing I should like to say to you before I leave, Mynheer. Your ship now boasts the lovely carving of the Sea Siren. Do you really think that the lovely pirate lady riding the seas of late, these past months, will not molest you or your ships if she sees her likeness on the bow of your vessel?" The Spaniard laughed quietly. "She has you bewitched, my friend. Ah, I see by the look on your face that it's true!"

"I think no such thing. I merely wanted a figure-head for my ship, and the Sea Siren — beauty that she is — seemed ideal for it. Make no more of it than that, sir! But there is . . . an item of true business that I called you here to speak of. Will you take a seat again?"

"For a moment I thought you were going to forget to detail what you merely mentioned to me in passing, the other day in town. You said then that you wanted to plot a trap that will be so well constructed, so escape-proof that the Siren will raise a white flag and fall to her knees, begging mercy!"

Regan explained his plan, which, Sirena heard quite clearly, was that each of them should take a convoy of three vessels, combined as it were into a fleet, and place a cordon around the western tip of Java, including the Sunda Strait and the coastline west of Batavia, along which the Sea Siren frequently disappeared. The ships' sails should be tinted black, as hers were; and they should maintain their vigil for a week.

"Several of my own ships have just been careened," Don Chaezar responded, "so that I'll have the sails dyed and will be ready to set them to sea within two days. However, in this joint expedition I have one condition: the Sea Siren is not to be killed, or injured in any way — though of course her ship must be dismantled and her crew hanged."

"I've no stomach for killing women, as you seem to think!" Regan shot back. "Of course I agree to your condition."

"I hesitate to ask you this, Regan, but who gets the prize? The Spanish or the Dutch?"

Sirena held her breath as she waited for her husband's reply.

"Don't hedge, Chaezar. What you're asking is who gets the Siren — you or me!"

"You *are* an uncouth lout, do you know that, Regan? Very well, that's what I want to know."

"It's quite simple," the Dutchman replied. "Whichever of us is man enough to take her. I rather think she shall be mine."

Well, is she now? Sirena smiled to herself. We'll just see about that!

Suavely, the Spaniard prepared to make his exit. "Shall we merely say that 'To the victor go the spoils'?"

With the grace and speed of a cat, Sirena raced out of the anteroom and across the broad main entranceway to the staircase, where she pretended to be in the act of coming downstairs. As the Mynheer conducted his guest to the front door, she did not see the Spaniard reach into his waistcoat pocket and produce a small package.

"By the way, friend Regan," the representative of the Spanish Crown said softly, "several months ago we agreed on a small wager as to which of our ships — the *Rotterdam* or the *Sevilla* reached Capetown first. As you recall, they began their journey at the same hour. Thanks to the indolent lout who captained the *Sevilla*, you have won the wager. I'm sure you'll find this token" — he extended the packet to his host — "a bit more valuable than the amount we agreed upon." And with that he left.

After a pretended survey of the kitchen, Sirena had returned to her room, upstairs, and had briefed Caleb on what she'd heard.

"They'll wait out there in the straits until they grow old — for the Sea Siren won't be ensnared by them! Then they'll each think a spy told her not to go to sea — and each will think the spy is in the other's camp, for they both want the Sea Siren for herself alone! Man are so stupid, so really stupid. Except for you, Caleb," she added hastily.

"Does this mean we won't go out to sea again for more than a week?" the boy asked.

"That's exactly what it means. But," she said quietly, "we'll set sail if — as I believe he will — Regan finally sends the convoy, both his ships and Chaezar's, home and then returns last, alone! We'll catch him with his fleet gone home. I doubt that the expedition — 'the fleet,' as they call it — will even last a week. Don Chaezar will not have as much patience as is needed. Furthermore, both men will believe the other let the plans become known, in some way, to the Siren; this will make for dissension among the Spanish and Dutch vessels of the fleet."

"You'll — you'll not harm the Mynheer, will you, Sirena?" Caleb asked anxiously.

She smiled. My, how the boy admired the loutish Dutchman. "Go to your room now, little brother. Back to your studies for a time. We will speak more later."

No, she would not "harm" Regan, Sirena told herself when the youth had left. But she would best the man! That was what she wanted, wasn't it?

Then, sinking down onto the soft coverlet of her bed, she let her thoughts race. What else did she want of Regan? Did she want to gaze into those steely eyes of his and murmur words of love to him? Did she, indeed, want to be taken on the wide deck of the *Rana*, the ship tossing and thundering against giant breakers to the rhythm of lovemaking? Yes . . . she admitted it to herself for perhaps the first time.

But, sitting up straight as a ramrod, she suddenly reproached herself: I *must* kill him. I've lied to poor Caleb! I swore to take vengeance on Isabel's killer. And, though perhaps only indirectly, Regan van der Rhys is that man. He may not have wielded the cutlass, but —

Perspiration broke out on her brow. The thought of taking Regan's life was so abhorrent that she trembled. What was happening to her? She rose and went to stand by the window overlooking the garden. Her hands were folded and her eyes glazed as she stared out at the exotic flowers beyond. And then a knock sounded at her door, jarring her from any further thoughts.

"Come in," she called, and Regan entered, his eyes raking the room.

Sirena willed her face to blankness. She waited, her heart thumping in her chest. What did he want now?

"I've just seen Señor Alvarez to his trap."

Her glittering green eyes looked directly into the mocking angry blue ones of her husband. "And how is Cha— Señor Alvarez?" she asked softly.

"At the moment he is well. However," he said harshly, "he may not remain in that state much longer if he does not put an end to the rumors that are floating about the island."

Sirena's lips closed tightly.

"And you add to those rumors by your visits to him?"

"I have entered his house but twice," Sirena asserted calmly.

"Twice is twice too many times!" Regan fired back. "Everyone in Batavia is calling me a fool. Why only last night, Gretch—" He caught himself, but too late.

Anger shot up Sirena's spine, her eyes smoldered as she gazed at her husband. Her eyes belied her soft tones, as she answered. "A 'fool'? But you were that, long before I arrived — and long before you married me. When one is a fool to begin with, nothing can change the matter, unless," she said coldly, "it is to be made still a bigger fool. And you, Mynheer, are quite adept. You need no help from me! What do you want with me? Why are you here?"

Regan's eyes narrowed to mere slits. Her words were infuriating . . . but why did she have this strange effect on him? He should, by rights, hate her — and whip her — for what she'd said.

Instead, he posed a question: "What is it . . . about Don Chaezar Alvarez that so fascinates you, my dear?" Then, quickly, as she lowered her gaze: "Don't deny it. I see it in your eyes!"

"Don Chaezar is a fellow countryman, as I've told you before. *He* . . . is a gentleman. He speaks my native tongue as it was meant to be spoken. I find him gallant. Do you know the meaning of that word, Mynheer?" she taunted him quietly.

And stirred him to his depths by that taunting.

He knew he must control his passions. "I shall

355

leave you to your prayers. In fact, that was my main reason for coming here." He reached deep into his pocket and withdrew a long circlet of pearls. "I broke your rosary, as you may recall. I thought you might like to say your prayers on these perfect, cultured pearls — which may give your laments more meaning than the mere stained glass beads you used before. But say some prayers for me — we 'heathens,' " he said mockingly, "need all the help we can get!"

Regan tossed the pearls on the bed. Curious, and with an expression of remembrance, Sirena walked to the bed and gathered them into her hands. "Where — where did you get these?" she stammered, turning pale.

Noting her shock, her husband said softly, "I won them in a wager." He didn't tell her who lost the wager to him. He did not want her to know she held in her hands something of Don Chaezar's. Then he turned swiftly on his heel and strode from the room.

Outside his wife's room, Regan stopped short and looked back at the closed door.

Sirena had not admitted to a relationship with Alvarez. Of course not, how could she have dared? The more he thought about the possibility of Sirena's loving Don Chaezar, the more Regan's mind whirled. Despite her mourning, despite her attitude of calm, might she not have . . . ? He raged inside. Had the cur Chaezar bedded her? Regan drew in his breath; a million small, wriggling worms seemed to be gnawing his belly.

He slammed one fist into the other. "I'll kill the

bastard!" he all but shouted. The vision of the two coupling, moaning in ecstasy was suddenly so vivid.

Anger getting the best of him, he stormed back into his wife's room, kicking the door shut behind him. Sirena now stood near the window, the pearls clasped in her hands, tears streaming down her cheeks.

Heedless of her torment, Regan yelled out: "*Have* you bedded Alvarez? Have you? I want an answer!"

With a swift movement, he tore the pearls from Sirena's hands and pulled her to him. Her eyes gleamed wet, her breathing was ragged.

"Answer me!"

Her lips remained closed. Savagely he pulled her even closer to his heaving body and brought his lips crashing down on hers, hot and blazing as he held her prisoner.

Sirena felt her breasts caressed by urgent hands. Felt, too, her own resistance to him melting —

Then, abruptly, she was thrust away from him. Mocking eyes laughed into hers.

"Alvarez may be a gentleman. But can he stir your blood as I just did?" He glared at her, sure of his conquest. After a moment, he changed his tack, and an acid pleasantry came into his voice: "But, remember, Mevrouw . . . ours is to be a marriage in name only . . . Until your period of mourning is over. And that will be some months yet, will it not?" he chuckled evilly.

Sirena stood stunned, her head reeling, her eyes deep pools of murky water. She knew that to retaliate in her present state would give her feelings for

357

Regan away. Sick and wounded, she turned her back to him, her head bent.

Watching her heaving back, Regan wished to grasp her, cradle that dark head to his chest and stroke that soft hair. He wanted to murmur soft, not harsh words to this lovely creature who had come to him, been contracted to him, from so far away . . .

Instead, he marched angrily from the room, muttering obscenities that she might hear. But, once outside, he took a deep and painful breath and gnashed his teeth. What is coming over me? he wondered. First I wanted Sirena . . . then the Sea Siren . . . and now Sirena once more. How she makes me forget even Gretchen! How this black-clad virgin controls me — I never thought it could happen to *me!* To me, Regan van der Rhys — my own master and slave to no woman!

The new role did not please him at all. With a steady hand he lit a cigar, shut his eyes briefly to avoid the blue-gray spiral of smoke.

Regan spent the next two days in a turmoil. He would issue an order and five minutes later countermand it. The crews of his private ships were beginning to look upon him as a madman.

Today he smoked cigars continuously as he paced the office rooms like a caged lion. Thoughts of Chaezar Alvarez and his wife lying naked in an opulent bed with lacy hangings set his teeth to rattling. Did she moan and breathe hard for that rutting pig? Did Alvarez make love to her like a gentleman, or like a savage? Regan wanted to strike out, to bludgeon, to kill, to rape, to ravage as

never before. After the Sea Siren was captured —
by dint of their joint fleet — he would kill the
Spaniard. He would show him no mercy. He
would slit his throat as if he were a stray piece of
wild game. Would Sirena cry over the villain's
mutilated body? The picture of her standing over
Chaezar's still form, crying unashamedly for all to
see, set him in such a frenzy that he kicked out at
the leg of a table that stood in his way — and the
pain in his foot was so excruciating he had to
clench his teeth to keep from crying out.

Regan cursed himself for a fool a thousand
times over. He had always prided himself on being
a man of his word; he never reneged. Why in the
name of Satan had he promised Sirena that the
marriage was to be in name only, until her mourning was done? I'll never be able to bed her now unless she comes to me, he thought, thanks to my
promise, and to Don Chaezar Alvarez! And
thanks to the cursed Spaniard she may not come
to me even after she doffs her black gowns!

Am I then to go through life staring at her across
the table, he asked himself, remembering the feel
of her fast-beating heart, the half-moans she
made. Is this — is this the punishment I've earned
for the life of sin I've led? he reproached himself
suddenly. For my whoring ways, as someone has
put it?

Sirena was now in his blood just as was the Sea
Siren, and he was doubly frustrated. And last
night, when he'd tried to bed the Javanese woman
he had been after for months, it had been a fiasco.
The woman had spat at him! Today the island was
doubtless buzzing with the tale!

Chapter Twenty-one

A week had passed, the joint fleet had departed Batavia harbor, and the town — deprived of its commissioners for the Spanish and Dutch crowns — seemed lifeless except for the mounting fear that the Spaniard and the Netherlander and their ships had met with some terrible end.

Sirena had no such fears.

She paced the elegantly hung bedroom, her fists clenched at her sides, in one of them the knotted rosary of cultured pearls. A hundred times since his leaving her room that night, nine days ago, she had asked herself how Regan himself had had the gall, the cruelty beyond measure to give them to her. To give to her her sister Isabel's precious prayer beads! It was beyond belief! And now . . . now she had no choice: she must bring him down. Yes, little brother, she muttered to herself, I must kill him after all. God help me, I must kill him! His giving me the rosary wipes out all doubt now that he might not have had anything to do with my sister's death!

At a timid knock on the door that connected her chamber to Caleb's, she called out ·bitterly, "Come in!"

The boy knew what was in Sirena's mind, and had become deeply saddened over the past few days. He looked up at her with tears in his eyes.

Heedless of his feelings, as she knew she *must*

be, she queried: "Caleb, is the *Sea Siren* ready to sail?"

The boy looked puzzled. Three times that day he had told her the crew were at the ship, all preparations made. "It's time to leave, Sirena — if we must make the tide. Aren't you ready?"

She sighed. "Yes, I am ready, Caleb. But this time I have little heart for our journey — though I know what I must do. You have seen the pearls, little brother, and I have told you whose they were."

"But the Mynheer told you that he won them in a wager."

"My husband, though an experienced liar, was not trying to deceive me. He was, indeed, challenging me. And . . . my young friend . . . this may mean that he knows I am not his intended!"

Sirena watched the stars with mixed emotions as she stood by the ship's rail. The stars were so far away and so bright. Isabel had been like them in a way: bright, shining, and a faraway object too — remote and ascetic. But Isabel's star had been snuffed out.

Jan, her first mate, touched her lightly on the shoulder. "Capitana?"

Snapping her thoughts back to the reality of her mission, she turned to the blue-eyed Dutchman.

"Willem has just come back from the end of the cove," Jan told her. "He says the fifth ship has passed by the mouth of the river. Thank the Lord for our good moon tonight — else he'd not have been able to see. He believes that the flagship, the Mynheer's own, will not be long in following."

361

"Then we must up anchor, leave our old hiding place here, and sail downriver to meet him — just beyond the shallows and rocks. It's a dark night, withal, and neither the five ships that have already gone by, nor those at anchor in Batavia, will spy us. If Regan is too close to shore, what's more, we'll lure him farther out into the open sea so that he and I may play out our battle unobserved and unhindered!"

Nevertheless, minutes later, as the *Sea Siren* eased out of the quiet waters of the cove into the swiftly moving river, Sirena's hands were clammy on the ship's wheel. Could she go through with it? Could she kill Regan van der Rhys? Then a vision of her sister Isabel floated before her, and her hands clasped the wheel fiercely as she straightened her back and squared her shoulders. She knew what she had to do, and she would do it!

The ship neared the mouth of the river and Sirena's eyes watched the threatening rocks as she guided the frigate through the narrow channel and eased it into the open sea once more.

At the cry that went up from the men — ever amazed at her ability to free the *Siren* from her hiding place — she sent down word with Jan that they should speak softly. Their words might carry over the water, and though their dark sails gave little hint of the ship's whereabouts, she wanted to surprise Regan's vessel.

And, suddenly, there it was — black-rigged like her own ship, alone on the inky-watered Java Sea.

"Take the wheel now, Jan," she called.

"Aye, Capitana." As he gripped the circle of wood, he continued: "She's in no hurry,

362

Capitana. See, she travels at a mere six knots or less — and with half-furled sail. A sad ship she'll be, too, returning after seven long days and nights with no sight of her prize! Her men will be anxious to see their wives."

"*If* they see their wives," Sirena said ruefully, and her first mate's smile vanished. He, as well as Caleb, knew her intent this time. "She's far enough offshore so that our encounter will not be seen," Sirena went on, "but we must be quick about it. We've the advantage: the breeze urges us toward her! Caleb," she barked to the boy who sat dejectedly near the stern rail of the *Siren*, "go below, so you'll neither be seen nor hurt. Off with you now!"

"Aye, Sirena," Caleb said as he extended his hand manfully to her. "Good luck . . . Sirena." With difficulty he had held back his tears.

"Caleb," she said softly, pulling him close to her breast, "if it is any consolation to you, at this moment I don't know if what I'm about to do is right, in the sight of God and man, or not. All I know is that . . . I have to do it." She pressed the boy close for a moment. Then: "Get below now. Hurry!"

She turned to Jan. "Pass the order to tighten sail."

In little more than a minute her command had been obeyed. They were a good crew, these Dutchmen she employed. Not one of them would defy her, even though their hearts might not be united on what she planned to do this night.

Jan was at her arm again. "We travel at eight knots, we'll overtake her in minutes. See, there she is — dead on our bow." Suddenly, the confident first mate showed alarm. "Look! She's sighted us, and — But, by the gods, she's sailing off — she's afraid of us!"

"Yes, Jan. Together with her fleet she had no fear of the Sea Siren. Alone, she's a coward!"

In the *Sea Siren*'s chase after the Dutch brigantine, her smaller and lighter hull gave her the advantage. Surely and swiftly the frigate gained on the Dutchman.

Then, with a resounding crash, the ram of the *Siren* pierced the stern of the brig. Shouts and curses rang out aboard the larger ship as Sirena's crew shouted joyously and ran to the side of the *Sea Siren*.

"Do not board the brigantine," Sirena shouted to her men. "Not yet. I want to speak with her captain."

Regan, stripped to the waist, stood near the brig's sterncastle, his eyes glaring, his breeches clinging tightly to the hard muscles of his thighs. Nimbly, Sirena swung herself up into the rigging of the *Siren* and stared down at him.

Suddenly, she heard one of Regan's crew shout breathlessly from the bridge: "But, Captain, she flew her black sails — and the moon was behind the clouds until a moment ago!" Then, silence, as a shot rang out and the crewman fell wounded to his knees.

"Ho, there, Willem! Enough! Await my orders!" Then she spoke to Regan: "Come aboard, Captain, if you like. I will set no foot on that rotten wood you command. She sinks in an hour's time with one good broadside shot from my crew. You are growing fat and lazy like all Dutchmen. A little alertness on your part and you may have outrun me. You see now that you have nowhere to go but the water. Can you swim, Captain?" she shouted.

Regan stood on the stern, his eyes murderous. So she was on the Spaniard's side after all! Why else did she lay in wait and attack him? And to use black sails! Damn! Why didn't the moon come out so he could get a good look at her? Suddenly he laughed, white teeth gleaming in the yellowish light.

"What do you want from me? You have almost single-handedly ruined me, what else do you want?" he shouted as he watched the long-legged creature nick the air with the point of her cutlass.

"Your life, Captain. Also the life of the one that carries a hook for a hand. Turn him over to me and perhaps I'll spare your life."

Regan laughed again, his arms raised, his feet sure on the rolling deck. "What do you want with the man who uses a hook for a hand? I carry no such man aboard this ship. Tell me why you seek this man," he demanded, his eyes taking in her scanty attire.

"The day I run him through I shall post a notice; until that time, it is my affair! Into the jolly-boats or you die. It's your choice, Dutchman!"

"You can't win. My men will kill the lot of you. Surrender to me and I'll see that it goes easy with you at your trial."

Sirena's laughter rippled across the water. "You seem to have made a mistake, Dutchman; it is I who captured you. I could run you through before

365

you could blink an eye. I should surrender to you? Fool!" she shouted.

"Wrong, lovely lady, look to your stern, it is I who have you captured. The galleon on your stern is mine. She weighed anchor in the mangrove swamp not far from here. Your mistake," he said bowing low.

Sirena swiveled and saw the cannons jutting from the gunwales. The Dutchman was right, she was outnumbered. She would have to fight. Firing cannons at this close range would imperil the frigate.

"All hands to the deck!" Sirena shouted. "It's kill or be killed! I would have let you go, Dutchman, now you leave me no choice," she said, leaping from the rigging to land, feet firmly planted on Regan's deck. She stood a moment, her breathing ragged as she brought up the cutlass in a jaunty salute. She felt a jolt of pain in her shoulder as steel met steel. The air rang with shouts and screams as metal clanged against metal. Shots seemed to come from nowhere and men toppled to the deck like flies. Out of the corner of her eye she saw her mate, Jan, drop his cutlass just as a cutthroat was about to run him through. With the speed of a cat, Sirena turned, leaped over a pile of rigging, and slicked her cutlass with a high wide arch; the man's arm as well as the cutlass rolled to the deck. Jan looked up at the woman in front of him and grinned. "Aye, Capitana, a fierce blow it was. I'll be in your debt."

Her men fought valiantly, as did Regan's crew. The battle raged, with the crew from the *Sea Siren* having the advantage. Great clouds of black, pungent smoke lay heavy in the air from the burning brig. Rubbing her eyes, Sirena turned to attack a crewman bent on cutting her down. Just as she drove him backwards over the rail a thundering shout ripped through the air. Breathing heavily, she strained to see through the thick smoke. It was Jan's shout that made her turn and see the man bent on slashing her in the back.

"Blackheart!" she shouted. "So," she screamed, bringing up the cutlass to hold him at bay. "Willem, Jan, Jacobus," she shouted, "I have a score to settle with this beast. Clear the decks!"

"No need, Capitana, the Dutch have shouted for quarter."

Never taking her eyes from the man in front of her, she called her order. "See to our wounded, theirs as well as our own. Lower the Dutchmen into the jolly-boats after their wounds have been seen to. Sink the galleon and gut the brig! Let no man interfere with what I'm about to do. Willem, stand guard over Captain van der Rhys."

All eyes watched the woman with the cutlass as she advanced to a point and then stopped before the burly Englishman. "So, you would have run me through from behind! Coward!" she spat. "I told you there would be a time and a place! This is it!" she said, her voice deadly in its calm.

"I'll give you a fighting chance which is more than you gave me. En garde!" she shouted as she flexed her knees and brought up the cutlass and slashed at the man's weapon. His arm flew backwards and he was stunned with the force of the blow. He recovered quickly and jabbed straight for Sirena's midsection. Nimbly she sidestepped as her weapon again struck out, this time glancing down the side of his arm. Blood spurted as she laughed at the look of terror on Blackheart's face. "How does it feel, Blackheart, to see your arm in tatters? Guard it well, for I shall strike till I lay the bone open." She feinted to the right, the cutlass finding its mark across the man's shoulder. The crack of the shattering bone brought cheers from the *Sea Siren*'s crew. Regan stood, mouth agape, awed by the woman's expertise. How in the name of God did she have the strength to heft and wield the heavy cutlass like a man? Before Blackheart could recover himself she slashed downward, ripping his leg from thigh to ankle. Crimson blood leaked onto the deck and he slipped, trying to regain his position.

"Let me hear you beg, Blackheart!" Sirena spat. "Shout for quarter and I'll throw you into the sea."

"Never!" the man hissed.

Sirena held the cutlass loosely in her hand as she watched Blackheart's agonized face. "You have one leg left, surrender to me, otherwise you give me no choice."

"Never!" the man spat, using his injured arm to strike out with the cutlass. His eyes never saw the blade as it ripped his other leg from thigh to toe. Sirena stepped backward. "You have just seconds to surrender." Glazed, hate-filled eyes stared into hers, the cutlass dropped from his hand.

"Stand like a man and fight! Damn your eyes! Fight, I tell you!" Sirena screeched. With one quick movement she had the fallen cutlass in her hand. She tossed the weapon to the man, and spoke softly: "I want that weapon in your hand when I kill you. I'll have no man say I ran you through unarmed!" Blackheart staggered, the cutlass hanging loosely in his wounded hand, the other hanging loosely at his side.

"This is the last time I'll give you the chance to ask quarter. What is it to be?" she menaced, the cutlass straight in front of her. For answer, Blackheart spat in her face. His weapon, thrust forward, aiming for the soft flesh of her midsection, took Sirena off guard.

In the instant reflex of protecting herself, Sirena sidestepped Blackheart's attack, her cutlass parried and found its mark in the flesh of his belly, and he crumpled to the deck, lifeless.

Trembling with the overpowering emotion of a long-sought revenge accomplished, Sirena's eyes were pinpoints of flame. "I gave him the opportunity to ask for quarter. He had his choice. I could have done no less than I did. Right or wrong, I'll live with my choice."

As a man, Regan understood this. Her grievance against Blackheart must have been all-consuming. No, he thought, she could have done no less.

Sirena's arrogance returned and she faced Regan with confidence. "Be truthful, Dutchman, have you ever known a woman like me? Admit you'd like me for your own. I see I've scored. Lust leaps from your eyes like frogs from a pond!"

Unable to control himself, Regan pulled free of his captors and planted his feet firmly on the deck within inches of Sirena. "You would challenge me, is that it? Has it become a matter of honor?"

"Yes," Regan menaced. The Siren had lost all

claim to womanhood in Regan's furious opinion. She cursed like a man and fought better than most men. He wanted to meet with her in the excitement of a duel. Then, when he had subdued her, cowed her, he wanted to meet her in the excitement of passion.

Sirena read his thoughts accurately and excitement coursed through her veins. "Willem, toss Captain van der Rhys his weapon!" Turning once again to Regan she said harshly, breathlessly, through clenched teeth, "There's no need for this duel." Suddenly she didn't want this duel to happen. Her mind sought frantically for another way to bring vengeance upon him. The idea of piercing his flesh, drawing his blood, was repulsive to her, but, if she must to save herself, she would.

The cutlass came up with lightning speed and slicked across Regan's chest, perforating his shirt and drawing blood. Regan did not take his eyes from the wild untamed she-demon before him. He brought up his weapon with slow deliberation and back-stepped, swinging the blade with a wicked flourish, nicking the buttons on Sirena's blouse. Her creamy, jutting breasts spilled from their confinement.

"You whoring bastard!" Sirena screeched as she fought to keep her blouse together. Being displayed before the crewmen's gawking eyes was too much like that other time aboard the *Rana*. Reckless fury overtook her, blocking out all reason. Beyond all feeling, she dully realized that in her aimless swings with the cutlass Regan's blade was slicing at her fingers and hands, the sticky wetness of her own blood making it impossible to hold her blouse together. Tears of rage blinded her as she brought up the cutlass and thrust it frenziedly at Regan's arm. "I said I'd kill you and I will!" she shrieked. "I hate you!" Again the blade flashed, and she lunged, driving the point of the cutlass through the sinewy muscle of his forearm.

His slate-blue eyes darkened as Regan sucked in his breath. Damn the witch! She said she would kill him and she meant it. There was no doubt in his mind that she was tiring, and were those tears falling down her cheeks?

"Kill me," he said softly. "I'll fight no more. Look to the stern, your men have been seized. We tricked you! You can't win, lovely Sea Siren. You may have me pinned to the halward but you still have to kill me, can you do it?" His eyes darkened and glints of admiration shone as he gazed at the woman breathing in ragged gasps, her jutting breasts rising and falling with each breath.

"You have wounded me as no man has ever wounded me," Regan breathed. "I'll fight to the death, is that what you want? For one of us to die, to spill more blood on these decks."

Sirena backed off. "If I loose you, what then?" Sirena gasped.

"My men will secure your men in the hold and return to Port Batavia."

"That is your bargain?"

"Yes, no more bloodshed."

"You lie," Sirena spat. "I don't believe you."

"I may be many things, but never a liar. You have my word. Even if you kill me now, this minute my men will draw and quarter every man in your crew. Make up your mind," he said harshly, "so I can see to my wounds."

Indecision overwhelmed Sirena. The men watched and listened carefully for her reply.

Slowly and deliberately, Sirena advanced one step, then another. She looked deeply into the man's eyes. She leaned still closer and at the moment she withdrew the cutlass she smiled. "I bested you, Dutchman, admit it. Admit it to your men. Now! For if you don't then I shall pierce you again, this time where it will do the most good."

Regan threw back his head and roared with laughter, his injured arm hanging limply at his side. "All hands," he shouted, "the Sea Siren bested me in a fair duel. Toss her men in the hold, board ship, and a pint of grog for every seaman."

"First," Sirena said, bringing up the point of the blade against Regan's back, "first, you will see to my wounded. When their wounds have been dressed, you will give every member of my crew ale. Understood, Captain," Sirena said softly, the point of the blade nicking the broad back in front of her.

"*Ja,* you heard the . . . lady. Heave to, lad. Who is to dress my wounds?"

"Don't look in my direction, Captain. For if you do, I fear it may be salt I pour in your wounds." Regan laughed as if it were a joke.

"I believe you, Siren. You never give quarter, do you?"

"Never," Sirena cried passionately. "This battle was not necessary. I told you I was finished with you. The wounds you carry are of your own doing. I feel no remorse. Die for all I care! You'll get no help from me!"

"So it's an impasse, is it?"

Sirena laughed, her eyes dancing as she answered: "An impasse? Hardly, Captain. You are almost bankrupt, your cargos are at the bottom of the sea along with ten of your ships. You stand before me with wounds I inflicted and you call it an impasse?" She laughed again. "Hardly!" Regan clenched his teeth at the musical tinkle of her laugh. Damn her eyes, she wasn't human. Or was she . . .

Caleb, hiding in the shadows behind the frigate's rigging, watched in alarm as Regan dueled with the Sea Siren. A thick dense fog was rolling in, adding to the apprehension fluttering in his chest. If either Sirena or Regan should be killed, how would he feel about the survivor? So engrossed in his own thoughts was Caleb that he failed to notice the turnabout of events which saw the crew of Regan's brig become the captors of the *Sea Siren*'s men.

Each minute seemed an eternity. Nervously, he pulled his cap lower on his head, his tumble of hair tucked beneath it. What a fool he'd been, why had he been so mesmerized by the duel he had failed to notice the Dutchman's crew take the advantage over his fellow crew members! Hardly daring to breathe, Caleb heard Regan order his seamen to take Jan, Willem, and the others to the ship's hold. His quick ear also picked up Sirena's demand that her men be given their pint of ale. The message was clear! Silently, on cat-feet, Caleb darted in and out of the shadows to the *Sea Siren*'s galley. Somewhere in the kitchen's stores

Martin had placed the dull, green bottle of laudanum.

Hiding behind the forecastle rail, he wondered how he could board the brigantine without Regan's notice. The thick lines that lashed the *Sea Siren* to the Dutch brig tightened and slackened, squeaking with protest as the heaving sea closed and separated the gap between the two ships.

Sirena must have been reading his thoughts, when next she spoke to Regan: "Surely you'll allow me to change my blouse, Captain van der Rhys. I hope you are gentleman enough not to expose me to the crew this way."

Caleb couldn't hear Regan's reply but he must have agreed, for Sirena leaped to the rail of the sterncastle, waited for the gap between the ships to close, and deftly leaped aboard her frigate, Regan in her wake. As they stepped across the deck toward the captain's cabin, the boy heard Sirena tell Regan she had an ointment for their cuts. First she said she wouldn't help him with his wounds, now she was offering ointment. He smiled to himself; this must fall under the heading of 'wily woman.'

As soon as the cabin door closed, Caleb put the laudanum bottle between his teeth and boarded the brigantine, confident Sirena would occupy Regan long enough to give him time to dose the ale.

As Sirena leaped aboard her frigate, she spied Caleb's slight, crouching form hiding in the shadow of the forecastle rail. She had every confidence in the boy and was positive he had picked up his cue and would soon be aboard the Dutch-man's brig mingling among the seamen and offer-ing to help serve the apportioned pint of ale. It would be up to Sirena to detain Regan long enough to allow Caleb free movement. A thick, al-most tangible bank of fog was drifting in from the horizon, its web of gray already obscuring the moon.

Regan was close behind her, she could almost feel his breath on the back of her neck. She has-tened her step and pulled open the cabin door, her mind racing backward to remember the condition of her quarters when she had seen them hours ago. She desperately tried to recall if she had left any-thing about which would reveal her identity. It had occurred to her before this how foolish men were. Change a woman's hairstyle, her clothes and manner, place her in a location or situation where she wasn't expected to be, and a man wouldn't recognize his own mother! The only thing a man recognized was whether he found a woman desirable or not.

Stepping into the dark cabin, groping for the ta-ble on which rested a lamp, Sirena grasped the glass and sent it crashing to the floor in what seemed like an accident. Murmuring a vague oath which cursed her clumsiness, she picked up the flint box and after much fumbling managed to light the small lamp on the wall at the far end of the cabin, noting with satisfaction the low level of oil and the weakly flickering flame. Turning to keep her face in the shadows, she moved over to her bunk and withdrew a coffer of medicines from beneath it.

"If you'll come over here, Captain, I'll bind your arm."

Regan seemed doubtful, even suspicious. Using his foot, he knocked a three-legged stool against the door to keep it open. His frosty blue eyes raked the room looking for hidden weapons. Seeing nothing to cause alarm, he stepped toward Sirena, who was sitting on the bunk unrolling a length of dressing. As he moved, glass from the broken lamp crunched beneath his foot, the only sound in the heavy, moist air.

It was then Sirena noticed the absence of another sound, that of the frigate's bow bumping against the sterncastle of the Dutch brig. Good work, little brother, Sirena thought with delight, realizing that Caleb must have cut the lines connecting the two ships. The frigate was now drifting free, each wave widening the distance from the brig.

She had meant to change her blouse to cover her near-naked bosom, but on second thought negated the idea. Perhaps the expectation of seeing rosy-tipped breasts spilling from her tattered blouse would divert Regan enough so that he wouldn't notice that each wave separated him further from his men.

Regan sat beside her on the bunk, as she silently smoothed an ointment on his wound and bound it with slow and deliberate movements. Sirena felt his eyes upon her and was becoming more and more aware of his nearness.

He broke the silence. "This is unheard of in naval history, I'd stake my life on it," he growled. "Two adversaries doing battle then binding each other's wounds. Perhaps we're both more civilized than we imagined. It's a wicked scar you carry on your arm, Siren, and fairly recent from the looks of it."

"Aye," Sirena grumbled, a harsh note deepening her voice, "a memento from the scurve Blackheart."

"You've taken your revenge on him now, does it make you happy to know he's dead?" Regan asked, his tone mocking.

Sirena stood up and, with her back to Regan, clenched the back of the chair near the table. "Happy? It delights me!" Her voice held a hatred so intense it raised the hackles on Regan's neck. "His death is food for my soul, nourishment for my spirit. I only regret I cannot kill him twenty times over and twenty times more! I'd dreamed of the moment, yearned for it as a thirsty man longs for water. But the scum even denied me this! He chose to die a coward and rob me of my victory. I find no victory in killing a coward."

As she spoke her supple spine stiffened, the muscles in the backs of her incredibly long legs tautened, accentuating the delicious curve of her buttocks. A deep curl of heat arose in Regan's middle and he was conscious of his prophecy that one day he would bed the Sea Siren. It was then Regan noticed a dark stain on the back of her blouse. "You could do with a bit of that ointment. Come here!" he commanded.

Sirena bristled at his tone, was ready to turn on him and loose her wrath. But she was tired, every nerve within her clamored for relief. Also, she reminded herself, she had to give Caleb every chance. Wearily, she joined Regan on the narrow bunk allowing him to bathe the backs of her hands with the water from the ewer and apply the ointment.

His attitude as he went about seeing to her cuts was so serious, so intensely solicitous, he made her laugh. Regan was embarrassed by what he imagined was an unmanly picture of himself tending to her wounds like an old nursemaid. Gruffly, he ordered her to turn around.

Sirena stifled her laughter when she heard his forbidding tone and obediently turned her back to him. Roughly, he pushed her down on the bunk and, before she could protest ripped the bloody, tattered blouse from her back.

Sirena's petulant mouth opened in a silent scream of protest, her body flexed and arched attempting to break free of his grasp. Her eyes squeezed shut, her sob was muffled against the coverlet. No, she pleaded silently, not again! Dear God, she prayed. Please don't let me be raped again!

"Hold still, Sea Witch! I don't mean to hurt you. Blood from the cut on your back dried to your blouse. There was no gentle way to remove it!" Pressing her down against the mattress, Regan bathed away the blood, gently cleansing and tending the cut.

Slowly, Sirena felt the tenseness and the fight drain out of her. The feel of his fingers on her flesh was soothing, delivering her into a state of mind where she felt warm and peaceful. Through half-closed eyes she saw the lamplight flicker and become more diffused. No doubt due to the fog creeping in through the open cabin door. The flickering, dimming lamplight was hypnotic, lulling her into a dream-like state. She felt him apply the soothing ointment, tenderly dabbing it on with his fingertips.

Regan cursed the dimming lamplight, and hurried at his task before the lamp gave out altogether. Wiping the greasy salve from his fingers on her torn blouse, he stood at his full height and gazed down at the Sea Siren.

Her wealth of heavy dark hair covered the side of her face, obscuring all but the tip of her chin and a glimpse of her brow. Her body had relaxed, the taut readiness abated; her arms extended over her head, with her hands open and still.

Beneath her upstretched arms the soft spill of her full, round breasts was visible. The long, low slope of the small of her back, rising again to the firm, spherical hillocks of her bottom, ending in the firm-fleshed lines of her slightly parted thighs, aroused him, beckoned to him as sweetly as the song of the legendary sirens for which he had named her. Quietly, gently, he leaned over her and pressed his lips to the hollow of her spine.

Sirena felt him touch her again, gentle teasing touches, warm, warmer than the night air. Forcing her heavy-lidded eyes open, she saw the lamp had finally flicked its last light, the cabin was in a gray-black darkness, swathed in a haunting, isolating fog.

She sighed, reveling beneath his light touches, feeling him lean against her, aware of the comforting weight of him. He lifted her salt-scented hair off the back of her neck and shoulders and suddenly she realized the touches she felt were kisses, trailing warm and moist across her shoulders, the nape of her neck. Feeling his breath on her skin, she heard a barely audible groan escape his lips.

With an indrawn breath, Sirena turned onto her back, encircling him in her arms, offering her mouth for his kisses. His powerful hands were in her hair, his lips burning hers. Her arms cradled his head to her breasts, her body arched beneath him. She wanted him, needed him as she was sure no woman had ever wanted a man.

His mouth was on her throat, her breasts, eliciting moans of ecstasy from somewhere deep in her soul.

When he pulled away from her she clung to him, enticing him back with her passion-bruised lips, gentling away his remaining reserve and her own with daring, intuitive caresses of her tongue.

Forcefully, he pulled out of her embrace. He removed his boots and appreciatively grazed his hands over her firmly fleshed legs. Slowly, he worked the buckle of her belt, sensuously he tugged her cutoff trousers over her curving hips, delighting at her grace and strength of limb when she lifted her haunches to aid him. Finally, he pulled the clothes from his own body, tearing and ripping them, having no patience for their restrictions.

Sirena's senses whirled and soared, making her dizzy with passion, bringing her to the borders of lust. There was no escape for her now, she had lost her resolve just as she had secretly known she would have lost it on her wedding night had he come to her then. But all that was behind her now.

His lovemaking was driving her to the brink of wantonness.

She answered his caress with sensuous embraces, responded to his kisses with a sizzling animal passion she never dreamed she possessed.

Unabashedly, she invited him to awaken her sexuality. His lips covered her breasts, her stomach, her thighs . . . She moaned with exquisite joy as she turned her welcoming body this way and that, pliant to his demands, relishing the new-found sensuality he awakened in her.

Regan delighted in his bewitching Sea Siren, withholding the moment of completion to further savor her charms. He rejoiced to find his passion matched by her own.

He could barely see her in the dim light of the cabin. The fog had enveloped the moon, quenching its light in a bath of gray mist. Her lissome, supple beauty was perceived through his fingers. The delicious fragrance of her, the silken texture of her skin heightened his desire as he fondled and explored her secret charms. Her lips tasted of the sea, and her pleasure in him was unaffected, her responses genuine and unpracticed.

Almost innocently she would seek and find the most sensual caress, exalting in the pleasure and inspiration she gave him. Against his lips she moaned, begging, imploring, "Have me! Have me now!"

Afterwards they slept, entwined in each other's arms.

Sirena awakened at the first light of dawn. The

381

hazy mist still lingered in the cabin, but she knew that in a few hours the sun would burn it away. Regan still slept beside her, his body emanating a feverish heat. His face was flushed with fever, his lips appeared parched and dry.

Her eyes flew to the bandage she'd wrapped around his arm the night before; a yellowish, bloody stain seeped through the linen. Tears welled in her eyes. *"Querido,"* she whispered against his feverish temple, "I did this to you!" With horror she realized that the blade she had cut Regan with was the same with which she had killed Blackheart. Coming from that hulk of evil and into Regan's arm, no wonder the wound was unclean.

Disentangling herself from his embrace, she climbed out of the bunk and dressed quickly. On deck she scanned the horizon for signs of the Dutchman's brig, praying that Caleb had been successful. There, coming toward her from the north coast, was the brig's silhouette. Now she would suffer the ordeal of waiting to see who manned the brig, her men or Regan's.

Sirena went back to Regan and placed a cool cloth on his feverish brow. She contemplated changing the bandage on his arm but her ignorance of whether she would be doing more harm than good stopped her. As she changed the cloth on his forehead she attempted to sort out her feelings for this man, her husband. In the end her emotions were still unresolved.

She only knew that he was her enemy, one she had started out to kill. When had she changed her mind? Was it when Caleb wished her luck. How could she kill him . . . she loved him! Her beloved enemy!

A shout reached her ears. "Ahoy *Sea Siren*!" She recognized Jan's hoarse shout. Caleb had succeeded! In that instant she determined she would return Regan to the care of his own men, aboard his own ship.

Sirena and Caleb stayed below in the galley as Regan was lifted aboard his brig. Should he awaken she had no wish to see him, she felt too vulnerable to face him in the light of day.

As she instructed, she heard Jan warn the Dutchman's first mate to head directly for Batavia if he wished to see his captain live. Later, when the Dutch brig was safely out of sight, Sirena went on deck and changed course for the mouth of the River of Death between the "Sisters of Fire."

Leaving the wheel to Caleb, Sirena then went to her cabin and threw herself down on her bunk. While she lay there, exhausted by emotion, fraught with anxiety, she slept . . . and dreamed of the passion and ecstasy she had shared with Regan the night before.

Caleb gently shook Sirena's shoulder. "We're home. If we ride swiftly we can arrive just as dusk settles."

Sirena rubbed at her sleep-filled eyes. "I must have slept a long time," she said, puzzled.

"I told the men to allow you to sleep. We managed well. The decks have been scrubbed and the wounded are taken care of. I'm sorry, Sirena, I guess I am still a boy. I was so frightened I could not make my mind think. If I had been quicker, perhaps none of this would have happened," he chastised himself. "Will Regan die?"

"He won't die, Caleb. He carries a vengeance in him that won't allow him to die just as I do. Have no fear, little brother, when we arrive home under the cover of dusk, he will already be under the mothering influence of Frau Holtz." As Sirena spoke those reassuring words, she prayed to the God she had renounced that the man she loved would live to hold her again.

Chapter Twenty-two

"Gretchen!" Chaezar exclaimed his surprise. Not so much because of her explosive entrance into his private office but because of the early hour. A small, knowing smile tugged at the corners of Chaezar's mouth. Obviously Gretchen had spent a restless night alone in her bed, a rarity which always left her in ill humor; otherwise, she would have lain abed till noon recovering from the strenuous activities of the previous evening. Still smiling, he soothed, "May I say you are exquisite this morning?" Chaezar's black, heavy-browed eyes slid over her body familiarly. It had been too long since he had shared her bed, a situation he would hasten to remedy.

Seeing the light of appreciation in his gaze, Gretchen preened and was slightly mollified as she could be by the flattering glance of a handsome man. "You may," she said finally.

She had chosen a lightweight, handwoven fabric from India, artistically dyed in great splurges of green and blue on a background of palest yellow. A widebrimmed straw hat festooned with yellow tea roses protected her flawless, clotted-cream complexion.

"To what do I owe this visit?" Chaezar asked. "Isn't it early in the day for you to be abroad? Is something wrong?"

"Everything's wrong!" Gretchen pouted as she

paced Chaezar's office nervously. Turning on him suddenly, she threw her gloves on his desktop. "You said you'd hear something about that boy! That was weeks ago!" She stamped a pretty, silk-shod foot on the red Oriental carpet.

"And I have, just before you arrived," Chaezar said smoothly, impervious by now to Gretchen's display of temper. "I would have paid you a visit a little later in the day, when I could be certain you were alone." Any other woman on Java would have either been insulted or at least blushed at his obvious slur on her morals. But not Gretchen. She never minded comment on her sexual activities, in fact she welcomed them. "You won't like hearing what I found out, Gretchen. The boy is gone."

"What?" she shrilled. "How?"

Chaezar repeated what he had learned in a voice devoid of emotion. "As we already know, the child was merely a baby, not more than four when we arranged to relieve Regan of his wife. 'The Hook,' as our mutual friend is popularly referred to these days, made the agreed-upon arrangements to see the child was cared for. This he did by *selling* the child to a rich Shintu chief. This chief purchased the boy for one of his wives, who was barren and desired a child. The boy was well cared for, doted on actually until he was somewhere around the age of six. At this time it is purported there was a war between feuding tribes and the child was taken as a slave. After this point all trace of him is lost. The boy's former owner is convinced the child was press-ganged, as all trace of him stops at the Banda quay in the Banda Islands.

"Oh my God," Gretchen wailed. "Now what do we do?"

"Do? There's nothing for either of us to do. We wait."

"Wait? Wait for what? For Regan to find out and have him kill us? You're insane, Chaezar! You've played me false from the beginning. From the moment the *Tita* set sail you had no intention of letting Regan go free. I thought then that you gave in to me too easily. You wanted Regan out of your way in that damn Spanish prison. True, you managed to kill his wife for me, but that was just so I would be indebted to you. All along it was Regan you wanted out of the way. You weren't helping me at all, you greedy swine! It was convenient for you to kill Tita, so you did. But never for me! For yourself! And now that it has come time for us to pay for our . . . sins, you'd let me hang for yours as well. You won't get away with it, Chaezar! If it comes to Regan finding out, I'll tell him your part in it. If I have to die, so will you. Why in the name of God didn't you place the boy with a missionary?"

"If you'll remember correctly, we had little time to do more than we did. I don't much care for the tone of your threats, Gretchen," he said softly, stroking his luxuriant beard.

"You'd sell your mother for a piece of gold, don't deny it," Gretchen sneered. "And 'The Hook,' what did you find out about him? If Regan finds him, the charade is over!"

"Pray God the Sea Siren finds him before Regan does." Chaezar's voice betrayed a hint of his inner agitation. "The man must have been warned and has taken to land again. Otherwise, he would have been sighted long ago."

"Do you think an inner-island search would help?" Gretchen asked hopefully.

"It's worth the effort."

"When will you send someone to the islands to start inquiries?"

"Would today suit you?" Chaezar smiled wickedly, drawing her close to him. "Perhaps in the meantime we could . . ." His words were muffled against her lips.

So overpowering was the wave of revulsion that washed over Gretchen, she had the feeling she was drowning. Once again she must barter her flesh as a means to her ends. Her mind hated the Spaniard's soft, caressing touch, but her traitorous body welcomed it. If only Regan knew how she sold her body time and time again with only one thought in mind: to make him hers.

Chaezar's lips were soft and demanding as they sought the warm, moist recesses of her mouth. Shuddering inwardly at the close physical contact, she forced herself to respond, at first unwillingly then willingly as desire coursed through her body. It was a simple matter to pretend these were Regan's arms that were holding her. Soft moans escaped her as the pressure on her mouth became more insistent.

Chaezar released her suddenly. "Not here," he said thickly, "the servants." Half dragging and half carrying her, he led her to his chambers and immediately ripped the gown from her body.

Gretchen, her passion momentarily abated, narrowed her eyes and forced back the screams of protest at the damage done to her newest gown. If it had been Regan who tore her gown to shreds she would have helped him. She would do anything for Regan. She would give up all the gowns in her massive wardrobe. Her sultry eyes narrowed again — well, perhaps not all the gowns, but half of them. If only Regan would say just once, I need you, I want you, she would do anything . . . anything!

Desire once more coursed though her as Chaezar's nakedness met her flesh. His dark hands grasped her long golden hair. He twined it about his fingers, as he suckled her breasts with their rapidly hardening cherry nipples. Slowly, insidiously, he manipulated every part of her silken softness till she cried out with frenzied desire.

Fire danced and rippled through her, threatening to engulf her, and still he caressed her at this maddening slow pace, exploring every inch of her warm, wet flesh with his nibbling lips, darting tongue, and plying fingers.

Lost in her moment of desire, Gretchen imagined herself once again under the stars with Regan, making wild, passionate love. A small cry escaped her as she felt the familiar pressure within her. The world exploded as Regan's name escaped her parted lips.

Shocked, she found herself in a heap on the floor, staring up into the wild, rage-filled eyes of Chaezar Alvarez. "So, I come out second best with Regan's whore," he spat with controlled fury. His tone softened abruptly, frightening Gretchen still more. She could handle his fury but never this soft, dangerous mood. Slowly, she got to her knees and backed away from his outstretched foot. She had no desire to have her face disfigured.

Chaezar bent down and pulled her to her feet. He would kill her, she was sure of it. With the instinct of a trapped animal, she lashed out, gouging and kicking, raking her nails down the Spaniard's chest, drawing blood. "Bastard! You'll not kill me!" she hissed, her breasts heaving with the exertion.

She lashed out with her foot, only to have it become caught between his legs and they both went down in a tumble on the floor. Gretchen grabbed handfuls of the black, curly hair on Chaezar's chest and yanked. A womanly, high-pitched shriek tore from the Spaniard's throat.

Rolling across his nakedness to make her escape, she was stunned to feel his hardness beneath her. Her fear was replaced with disgust. Instinctively she knew what she had to do. Once Chaezar was lulled by his satisfied passions she could escape.

Her strong, slender hands gripped his shoulders and forced him back onto the floor. She gazed deeply into his passion-filled eyes as she pinched his nipples. Slowly she raised herself and mounted him.

Chaezar closed his eyes as she took him in, a saturnine grimace distorting his features as Gretchen rocked back and forth, first taunting him with slow movements, then faster and faster as she was engulfed in the delight of her own pleasure. Spasm after wild spasm gripped Chaezar's body and soon he was breathing deeply with satisfaction. He was lost to a world where he indulged his aberrations.

Seeing her chance, Gretchen scrambled to her feet and donned her torn and ravaged clothing. Without a backward glance she quietly left the room, knowing she would never return.

Chapter Twenty-three

Frau Holtz stood next to Regan's bed in the darkened room where the sun-bronzed giant thrashed about in delirium. Her expression was more dour than usual, reflecting the pain and pity churning within her. Lifting her eyes, she gazed at the doctor and read worry and indecision in his face.

Clearing his throat, the short, outmodishly dressed physician turned to avoid the housekeeper's accusing glare. "The wound is to the bone, but it will be a miracle if he doesn't perish of the fever. Regan will become a madman if he loses his arm. Someone must stay with him every moment. Where is Mevrouw van der Rhys? She must be told."

"The Mevrouw will come shortly. She's been in retreat, and shortly before the Mynheer was brought home she called for her bath water. It won't be long now." Frau Holtz's disapproval of her mistress was evident in the tone of her voice.

"I can't wait about for her, Frau Holtz. Night has already fallen and Mevrouw Sankku, the clerk's wife, is ready to birth her first child. Follow the instructions I gave you and I'll be back in the morning. If his fever hasn't broken, I may have to take his arm." The doctor's voice said this was more than a possibility, it was inevitable. "Hurry the Mevrouw along. Make her understand the situation. Tomorrow's sunset may see her a widow!"

Picking up his heavy, black bag, he followed Frau Holtz to the door.

The housekeeper muttered to herself as she retraced her footsteps to Regan's door. She looked in and satisfied herself that he had not changed position. The drug the physician had administered was taking effect.

Sirena hurried down the hall toward Regan's room. Frau Holtz seemed to be guarding the door, a worried, forbidding expression lining her plain peasant's face. "The doctor has just left. He'll return in the morning. He's worried he may have to take the Mynheer's arm . . . if he lives!"

Sirena gasped, "I'll go to him at once!"

Frau Holtz moved to block the doorway. "The doctor said I was to stay with him and nurse him." The housekeeper's tone was guarded, her expression suspicious.

"I will see to my husband, Frau Holtz, I won't be interfered with! You will repeat the doctor's instructions of what must be done and I will do it. Quickly now!"

The housekeeper's eyes were cold and unreadable as she stepped aside to allow Sirena passage into Regan's room. In a bone-chilling tone she repeated the physician's instructions.

"Mevrouw, how will you manage if Mynheer needs to be restrained?"

"My brother Caleb will help me, Frau Holtz."

Stepping closer to the bed, Sirena stared down at Regan's fever-flushed face. She clenched her fists to still their trembling and forced her face into lines that would not betray her inner emotions. She had done this! Unable to restrain herself any longer, Sirena dropped to her knees and gently touched Regan's feverish brow. He lay so still, so quietly, as quietly as death must lay. Her fingers felt scorched by their fleeting contact with his brow. Her eyes traveled downward to his bandaged arm which lay atop the coverlet. Blood and pus were already soaking through the bandages. Tears glistened in her eyes, illuminating them like stained-glass windows in a chapel. She had done this! She must help him!

Sirena lifted her eyes and held the housekeeper in a steady stare. In a voice that was stronger than she felt, she ordered, "On your way back to the kitchen send my brother to me." In that one simple sentence she had challenged Frau Holtz's right to be with Regan. Sirena imagined she could almost hear Frau Holtz's nerves crackle with rage but she kept her gaze steady, with an imperious lift to her chin. Whatever Frau Holtz was about to say in retaliation, she apparently thought better of it and accepted Sirena's dismissal. Head held high, her coronet of salt-and-pepper braids adding to her regal bearing, Frau Holtz left the room.

Regan began thrashing about on the bed again and Sirena attempted to soothe him with cool compresses and gently reassuring murmurs. Caleb quietly entered the room; he took in the scene, and winced when he saw the tears shining in Sirena's eyes.

"How . . . how bad is he, Sirena?"

"Very. Look at his arm. Frau Holtz told me the doctor's instructions and gave me these powders he left. But I don't trust them. Go to my room and bring me those powders in my medicine chest.

They're the same kind you used to save my arm; pray God they'll help Regan."

"But . . ." Caleb began, indecision flashing in his eyes. "Perhaps the doctor *did* know best."

"No buts, Caleb. We have to take the chance. The doctor has so little faith in the prescription he left that he fully expects to amputate in the morning."

Regan again stirred fretfully, and tried to speak. Sirena grasped his hand in a firm grip and spoke soothingly. Her soft words seemed to calm him and he quieted. Placing a cool cloth on his forehead, she gently wiped his face and neck. "I've done this to you, Regan, but I won't let them take your arm. I won't let you die like that, you have my word on it," she said quietly.

Regan's blue eyes opened, and were cloudy and pain-filled. He looked up and tried to focus on her face. But the face was a blur as were her words. Nevertheless, he felt comforted by her presence and by her gentle touch. His heavy fringe of eyelashes fluttered and closed.

Moments later, Caleb reentered the room, Sirena's medicine chest under his arm. "Sirena," he said, "the smell in here is worse than bilge! What is it?"

"It's his arm, Caleb. I think what you smell is the onset of putrefaction. That's probably why the doctor feels the arm must come off. We'll have to reopen the wound to clean it and when we do he'll scream to the high heavens. You'll have to hold him down and he'll fight like a tiger. First secure his good arm to the bedpost, then the injured arm. You'll have to straddle his chest to keep him down on the bed. Do you think you can do it?"

"I'll do it," Caleb said, his young mouth set in a grim line.

Within minutes Regan was securely bound to the bedposts. Caleb was in position across Regan's chest, pressing the hard, muscular shoulders down into the mattress. Sirena quickly unwound the bloody bandage over the wound, drawing in her breath at the sight of the gash. "Caleb, was my arm this bad? Look quickly!"

Caleb gulped when he saw the festered opening oozing blood and infected pus. "It might have been, but we didn't let it get this far. What kind of scurves does Regan employ on his ships that not one among them knew how to treat the wound until they could get to port?" Sirena sympathized and understood the anger she saw in Caleb's face. The boy admired Regan and it was inconceivable to him that Regan's men could have neglected their captain this way.

Steeling herself for what was to come, Sirena withdrew a sharp knife from her medicine chest. She lit a candle and drew the blade through the tip of the wavering flame. Without hesitation, she slit the wound along the original cut with a fluid motion. Blood and pus spurted and drained from her lancing. Caleb forced Regan down on the bed, exerting all the strength within his sturdy twelve-year-old body. Regan growled and cursed and damned the monster eating his arm. In his delirium he imagined he was the object of a shark attack. This, Caleb understood from Regan's ramblings and the boy was once again in awe of the bronzed sun god who would curse and swear and fight like the devil and never give in to the most feared fate of any seaman, death by those greedy demons of the sea — sharks!

"I have to drain the pus. Hold him Caleb, he'll rave like a madman." Drawing in a great breath, Sirena pressed the edges of the wound together. Regan's cries and thrashings jolted her backwards. When she regained her position, she swabbed away the fresh blood which was now free of the yellow-green pus. Her movements were hurried as she lavishly sprinkled a dull-yellow powder over the wound and covered it with a thick strip of bandage.

Caleb and Sirena were totally engrossed in Regan, so much so that neither of them heard Frau Holtz enter the room. Suddenly Sirena was jerked back away from Regan and soundly slapped across the face. "Witch!" the housekeeper spat vehemently, "what do you think you're doing to the Mynheer?" Wildly, Frau Holtz yanked Caleb off Regan's chest.

Sirena retaliated angrily, grasping Frau Holtz's arm and flinging the woman against the far wall. Panting from the exertion, Sirena gasped, "Are you mad? The Mynheer is fighting for his life. Why are you behaving this way?"

"I saw what you were doing, you're a witch! What have you and your brother done to him? He's as still as death! The doctor will hear of what you've done!"

"If left to that stupid doctor's devices, I would be a widow by morning! Now get out of here and don't come back!"

The stately housekeeper rubbed her shoulder.

"You'll regret this, Mevrouw," she hissed viciously.

"Perhaps I will," Sirena retorted, "but the order still stands. Get out and don't come back!"

The sharp slam of the closing door made Caleb sigh with relief. "We must have looked like a coven of witches sacrificing Regan in a ritual. I can understand what she must have thought when she saw me sitting on his chest and you leaning over his arm, your hands smeared with his blood!"

A slow smile broke out on Sirena's face as the ridiculousness of the situation hit her. "I can see your point, Caleb. Nevertheless, that one takes too much upon herself!" Sirena's cheek was beginning to smart and she knew there was a brand from Frau Holtz's fingers on her face.

Caleb and Sirena decided to alternate their watch over Regan. Taking the first watch as Caleb slept atop a quilt in the corner of the room, Sirena sat next to the bed, her slim white hand covering Regan's.

From time to time Regan moaned and thrashed on the bed. Sirena would speak in a low, soothing tone and he would quiet. At one point, his sun-darkened hand sought hers and he tried to grasp it, only to have his strength ebb. Moans of pain darkened his features. Sirena's eyes were tortured as she watched Regan fight the fever. Again she changed the dressing on his injured arm. Something was wrong, the signs of putrefaction were more evident than before. Frightened, she bent to look closer with the aid of the lamp. Merciful God!

On trembling legs she raced to the corner to

wake Caleb. "Quickly! Come see his arm." Shaking with fear, Caleb looked at Sirena.

"Lock the doors and come back here!" Sirena rapidly told Caleb what had to be done. "It will take strength you don't have, Caleb. You will have to find a way to be strong. He can't move the arm. I'll do it," she said through clenched teeth. "If he's not to lose his arm, it's the only chance he has." Before she could think twice or change her mind, she held the long, flat blade of a knife to the candle flame. Regan struggled and writhed beneath Caleb as he fought for escape from the pain. Caleb sat atop Regan's chest with his hands pressed into his hard, sinewy shoulders.

"It's done, Caleb. Put cool cloths on his forehead, while I see to the dressing. I think you can untie his arms now."

"No!" Caleb said fearfully, "leave him tied till the fever abates." Sirena agreed while she sprinkled the yellow powder over Regan's seared flesh and laid a clean dressing on the arm.

"Will it work?"

"God only knows. There isn't anything else to do. Now all we can do is wait. Go back to sleep."

Regan lay quiet, breathing in uneven gasps. Sirena held his hand and dozed from time to time. Toward dawn, she fell into a quiet sleep.

Regan opened his eyes and focused on the woman on the chair next to him. Wearily he closed his eyes, his arm wracked with pain. What in the name of God was wrong with him? Where was he? His vision blurred as he tried to look around the room. He needed help. His glazed vision settled on the sleeping woman on the chair with her hair hanging loosely from its pins. The Sea Siren! Would she help him? He opened his mouth to cry out when she woke and leaned over him. Soft soothing words were being said but he was unable to distinguish what they were. Somehow they were like a balm to his ear. Gentle hands wiped his face, cool lips touched his forehead, his cheeks, and his mouth. Opening his eyes he stared into the depths of green-water pools. Why would the Sea Siren cry for him? He had to speak, to ask what was happening. Gasping, he opened his mouth only to have those same cool lips cover his. His head swam dizzily as remembered sensations flooded his body.

"I'm sorry, I'm so sorry," Sirena said softly. "I didn't mean it to come to this. It would have been better if I killed you." The tears she had long held in check were now streaming down her cheeks.

"You bested me, Siren," Regan said, his voice rough and hoarse, his head whirling.

"Shh," Sirena said, laying a finger to his lips. "You must rest now to regain your strength." Regan slept, his mind whirling backwards in time to the decks of the black ship and the embrace of the Sea Siren.

"It is time to change the dressings. I'm almost afraid to look, little brother. The doctor will be here soon and we may have some problems."

Her first thought was to pull the dressing away with one motion. Some inner voice warned her to ease it off. "Look, Caleb," she whispered excitedly, "a scab is forming."

Caleb breathed a sigh of relief as he looked at

the thin crust which was forming over the wound. Sirena herself closed her eyes in relief.

"What of his fever?" Caleb asked anxiously.

"We can do nothing but let it run its course. We'll continue with the cool cloths and the medicine."

"I'll watch him if you want to bathe and change your clothing," Caleb volunteered.

"Don't take your eyes from him, Caleb. Continue with the cool cloths and I'll return as soon as possible."

Sirena was in the process of buttoning the sleeves of her gown when Caleb burst into the room. "The doctor says he'll have to amputate his arm and Regan is half awake! Hurry, Sirena!"

"What! The fool! Did he look at the arm?"

"Aye. But he says the poisons are in Regan's body from the arm and that is why the fever still rages. Don't, please don't let them cut off his arm!" Caleb pleaded as they laced down the corridor.

Sirena flung open the door, her eyes wild, her hair streaming down her shoulders. "What is this my brother tells me that you will take the arm? What foolish talk is this?"

"Look to your husband, Mevrouw. Do you see how the fever engulfs him? The poisons from the arm are all through his body!"

"The arm is on the mend! Open your eyes, old man, open them wide! The dressing is clean and the wound has crusted!"

"I have been Mynheer van der Rhys's physician for many years. My judgment has never been questioned before!"

401

Regan lay, his eyes half open, listening to the exchange between the doctor and the Siren. They wanted to cut off his arm. No, that wasn't right. The doctor wanted to cut off his arm and the Sea Siren was opposing him.

"You will not take his arm," Sirena said coldly.

"It's necessary. Do you think I like the idea of taking off a man's arm? Especially a man like Regan? I tell you, it's necessary!"

"And I tell you it's not necessary. The fever will run its course. The arm mends. My husband is half lucid, why don't you ask him before you make any more decisions?" Sirena said quietly, her eyes chips of frozen seawater.

"The man is in a delirium, he can't know what is going on. I am the physician!"

"And I, Mynheer Doctor, am his wife. I say the arm stays."

What were they babbling? Regan thought. Why was the Siren saying she was his wife? And that fool of a doctor, why did he want to cut off his arm? Why was the Siren saying the arm was to stay? Hadn't she been the one who laid it open? Did she want him to suffer still more? What good would he be with only one arm?

Regan tried to motion for silence. His mouth felt dry and full of lint. He had to make them understand the arm was to stay. He would rather be dead than lose it!

Sirena, seeing Regan's desperate condition, bent low and whispered soothingly, "Have no fear, I'll not allow him to take your arm." Her calm, soft tone reassured Regan and he closed his eyes and slept.

"The matter is ended. I will care for my husband myself. When my husband recovers, you may discuss this matter with him. Till then, your services are not required. Good day, Mynheer Doctor. Caleb, show him to the door."

Left alone with Regan, who seemed to be resting quietly in spite of the ferocious fever, Sirena sank down into a chair. Quaking with anger, fraught with anxiety, she couldn't suppress the one thought which kept surfacing: What if I'm wrong! Have I saved his arm from that blood-thirsty physician just so Regan can take it into his early grave?

Tears came unbidden to her emerald eyes as her mind rebelled from the thought that she might never again know his caresses, perhaps someday, his love . . .

Chapter Twenty-four

Sirena and Caleb occupied themselves in Regan's room. Quietly dusting tabletops that needed no dusting, opening or closing the shutters on the long windows, bringing fresh water, adjusting the bedcover, changing wilted flowers for fresh, doing all sorts of busywork in an effort to keep themselves from thinking about Regan. His fever had broken the night before and after one or two lucid moments he had fallen back into an exhausted but natural sleep. Now Caleb and Sirena hovered about him, anxiously awaiting signs of Regan's awakening.

The faint rustling of the covers brought Caleb scampering to the bedside. "How are you, Regan?" Caleb asked, trying to restrain his exuberance.

Regan frowned and tried to bring his vision into focus. "You've been very sick, Regan, but you're on the mend now! Your arm gets better every day and you've been without the fever since yesterday."

Regan's eyes roved the room frantically and came to rest on Sirena, who was calmly seated in a chair, rosary in her hands. Wearily, he closed his eyes again. Why had he expected to see the Sea Siren? How ill had he been? "How long have I been home?" he asked, his voice hoarse and low.

"Six days, Regan," Caleb replied. "Sirena's

been taking care of you all that time." Vaguely, Regan was aware Caleb had dropped the title "Mynheer" and was using his Christian name. A certain satisfaction permeated his weakened body. Once again his blue eyes closed and he heaved a deep sigh.

Satisfied Regan was lucid, Sirena stood next to the bed and looked down at him.

"We Dutch are hardy stock," Regan said hoarsely.

"Hardy stock is it?" Sirena laughed with a hint of mockery in her voice. "And I thought perhaps it was my prayers on the cultured pearl beads you gave me. You did say that perhaps if I prayed on real pearls my prayers would carry more weight." She lowered her head a trifle and said, "I am happy you're better, Regan. Come Caleb, he still needs much more rest."

Regan regained his strength quickly, and Sirena found he required her ministrations less and less. She soon began devoting herself to his affairs outside the house: delivering messages to the clerks in his office, dealing with the most urgent business matters. She had learned from Caleb that Regan asked every day if there were any word of the Sea Siren. It gave her a certain vicarious pleasure to know Regan was obviously hopelessly enamored of the ruthless female pirate. When she realized to what extent Regan dwelled on his fascinating "mistress of the sea," Sirena took extra pains with her appearance to obscure the most obvious similarities. She kept her hair brushed sleekly back into the heavy knot at the back of her neck; a black lace mantilla covered her head and cast dark, lacey shadows on her whitely powdered face. Cumbersome, black gowns cut to obscure her figure were as integral to her wardrobe as her softly modulated voice and prayerful manner were to her demeanor.

Every now and then Regan would look at her speculatively, almost searchingly. At these times Sirena would practice a little trick she had been employing for the months since she had arrived in Regan's house. Just a humble little dip of her head and the sides of her mantilla would fall against her face, obscuring her features behind a web of mystery. Before her mirror she had experimented with more elaborate hairstyles, but in the end had decided the sleek style brushed severely back from her high forehead suited her purposes best.

As the Sea Siren, her fine-boned face was largely concealed by a brightly colored bandana tied around her head just a few inches above her delicately arched eyebrows. Still, when Regan's eyes swept over her face searchingly, she experienced a chilling fear of discovery.

One month to the day of being laid low by the Sea Siren's blade, Regan, who had been ambulatory for several days, sent word to Sirena that Chaezar was giving an impromptu dinner that evening.

Sirena smiled to herself, looking forward to the dinner party. She had been more or less housebound since Regan's illness. It would be good to get out again. Leave it to Chaezar to give a party to take his guests' minds off the ominous rumbling which had been emanating from the Sisters of Fire for several weeks. The whole of Java was uneasy about a possible eruption. In fact many families had left the island, pleading the need for a change of scene. No one was fooled, an inner panic lay beneath the public actions of most Batavians.

At the appointed hour Sirena descended the stairs to join Regan, who waited for her in the drawing room. His eyes flicked over her approvingly as he offered his arm to escort her to the carriage. As always, Sirena wished she could dispense with the drab figure-concealing black gowns. She would have loved to wear something more colorful and revealing to dazzle him.

Seated next to Regan in the carriage, Sirena asked lightly, "What's the purpose of this dinner? I assume there's a purpose, isn't there?"

"So, at last you've discovered there are few things Chaezar Alvarez does without an ulterior motive."

Not caring to engage in an argument concerning Chaezar, Sirena bandied, "Does this dinner concern the Sea Siren?"

"Yes, it does. She must be captured and brought here to Batavia." Even while speaking of the Sea Siren's capture, Regan's face revealed his desire for the infamous piratess.

"How do you plan to capture her? She's slipped through your fingers time and again."

"I'm not sure how yet. Tonight some scheme will be arrived at. I don't understand her motives. She could have killed all my men and me along with them. Instead she allowed my brig to sail to port because I was wounded and needed a doctor.

If I only knew why she hunts this man called The Hook perhaps I would almost accept this havoc she enjoys creating. I saw a look in her eye I can't name. She's possessed by a devilish drive to find The Hook!"

"Is she as beautiful as they say?" Sirena asked cautiously, watching his face covertly under cover of the dark night.

Regan spoke slowly and carefully, as if he were carefully choosing each word. "I've seen many beautiful women but the Sea Siren is something more. She's as wild as the seas she rides, as sultry as the equatorial air, dangerous as the seasonal monsoons, as hauntingly beautiful as a rare gem. There's liquid fire in her veins and a promise of a kiss plays on her lips. There's no other like her if one searched the world over."

Sirena's pulses quickened. She knew Regan was thinking of the night aboard the frigate, alone in each other's arms, separated from the world by a blanket of isolating fog. His voice was warm and husky, his frosty blue eyes looked far off into the distance.

"You seem to be enamored of her, Regan, are you?" Sirena asked softly, thrilling to his low, intimate tones, wanting him to continue speaking of the Sea Siren, forgetting for the moment that he thought he was speaking of a totally different woman.

Instead, Regan turned to her in amazement. "You have a bold tongue! Strange question for a wife to ask her husband!"

"Not really. What I find strange is that you haven't answered me!"

Regan was saved from a reply by their carriage arriving at Chaezar's palatial home.

After the elaborate dinner at Chaezar's table, Regan and Sirena, along with Chaezar, and Gretchen and several captains and their wives whom Sirena vaguely remembered meeting before at her wedding and Chaezar's elaborate ball, retired to the drawing room.

In this room Chaezar's distinctive tastes were successfully mirrored. Cool blues and pale yellows dominated the color scheme, enhanced by the delicate teak and ebony tables clustered close to the white damask upholstery on the spindly-legged gilt chairs.

Gretchen was resplendent in a low-cut gown of silver net atop a shimmering blue petticoat. As in the dining room, she contrived to place herself at Regan's elbow, ready at the smallest provocation to smile up at him, dimpling her chin and displaying her splendid startlingly white teeth. It wasn't Gretchen's shameless flirting that rankled Sirena, because she knew Regan was obsessed with the Sea Siren, it was the pitying glances Gretchen tossed at her that made Sirena's nails itch to rake that pink face.

Chaezar moved to the center of the room and held up his hand for silence. "Mevrouw Lindenreich has kindly agreed to sing for us this evening. Any business can be discussed later. Gretchen, if you please."

Pretending a coyness which didn't become her, Gretchen allowed Chaezar to lead her to a position next to the spinet. Seating himself at the instrument, Chaezar ran his fingers lightly over the keys. The tune was unfamiliar yet hauntingly lovely. At her cue, Gretchen began to sing, in French, a love ballad about the undying love of a pretty street urchin for a grand duke.

If she were to be honest with herself, Sirena had to give Gretchen her due. Her voice was a high, clear soprano, colorful and rich. The room was hushed, every eye on the beautiful Gretchen who only had eyes for Regan.

Sirena, whose back was to Regan, imagined he was preening in Gretchen's bold flattery. Slowly, Sirena turned to steal a glance at the effect Gretchen was having on him.

Regan, with his usual easy grace, sat on the delicate gilt chair holding a snifter of Chaezar's rare brandy, long legs stretched out before him. His agate gaze was centered on Gretchen, the lines about his square lean jaw relaxed and softened, a smile played about the corner of his mouth. The looks traveling between Regan and his silver-blond mistress excluded everyone else in the room. How many times had Gretchen sung for him when they were alone and free to indulge themselves in the promised sensuality of her songs?

Several gentlemen shifted uneasily in their chairs. Regan's connection with Gretchen was well known and before Regan's marriage to Sirena these same gentlemen were happy enough to jab elbows into one another and smile knowingly. But now! The glances traveling between Gretchen and Regan were making them most uncomfortable, especially before their wives who, pitying Sirena, would take great care not to suffer her embarrassment themselves. The reins would be tightened in many Batavian households.

Sirena's body temperature rose several degrees. How could Regan denigrate her this way? she thought hotly. I wonder if Gretchen would find him so attractive if he'd lost his arm? Somehow Sirena knew Gretchen would want Regan if he were armless and legless and a mindless idiot. Beneath that blond, voluptuous almost vulgar beauty was a passionate woman who, despite her amoral behavior, truly loved Regan van der Rhys. Realizing this, Sirena felt almost sorry for Gretchen. Regan had used Gretchen, had toyed with her and would continue to do so, never for a moment taking her seriously.

Gretchen concluded the last of her songs and basked in the applause and compliments paid her. At last she turned her triumphant hazel eyes to Sirena. "Your voice is lovely, Gretchen," Sirena said truthfully.

"Thank you," Gretchen said simply, a shard of ice in her polite pleasantry. Gretchen's eyes sought Regan, who was still sitting easily on his chair contemplating the burnished liquid in his glass.

Chaezar stepped over to Sirena, and said in a clear voice, "And now, Sirena, perhaps you would honor us likewise."

"Oh no, I couldn't," Sirena protested meekly over a chorus of gentle pleadings from the party guests. She was about to plead a headache when she looked into Gretchen's eyes. Hate spilled from them and had the look been a tangible thing,

411

Sirena would have been struck from her chair.

"I'd love to play for you," Sirena said, smiling up at Chaezar. He drew her to her feet and led her over to the far end of the room. Seated near the spinet, the glow of the lamplight illuminating her complexion to perfection, Sirena softly strummed Chaezar's ornate Spanish guitar, testing the chords, reverberating the deep tones, playing staccato on the high notes. Her audience complimented her with rapt attention.

She played a succession of short, lilting, melodious folk songs which induced her audience to tap their feet and clap their hands in rhythm, caused their faces to be wreathed in lighthearted smiles. The tunes ended, Chaezar and his guests applauded with delight, and yet Sirena sat, her head bowed in concentration, her fingers poised on the strings. The room became hushed, everyone was alert with expectation. Suddenly, Sirena's fingers flew over the strings, and the music was alive and vibrant. Chaezar moved close to Sirena and dropped down on one knee, his dark, brilliant eyes intent upon her face. He knew from the opening strains she was about to play for him the flamenco, food for the passionate Spanish soul.

It was then he heard it, so perfect in tone at first he thought it was the guitar. Then the sound blossomed and poured forth, spilling into the hushed corners of the room with perfection and clarity of pitch — Sirena's voice.

She sang the flamenco with inspiration, and her audience was caught up in the music's sensuousness, especially Chaezar, who understood its sweetness and poignancy, and could follow Sirena through each movement knowingly, savoring its promise.

As Sirena sang, she looked at Chaezar. He seemed to be transported, her music moving him across the thousands of miles back to Spain.

Regan watched his wife and Chaezar through flashing cold eyes, his mouth set in a tight, grim line. What did Chaezar think he was doing poised on one knee inches away from Sirena and gazing up adoringly into her face? And Sirena! His cool, aloof Sirena. Was her poise, composure, and cool reserve only for him, Regan? Was there a fiery nature and passionate soul, as passionate as her music, beneath that mask of constraint? Was it only for Chaezar the mask was allowed to slip, revealing beneath it a temptress, bold and exciting?

Regan quickly swallowed the remainder of his brandy and frowned. The heat from his hand had warmed the liquor beyond what he considered a pleasing temperature. Bah! he thought, treacherous friends, a flirtatious wife, warm liquor!

When her song ended Sirena lifted her head and looked across the room to Regan. His face was flushed with anger, his sheaf of white-blond hair spilled across his sun-darkened brow, emphasizing the burning rage in his eyes.

Chaezar and his guests gathered about Sirena, applauding her enthusiastically and declaring their praise — everyone save Regan.

Later in the evening, Sirena found herself bored by all the talk and speculation about the Sea Siren. She found herself squirming and fidgeting on the gilt chair. Her back ached with strain, her stomach was queasy and she was feeling light-headed. She'd experienced this feeling quite often during the past weeks and, having no patience for illness, attributed it to being confined to the house nursing Regan and missing the fresh, free-spirited air of the open sea. Perhaps if she refreshed herself she'd be better able to tolerate the balance of the evening.

Excusing herself, Sirena made her way to the ladies' chambers to splash cologne on her wrists and neck. Sirena was smoothing her hair when she looked up to see Gretchen enter the room.

"You did it purposely, didn't you?" Gretchen hissed.

"Did what?" Sirena asked, puzzled.

"Made a fool of me by strumming on that box! You did it on purpose! You won't win, you know; Regan is mine! He's been mine for years!"

"Now I see what you're talking about. The songs you sang were an excuse to bait me. I hesitate to remind you that I am married to Regan. If he had wanted to marry you, the choice was his." Sirena knew her calm, unruffled attitude was infuriating Gretchen.

"There wasn't any choice and you know it! The contracts were arranged long ago!"

"Contracts have been broken over less trivial things. If he wanted you he would have sought you out. I find this discussion in poor taste. If you'll excuse me," Sirena said, gathering her skirts in her hand to pass the angry-eyed German.

"I'm not finished!" Gretchen spat, as she jerked Sirena's arm to push her backwards.

"That was a foolish move, Gretchen. What if

one of the other ladies were to enter the room?"

"I don't care. I have more to say!"

"I have nothing to say to you. Now let me pass."

"You're so cool, so confident. Why is that? If I had a husband who bedded every whore from here to Cape Town regardless of her color I wouldn't be so smug."

"Why are you concerned? Regan isn't your husband."

"He would have been if it weren't for you," Gretchen spat.

"I find that hard to believe."

"Bitch!" Gretchen hissed angrily as she reached out and grabbed Sirena's arm, throwing her off balance. Sirena collided with the wall and brought up her arm to shield her face from Gretchen's clawing attack. Sirena's hand bore deep, bleeding gouges. The German poised for still another attack and Sirena found her hand instinctively reaching for the hilt of her cutlass. With a lithe movement she brought up the inside of her arm and jarred Gretchen's hands away from her face and rendered the blonde a stinging blow. Sirena, having the advantage now, gave Gretchen a push and yanked at her heavy blond hair. Sirena wasn't surprised to see a handful remain in her hand. She was gazing at the curls in her hand when the door opened and Chaezar and Regan entered.

"Two spitting cats," Chaezar grinned. "Who was the victor? Ah, Gretchen, it would appear it wasn't you. Tidy yourself and come join the party."

"She doesn't even fight like a woman," Gretchen spat. "Look at her. Not a hair out of place!"

Regan's blue eyes traveled to his wife and was puzzled. How could Sirena have fought a cat match and been the victor? Gretchen was right, there wasn't a hair out of place.

Regan found his glance traveling to Sirena for the remainder of the evening. There was something about her that made his blood rush through his veins. He knew he had imbibed too freely of Chaezar's excellent brandy. Perhaps he wasn't fully recovered from his illness. Was it the alcohol that made him imagine the Sea Siren's beautiful laughing face superimposed over his wife's aloof, reserved features?

Apprehension knotted in the pit of Sirena's stomach each time she felt Regan's eyes on her. He was looking at her almost as if he knew of her secret identity.

The party ended close to midnight. Regan and Sirena were the last to leave. Courteously, Regan apologized for his wife's behavior.

Angrily, Sirena interrupted, "I need no one to make apologies on my behalf. I merely defended myself. You men defend yourselves against the Sea Siren, don't you? Should I have allowed Gretchen to scratch my eyes out and rip my gown down the front as was her intent?"

"Indeed not!" Chaezar said, bowing low over her hand. "You never need to apologize for anything in my house. I must be allowed to reinstate my hospitality, Sirena. Say you'll be my guest for lunch this week. That is if you are permitted," Chaezar said, looking at Regan defiantly.

"You seem bent on ignoring my wishes, Chaezar," Regan said coldly, his words slightly

416

slurred because of the brandy he had consumed. "I have no desire to insult you in your own home, but I've warned you once and I won't repeat myself. The Mevrouw has many duties to occupy her time."

"What duties?" Sirena challenged. "I'm bored to tears. Chaezar," she addressed the Spaniard airily, "next you know Regan will have a chain about my neck to lead me to and fro." Her laughter tinkled out into the dark night.

Regan drew in his breath.

The ride home was made in silence. Regan seethed inwardly because of her open defiance and ridicule. If he ever knew for certain she had taken the Spaniard as a lover, he would kill her!

Sirena rode next to Regan and tried to keep from being jostled against him. She hoped she was wrong about what she was reading in her husband's eyes. She inched further away from him, sensing she could smell his open lust.

In her room with the door locked, she shed her gown and was in the process of loosening the pins from her hair when a knock sounded at the door. Clutching the gown to her, she approached the door fearfully, hoping against hope that her maid Juli had stayed awake and was coming to brush her hair.

Sirena called softly through the door, "Yes?"

"Open the door, I want to speak to you."

"I'm preparing for bed, Regan, and I've many prayers to say before retiring," she explained in a calm voice that belied her inner turmoil.

"You'll find this door at your feet if you don't

open it! You've got til the count of five!"

Sirena gasped. She had been right! God, where was Caleb — Juli — anyone! Quickly, she pulled the gown over her head and fumbled clumsily with the long buttons. On the count of four, with a yard of buttons still to go, she swung open the door and stared up into her husband's face.

Regan measured her disarray and the panic in her eyes. Why in the name of God should she fear her husband and not that bastard Chaezar? Incensed by fury and too much brandy, he sauntered over the threshold and locked his arms across his massive chest. "It's occurred to me, Sirena, the last time I was in your room I asked a question and didn't receive your answer. I want it answered now!"

Sirena pleaded ignorance, though she knew full well what he was asking.

"Your memory seems to be as convenient as Chaezar's. He also pleads ignorance when I discuss the matter with him," Regan said bitterly.

"Regan, I don't know what you're talking about," Sirena protested.

"Have you taken the Spaniard for your lover? This evening you made a fool of me again with your coquettish looks at the Spaniard. Everyone noticed and Chaezar himself was the cat in the cream crock. I won't have it!" he raged, unlocking his arms and stalking her.

Sirena frantically clutched the gown over her heaving breasts as she tried to figure a way to elude him.

"Answer me, damn you! Is Chaezar your lover?"

"I refuse to answer you, you're drunk and don't know what you're saying. You'll be ashamed of yourself tomorrow."

Regan's face showed his uncertainty. What was it about this woman that could cow him as if he were a child? Roughly he reached out and pulled her against him.

"I want you," he murmured huskily, his lips seeking hers.

Sirena fought his embrace, but her struggles were useless against his powerful arms. Ignoring her protests, he picked her up in his arms and cradled her head to his chest, all the while whispering soft, indistinct phrases.

Almost tenderly, he laid her on the bed and began to remove her gown. Head reeling, Sirena gasped, "Please, Regan, you mustn't. Please don't do this to either of us! We won't be able to face each other tomorrow!"

His lips found hers again, his hands worked at her gown. Lost in the moment, Sirena could only surrender to the feelings engulfing her. All was forgotten and she was again in the cabin of her frigate, the *Sea Siren*, surrounded by the isolating fog. Then she remembered the wicked scar on her arm — if he saw it the game would be played and she the loser.

"Regan! Stop!" she cried hoarsely, pushing him from her as she rolled across the bed to escape him. He said nothing, his eyes said it all. She was his wife and he meant to have her.

Drunkenly, he stumbled toward her. She knew if he got his hands on her she would be powerless against him. She backed away, groping behind her for a weapon to stave him off. Her hand closed over a silver-backed hairbrush. "Don't come any closer, Regan," she threatened, hefting the brush.

Still he advanced on her, tearing his shirt open and removing his belt.

Hysterically, she cleared off her dressing table, throwing each object directly at his head.

Fists clenched so tightly his knuckles stood out starkly white, he fended off her attack. When her supply of weapons on the dressing table was exhausted, he watched to see her next move. Menace glowed in his eyes, there was a smirk about his mouth, he looped the end of his belt through the heavy brass buckle, making a noose.

"The devil take your soul, you filthy scurve!" she shrieked.

Still he advanced, portending lust making his eyes as indigo as the night.

"You're not man enough to make me come to you, to make me want you, so you think you'll rape me! Never! You pig of a whoreson!"

Still he advanced.

Her only escape was the door. Regan seemed to realize this. Hampered by her dragging skirts, she stumbled, her arm reaching, clawing for the knob.

In a flash of motion, Regan looped the belt around her wrist and yanked her to him, the threatening smile playing about his cruelly twisted mouth. Half dragging, half carrying her to the bed, he flung her upon it, looped the long end of the belt around the bedpost, and ran it back through the buckle, fastening her securely.

Panting with exertion, Sirena lay there wild-eyed, anticipating his next move. Still glaring at

420

her, he knocked the glass chimney from her bedside lamp and extinguished the smoky flame with the palm of his hand.

After a moment he came to her, locking her kicking legs between his knees. He fell on her, naked now, ripping and tearing the clothes from her body. She could feel the hard network of muscles beneath his sun-ravished back.

Despite her struggles, his hand grazed her body, his fingers tangled in her hair, his lips sought hers, parting them and seeking out the warm recesses of her mouth. Wearing little else but her silk stockings, her body was covered by his, which pressed her into the soft bedding.

His kisses covered her lips, her cheeks, her eyes, her throat. In spite of herself, Sirena was aware of a building response. This was Regan, the Regan who had taught her about lovemaking aboard the gently rocking frigate. She closed her eyes, she imagined she could smell the thick, pungent, salt tang that rolls in with a sequestering fog.

Like the sea, Sirena felt her resistance ebb to be replaced by a surging tide of passion. Her lips answered his, her body arched against him. Just as she felt herself succumb, drowning in a sea of desire, she heard him whisper against her ear, "Not man enough to make you want me, am I?"

Her answer was to pull his head down and press her warm, passion-bruised lips to his.

Chapter Twenty-five

Sirena felt rather than saw the man at her side stir and move from the bed. His movements were quiet as he dressed. Completely awake and aware of the happenings of the past several hours, she could only wonder if the man who stood so quietly looking down at her was aware of her dual identity.

Locked in the throes of passion, some inner warning had penetrated her mind, warning her to keep the wounded arm out of sight. Drunk on brandy and passion, Regan could well have missed the telltale scar. Pray God he did.

Her heart ached as she watched him walk to the door. In the dim moonlight she saw him stop, turn and gaze toward the bed where she lay. She wanted to scream, to call him back, to have him come to her bed and lay next to her where she could cradle his head to her breasts and kiss his mouth in forgiveness.

She forced her breathing to be steady and moved slightly, as if asleep. The sound of the closing door forced her head into the pillows to choke the tears and sobs that racked her body.

Regan stood outside the door, uncertain of the sound coming from the room. Quietly, he opened the door and flinched when he heard her heartbreaking sobs in the darkness. He forced himself back into the dimly lit corridor. His shoulders slumped dejectedly as he made his way to his room. Inside he poured himself a generous glass of rum and stood staring out the wide windows. He was angry, puzzled, and indignant. Another glass of rum and his blue eyes darkened, taking on a murderous look as he gazed out into the dark shrubbery.

Caleb woke, his hair tousled and damp. Trembling with fear, he crawled from the high bed and walked to the wide windows. Why did he have such murderous dreams? The last, which woke him, had sent fear coursing through his veins. They had been sailing the *Sea Siren* home when Sirena called him to show him her arm. Only it wasn't her arm, it was Regan's growing from her shoulder and it was laid open to the bone. Sirena was asking his help in winding the cultured-pearl prayer beads around the wound to close it. He had gasped in fear because the shimmering pearls were covered with the thick oozing slime that ran from the wound. One of the seamen was shouting from the shrouds that the Dutchman was returning for his arm. Then Caleb had wakened.

Though it was barely dawn, he knew he would never be able to return to sleep. He would go to the kitchen and take some cheese and walk to the wharf. Perhaps some cheese and fruit, he thought as his stomach grumbled hungrily.

Dressing quickly, he descended the steps quietly and felt his way down the dark corridor. He stopped in midstride as he saw a faint light shine from Regan's office door. Was Regan working or did he also find it impossible to sleep? Perhaps they could talk. He'd offer to get cheese and fruit for Regan. Caleb tiptoed into the room and stopped short. Regan was sprawled in his big chair behind his desk, a rum bottle clutched in his hands.

"What are you doing up at this hour, Caleb?" he asked, his speech slurred as he brought the rum bottle to his lips.

"I couldn't sleep. It's too hot and I had a bad dream. I thought I'd get some cheese and fruit, then go for a walk to the wharf. Can I get you something to eat?" he asked, eyeing the rum bottle.

"It's not food I need, boy. Sit down and talk to me."

"Is something the matter?" Caleb asked hesitantly. "Is something wrong at your offices? I see you've many papers on the desk before you."

"Many papers," Regan answered solemnly, taking another pull from the rum bottle. "Do you see this paper?" He fumbled among the sheaf on his desk.

"Yes, I see it. What is it?"

"It's my copy of the marriage contract with your sister. It's the first time I've looked at it. I never wanted to see it before. I never wanted this marriage." Suddenly Regan laughed as he waved the paper and the rum bottle in the air. "Do you see this? I haven't read it, I can't read it! This damnable curly Spanish writing. You read it to me, boy."

Regan waited for Caleb to begin. He wanted to hear the words that would absolve his guilt for forcing his way into Sirena's room and demanding his rights as her husband.

Worms of fear crawled over Caleb's belly as he

424

heard the demand. He knew the words on the contract as well as his own name.

"Read it to me," Regan said, tossing the paper across the desk, spilling the rum at the same time. Again he laughed. Nervously, Caleb reached out to pick up the marriage contract and, with a slight hand motion, maneuvered the paper onto the sticky puddle of rum.

"I'm sorry," he muttered, as he picked up the contract and smeared the rum over the written words. "It's difficult to read," he murmured, "with rum soaking the paper."

"You'll manage," Regan said, watching Caleb suspiciously, "read me the words!"

"It . . . says that . . . Sirena Elena Esthera Ramos y Córdez," Caleb whispered, substituting Sirena's name for Isabel's, "oldest daughter of Don Antonio Córdez Savars, is promised this day to Regan Pieter van der Rhys. It says . . . that both elders are in agreement, that joining these two old, revered families is an honor for them both. Then it goes on to define the financial agreements."

"Is that what it says?" Regan laughed drunkenly.

"Yes," Caleb whispered. "Shall I put it away?"

"Don't put it away, throw it away! I'll replace it one day with a divorce paper!"

"Why would you do that?" the boy quivered.

"Why? Because I would, that's why." Rum dribbled down his chin and he wiped it away with an angry gesture. Hearing that Sirena was legally his wife had in no way assuaged the guilt he felt because of the way he had forced himself on her.

"You see before you a broken man. My business

425

has been ruined by that damn devil Siren. I've lost face with my men. I've been bested by a woman, wounded nearly fatally. And . . ." the rum bottle found its way to his mouth again, "and I'm no longer a man of my word. Today was the first time I ever went back on something I gave my word on."

"One little mistake, Regan. Perhaps the problem can be mended. Right now you're not thinking straight. Tomorrow you may feel differently."

"When a man loses his honor, there's nothing left," he hiccuped drunkenly.

The man looked so lost, so humble, Caleb was off the chair and behind the desk in a second's time. He knelt at Regan's knee, his brunette head raised to look into Regan's blurred eyes. "What is it you did, Regan, that you feel cannot be mended?" He wanted to comfort this strange man with the sad eyes. What could he do? What could he say?

"To speak of the matter only makes me . . . fetch me a bottle of rum. I don't wish to speak of my dishonor."

Caleb uncorked the bottle and handed it to Regan. Regan tilted the bottle and drank greedily.

"Perhaps if you speak of the matter it won't be so bad," the boy said softly.

The Dutchman looked down at the boy at his knee and frowned. A large bronzed hand reached out clumsily to touch the dark head. He drew the boy closer to his knee and spoke simply, all signs of drunkenness gone. "Perhaps you would understand, you're almost a man. I gave my word to your sister that our marriage was to be in name only. Tonight I violated her like a madman. I used

426

her. I was an animal. I'm torn two ways. At first, I had thoughts of only the Sea Siren. She was in my blood, she still is and will remain so forever. She will always be a part of me. And then there is your sister, my wife. As each day goes by, I see in her things that please me. She crawled into my blood when I least suspected it. One woman pulls me one way and the other pulls another."

"But the Sea Siren tried to kill you! How can you love her?" Caleb tried to distract him from his comparison.

"She could have killed me, but she didn't. I think now I understand what drives her. She carries a vengeance in her as I did. I know now I can never bring my wife back from the dead. The ship which was named after her lies at the bottom of the seas. And my son . . . I don't know if he's alive or dead.

"If he's alive, I can only hope someone cares for him and gives him a good life. I no longer carry vengeance in my heart. It is over and done. The Sea Siren taught me this. I see what vengeance has done to her, what it did to me. One day she'll find her quarry and then she'll be at peace. Till then, she'll never give up. I respect this in her."

"If you could capture her, what would you do?" Caleb asked hesitantly.

"I don't know. Perhaps I'd kill her so I could rest without her on my mind every second of the day. She can never be mine. She's as free as the wind and the seas. I doubt there's a man alive who could tame her and call her his own."

"I think you're such a man, Regan. I think you could capture her and make her love you."

"One cannot make someone love them. On the other side of the coin is your sister. She crept into my blood and she is possessing me like the Sea Siren does." The bronze hand idly stroked Caleb's dark head as he spoke.

Caleb was still, the sensation so pleasing he never wanted to move. It was almost like having a father. "What will you do now?"

"Now I'm going to sleep. And you, my boy, get some food in your stomach and go for that walk to the wharf. But before you go, I have a present for you. Open the drawer of the desk. It's yours."

Caleb reached into the drawer and withdrew the small model of the *Tita*.

"Regan, you mean to give me this?" the boy asked, his eyes lighting with happiness. "But I can't accept it. It's all you have left of the *Tita*, your wife and son."

"That's why I'm giving it to you. There's no need for me to stare at it every day and torture myself. Didn't you hear me when I said the Sea Siren taught me something? There's no room in this world for vengeance. It's over. The *Tita* is yours. What do you think of the carving on her bow?"

Carefully, the boy turned the ship around in his hands. His eyes widened at the carving. "She's beautiful. Was this your wife? Did the same man who carved the *Java Queen* do this?"

"The same man. Tita was the most beautiful girl on the island when I married her. It's an exact likeness."

"She . . . she looks like someone . . . ." Caleb shook his head, unable to place the likeness in his mind. "I'll treasure it. Thank you, Regan."

428

"There's no need for thanks. I wanted you to have it. Perhaps it will give you pleasure. It gave me only pain and vengeance. Go now and see to your stomach. I can hear it howling from here."

Regan leaned back in his deep chair and rubbed his temples. His brain felt as if it were on fire. He needed sleep. With one sweep, he gathered all the papers, including the marriage contract with its wide stain of rum on it, and slipped them haphazardly into the box. Why look at them again? The boy had read the words. Why continue to torture himself?

Chapter Twenty-six

Chaezar leaned back and crossed one elegantly clad leg over the other, his cigar held loosely between long, slender, graceful fingers. His dark eyes were warm and soft as he gazed at the woman seated across from him.

"Your beauty leaves me almost gasping for breath," he said suavely as he stroked his pointed beard. Sirena watched, fascinated at the soft sure strokes he gave to his luxuriant beard, much the way a man would caress a woman. Sirena leaned back languidly and said, "I'm pleased, Chaezar, that you find me beautiful. But then we Spanish have always had an eye for beauty." Why was she so relaxed? Was it the wine? She felt so . . . so delicious. Chaezar smiled sensuously, his dark eyes lighting.

Sirena basked in the warm tones of her native tongue. An attractive man, a glass of excellent wine, and . . . She was jarred from her wicked thoughts as Chaezar spoke:

"I've desired you from the first moment I saw you. You're the most beautiful woman I've ever seen. Let's not fence, beautiful lady. I want you for myself. Divorce Regan! I'll whisk you away to a place where we'll live a life of luxury and ease. I'll treasure you as one does a rare work of art."

Sirena was shaken. What was she to say? She wouldn't fence. "Chaezar," she said lightly, "you

430

covet another's wife." She smiled and sipped at the wine she held in her hand. It was an effort to keep her eyes open. Shaking her head to clear it, she said softly, "I find you most . . . gallant. When we speak our native tongue, I warm to you. I appreciate the way you have befriended me. However, I don't think that Regan will be too quick to give me a divorce." She held up a hand to ward off Chaezar's outburst. "He takes his pleasures where he finds them. I know this. But, he will never agree to a divorce. Yes," she said teasingly, "I am not above a little dalliance on the side. When I am ready," she added hastily as she noticed his eyes grow hot and wanton.

"I wouldn't want to rush you into any decision you were unable to carry out." His voice was soft and sensuous as he rose to his feet and looked down at Sirena. Her heart whipped in her chest for a moment as she gazed into his smoldering, dark eyes. She blinked again as Chaezar helped her to her feet. She swayed, held his arm for support. What was wrong with her? Why did she feel so . . . so delicious and abandoned? She smiled to herself. Why was Regan looking at her like that? No . . . not Regan, it was Chaezar who was looking at her with passion in his eyes. Why was she so confused? She licked dry lips as she tried to focus her eyes. Her vision seemed blurred and a strange feeling was engulfing her. Suddenly she wanted to rip the clothes from her body and stand naked before Regan. Would he like her body? Regan didn't have dark eyes and olive skin. She shook her head to clear it. Regan had blond hair and blue eyes. What was Regan saying? Whatever it was, he was speaking Spanish fluently. He must have learned Spanish secretly to please her. Regan would never do anything to please her, what was wrong with her? She felt herself being half led, half carried down a dim corridor. Soft murmurings as she felt a warm breath on her neck. She had to get these clothes off. The compulsion was so strong she tried to quicken her step. She felt herself picked up bodily and carried through a doorway. She tried to focus her eyes but she could only see vague shadows in the semi-darkened room. How was Regan to see her body if the curtains were drawn? She smiled. What did it matter as long as he could feel?

She felt her clothing being removed. Her own hands fumbled with the small hooks as she tried to remove her gown. Within moments she was standing naked and erect, her arms outstretched to welcome the man opposite her. Gently, he lowered her to the bed and immediately was atop her. She cried out as soft hands caressed her body slowly at first and then more urgently. The urgent caresses were unleashing some wild, clamorous passion so far held in abeyance. Her glistening, demanding body writhed on the bed . . .

Sirena woke to bright light streaming through the wide windows. She stretched luxuriously as she let her eyes rove the room. Where was she? Startled, she sat up in bed, the thin cover falling from her. She looked down at her nudity and again let her eyes circle the room. Memory flooded her as she pulled the cover to her chin. "Mother of God!" she cried out in anguish.

Hiding her face in the mound of pillows, she let her thoughts race. Did she . . . ? Weakly, she brought her hand to her mouth. Yes, she remembered everything now. Regan — no, not Regan, the Spaniard . . . How could he . . . ? How could she have . . . ? The wine . . . after she drank the wine she started to feel . . . there must have been something in the wine . . .

Tears formed in her green eyes as she recalled how she had fumbled with her gown. Merciful God, how could you let this happen to me? she cried silently. Slowly, she threw off the thin covering and looked at the nakedness that betrayed her. Gradually, the green eyes darkened till they resembled chips of jet. Lust! She spat the word. Men were the animals of the earth, not the four-legged beasts which roamed at will. Chilling anger at her circumstances washed over her as she rose and dressed. What would the servants think? What would Frau Holtz say when she returned? How long had she been here? Where was that bastard Spaniard? How would he look upon her now? Did he leave to save her the humiliation when she woke?

Sirena shuddered as she remembered the feel of his hands on her body. She had to leave this house! She had to get home! Home! Where and what was home?

In her daze, rushing to leave the house, Sirena took a wrong turn and found herself in a large, sunlit room lined with shelves and decorative display cases. The sunlight streamed through the iron-meshed windows, glancing off the various objects carefully arranged atop the shelves.

Chaezar's treasures. The display was so ostentatious that despite her hurry, Sirena stopped a moment. Knowing Chaezar's liking for the accouterments of wealth, she wasn't really surprised to see rows of precious crystal goblets, intricately carved figures of jade from China, wrought-gold serviceware from India, tiles set with semi-precious stones from Northern Africa. In the back of her mind she thought that Chaezar would be very upset when he discovered he left the heavy ebony door unlocked.

Just as she was about to leave, the light dazzled off an object on a lower shelf, catching her eye. Stunned, gasping with shock, she walked slowly toward it, her mind denying it was what she thought. Slowly, almost hypnotized, Sirena stepped across the room. It couldn't be! Disbelievingly, she took it in her hands and turned it upside down. It was! Isabel's confirmation crucifix. There were her initials engraved under the base — I.T.C., for Isabel Theresa Córdez.

Sirena's mind raced in circles. When she reached the obvious conclusion, she was staggered. Nevertheless, she knew her assumption to be correct. Regan *had* received the cultured pearl prayer beads in a wager. A wager with Chaezar! Chaezar, not Regan, was Isabel's murderer!

Regan was innocent and she had come so close to destroying him! Killing him! All the while it was Chaezar's cutthroats acting under Chaezar's orders. That's why Regan was so puzzled when she ran Dick Blackheart through! Regan had absolutely no knowledge of Blackheart captaining the ship that assaulted the *Rana*.

Thank God she had been spared killing Regan. Now she would never have to put herself to the test. Could she have actually done it? Could she have pierced that beloved flesh and watched his life ebb before her eyes? No! her mind screamed out in agony, she knew now she never could have done it. Regan's death would have been her own. The realization was string yet she knew it was a fact. She loved him! Hopelessly, desperately! She loved him.

It all fit. Chaezar would naturally have dismissed Blackheart for losing the *Rana*. A little paint and new sails and Chaezar would have had another ship to add to his fleet. Perhaps that was what happened to Regan's *Tita*. Chaezar was behind that, too! Refurbishing the *Tita* and renaming her *Wanderer*, Chaezar was richer by another valuable ship. Only he hadn't known about Regan's son's initials carved on the quarterdeck. If Regan suspected as she did, it was small wonder he hated Chaezar so.

Sirena glanced once more at the heavy gold and mother-of-pearl crucifix. She would have liked to take it with her. It disgusted her to think of it resting on Chaezar's shelves like a trophy. But she replaced it on the shelf. Under no circumstances could she take the chance of arousing Chaezar's suspicions. First she must decide how to gain revenge against the despicable Spaniard.

Boldly, she opened the door of the house and came face to face with Frau Holtz. The old housekeeper did not fail to notice her glittering green eyes or the triumphant set of her firm chin. She al-

435

most looked like a satisfied . . . The Mevrouw had been gone over four hours. Luncheons rarely lasted more than a socially respectable two.

Sirena noticed the suspicious look immediately and spoke coolly: "It was such a lovely day I decided to take a drive to the wharf and see the Mynheer's new ship. Was there something you wished to say, Frau Holtz? No, then I suggest you continue with your duties."

A glib story. She would wager her last gulden that the Mevrouw had been nowhere near the wharf today or any other day for that matter. What kind of religion did she embrace that she would pray with the beads, then go to the Spaniard's house unchaperoned and stay for four hours? Next she would say she was going to have a retreat in her room. What did she pray for? Surely not divine guidance. What would the Mynheer say when he was informed of this affair? A smile played around the corners of her dour face as she envisioned the master's anger.

Angrily, Sirena ripped off her gown and flung it in the corner. She would have to find a way to dispose of the offensive-looking garment. A feeling akin to hatred raced through her blood as she recalled the look on the housekeeper's face. She had looked as if she could read her mind and see into her soul. How could she have let the Spaniard do what he did? That she wasn't a willing partner — indeed, a drugged partner — didn't enter into it. Would he hold the events of the afternoon over her head in some way to get to Regan? Now she knew what Chaezar wanted, to ruin Regan! What a fool she had been! The green eyes were cold with hatred and vengeance as she looked out the large windows into the lush tropical garden. Chaezar would pay, countryman or not! She realized the enormity of her plan. How would she learn of the Spaniard's activities? She would send Caleb to the wharves to watch and listen. There would be a way, she would see to it!

What was happening to her? First Regan comes to her room and then Chaezar drugs and rapes her. Then she discovers Chaezar was responsible for Tio Juan's and Isabel's deaths! God in Heaven, was this what I was put on earth for, to be a receptacle for men's lust?

The desire to kill the Spaniard was so great she had to force her hands to remain still. She could picture her hands around his neck, choking the life from his body. When he gasped and turned blue, she would ease up the pressure, let him gulp for air, then exert more pressure. She would continue this until his lungs burst from the effort. Tears burned her eyes at the injustice of it all. Flinging herself on the bed, she cried great heartbreaking sobs.

"Where has Regan been all this time?" she asked a worried-looking Caleb.

"He's gone to the inner islands for some business matters. He'll be gone ten days."

"Ten days! And you didn't tell me! Why?"

"He just left this morning. Please don't, Sirena, please! Leave him. You've ruined him. No more."

Sirena stood quietly and looked at the boy. "I understand how you feel. I also feel the time has come when you don't tell me everything Regan says to you. It's all right, I told you I understand. This time it's the Spaniard's turn. With Regan on land we shall take on the Spanish fleet. Chaezar set sail two days ago with an escort of three. This time, since I have no definite plan of return, we'll say we are going to visit a friend of my father's on one of the islands. There is no one to dispute either of us. Take the message to Frau Holtz and if she questions our return, simply tell her we will return when we have become bored, no more no less. We'll leave the carriage at the wharf for safe keeping and from there we'll ride to the *Sea Siren*. We'll leave under cover of darkness. I promise you, I shall not attack any Dutch ships."

One day was much the same as the next. The *Sea Siren* would lay in wait in a cove or inlet and, at the passing of a ship, would sail out of her hiding place. If the ship were Spanish, in the blink of an eye it would be attacked and her crew scattered on the seas. The *Sea Siren* would then retire to her haven and await the next passing ship."

On the evening of the eighteenth day, Sirena gave the order to tighten sail and head for the straits. They were going home.

"Sixteen of the Spanish fleet at the bottom of the sea. Not bad, little brother, we averaged almost one a day."

"But you still haven't found the man with the hook."

"I will. It's just a matter of time."

"Ten knots and we arrive at the mouth of the river," Jan called.

"Sail ho!"

Sirena swiveled and saw the sail, a bright speck in the noonday sun. "Sight her flag!"

"Dutch," came the reply.

"Rest easy, little brother, I gave my word that I'd leave Regan be. It's the Spaniard who's responsible for the events aboard the *Rana* and Isabel's death. Straight ahead, tighten sail," she called her orders.

"What if she fires into us?" Caleb asked anxiously.

"A promise is a promise, yet what would you have me do?"

"Run!" he answered.

"I run from no ship. I said I wouldn't attack the Dutch ships and I'll keep my word. You haven't answered me. If she fires into us, what will you have me do? Think carefully, little brother, it's our lives you answer for."

Caleb nodded. "We fight but only if she attacks us."

"She had us in her sights, Capitana," Jan shouted. "I see her cannon on the port." The air split with the sound of cannon. One, two, then three in quick succession tore the decks of the frigate.

"Fire!" Sirena gave the order.

It was of no use, the frigate had lost her maneuverability and limped along in a frantic effort to elude the Dutch brig. But it was not to be. The brig sailed true and berthed alongside the frigate, evidence of the *Sea Siren*'s attack smoking her decks.

"So, we meet again," the blue eyes were no longer mocking, but sad.

Sirena looked into his eyes and wished she could brush away the pain she saw there. She felt helpless in the face of his pain. Her love for him had disarmed her to a greater degree than if she had been stripped of her weapons, the ship, and her crew. Her love held her prisoner. Not by word, gesture, or glance could she reveal her feelings. She must play out this farce, her role as the Sea Siren, one last time. More wounding than a scabbard's edge would be Regan's mocking laugh if he should suspect her tumultuous emotions.

"You seem to have lost your appetite for fighting, Captain van der Rhys. I, too, have had enough of this bloodshed. I was homeward bound. I wouldn't have attacked your ship. You're wounded as am I. Your ship is in no better shape than mine. Both will sink within hours if they're not shored up. What's it to be? I can sail on with my men or I can fight till one of us dies. The decision is yours."

"There's nothing to fight for, Sea Siren, I went in search of the man with the hook. I found him on one of the inner islands. He's aboard my brig. I'm taking him to Batavia to be judged and sentenced."

"You have the man?" Sirena asked, shock marring her green eyes murky as the water beneath her, all thoughts of Regan and love erased by her desire for revenge.

"He's my prisoner."

"He belongs to me, hand him over! This time I won't play the weak-kneed woman."

"Neither of us is fit to judge this man. Let others do it."

"I'm his judge and I'll sentence him! Don't let all this have been for nothing. I can't give up now. Hand him over to me. I promise you if you do that, this is the last you'll see of me."

Regan frowned. "Tell me why you want this man and then I'll decide."

"I'll tell you nothing. We hold the advantage," she said brazenly, knowing she lied. "It's a personal matter of mine and mine alone. Turn him over to me and I'll allow you and your crew to go unharmed. If you don't," she shouted clearly, "I'll run you through. Make fast work of your answer, for I have no patience this day."

Regan stood on his collapsing stern mere feet from Sirena on her bow. Perhaps if he gave her what she wanted he could get her to let her guard down and then attack her and bring both the Sea Siren and The Hook to Batavia.

"Well!" Sirena shouted.

Regan nodded. He called an order and the man with the hook was standing next to him.

"Give him a cutlass and swing him aboard," Sirena shouted, her eyes glittering in anticipation of securing her quarry.

"No, Captain; no, Captain. Quarter! Quarter!" The Hook shouted.

Sirena laughed. "Why is the coward yelling for mercy? I have not made my objective known." She laughed, the tinkling musical sound carrying over the water and bouncing back with an eerie shriek. She leaned nonchalantly into the rigging, her cutlass held loosely in her hand. Fearfully, the man with the hook tried to edge away from Regan, only to find himself with a hold on the rigging and swinging toward the bow of the *Sea Siren*.

"Don't move!" Sirena ordered sharply, her cutlass pointed at his midriff. "Captain van der Rhys, I think it would be best if you lowered your jolly and had your men descend the ladder before I forget my generous offer. You're to follow them directly. If you don't," she shouted, "I'll keep my promise and run you through. You could salvage your ship if she was shored within the hour; if not, she sinks. I prefer that she sinks. Look lively now. Till we meet again!" Sirena raised her cutlass in a salute and gave him a mocking bow. Regan stood as if carved from stone. She was as tricky as a fox and wily as a minx. Briskly, he gave the order to leave the ship.

Sirena turned and jumped from the tackle box with the stealth and speed of a panther. Her eyes glittered as she swung the cutlass in wide swaths in the air. The breeze ruffled the greasy ranks of hair on the man's head. His eyes held fear as he brought his own cutlass up to ward off a blow.

Sirena lashed to the right and to the left, giving no quarter. The man fought valiantly but he was no match for the hate-filled woman who swung her blade with an expertise Regan had yet to see matched anywhere. Sirena darted to the left and slashed downwards with the cutlass, ripping the man's boot to the toe. She brought up her hand and the cutlass sliced at the man's ear. When it dropped to the deck, Sirena lowered her cutlass and pierced the flesh and taunted the man.

"You bleed like a pig!" she shouted. "Already your head is covered with blood. The sight sickens me. Let us get this over with. I'm tired of this play!" With a lightning movement she jabbed to the right and the sound of steel against steel rang in the bright sun. Quickly, she withdrew and brought her arm up with all the might she could muster, knocking the cutlass from the man's hand. Sirena drove the point of the cutlass through the man's shirt sleeve and pinned him to the wall.

The man's eyes were filled with fear as he gazed into the glittering eyes of the woman before him. He looked from one man to the next. He would get no help from them.

"Why do you want to kill me?" he whined. "What did I do? I do my job and take my pay."

"And a few other things along the way," Sirena said softly. "I want to hear you say the name of the man who employed you when you sailed with that pig Blackheart and attacked the Spanish frigate *Rana*, killing her crew and raping the women. Finally you murdered one of the women with your hook. You slit her from her throat to her gullet. Remember? Now! The name of the man!"

"Chaezar, Señor Chaezar Alvarez!"

"I already knew. I wanted to hear it from you!"

"What do you want from me?" The Hook whined.

"I want you to pray."

"Wha— what?"

"Pray! I want to see you pray!"

"I — don't — know how —"

"Then you had better learn quickly. I won't tell you again. Now pray!" Sirena nicked the cutlass, making small knicks on the man's arm as he attempted to do her bidding.

443

"Holy God —"

"Go on!"

"Holy God —"

"You said that before, now pray!" She jabbed the cutlass, drawing blood from the man's arm.

"Holy God, help me —"

"Your God doesn't seem to hear you. Louder, much louder."

"Merciful God, help me —"

"Louder! He still doesn't hear you! You appear to have a problem. Where is this God you pray to? One would think he would answer so heartfelt a plea. Try again, this time on your knees! Loudly and clearly. I want every man aboard this ship to hear your prayers!" Again she knicked the man's arm and, to his horror, more blood spurted. "I want them to hear your prayers just as they heard my sister's when you raped and killed her!" Fear at her words was like a live thing in the man's eyes.

"You're not praying. Loud and clear!"

"Merciful God," the man whined, "help me, don't let this crazy woman kill me! Help me!"

"For some strange reason this God of yours isn't paying any attention," Sirena said softly. "Why is that, do you think?"

"Don't kill me!" the man whined.

"I'll be your God!" Sirena shouted. "Pray to me!" She reached into the pocket of her blouse and withdrew the pearl rosary. With one movement she had it looped around the man's neck.

"I'm waiting!"

"God help me," the man pleaded.

"Yes," Sirena said conversationally, "I'll help you, just the way you helped my sister. I'm going

444

to listen the way you listened to her."

Sirena gave the cutlass a vicious swing and brought the end of it down on the man's shoulder. The loud crack of the splintered bone was fierce on the quiet deck. "Pray!" she demanded coldly.

"Mother of God . . ." *Crack!* and the cutlass sliced the air.

The man's face convulsed in pain as Sirena brought up the cutlass a third time. "Kill me!" the man groaned. "I can't stand the pain." Sirena stood and looked at the man.

"Throw him overboard. Let his compatriots see to him."

The man's screams would ring in Sirena's ears for a long time as her men grasped him under the armpits to heave him over the side. Suddenly there was bedlam and — Regan and his men on the deck of her ship.

"You made one mistake too many, my lovely Sea Siren," Regan said mockingly. "You were so set on your vengeance you thought we would do your bidding, and accept your generous offer of our freedom after you sacked our ship. The tables are turned now!"

Coldly, in a ringing voice, he issued orders and the frigate's men were secured in the hold. She was defenseless.

"Swing aboard ship, shore her, and secure her tight as a drum. You have less than an hour — heave to, lads. Now," Regan said briskly, "we'll go to your quarters and see what this is all about."

"Take your hands off me or I'll kill you!" Sirena spat, her green eyes shooting sparks of flame.

"With what? I have your cutlass," he laughed,

swinging it in the air.

Sirena followed Regan to her quarters. She defiantly stared into his eyes. "Are we to play your game of lust again? Will you make love to me here in this room or will you do it on the decks, like the animal you are, for all to see? You'll have to rape me, for you'll never take me of my own free will. I'm finished. There's no feeling left in me. I found that which I sought. I completed my mission and the end is here. Monies will be paid to your bank account for all the damages you suffered at my hands. Get on with whatever it is you have to do."

Casually, Regan tossed her a rapier. Instinctively, she reached up to grasp the hilt. She eyed the long, slender weapon and laid it down next to her. "I told you I was finished. I'll fight no more."

"The tables are turned now. I have the upper hand and now you have lost the desire to duel." Regan laughed, the sound harsh and guttural in the still cabin.

"Think what you will, I'm finished. At this moment I don't care if you rape me or kill me."

Regan frowned. She meant it. The mocking green eyes he remembered were now dull and flat and . . . lifeless.

"What if I take you back to Batavia?"

"Then do it, don't just stand there making idle threats. I told you that I was finished, how many times do I have to repeat myself? You Dutch are a stupid lot!" Sirena leaned back on the hard bunk, her long tawny legs extending in front of her. Nonchalantly, she toyed with the handle of the rapier at her side. Regan stood mesmerized at the sight of her long, creamy legs. His eyes traveled to her thighs and stopped, the rapier almost dangling from his hand. When he raised his eyes to look into hers, her hand grasped the hilt of the rapier and, with one fluid motion, she knocked his weapon from his hand. The tip of the silver blade rested directly below his navel. "It would be advisable if you didn't so much as breathe, Captain van der Rhys, for if you do this weapon will travel downwards at an alarming rate of speed. I'll castrate you without a second thought. Now back off slowly if you desire to have your manhood remain intact. Breathe softly, Dutchman, for I have no patience left. To the ladder now and shout your orders to board your ship. If you hurry you may save her."

"All hands board the brig," he shouted loudly. Silence greeted his order and a burly head appeared at the top of the ladder.

"Aye, Captain," he said as he jumped with the aid of the rigging to board the brig. The other seamen followed him and then Regan departed.

Sirena stood on the bow, her green eyes laughing merrily. "Good-bye Dutchman! Remember what I said about the monies finding their way to your bank account. A notice will be posted at Batavia announcing my retirement! My apologies," she said, bowing low.

"Tell me something before you leave. Would you have . . . ?"

"Castrated you? You'll never know, will you?" she replied, laughter bubbling over in the sea-green eyes. "You're free, Dutchman, as free as I am. Perhaps now we can pick up and try to live what passes for a normal life." Each gave the other a mocking salute with the tip of their rapiers as the two ships sailed away. Tears formed in the emerald eyes for the things that might have been.

The Sea Siren was dead.

Chapter Twenty-seven

Regan sat in his office, his face a veritable thunder cloud as he looked at the empty space where the model of the *Tita* had rested. Would he ever be the same again? The Sea Siren had found that which she sought and she had conquered it. Was it a mistake to hand over The Hook to the woman? He thought not. If nothing else, he gave her peace. He would never forget that glorious, long-legged creature. Never as long as he lived.

He had other matters to occupy his mind now. His son. He now knew that his son lived somewhere. His journey to the inner islands had been fruitful. If he had to, he would move heaven and earth to find him. When he had been bearing down on The Hook, the scurve had babbled like an old woman, and revealed the fate of his son on that horrible day aboard the *Tita* so many years before. He should have known, if not at least suspected the wily Gretchen and that bastard Chaezar. He would kill them both with his bare hands!

He knew he had to think carefully before he made a move. He would attack the Spaniard on his home ground and kill him! And Gretchen, that bitch! He'd draw and quarter her and hang her on the wharf to rot in the sun! His thoughts were interrupted by a sharp rap on the door and the entrance of a tall, blond man.

"Captain Dykstra, how go the repairs on the

Whispering Wind?"

"The galleon will be ready next week. What's this scuttlebutt I hear?" the man asked.

"What was it you heard?" Regan asked.

"Scuttlebutt has it you found The Hook and turned him over to the Sea Siren."

"What you heard is true. She gave her word she retires from the sea."

"And you believed her?" Dykstra asked, amazement lifting his voice.

"Yes, I believe her."

"They say her treatment of The Hook was brutal!"

"Yes, it was. But she didn't kill him, she threw him overboard and my crew picked him up. He'll do no more harm, so battered is he. You must remember something, Dykstra, men have been fighting wars and destroying their enemies since the beginning of time. And men have, through the ages, arrived at a formal code, a set of ethics and honorable conduct. Not so women. War is new to her, power to destroy her enemies untried. When a woman meets her enemy she has no code of ethics. She's unhampered by a sense of honor. She has a much keener sense of kill-or-be-killed than we men. A woman faces her enemy and destroys him."

Seeing Regan's serious, reflective mood, Captain Dykstra changed the subject. "Chaezar Alvarez left the island. There's a great deal of speculation as to where he's gone, but nothing definite. The only thing certain is that he'll be gone at least two months."

Regan glared at Captain Dykstra and the man groped for another subject. "Frau Lindenreich,"

450

Dykstra said more confidently, "has accompanied her latest lover on a buying trip to India. The man's a merchant and has promised to supply her with the richest silks in the East to refurbish that endless wardrobe of hers."

Regan's scowl deepened, his mood became blacker. "Chaezar will be gone for two months, you say? Why, do you think?"

"Personally, I believe Señor Alvarez is to meet his superiors in Cape Town to give an accounting of his losses. He'll have a lot of explaining to do."

Regan, Dykstra in his wake, strode through beaded curtains and into the anteroom of the most exclusive brothel in Batavia. "Clarice!" he shouted drunkenly, "where the hell are you? As madam of this whorehouse, get your ass in here! I've brought you a new customer and don't send me any of your disease-ridden hags. Nothing but the best for my friend," he said, reeling into the beads. Frustrated, he grabbed a handful of the colorful beads and ripped them from their hangings. Hundreds of beads scattered and rolled across the floor. He laughed at his destruction and, wobbling on unsteady legs, he muttered to Dykstra, "I always hated those damn things. They remind me of prayer beads."

Clarice ran into the room. Regan van der Rhys had taken the place apart more than once. "Stop calling my brothel a whorehouse! What you do here is your own business, but I thought you gentleman enough to keep it to yourself. This is an establishment. Your money alone has made me fat and rich." She kicked angrily at the beads with her plump, slippered foot. "In the future, treat my furnishings as if they were your own. I'm tired of redecorating after your visits."

Regan laughed uproariously at her little joke. "Dykstra, old friend," he said, clapping the nervous captain on the back in an expansive mood, "I've kept this 'establishment' operating. I'm their most valued customer. Don't believe anything Clarice tells you. All she does is bank what I spend here. She's probably worth more than the two of us together."

A smirk on her plump, jaded features, Clarice was busy pouring rum into ruby crystal goblets. Regan could burn the place down, for all she cared. He'd always make good and then some, in retribution. "Luanna isn't here right now." Clarice smiled slyly. "I have two new girls, both of them are virgins, perhaps they could profit from your vast experience." She hoped she had sparked Regan's interest. It was time Luanna, Regan's favorite whore, was set back a few steps. She was getting caught up in her own importance lately. Regan's preferring someone else could shake some sense into her.

"Two virgins," Regan hiccuped drunkenly, "I'll take them both!" Seeing a flame of interest in Dykstra's eyes, Regan said magnanimously, "On second thought, Clarice, give them to Dykstra. I'll pay!" he said, downing the glass of rum. "What have you got left?"

"Nothing," Clarice answered flatly, "the other girls are otherwise engaged."

"Well, disengage them," Regan boasted, "all of them!"

Worried for her trade, Clarice soothed the impetuous Regan. "Regan, why destroy your image? In your condition you wouldn't be much use to one girl, much less seven. Let me get you a room for a few hours. Sleep and then I'll send in everybody and anybody you want."

Regan looked at her with drunken suspicion. "I'll wait for Luanna."

Clarice led the two "virgins" into the room. They were beauties, there was no doubt about it. They were small, and delicately boned, almost childlike. Slim narrow hips extended into lean, lightly muscled thighs. Nubile, budding, coral-tipped breasts peaked out from gauzy shifts. They were a smooth skinned ochre-color. Their eyes had an Oriental slant. Clarice introduced them to Captain Dykstra, ignoring Regan. Eagerly, they began to paw and pet the perspiring Dykstra.

The girls led him up the stairs to the second floor. Regan, standing at the bottom of the steps, appraised their gracefully swinging hips and saw one of the girls reach back to caress Dykstra's haunches. "Virgins, my ass!" he mumbled accusingly to Clarice.

The madam shrugged and gave Regan a conspiratorial wink. "He'll never know the difference."

Regan wiped the smile off Clarice's face by issuing an edict: "I'm only paying for one! Now get me that room, I'll sleep off this drunk and then I'll take care of your girls, all of them!"

Luanna was tiny, a porcelain doll. Jet hair flowed to her waist. Her small, naked breasts were firm and high. Her body was hairless in the Javanese tradition. "Regan," she cooed softly, "Madame Clarice told me you were here." She smiled beguilingly, her small, white, sharp-pointed teeth nibbling at her full, lower lip. "Have you been waiting long?" Regan grunted, neither an admission or a denial. Because of the rum he had consumed he didn't know how long he had been there. Only his aching head told him it had not been long enough.

Luanna slid into the bed next to him, wiggling her hips seductively as she slid into his embrace. She put her mouth against his and nibbled his lips, searching his mouth with her tongue. Regan lay still, accepting her caresses, willing himself to concentrate on her charms.

What was wrong with him? Luanna had always excited him, heated his blood to boiling, he could never get enough of her. Now her charms were ineffectual, her body was too thin, too small, her breasts too hard and lacking voluptuousness. Her musk scent was unpleasant to him. His mind kept searching for fuller, softer breasts, lean, long haunches, the scent of spindrift. The Siren! That's who he longed for, the damnable Sea Siren who was his nemesis.

Luanna's hands caressed him searchingly, sliding over his body in a hot embrace. Realizing her failure to arouse him, her lips became hungrier and she pressed her body still closer.

Suddenly, abruptly, she sat up in bed, her eyes accusing and murderous. "So, you didn't wait for your Luanna after all," she hissed. "How dare you come to me spent and exhausted from the embrace of another?" She was enraged, seething with jealousy. She eyed him calculatingly, her lips curled back over her pointed little teeth, which now seemed carnivorous and deadly. She would rather have him dead than have him solicit another whore. To be rejected by Regan for another one of Clarice's girls would mean the toppling of her position in the ranks. A position she guiltily knew she had abused. As Regan's favorite she had enjoyed being pampered by Clarice and looked at with envy by the other girls. Rather than pay homage to her successor, she would kill him first!

A slight snore filled the small, otherwise silent room. In a frenzy, Luanna was off the bed and reaching for the stiletto she kept hidden in a dresser drawer. She pounced on the bed, the knife poised. Her movements jarred Regan awake. He leaned over and grasped her arm, knocking the stiletto to the floor.

Chaezar's words rang in his ears: "You have to be careful, Regan, these Javanese whores are well versed in the art of murder." Regan shuddered at how close he had come to fulfilling Chaezar's prophecy. Luanna was up and reaching for him with sharp, talon-like fingers. He threw her against the wall, grabbed his clothes from the chair near the door and made a hasty exit.

As he raced down the stairs, naked, his clothes in his arms, he bellowed, "Dykstra, you son of a bitch! It's time to get out of here! No virgin's worth your life!"

His near-white thatch of hair practically standing on end, his face flushed, he was completely sober now. He passed in front of Clarice, who was laughing uproariously.

"I see you're in a hurry, Regan," she shouted as he leaped through the door. "We'll settle up the bill another time!"

Sirena passed her days in distracted idleness. Chaezar's sudden departure had left her feeling frustrated and empty. Time dragged and would continue to drag until he returned and she could plot her revenge.

Occasionally she dined with Regan, but neither of them had much to say. That night in her room stood between them and made communication impossible.

One afternoon Caleb came to her room. "What is it, Sirena? What's wrong?" he asked. In the six weeks that had passed since she had found The Hook she had become irritable and demanding. Restlessness created a hollow look about her eyes.

"I think I'm going mad," she answered. "Are you happy, Caleb?"

"Happy enough," Caleb confessed. "Regan keeps me busy. He's taking me on a cruise to the inner islands. He says he wants someone to meet me. Why is that, do you suppose?"

"When did he first mention this to you?"

"It was just after you dealt with The Hook. Remember, Regan was returning with him from the inner islands? He called me into his office and told me. His eyes were so sad, I know he grieves for his son. When I was there he told me he knows his son is alive and he's determined to find him. Regan's eyes are haunted and he drinks more than what's good for him. You must have noticed the change in him, Sirena."

"I rarely see him, how could I notice a change in him?" she replied bitterly.

"Regan asked me if I remembered who the carving on the *Tita* reminded me of."

"And did you?" Sirena asked vaguely.

"No, and it bothers me. It seems so familiar. Let me get it and show it to you. Perhaps you will notice something."

Caleb was back in minutes, the small model held securely in his sun-browned hands.

"It's beautiful," Sirena said, taking the model from his hands. "Whoever did the carving is a master craftsman."

"Regan said it's an exact likeness of his wife Tita. Look at the carving around the eyes. You can see separations between her eyelashes. Isn't she beautiful?"

Sirena ran her hands over the small carving and looked into Caleb's eyes. Her own were narrowed as she gazed at the boy. It couldn't be. Yet . . . "Tita was a native princess, I imagine her eyes were inky-black."

"Brown," Caleb corrected. "Regan said they were soft as a dove's, and her hair was like silk, her skin was like spun honey."

"She must have been very beautiful," Sirena said sadly.

"What is it, Sirena? I see such sadness in your eyes."

"It's nothing. I guess I'm just bored."

"Does the carving remind you of someone, as it does me?"

"Yes, it does look familiar. I think it's the eyes.

What do you think?"

"I agree. That's what I told Regan was familiar to me. He just looked at me and smiled."

"I'll think about it and if I decide who it is I'll let you know," she said, handing back the model to the boy.

Caleb scampered off happily, his model clutched in both hands.

Sirena sat frowning. It was impossible yet everything would almost point in the direction of . . . Had Regan noticed the resemblance? If he had, her game was up. Suddenly she gripped her stomach as a violent attack of nausea overcame her. God in Heaven, not again. What ailed her? Suddenly her eyes widened and she gasped. Her mind raced as she gripped her stomach and fought back the retches. Wearily, she lay down on the bed, tears streaming down her cheeks. Please, God, no, don't let it happen. Not now, not after all I've been through.

Sobs shook her body as she buried her face into the smoothness of the pillow beneath her head. How would she explain it? Regan would never believe her. Would he kill her? Did she care? Yes, she whispered, I care, for I love him. I love him too much to let him know. I'll have to leave. Soon she wouldn't be able to hide the obvious. Already she had noticed Frau Holtz looking at her with more than her usual suspicion. I have to do something. And Caleb. What of Caleb? What would be best for the boy? Her head whirled and the only consolation she could offer herself was the certainty that this child was Regan's. The signs had appeared long before that afternoon with Chaezar but long after the events aboard the *Rana*.

"Sirena, I'm going to the inner islands with Regan today. I don't know how long we'll be gone. Will you be all right alone?"

"Of course, why do you ask?"

"You don't look well to me. The circles under your eyes get darker each day. Is there anything I can do?"

"I don't think anyone on Java has been getting much rest! Not with these nightly tirades from the volcano." The Sisters of Fire had been reminding the islanders of their presence more frequently with their ominous tremors and belches of hot cinders. Many natives had escaped from the Dutch plantations, slipping away by night in their dugout proas. Still, the stubborn Europeans refused to acknowledge the threats. They doggedly remained on Java, fearful of losing the fruitful properties they had amassed.

"When do you leave, Caleb?" Sirena asked, anxious to divert his attention away from herself.

"Sometime this afternoon. Regan says he must be here when Señor Alvarez returns. He has a score to settle with him. He blames Chaezar and Frau Lindenreich for his son's disappearance."

"Caleb, if for some reason I'm not here when you return, I want you to stay here with Regan. This is to be your home from now on. Someday you'll understand. I promised you the *Sea Siren* and she'll be yours, when you're of age. I'll see to it that she's sent here for you."

"Where are you going?" the boy asked, fear leaping into his eyes as he clutched her arm.

459

"I'm not sure. You must trust me and tell no one what I just said to you. I can't stay here any longer. For Regan's sake I must leave. Please believe me when I tell you that I don't want to hurt him anymore."

"Will you take the *Sea Siren*?"

"Yes, I shall take her. Alone."

"Alone!" Caleb gasped.

"Your promise, little brother."

The boy gulped but promised, his body shaking with fear.

"There's something I must tell you. I'm almost positive that what I am about to tell you is true. I couldn't leave and not let you know. I think Regan suspects but isn't sure. Until that time, you have a right to know but you must not let Regan know and you must guard this secret until such time as Regan acknowledges it."

"What secret?"

"Remember the carving on the bow of the *Tita*?" The boy nodded. "You thought it reminded you of someone and so did I." Sirena grasped the boy's shoulders and looked lovingly into his eyes. "Tita was your mother and Regan is your father. I've suspected for a long time but wasn't sure. You say Regan is taking you to the inner islands today. He'll want someone to look upon you and give him details. You must not let on that you know. If you do, he will think it is some sort of trick. He has to acknowledge you himself. Once he realizes that you are not my brother, he will know that I am not what I pretend to be. Now do you see why I must leave? Don't cry, little one, you'll soon gain a doting, loving father. Already I see the love creep from his eyes when he looks upon you. You'll have a full, rich life."

"And you, what will happen to you?" Caleb looked worriedly at the woman who had been his Capitana and his sister.

"I will be fine. You mustn't worry about me. Will you keep the secret?"

Caleb nodded dejectedly. "I'm too big to cry," he blubbered.

"You're never too big to cry," she said, holding him close to her chest. "You have to hurry now, it's almost the noon hour. Don't look back, little brother, go out that door and join your father." You'll always be my little brother, she whispered to herself as the door closed on her gathering tears.

Sirena looked around the small cluttered room and forced herself to walk through the door. She would go downstairs and leave by the front door. Who was there to question her, certainly not Frau Holtz? And if she did, what could she do about it?

Walking around the courtyard, she saddled her horse and mounted it. She sat for a moment, looking at the house. Who was there to miss her? Perhaps the boy, but in time he, too, would forget her. She spurred the horse and narrowly missed colliding with a dark shadow emerging from the driveway.

"Chaezar! What brings you here?" she demanded coldly.

"And what brings you out at night, atop such a fiery steed?"

"I'm bored," she lied. "Regan isn't here. He took the boy to one of the inner islands this afternoon."

"To the inner islands?" Was she wrong or did she detect fear in the man's voice?

"Yes," she answered him simply.

"Is it true he turned the man with the hook over to the Sea Siren?"

"Yes, it's true. Have you just returned, Chaezar?"

"Several hours ago. I came as soon as I heard. Now you say that Regan has gone to the inner islands. That's strange, he rarely goes there."

She knew Chaezar was baiting her for more information. "But you're wrong, Chaezar. He's been going there every week for the past month." Sirena sensed the man's fear at her words and enjoyed it. Nevertheless, this wasn't the time to deal with Chaezar. To take her leave of him, she said, "If you'll excuse me, I'll continue my ride. I'll leave a message for Regan saying you called."

"That won't be necessary. Perhaps you'll allow me to join you on your ride. The evening is much too lovely to be alone."

"Your pretense is admirable; however, I prefer to ride alone. I have many things I wish to think about. I haven't forgotten our last meeting, Chaezar, nor will I forget it in the future."

"Ah, my little dove, what can I say?" He threw his hands up in a helpless gesture. "I'm a man, you're a beautiful woman. I was lost in the moment, and may I say it was a memorable moment?"

Sirena flushed. "You tricked me! The wine was drugged and you were the one who drugged it.

You knew I'd never crawl into your bed otherwise!"

"Dear Sirena, you sound like an angry virgin. If I recall correctly, you were quite enamored of me that afternoon and surprisingly experienced, despite the rumors of Regan never having bedded you."

"Pig!" Sirena spat. "You want only to ruin Regan and you thought by seducing me you could break him and achieve your ends. I could understand an honest seduction, but not this contrived affair. I think Regan has something to settle with you."

"What sort of threat is that?"

"It's not a threat. I don't know what he's been doing, but my brother tells me that these trips to the islands have something to do with you. And that's all I know," she said, jerking the reins from his fingers.

Chaezar gripped her wrist, twisted it, and nearly dragged her from atop her horse. Sirena kicked out, struggling to free herself from his surprisingly strong grasp. Pulling backward, Chaezar's grip ripped her sleeve, baring her arm to the moonlight.

Viciously, Sirena lashed out, aiming for his eyes. Shocked, Chaezar stepped back, giving Sirena her chance to escape. Spurring the animal, Sirena's heart hammered in her chest. Even though it was dark, the moon shone quite brightly and his face had been hate-filled. Had he seen the scar? Would he have recognized it as the wound a slicing cutlass leaves? There was no doubt in her mind that if he wanted to he would overtake her and . . . What would he do?

Unknown to either of them, a tall stately figure had watched them from the window. She had been so near she might have reached out and touched them. Frau Holtz's face was set in dour lines. She had suspected for some time the Mevrouw was hiding some terrible secret. She had noted that every time the Mevrouw went into retreat the Sea Siren wreaked her havoc.

Juli said the ailment the Mevrouw claimed to suffer left a film, white and salty like spindrift, on her skin and hair. Then finally, spying from the garden, she had seen the Mevrouw and Caleb climb into the house through the window.

Frau Holtz had secretly championed the Sea Siren and had admired the piratess's triumph. Frau Holtz, along with all the female sex, knew what it was like to be impotent in the face of men's strength.

The main reason Frau Holtz disapproved of the Mevrouw wasn't because of her deeds at sea, but because she believed Regan was being cuckolded. Now, seeing the wild hatred in Sirena's face, the viciousness of her escape from Chaezar, Frau Holtz admitted her mistake. Swiftly, she calculated the days till Regan's return. She must tell him. Frau Holtz knew another secret — Sirena was pregnant with Regan's child.

Chapter Twenty-eight

The cool night air cloaked Sirena as she spurred the beast beneath her. Twice she reined in the gelding when she thought she heard hoofbeats behind her. Satisfied, she continued her journey to the *Sea Siren.*

She dismounted and stood quietly listening for any sound other than the usual night cries of the birds. The frigate lay in her berth like a dark, ghostly phantom. She gave the gelding a hard slap to its rump and prayed he would find his way back home.

Quietly, she crept aboard the dark ship and headed for her cabin. The night lay before her like an oblong grave. She would have to ready the ship under cover of darkness. Her nausea was returning and she felt decidedly weak as she bent to hoist the sail. Her feet were sure on the gently pitching deck and she gave a startled cry as her toe touched something soft and yielding.

"Who goes there?" came a hoarse sleep-filled shout.

"Jacobus! What are you doing here? You startled me."

"I didn't think you would mind if I slept on the deck. It seems the older I get the fancier my notions. I can't sleep on land. I didn't think you'd mind and at the same time I keep my eye on the ship for you."

"No, I don't mind," Sirena said, trying to fight down the nausea that threatened to erupt. "I'm taking the ship back to Spain. If possible I'd like to set sail before midnight."

"You'd sail without a crew? But Capitana, that is not wise! Do you know what the bounty on your head is? It was posted two days ago. You won't stand a chance on the seas alone. It will take but an hour to get the crew together."

"How much is the bounty?"

"An outrageous sum," Jacobus said, grinning.

Sirena raced to the rail and retched till she had to hold her ribs for support.

"And you think you can sail this ship in your condition? Wait here, Capitana. I'll be back in an hour." Sirena nodded weakly. She sat in a pile of rigging, her head between her knees to stop the whirling dizziness. Jacobus was right. What in the name of God had possessed her to think she could make the trip to Spain alone? It would take months and she had given no thought to provisions. Fool, she chided herself.

Tears welled in her emerald eyes as she let her thoughts wander to Regan. Soon he would know everything. What would he do? What could he do? Perhaps he would be satisfied to find his son and forget about her. Would he be able to forget the Sea Siren or his wife? Was she in his blood as he was in hers? It didn't matter now, nothing mattered except getting back to Spain. Back to her homeland where she could lick her wounds in private and give birth to Regan's child. She would go into seclusion on her country estate to give birth, and there she would remain. She thanked God for the financial security which would enable her to provide for their child. Their child, hers and Regan's.

The tears continued to roll down her cheeks as she let her mind dwell on Regan and the child she carried within her. Was this then to be the punishment doled out to her by the God she had renounced so long ago? She would live out her life in solitude with every luxury money could buy, but her life would have no love, no meaning, save that of the child, Regan's child. A lonely succession of days floated before her eyes, each one longer than the next. Would she be able to survive without the love she carried in her heart for the tall, blond Dutchman?

Swaying dizzily, she grasped the rigging for support as Jacobus quietly came aboard.

"Food, Jacobus, I didn't think of food. It's to be a long journey and I forgot."

"Aye, Capitana, we brought the provisions. Go below and we'll get the ship underway. Jan can take the wheel. Do you need help?"

"I'm afraid I do, Jacobus," she said, extending her hand. How strange, she mused to herself as the old man led her to her quarters, never before did I ask for or accept help. "Raise the Spanish flag, Jacobus. I'm going home!"

"Aye, Capitana, the Spanish flag it is."

"It would be well if you secure this ship before we set sail. There'll be a storm before the new day is out."

"And fierce it will be. I noticed the other day that the waters are warmer than usual."

"I fear what it means, old man."

"There is no need to be afraid, Capitana, I've ridden these seas all my life and those volcanos haven't spit out yet."

"There's always the first time, Jacobus. Never before have you noticed the water so warm either, am I right? And the mist, even in my sickened condition, I can tell that thick yellow fog is unnatural.

"Jacobus," she said, clutching his thin, sinewy wrist, "first we sail into Batavia. I made a promise to post notice that when I've caught The Hook I'm retiring from the sea. I wasn't serious at the time I made it, but I am now. To Batavia first, Jacobus. Speaking of posting, who posted the bounty on my head?"

"Captain van der Rhys. It is said that he borrowed heavily from all of the merchants and cleaned out his bank account. He said he would have you one way or the other."

"What's to happen to me if I'm caught?"

"He said you would belong to him and he would decide then what was to be done with you."

A vision of herself slit from throat to navel floated before her eyes as she drifted into an uneasy slumber.

Chaezar rode home in a fury. How did Regan find out? The Hook, of course, but would he have been fool enough to tell everything? Yes, the man was a coward. How fortunate that Gretchen had left the island for a visit. If he were to blame the whole of it on the German woman, would Regan believe it? Not likely, he was no fool.

There was only one means of escape, and although it was premature, he'd have to take it. The

African Gold Coast, to the beginnings of his latest enterprise. A nutmeg plantation that would undercut the East Indian trade, built from the fertile nuts he had been smuggling out for the past four years. His first crop would be in soon and, although small, it would rock the trade foundations of the Dutch East India Company. The house he had built was there waiting for him, and if he ever hoped to live in it he must get away from Regan, now.

Her face grim and purposeful, Frau Holtz stood on the edge of the wharf shielding her eyes from the smoky cinders falling about her. She squinted through half-closed lids and willed a sail, Regan's sail, to appear on the horizon. Where was he? It was time she opened his eyes, told him that his wife was actually the infamous *Sea Siren*, and was carrying his child. The tall, imposing woman blanched when she thought of the expression on his face when she told him that his remarkable wife had also left him. A look of utter hopelessness crossed her face as the vague rumblings beneath her feet increased in tempo. She always feared the Sisters of Fire erupting — the whole island would burn to a crisp and her with it.

Frantically, she paced the wharf, her arms crossed over her heavy breasts. She couldn't just stand waiting here forever. She had to do something. The falling cinders were already clouding the air, making visibility almost nil. Clenching her strong wide teeth in an agony of indecision, she marched purposefully toward the offices of the Dutch East India Company.

Panic had taken hold. Evacuation of the island was all that mattered. As fast as a ship left the harbor another was filled to capacity, making way to the open sea with its cargo of terror-stricken humanity. Men, women, and children, their belongings in sacks, raced to the wharf to board the waiting ships. Others looked skyward, their faces filled with a mixture of fear and disbelief. Would the Sisters erupt? Brushing impatiently at a stray cinder that singed her bare arm, Frau Holtz opened the door of the offices and stepped inside. Chaos reigned. Captains and merchants were busily stuffing papers and ledgers into satchels and gathering their personal belongings. She listened to the babble of high-pitched hysteria with alarm.

"I tell you, it's only a matter of hours," Captain Dykstra said harshly. "There's no way we can escape this time. The entire island has to be evacuated. The question is, can we do it in time?"

"Women and children first," Captain Kloss said quietly. "Has anyone heard from Regan?"

"I wish to know if Mynheer van der Rhys has made port," Frau Holtz interrupted anxiously. "I'm Frau Holtz, his housekeeper, and have messages of grave importance to deliver to him personally."

"No one's seen or heard from Regan. Not since yesterday, when he took the boy to the inner islands. I happen to know he expected to make his trip a short one. He should be returning some time today. God, I wish he were here now with his gift for organization. It would be best for you, dear woman, if you went to the wharf and got aboard a

470

ship. When I see Regan I'll tell him that you wish to see him. Go now, while there's still time!"

"*Ja*, I go," Frau Holtz said wearily. So, these men also knew what she knew in her heart. The Sisters would erupt and place everyone on Java in danger. She had tried, what more could she do?

Sirena gave the order to weigh anchor. Jacobus looked at her questioningly. "Are you sure, Capitana, that you know what you're about to do? The *Sea Siren* won't find a welcome in Batavia."

"I know that, Jacobus; however, a promise is a promise. I said I'd post a notice in the offices of the Dutch East India Company when I settled matters with The Hook. I must keep my word. That will end the matter once and for all."

"The cinders and the ashes are falling more heavily. You'd best make quick work of your mission. We must be safely out to sea when the Sisters spew their hot rocks and lava. Pray God there isn't a tidal wave, for then we're all dead!"

Sirena, her mind elsewhere, barely heard the warning Jacobus issued. Nimbly, she jumped from the ship and almost collided with Frau Holtz. The housekeeper was standing on the wharf, shielding her eyes with her strong hands. What in the name of God was the woman doing here in Port Batavia? Sidestepping her, Sirena raced to the offices of the Dutch East India Company and rushed inside. Bedlam greeted her. Her eyes raked the wall for some sort of board to hang her notice on, when she spied a slab of cork with a reward notice posted for her. She blanched slightly at the grim words of Regan's: Dead or

Alive. Quickly, she posted her own notice. Swiveling around the noisy room, she noticed two sea captains staring at her, their hands full of papers. Quickly, she placed her hand on the hilt of the cutlass that hung at her side and spoke quietly: "I came here to post my notice. I see that the time is not quite appropriate; however, it was a promise I made and one I felt honor-bound to keep. The *Sea Siren* is now part of the past." Both captains looked at her with strange expressions on their ruddy, weather-beaten faces. Was it safe to turn her back on them? Undecided, she backed up, her hand sure on her cutlass. No man made a move to follow her, or comment on her statement. So be it.

Outside, she saw women dragging small children by the hand as they wailed piteously and brushed at the hot ash dripping from the skies. Absently, she brushed ash from her bare arms. As quickly as she brushed it away, it covered her again, sometimes leaving small scorches on her soft flesh. Jacobus was right, they had to get to sea! She must think of the child, Regan's child! She had to protect the unborn babe!

She raced to the wharf unmindful of the people who stopped to stare at her near-nakedness, the cutlass swinging at her side. As she neared the wharf she noticed Frau Holtz turn in her direction. Should she leave the woman here? If she did, what would become of her?

"Frau Holtz, you must come with me. The island is no longer safe. Are you leaving on another ship? Are you waiting for someone?"

"I . . . I must find Mynheer van der Rhys. I must tell . . ."

"There's no time for that now. Come with me! Regan is at sea. Come, there isn't much time." Forcefully, she tried to grasp the housekeeper's arm, only to have her jerk it away.

"Jan," Sirena called, "come here! Bring some of the men, hurry, there's no time to lose." Soon her men stood on the dock next to her.

"What is it, Capitana, what can we do?"

"Get this woman aboard ship, even if you have to carry her. She won't be safe here. Use force if necessary."

"Aye, Capitana," Jan muttered as he grasped one arm and Willem the other. The two seamen struggled with the tall, heavy woman, eventually getting her to the plank leading to the ship. Sharp curses rang in the air as they grappled with the housekeeper. To her dismay, Frau Holtz found that she was no match for the burly seamen and, in the end, acquiesced.

"Capitana, perhaps we should offer the services of the *Sea Siren* to help evacuate the island. What do you think?"

"What do I think, Jacobus? I think the smell of blood is still too strong on our decks for these good people to want to set foot on our ship," she said mournfully. "I'll go aboard. You can ask if anyone wishes to sail with us. We'll take as many as wish to go. Try!"

"Aye, Capitana."

Nimbly, Sirena leaped aboard the frigate and looked around her. Already there was a dull-gray carpet of ash aboard the decks of the frigate. Small mounds smoldered and smelled of sulphur.

Shielding her eyes from the cinders, she

473

watched for Jacobus's return. She was not surprised to see him climb the plank alone.

"They say this is a ship of death and they don't wish to be saved by a devil woman. In all honesty it was the men who said it, Capitana. The women and children were willing to climb aboard, but the men said there were two galleons waiting for them."

"It's just as well," Sirena said glumly as she kicked at a mound of smoldering ash. "Hoist the anchor and let's leave this godforsaken island before she burns to a cinder."

"Capitana," Jacobus asked hesitantly, "is the bounty notice still hanging in the offices?"

Sirena laughed mirthfully. "It lays in shreds on the floor amidst the smoldering ash."

Chapter Twenty-nine

Gretchen Lindenreich looked around her empty rooms and swore viciously. They had all deserted her, every last stinking one of them. Slaves! Ingrates! Give them a home, food and honest work, and they turned on you for their thanks! Fear cloaked her perspiring body as she peered at the falling ash through her wide window. What did it mean? Never in her wildest dreams had she imagined that this time would come to pass. Now, the damn volcano was finally going to spew forth all the venom it carried in its bowels.

She had to pack and get out of here without any help. Damn Sudi, damn the houseboys, damn everyone to Hell! Trunks! Where were the trunks? Damn Sudi.

Close to hysteria, she raked her fingers through her thick golden hair as she tried to recall where the trunks were stored. Behind the kitchen wall. Running to the kitchen, she slipped and fell. Cursing Sudi and the houseboys, she picked herself up and dragged the massive trunks into the middle of the floor. She bent down to open one and was revolted by a layer of mildew spotting the trunk's lining. Frantically, she searched for a rag to wipe at the hateful black stains. Damn Sudi, she should have cleaned the trunks — all those beatings and still she didn't learn. Damn her soul to Hell! She couldn't put her expensive clothes into those moldy trunks. She rubbed at the offensive stains only to find that she could not remove the black spots.

She found a large towel and laid it on the bottom of the largest trunk. It would have to do. When she arrived at her destination, wherever that might be, she'd remove the clothing and air out the trunk. That would be her first order of the day, to have her trunks cleaned and aired and some sweet-smelling cologne placed inside. It was a wonder vermin weren't crawling inside. Damn that Sudi!

Where was Regan? Would he come for her, knowing she was alone? And Chaezar, where was he? Busy saving his own neck without a thought of her. Damn his soul to Hell, too! If it weren't for his slipshod maneuvering she'd now be married to Regan and he would be saving her precious gowns. And there wouldn't be mildew in her trunks. She would never forgive him for the mildew. "Damn Chaezar! Damn Sudi!" she muttered as she pulled at her hair and tried to think what she should do next.

Should she go to Regan's house? If she arrived there with her trunks he couldn't send her away, he would have to help her. Regan's broad back would get her trunks to the wharf where he would load them on one of his ships. Yes, she would go to Regan's. Stopping in midstride she negated the idea. What if he knew? Instead of carrying her precious trunks he'd kill her and stuff her into one of them. Oh, Regan, damn you! Why didn't you marry me?

She started pulling first one gown then another

from the depths of her spacious wardrobe. What to take? Everything! She'd leave nothing behind. That damn Sudi would come back and steal everything in sight. Self-pity welled in Gretchen's eyes as she sought each dress and carefully looked it over for the odious mildew. She wondered if the fungus in the trunk would creep up on the garment.

Tears spilled down her cheeks as she fumbled with each item of her elaborate wardrobe. Frantically, she rubbed at each and every hemline and then carefully folded the gowns and laid them tenderly in the trunk at her feet. She needed help. She was tired and her head ached. Her eyes felt puffy and she must look a sight.

Where in hell were all the men who had professed to love her when she lay in their arms? Where were they now when she needed help with this damnable mildew? Home with wives and families, that's where they were. No one cared about her. Not one person on this whole godforsaken island cared about her. She was alone and she would have to manage all by herself. She'd show them all! Tears formed anew at this silent declaration and she brushed angrily at the salty streaks.

She stretched her long neck trying to brush her heavy hair back off her face. The heat was suffocating. She didn't ever remember it being this hot. God in Heaven, did it mean the Sisters were due to erupt? The smell of the smoldering shrubbery was creeping into the house, making it difficult to breathe. She had to hurry.

Quickly, she raced to the kitchen and returned dragging the second largest trunk, then another trip for the third and last. This time she didn't bother to try to wipe the mildew from the trunk's lining, she just ripped the sheets from her bed and threw them into the trunks, hoping they would protect her gowns. Sweltering in the unbearable heat, her silk stockings curling and twisting about her slim legs like snakes, she cursed the abysmal heat and everything and anything that came to her mind as she continued her packing.

The trunks were filled to overflowing and there were still gowns in the closet. What to do? Raging with the injustice of her plight, she draped a gown around her neck and tied another around her waist after carefully rubbing at a dark black spot. She would have to take extra care that the gown didn't come loose and trail on the ground. Angrily, she stamped her feet and wiped at her brow.

Jewels! She hadn't packed her jewels! Stomping over to the small coffer, she grabbed brilliant stones and placed them in a drawstring reticule and carefully pulled the ties. She looped it around her neck, heedless of her appearance. The ribbons and pretties with which she loved to adorn herself — what of those? They weren't packed either. Another drawstring purse was filled and then it too was looped around her neck. Wailing, she dragged the heaviest of the trunks outside to the cobblestone courtyard, where her fleeing staff had left a broken-down, flat-back wagon used for hauling food and sundries from town. Someone had hitched a broken-down old nag to the wagon, then abandoned it, preferring Gretchen's spirited team of greys and her comfortable carriage which had a roof to act as protection against the falling cinders. Pushing and shoving the massive trunk, she cried to all the gods in the heavens to help her. Receiving no reply, she again pushed the trunk, only to have it lurch against a large boulder next to the wagon. How was she to get it to the wagon? Even a man would be hard pressed to lift it down.

There was only one thing to do. Quickly, she opened the trunk and ripped out her gowns and then heaved the heavy trunk aboard the wagon. Helter-skelter, she piled the gowns back in only to find that the lid wouldn't close. She banged with her fist, breaking one long tapered nail and then another. Blood gushed from one rosy-tipped finger and she stared at it, mesmerized. Tiny red drops fell onto the yellow gown she had tied around her waist. Choking with the acrid smell in the air, she ripped the yellow gown from her side and tossed it onto the smoldering shrubbery. Angrily, she stomped back into the house and repeated her actions with the two remaining trunks.

The trunks secure, Gretchen climbed into the driver's seat and stared at the nag that was to haul the wagon. The old roan looked as if she could barely stand. The muscles in her flanks twitched involuntarily from the stinging hot ash singeing her worn, fraying coat. The animal's eyes widened in alarm when she pulled on the leads. The old roan was practically beyond feeling. The noxious sulphur fumes and the asphyxiating heat were fast becoming beyond her endurance.

Gretchen fleetingly wondered if the animal would be able to make it to town, hauling the heavy wagon and cargo of precious gowns. Her trunks would get to town if she had to beat the dying nag every step of the way. An image of Chaezar flashed through her mind — an old nag begging to be beaten! If he were here, she'd oblige him gladly — damn him!

As she flicked the leads, the beast moved at a slow, dragging pace. Impatiently, Gretchen wiped at her soot-streaked face and squirmed in her seat. She was soaking wet, perspiration dripping down her back and under her breasts. Irritated, she moved her neck, heavy with the dress and the drawstring pouches. She would never give any of them up! Never! She would suffer!

Gretchen was thrown off balance and at first was at a loss to explain what happened. Convulsing with hysteria, teetering on the brink of madness, she gritted her teeth and strained to tighten her hold on the slippery thread that connected her with sanity. The earth lurched and shook and Gretchen with it. A scream was birthed in her soul and welled up through her breast, pushing against her tightly clenched teeth, wrenching her jaws apart, finding its release in a highpitched, almost inhuman yowl.

Cruelly, Gretchen snapped the leads over the stumbling horse. How was it those damn servants had left it behind? Because, she answered herself, it was half dead. Just as the wagon reached the town the horse stopped dead in his tracks and lay down in the middle of the road. Gretchen climbed down from the wagon. "Get up, you stinking piece of horse-flesh, get up, do you hear me?" Savagely she kicked at the animal. The beast lay perfectly still. Again she kicked, screaming at the top of her lungs. "We just have a little way to go, get up, get up this minute before I take the whip to you!"

Crawling on her hands and knees, she inspected the beast and willed a sign of life to stir the animal. "Get up, you useless old nag!" she screamed, pulling the carcass's ears. Her sweating palms lost their grip and Gretchen went sailing backwards, tumbling head over heels to land sprawled out and staring dumbly at the dead beast of burden.

Furious, she realized she would have to go the rest of the way on foot. Climbing aboard the wagon she pushed and tugged at the heaviest and largest of the trunks pushing it over the side. To her dismay, it landed in a pile of sooty ashes. She then pushed over the other two trunks, their contents spilling into the dark, curling ash. Rage gripped her as she climbed down from the wagon and she gave her shin a vicious scrape from ankle to knee, tearing and chewing the last of her silk stockings. She remembered she had forgotten to pack the others.

For the first time she realized that she was just past the outskirts of town. She had passed through the gates in the thick walls that surrounded Batavia. Coming into town by a little-used road, she had not seen anyone.

A heavy blanket of cinders fell from the sky and settled on her skin. She looked around at the buzzing town. Women held children by the hand, dragging them toward the wharf and carrying parasols to ward off the the falling cinders. She watched in horror as a particularly large cinder fell on a brilliantly colored parasol, setting it aflame. Servants — loyal servants who didn't desert their employers — helped with baggage and carried small babies as their parents carried the most necessary belongings. Gretchen wondered vaguely how many times you had to beat servants before they became loyal. On the verge of hysteria, Gretchen managed to drag one of her trunks a good eight yards before she collapsed at the side of the road. She would never make the wharf this way. She looked down at the soot-singed gown she wore and recalled its cost before she ripped it into thick slices. She tied a flimsy knot and looped it through the handle of the trunk. She then tried to drag the baggage by placing the rag over her shoulder. She hadn't gone two feet when the rag came free of its knot and she was right back where she started.

Mad with fury, she shook her head to free it of the odious cinders. She could feel the singed, brittle ends of her lush blond hair. Her skin not only smelled scorched, it actually was in many different places. She would go to the wharf and ask for help. There would be men there, strong men, who would be able to carry her trunks. She would ask, she would beg, she would barter her body, something she had always done successfully.

The first man she saw was a tall, dark-skinned native holding a child. "Help me!" she screeched. "I need someone strong and big like you to carry my trunks. See, there they are back there in the middle of the road." Getting no response to her plea, she cursed the man, telling him to put the child down and demanding that he help her. The tall man glared at her with hatred, gathered his child closer to him, and walked silently away, leaving her standing alone cursing. Gretchen raced to the farthest edge of the wharf where men were helping women and children into the jolly-boats for their brief sail to the galleons.

"You must help me," she cried passionately. "Someone has to help me. What am I to do?" The faces that looked at her were cold and hard. Finally she came to a bent old man helping two small children aboard the jolly-boat. "Help me," she begged. "It won't take long."

"I'll help you as soon as I get the children safely aboard."

"Never mind the children, their mothers can see to them! My trunks are all I have left! You must help me!"

"There's no reason for baggage. We take only children on this trip. You'll have to leave all your baggage behind. Save yourself. Help me with these children, they're orphans and have no parents to look after them."

"Help you with those sniveling brats after you tell me you won't take my trunks? You must be insane, old man!"

Why wouldn't anyone help her, she muttered to herself as she trudged back up the road, all the while brushing the hot cinders from her scorched flesh. She stumbled, breaking a heel on one of her slippers. Limping in a lopsided manner, she reached her trunks and heaved a sigh of relief that they were still intact. What if someone had stolen them while she pleaded with that old man? Why wouldn't anyone help her?

Suddenly she laughed, a harsh cackle that grated on her own ears. Of course! Why hadn't she realized before? She could have saved herself untold agony. She didn't look beautiful! She was dirty and messy, that's why everyone was looking at her so strangely. She would change her gown and go back to the wharf and then all the men would fall all over themselves with offers of help. That was all she had to do, change her gown and dress her hair.

With her last ounce of strength she dragged the largest of the trunks into a secluded spot along the road. Almost reverently she raised the trunk's lid. Which one to choose? They were all so beautiful and each did something special for her. Preening, she cocked her head this way and that, finally deciding on a pale lavender with gold threads.

Angrily, she flicked at a hot ash. She was in the process of extracting the lavender gown when a large, smoldering cinder fell on the gauze-like material, catching it in a winking, pinpoint of flame. Hastily, she tried to beat it out with her hands only to spread the flame further along the fabric. The faster she pummeled the gown the faster the flames seemed to spread, till a spark flew upward to land in her hair. In her frenzy she tried beating at the gown with one hand and raking the other through her wild, burning hair.

"Not my gowns, I can't lose my gowns!" The hungry flame devoured her gown, nipped at her soft white body. Where was Regan, the man who loved her, adored her? All reason gone, her fingers scorched to the bone, she beat at the flames. Two men noticed her dismay and raced to help her.

She was a walking incendiary, it was impossible to recognize her. The men tried vainly to smother the flames, but Gretchen, raving in her lunacy, fought them off. "My gowns, my gowns, save my gowns!" she cried before she collapsed on the ground, a mass of charred flesh more dead than alive. They heard her say calmly, pathetically, "I'll never be beautiful again."

Regan settled himself behind the desk in his captain's quarters aboard the swiftly homeward-bound brigantine. His feet propped on a desk corner, a cigar held loosely in one hand, he was a picture of complete relaxation, but his eyes were dark and angry.

"Wha— what do you wish to discuss?" Caleb quivered.

"We both know that the missionary said you were the child the man with the hook left in his care. He also said that a blond German woman and a dark Spanish man were asking questions about the same child. You. We both know you're my son. I think I knew in my heart you were of my blood the moment I set eyes on you. I was temporarily blinded by other things and took my wife's story at face value. Now I am fully awake and aware of what goes on around me. Now you will tell me the meaning of this charade. We will get down to father-and-son business later. For now the truth and nothing but the truth."

Caleb gulped and brushed at his eyes. His fists clenched, he started his story. "Two years ago I was on an errand near the wharf. I was hit on the head and when I woke, I was aboard ship and out to sea. And there I remained till about a year ago when one day we had made port and I was being flogged for not doing my duties fast enough. A very kind gentleman, Señor Juan Córdez, rescued me and offered me passage home if I would serve aboard his ship. I said yes and we set sail. He nursed me and took care of my back. I felt I owed him my life for the way he intervened in my behalf. We were within one week of Batavia when our ship was attacked by pirates. The marauding ship carried a Dutch flag so everyone aboard thought she was one of your ships."

"My men have no orders to attack ships at sea," Regan said angrily.

"She flew the flag of the Dutch East India Company," Caleb said stubbornly. "We all believed she belonged to you. The men attacked and killed Señor Córdez, my benefactor, and they raped and killed one of the women aboard. It was the man with the hook. He raped her and even after she was . . ." the boy shook his head. "I don't want to talk about it."

"You must talk about it! Now tell me the rest," Regan said.

"He cut open the woman from her throat to her navel with his hook and threw her overboard. Her name was Isabel. She was promised to you in marriage. Her sister told me as did her uncle that she was a holy woman and wanted nothing more than to lead a life of prayer. She accepted the marriage she was to have with you but she would have preferred to go to a nunnery. Her sister . . . Sirena, fought like a wild woman but she was overcome and severely wounded, much as you were wounded. You both carry like scars down the arm. They . . . they took turns raping her, one after the other, day after day. She was sick and burning with fever and wanted to die, but God wouldn't allow her to have such an easy death. I managed to steal some medicine from the captain's quarters and I did the best I could for her. Twice she almost died and twice God spared her. When she was delirious, she spoke of strange things. She said she would take Isabel's place and marry you and . . ."

"Finish it, boy."

"She said she would ruin you as you had ruined her sister and herself. She said she would never be able to hold her head up again. She said no man would want her if they knew what had happened to her. We agreed to pretend she was my sister — and you know the rest. Sirena is the Sea Siren."

"Yes, I know."

"You know?" Caleb's eyes boggled at the calm statement.

"I've suspected for some time, but I knew my suspicions were correct only a few days ago."

"You won't kill her, will you?" Caleb pleaded. "Please. Time after time she spared your life when she could have killed you. Please, Father."

"And the Spaniard. What of him?"

"She hates him. She only went to his lunches to glean information about his ships. She said he's a traitor to Spain. If she could have, she would have killed him. It is you she loves."

"Has she said this to you, boy?"

"No. She didn't have to say anything to me. I could read it in her eyes. She told me you were my father before she left. She said I was to let you tell me yourself."

"Left!" Regan shouted. "Where did she go?"

"Back to Spain. She left the day we sailed to the inner islands. She took her frigate and plans to sail alone."

"Alone! It's impossible!"

"Sirena can do anything she sets her mind to," the boy said confidently.

"She can, can she?" the Dutchman barked. "You know everything about this woman who is my wife."

"Aye, I know her well. Better, perhaps, than you, and you're her husband. Did you know that she carried your child, Father?"

"What?"

"Sirena's going to have a child. I heard Frau Holtz ask Juli all kinds of personal questions about Sirena. I haven't exactly been sheltered, Father, I know what she was asking. And," he added ominously, "she wasn't feeling well the last time I saw her. Again, she didn't tell me this. I've watched her and I've seen the sickness overcome her and the way she tried to hide it from me. It was in her eyes. There was so much sadness there I wanted to run and tell you, but she forbade me. I swore my allegiance to her aboard the *Rana*. I owed it to her and her uncle. I could do no less."

"Blind! I've been so blind!" Regan's voice was tormented.

"You must go after her and make her come back! She'll never be able to sail to Spain in her condition."

"I thought you said she could do anything!"

"Well, almost anything when she is feeling well. When she's sick, like on board the *Rana*, she

488

needs help. Please, Father, go after her."

Regan drew the boy to him. "We should be discussing how happy we are that we found one another and here we stand, you pleading for the Sea Siren and me feeling like the blind fool I am. Do you know I posted a bounty on her head that . . . God," he groaned, "what if some wild marauder finds her and kills her? Fool, fool," he cursed himself. "Come, we'll go after her."

The boy looked at his father, his jaw just as stubbornly set. "Why?"

"Why what?"

"Why are you going after her?"

"Because you said she is ill and needs help. You pleaded with me!"

"Then I won't go if that's your only reason," the boy said angrily.

"But you . . . what is it you want from me? One minute you asked me to go after her and then when I agree you refuse to go."

"I'll go only if you tell me the real reason why you seek her out."

"I thought you were only twelve years old. You think like a man," Regan said, clapping the boy on the back. "You want to hear me say I love her, is that it? I do, son, I love the Sea Siren and I love Sirena, my wife. It is well that I didn't have to make a choice between the two of them."

"You love the Sea Siren after what she did to you?"

Regan nodded. "I too saw strange things in those green eyes. The things I saw in my wife's eyes. That was the one thing she couldn't change."

Chapter Thirty

As Caleb stood at the wheel, Regan watched him, a lump in his throat. A feeling of pride filled him as his gaze lingered on the raven-haired boy. He shuddered at how close he had come to never finding him — and without Sirena, he probably never would have. His heart ached for the sight of her. Was the boy right? Had she left the island? Would he ever see her again?

Was it possible Caleb was mistaken about Sirena being pregnant? No, he discounted the notion, Caleb wasn't mistaken. But how? When?

His memory soared to a night of darkness and shadow, the sound of breezes in the rigging; the warm, moist blanket of sequestering fog; the rocking of the quiet ship on the silently rolling waves. She had been magnificent that night! The excitement of their duel, the sparks dying from her eyes, her sense of drama, her exultant victory over that coward Blackheart. Regan could understand, now, why she had to kill the man. He, himself, could not have done less.

She was a paradox, an enigma. A fighting, snarling cat one moment, then a ministering angel the next as she tended his wounds.

Regan's memory of that night was acute and distinct. So acute that it seemed as if he could conjure her out of the spindrift. His concentration was so great he seemed to feel her presence and he found himself listening for the sound of her laughter. His eyes ached for the sight of her as she had appeared that night, his hand burned for the feel of her satiny, cool skin. He remembered, the sweet, salt-fresh perfume of her billowing dark hair, the sensuous, lissome length of her body, the voluptuous spill of her full breasts, the soft, gripping strength of her thighs . . . All this and more called to him, arousing the familiar deep curl of heat in his middle.

Her passion had equaled his own, he knew she wanted him as much as he desired her. Their union had been complete and total in its perfection, and because of it she had conceived his child. Their child, Sirena's and his.

The vision of the Sea Siren dropped away and in her place was Sirena, his wife, reserved and aloof. Sirena, his wife, who spent more than one afternoon engaged in lengthy lunches with Chaezar Alvarez. Every fiber of his being rebelled at the thought that the child she carried could be Chaezar's.

Forcing his attention away from the murderous thoughts he was entertaining, his eyes searched the sky hoping for some sign that he was wrong about the threatened events. Never during the period since the white man's arrival in Java, had the Sisters of Fire erupted. The most they had done was growl their ominous warnings and then subside like great sleeping cats. But the smell of sulphur was heavy in the air and it was becoming more difficult to breathe. Was it wise to go back to Port Batavia and hope against hope that Sirena would still be there? Would she know enough to

491

go to the wharf and get aboard ship? He *had* to know. There was no other choice but to return to his home and see for himself.

Besides, he needed provisions if he was to sail for Spain. He had explained to Caleb that you couldn't sail blindly without preparation. The long journey would not be an easy one. Perhaps he would be able to overtake her and save some precious time, but first he had to see if she had really left the island. Surely if she stayed, Frau Holtz would have seen to her and, along with the rest of the household help, aided her evacuation. Frau Holtz could be depended on. He was sure of it. But would Sirena listen to her?

"We've lost sail, there's no breeze . . . Father," Caleb complained. "We're losing time and . . ."

"And you feel that I am not doing anything, is that it?"

"I think we should be searching for Sirena. You promised," the boy said accusingly.

"Listen to me, son. You can't just take to sea blindly. Look to the skies, the Sisters could erupt momentarily. What if you're wrong and Sirena didn't follow her plan and go to sea, what if she's still at the house waiting?"

"Sirena does what she says she will do," the boy replied stubbornly. "She's sailing the frigate alone. She needs help, your help."

No sooner had the boy spoken than Regan shouted, "Look at the sky!" Flames were on the horizon and a loud thunderous boom split the air.

"Pray God that everyone left the island," Caleb said piteously. "What happens, Father, if Sirena is at sea and there's a tidal wave? She told me she sails alone!"

Regan's eyes took in his son. "I thought you told me she was a better sailor than any man, those were your words to me, weren't they?"

"Yes, but . . ."

"No buts, Caleb. Is she or isn't she a better sailor than me or any man?"

"Yes," Caleb answered defiantly. "Sirena can do anything!" he said loyally.

"Then there's no problem, is there?"

"But this time she sails alone. What if the tidal wave comes and she's washed overboard. She could capsize."

"I doubt there will be a tidal wave. You're going to have to trust me, son. I'm doing what I think is right. We're going to Port Batavia to see if she did indeed leave. We're only six hours from port. There may be others who will need our help. When we see what the situation is, then we'll go after Sirena."

"You promised, Father, you promised me," Caleb shrilled. "Sirena never broke a promise, she said honor is all-important. How can you, my father, and Sirena's husband, break your word? If you do I'll never forgive you till the day I die. I'll find her myself!"

"You must love her very much," Regan said quietly, as he looked compassionately into Caleb's eyes.

"Sirena is the reason I'm alive today. She's the reason I'm standing next to you on this deck calling you 'father' and you're calling me 'son.' Sirena is the reason for everything. I could never live in your house without Sirena even if you are my father. I have to find her! I have to see her!"

Fear crawled into Regan's eyes. The boy's tone frightened him. He'd find her one way or another. He would leave and search for her — of that there was no doubt. He must keep his promise to his son. He must search for Sirena and bring her home with him. Even if the child she carried was Chaezar's . . .

"Well," Caleb said stubbornly, "what's your decision, Fath—" The word stuck in his throat as a picture of Sirena floated before his eyes.

"I'll keep my word. As soon as we're sure she isn't at Batavia we'll sail for Spain. Agreed?"

"Agreed!" Caleb said firmly.

Helga Kloss, holding her parasol at a jaunty angle to protect her head from the hot, falling ash, marched down the road to the wharf. Behind her followed a laughing, singing parade of young, brown-skinned children.

Mevrouw Kloss led them in song, her short, round body stepping with a light rhythm. Though her lips formed the lyrics and her voice lifted in tune, her innards were twisted with fear. Dear God, she prayed fervently, though her face was wreathed in smiles, please God, help me get the children to the ships!

The children, ranging in age from infancy to six years, were all members of the Christian Mission of Batavia, where Helga spent a great deal of her time as a volunteer.

As they marched along singing, grief clutched at Helga's heart. The mission was gone, destroyed by fire, taking with it countless young lives and that of Father Miguel, who had come to Batavia to care for the orphans and bring them to God.

When word was brought to the mission that the ships were in the harbor ready for evacuation, Helga had been readying the little ones to leave with the help of a few of the older girls. The thatched roofs on the mission compound were already smoldering when Helga had lined up her young charges in the courtyard.

"Start the children on their way to the wharf, Mevrouw Kloss, they're so small they won't be able to walk very fast. The others and myself will catch up with you in no time," Father Miguel had said. "We still have preparations to make for our journey. We'll need our mattresses and fresh linen for the little ones." The tall, dignified missionary kept his voice light, almost jovial. It was important that the children not be frightened. Hysterical children would be impossible to handle.

So Helga, taking her cue from the dour-faced Father Miguel had burst into one of the children's favorite songs and led them singing along the forest path to the wharf. Half an hour later, while cutting across the hilltop, Helga peered through the falling ash in the direction of the mission. There, below her, she witnessed a holocaust of flames. The thatched roof of the main building had fallen in, taking part of the walls with it.

Quickly, almost without thinking, she turned the parade of children to the far side of the hill, *"Kinder!"* she called, "This way! Quickly!" Clapping her hands and singing louder, though she thought her heart would break, Helga led her children out of sight of the burning disaster below them.

She longed to go back, to help somehow, but when she looked upon the eager, trusting faces of her young charges, she knew she couldn't leave them. She must get them to the wharf. And so, she led them onward, her voice lifted in song, her heart swollen with grief.

At the back of the parade were the older girls and boys carrying the infants too young to walk. Glancing back, Helga saw their cheeks damp with tears, their lips trembling with suppressed sobs, but still they followed her example and sang on as they trudged down the hillside along the dusty road to the city. The air was rank with sulphur. Some of the children cried aloud, protesting against the scorching cinders that singed their tender, young flesh. Tremor after tremor shook the earth, but faster and faster they walked, louder and louder they sang. The wall surrounding Batavia was in sight. Hopefully Helga prayed that her husband, Anton, would be on his ship waiting for them.

A particularly violent tremor knocked a little girl off her feet. Snatching her up, Helga directed the children, "Lay down, *Kinder!* See! Do like me, *Kinder.*" To demonstrate, she lay down flat, shielding the little girl from the ash with her body.

The sky was dark and ominous, the air almost unfit to breathe. Distant thunder-like rumblings crashed through the sulphur-thick atmosphere. Her determination bordered on panic. The gates of the city were only yards away. "Hurry! *Kinder!* Hurry! To the ships!"

Herding the children along the streets, she saw one little boy fall to his knees, stunned. The back of his head was bleeding, at his feet rested a dark, gray rock. "Dear God!" she heard herself cry, "has it come to this? Please, Lord, they're only children!"

Picking the child up in her arms, she and the older children hurried the babes along to the wharf, to Anton. Helga ran till she thought her heart would burst. The burden of the child in her arms dragged her down, yet somehow she found the strength to go on.

The wharf was within sight. Soon, soon now, the children would be safe. People were running out to them, running to save the children. European and native alike, all with fright-distorted faces, were running to help her little orphans. "God bless them," Helga cried, tears burning her vision as she ran, "God bless them!"

Each child was swooped up into the protective arms of an adult. Sharp, rapping sounds vibrated the plank dock. The Sisters were spewing a pelting of rocks, hot and dangerous. They felled several people instantaneously, and children screamed in pain and outrage.

Helga caught several blows on her back, but she hardly noticed them in her determination to see the children safe. Working quickly, the children were handed into jolly-boats to be rowed out to the ships in the harbor. Thick, heavy tarpaulins were used to shield them from the hurling missiles. Happiness beat in Helga's heart when the last child was handed over.

People swarmed into the jollys after the children. Just as Helga was about to join them a wail of terror reached her ears. Turning about, she looked in the direction from which the sound came. From behind some crates stacked on the dock she saw a little girl, not more than five years old. Barefoot, her little mission dress hanging in tatters under which could be seen burns and blisters, the child's condition wrenched Helga's heart.

Running toward her, Helga surmised that the adult who had taken charge of the little one had been felled by falling rocks. Sweeping up the pathetic, wailing child, Helga ran for the jolly.

An explosive roar split the air. Instantaneously, the vicious pelting of rocks became heavier, knocking the breath from her, crashing against her body and head. Helga went down, the child beneath her shielded from the flying missiles by her bulk.

Several sailors, seeing what had happened, hoisted themselves out of the jolly and scrambled to Helga's aid. Cursing the wounding rocks, protecting their heads with their arms, they reached Helga's fallen body.

One seaman suffered a blow just above the eye. Bloodied and blinded, he fell to his knees. A second seaman went to his aid, a third reached for the whimpering child.

The little girl, fright widening her black, almond-shaped eyes, clung to Helga's body. Her arms reached for Helga's neck and held on tightly, refusing to leave her patron for the rescuing arms of the seaman.

"Hush, baby," the seaman said soothingly, despite the brutal beating he was receiving from the falling stones, "there's nothing to be done for her now. She's gone to be with the angels."

The little child seemed to understand. She was about to place herself in the sailor's arms when she turned back to Helga and placed a loving, grateful kiss on Helga's death-pale cheek.

Captain Anton Kloss watched the destruction of Batavia from aboard his ship where he waited for his wife Helga to join him. From beneath the protection of the overhung quarter deck, he witnessed buildings crumbling from the ravages of fires ignited by the red, glowing rocks showering from the sky. Trees were aflame, their trailing, dancing fires consuming everything in their hungry path. Burning portions of the deck hissed steamily as they toppled into the heated waters of the harbor. "Helga, Helga," his heart cried out.

Before his eyes he saw the land vibrating, the tremors causing high, frothy waves to rock his ship. The heat from the fires, even though a safe distance away, scorched his face and seared his lungs.

An ominous rumbling which grew into a roar, caught his attention. Off the horizon to the west it was possible to see the crest of the steaming, fire-spitting Sisters. As he watched, the horizon grew red, orange, yellow, then white with heat and smoke. The sound of the volcanos' roar was building to a crescendo.

The last thing Captain Anton Kloss was ever to see was the tops of the twin Sisters exploding. The last thing he would ever feel was the enormous shockwave that knocked him unconscious into the unnaturally warm waters of Batavia Harbor.

The yellowish, greenish water was churning beneath Regan's brig. A hot, humid breeze rifled the sails and the ship clipped along, each swell bringing them closer and closer to Port Batavia. Twilight's last pink streaks fought the yellowish air for supremacy as the day ended. Regan stood on the bow of the brig, the spyglass to his eye. The island looked devastated, not a soul stirred. He had a sinking feeling in the pit of his stomach. What if she were dead? Would he want to die too? If she lived would he fetch her back and could he live with another man's child in his house? He was pulled from his thoughts with the boy's anxious cry, "Land ho!"

The brig glided smoothly into what was left of the harbor. "Lower the jolly-boat," Regan ordered.

"There's nothing left," Caleb cried, his eyes scanning the charred docks and piers strewn with rubble of buildings that had toppled from the earth tremors and fire.

"There's a bit of the offices left — look, son." With a brisk order for his men to search the town for survivors, Regan joined Caleb in racing for what was left of the Dutch East India offices.

"Look, Father, here's your cigar box," Caleb said, handing a scorched brown humidor to Regan.

Regan looked around, his eyes settling on a large chunk of cork atop his battered desk. Relieved, he knew his captains had been here and taken everything with them. Caleb swung around to hand his father the cigar box and knocked the cork to the floor. "Look, Father," he cried, "look at this!"

Regan speared the rough paper pinned to the chunk of cork with the tip of the knife.

Caleb stood next to his father and quietly read the words aloud from the paper:

" 'I, the Sea Siren have retired from the seas. My mission is completed. I found that which I sought and now leave the Spanish and the Dutch to their business of trading.' " It was signed with a large sprawling *S.*

"You see, Father, I was right. This was the last thing she had to do before she left. This notice wasn't here when we left for the inner islands. I told you, Sirena never broke a promise."

Regan's eyes narrowed into slits as he looked at the boy. "You were right. I'll order the men to search out the root cellars and store all provisions on board. We'll set sail immediately." His eyes lowered to the scattered strips of charred paper at his feet: his personal bounty on the Sea Siren.

"Thank you, Father," Caleb said humbly.

Regan stood on deck, his thoughts whirling. Why was he doing this? For the boy or for himself? He admitted his love for the woman and it was a hard lump to swallow. How had she gotten into his blood like this? How had he allowed it to happen? Sighing he got to his feet, his eyes cold and hard. Somehow he blamed himself for all that had happened. Even for Sirena's present condition. If he had had his wits about him he could have stopped that bastard Chaezar. He realized now

501

that Sirena was like no woman he had ever known. If he had listened to her and . . . perhaps this never would have happened. How could she have fallen prey to that oily Spaniard? He must have taken advantage of her and she was afraid to tell him for fear of his wrath. "God help me, God help all of us," he breathed softly.

"Everything is aboard, Father," Caleb called.

"Then give the order to hoist anchor," Regan ordered grimly.

Chapter Thirty-one

Sirena lay on her hard, narrow bunk, her mind a beehive. Visions of Frau Holtz being dragged forcibly by Willem and Jan swam before her eyes. That it was for the housekeeper's own good sounded weak even to her own ears. The austere housekeeper had fought like some caged wild animal at which men were poking sticks. Eventually, with the aid of a few drops of laudanum, she had finally succumbed and was now sound asleep. What would happen when she woke? Sirena thought she wouldn't be surprised if the woman jumped overboard and attempted to swim back to Port Batavia. She grimaced as she pictured the aging Frau Holtz floundering in the water with sharks circling her. She would no doubt wag her finger and say, "*Ja,* I swim home, leave me be!"

Breathing heavily as if some ponderous weight lay on her chest, Sirena moved about on the narrow bunk trying to get comfortable. In the midst of her squirming, an ear-splitting boom shook the air. Panic gripped her as she slid from the bunk and raced up the narrow ladder to the deck. "God in Heaven, what was it?" she demanded of Jan, who stood at the wheel coughing and sputtering.

"The Sisters," he said curtly. "They had growled their warning once too often, now they've taken their revenge and are spewing everything in their guts on the villages and the wharves. God

503

help any of those who remained behind. I've heard of such things many times but never thought I would live to see it happen."

"What . . . How . . ."

"Capitana, the rocks she spills out will be glowing red with fire and set flames to anything they touch. When the rocks have finished falling then the lava will run and suck everything under it. The lava will cool before it reaches the town, but the plantation groves are finished," he said glumly.

"The children, the old people . . . what of them?" Sirena cried in alarm. Caleb and Regan! Were they safe? God in Heaven, she should have stayed and waited.

"Look about you, Capitana, as far as the eye can see are ships of every description. You saw for yourself the men were helping to evacuate the island."

"But there was so little time," Sirena protested.

"What you say is true. It's over now. When the lava cools the men will return to the island and try to rebuild and start over."

"But that will take years," she said in a muffled voice.

"Aye, years. Many years and then there will be years after that while they wait for the trees to grow again. If they grow at all," he said ominously. "It will depend on how much damage the lava did and how heavy it lays."

Sirena shook her head in wonderment at this bizarre happening. Thank God she had dragged the housekeeper aboard or she would no doubt be lying under the burning wharf.

"Jan, how long will this odious choking air be with us?"

"Till the wind shifts, and then it may be days. Go below, Capitana, where it is not so thick. I can manage the wheel."

"All right," Sirena acquiesced, "I want to look in on the housekeeper to see how she fares."

Quietly, Sirena opened the door of the cabin which had once housed Caleb and where now the aging housekeeper slept. For some strange reason, tears burned at her eyes when she gazed down at the sleeping woman. Wisps of iron-gray hair lay on her high, wide forehead and her skin was soot-smudged, giving her an old, haggard appearance. Without thinking, she brushed gently at the stray locks of hair and gently wiped the dirt from the housekeeper's cheekbones. Frau Holtz stirred fretfully, muttering under her breath. One long arm brushed the air and then lay still at her side. Sirena turned to leave when the faded blue eyes opened.

"Frau Holtz, it is I, Sirena. I just came to see how you were. Try to sleep, you look worn out."

"*Ja,*" the woman said harshly. "I am tired and find it difficult to breathe, why is that?"

"The Sisters erupted a while ago. The air on deck is horrendous. It is best to stay below and rest. I'm going to do the same. Have no fear," she said gently, "I'll put you ashore as soon as Willem says it's safe."

"*Ja,* I have no liking for ships and water. I want my feet on ground with trees and houses around me."

"I understand, Frau Holtz. I'm sorry that the men had to force you aboard. You see, I couldn't leave you behind to . . . die. I knew you must be on the wharf waiting for something, and everything was in such chaos I had to do something."

The housekeeper shook her head. "I was waiting for the Mynheer."

"Then he wasn't on the island?" Sirena said in a relieved tone.

"No, Mevrouw. He never returned with the boy." Boldly, her faded eyes took in Sirena's scanty attire and she pursed her mouth into a tight, grim line.

Sirena smiled slightly at her disapproving look. "I find that my . . . costume is . . . different and gives me much freedom. Perhaps if you wished I could fashion a similar one for you," she teased.

The watery eyes twinkled suddenly. "*Ja*, Mevrouw, and a sight I would be. If I was younger, perhaps, and with the body you have I might agree. As it is, I will have to keep these rags on my back," she said, looking at her scorched and tattered gown of gray silk.

Sirena laughed happily. "Tell me, Frau Holtz, how long have you known of my . . . dual identity?"

The housekeeper smiled. "From the moment I noticed the spindrift in your hair. Ailment indeed! You may have been able to fool your husband, but you couldn't fool me!"

"You knew and didn't tell Regan?" Sirena's voice held an incredulous note.

"*Ja* . . . I'm not the only one who knew your secret. Didn't you ever question the sturdiness of the trellis at your window or the stoutness of the vine which you climbed up and down? On the nights when you were gone, Juli and I lashed it to the trellis on more than one occasion. Caleb isn't quite as nimble-footed as you. Many times I stood in the courtyard and waited for your return. There was one time when I posted Juli at the top of the rise to be your lookout. I was worried," she said simply, "you'd been gone for weeks!"

"And yet you kept my secret from Regan? I can't fathom it, Frau Holtz."

"*Ja* . . . I was proud of your daring feats. I cheered you behind closed doors as did most of the women in the Indies."

"I don't understand, I thought the women most of all wanted to see me drawn and quartered. Now you say you were proud of me. Why?"

"The van der Rhys family always treated me well, but before I came to them I've had my share of suffering at men's hands." Her eyes became stormy as they seemed to be looking into the distant past.

Pulling herself back to the present, Frau Holtz continued, "Every woman has, at one time or another, wanted to strike out at men for the injustices imposed on us. But Mevrouw, some day that will all change!" Frau Holtz said earnestly. "The Sea Siren was a forerunner of the woman of the future. Now do you understand why I'm proud of you?"

"I . . . I think so." Suddenly Sirena laughed and bent down to embrace the older woman. "You knew all the time," she marveled.

"*Ja*," Frau Holtz smiled happily.

"Then that makes us compatriots of a sort, doesn't it?"

The housekeeper nodded, then asked: "Where

do you go, Mevrouw, when you leave me off at one of the islands?"

"Back to Spain. There's nothing left for me here."

"And the child you carry?"

"You know that, too?"

"I've lived a long time, Mevrouw. There's little that I don't know. Besides," she smiled, "there's that look in your eyes. You're in your fourth month. Have you felt the babe quicken?"

"Yes. But I'll arrive in Spain before my time is due. I'm sorry that you won't be with me," Sirena said sincerely.

Frau Holtz stirred from the bunk and tried to smooth her dirt-smeared, singed gown. Placing a gentle hand on Sirena's shoulder, she said softly, "Your husband should be with you at this time."

Tears gathered in Sirena's eyes. "It cannot be." The housekeeper nodded dejectedly and muttered obscenities about stupid men.

"I think I'll rest a while. Please don't go on deck till Willem calls and says we've sailed clear of the noxious air."

"Very well, Mevrouw, I'll see if there isn't something I can do about tidying myself. Rest well."

Weary to the bone, Jan slumped over the wheel, his eyes burning with the thick sulphurous vapor. His chest was paining him unbearably and by the minute he was finding it more difficult to take a deep breath. When was Willem going to relieve him? Soon, he prayed, otherwise they would be tossing his lifeless body over the rail. He forced his

508

eyes open and tried to stand erect, but the effort was too great and he found himself slipping . . . slipping into merciful oblivion. The wheel swung a full half circle and remained still as his heavy body slumped over, pinning it firmly to its base.

Below decks, Sirena slept while Frau Holtz, her tidying completed, lay back down to rest. Willem and the rest of the small crew stirred with the sudden lurching of the ship, thought little of it, and continued with what they were doing.

The frigate drifted for hours, miles off her course, leaving the cluster of evacuating ships behind. To the west of her stern a sleek galleon with an escort of two rode the churning, boiling waters. The frigate and her crew slept peacefully as the still thick yellow vapor began to dissipate.

Chaezar Alvarez held the glass to his eye, a satanic look on his face. He had known if he waited long enough he would find the frigate. At times it paid to be patient. From the looks of things there was no one aboard the small frigate, no one at her wheel, which was why she was drifting so aimlessly. With luck he could come up behind her and throw a grappling hook aboard and lash his bow to her stern.

Now that his personal victory was almost within his grasp, he could allow himself the luxury of relaxing. Regan was ruined! Port Batavia burned to ashes. Only the thick wall surrounding the city remained. The nutmeg trees were destroyed with no promise of more in the near future. He, and he alone, would command the entire nutmeg trade. He felt as if he, and he alone, had commanded the

509

Sisters to erupt to further his plan. With an evil smile, he cast his eye at the frigate's stern to see if anything moved on the decks. Soon, within minutes, the Sea Siren would be his. His and his alone! He'd take her to the kingdom he prepared in Africa. He'd reign as supreme ruler with the beautiful Sea Siren as his queen.

He had known for months the true identity of the Sea Siren. Dick Blackheart, who had captained the attack upon the Córdez family, had come to him with the sorry tale of how the spirited Spanish girl had outwitted him and sent him and his men adrift in a jolly. It all fit in with the unlikely story Sirena and that brat she called her brother told of a storm at sea and her miraculous rescue by fishermen. At that point he had accepted her story just as everyone else on Java had. To do otherwise would have dangerously implicated him in the crime of piracy and murder aboard the Córdez frigate.

Even after the Sea Siren launched her initial attack, he had no reason to suspect Sirena's duplicity. It could have been coincidental. But when he had Regan's figurehead of the Sea Siren stolen from the artisan who carved it, in order to smite Regan, he had naturally had a look at the carving: the likeness was unmistakable. That fool van der Rhys, who had aptly named the piratess Sea Siren, so close in sound and spelling to her actual name Sirena, appeared not to notice the resemblance between the figurehead and his wife. But Chaezar, with his sharp, appreciative eye for beauty, was certain of Sirena's dual identity.

Seeing Sirena raging against Gretchen, her eyes

filled with fire, had held further proof. So many times he had been tempted to reveal his knowledge to her. How often he had thought her to be on the brink of telling him herself. The Sea Siren had made his position as head of the Spanish shipping trade most precarious. She had brought ruin on the Spanish fleet, had cost him a small fortune in personal business losses. Yet he had done nothing. He had played along with Regan and the others in their plans to capture her, knowing that they wouldn't.

Chaezar's sense of drama had been tittilated. He intended to play the game out to the end. His fortunes did not rest with the Spanish trading fleet, they rested elsewhere with casks of fertile nutmegs and a kingdom on the African coast.

Chaezar's eyes narrowed to a menacing glare when he thought of his fertile nutmegs. By the time he had discovered the twenty-four casks were missing he had other matters on his mind. Regan had been closing in on Gretchen and himself, discovering bit by bit that they were ultimately responsible for the death of his wife, the loss of his son, and the long, hard years he had spent in a Spanish prison. Chaezar had been unable to pursue the loss of his nutmegs when he had been so concerned about keeping one step ahead of Regan to save his life.

The night he had met Sirena in the garden he had come to take her away with him, to offer her the life of a queen, to save her from Regan! But the foolish woman hadn't even given him the chance to speak — sharp points of hatred had shot from her eyes. She had still been angry about the afternoon he had drugged her and taken her to his bed to sample her passionate charms. Then she had become defensive of Regan, telling Chaezar that her husband had sailed to the inner islands. Chaezar had expected to hear that Regan had gone again in pursuit of his son, but not quite so soon.

Chaezar had been frightened, he had grabbed for her. His intent was to force her to go with him. In her struggle, Sirena's sleeve had ripped, baring her arm to the moonlight. There before him had been the ultimate proof that his deductions concerning her dual identity were correct. He had seen the wound on her arm, the one Blackheart had told him about!

Sirena Córdez van der Rhys was the indomitable Sea Siren! Chaezar licked his lips, he was aware of a stirring in his loins. He wondered what it would be like to be dominated by the infamous piratess. He would have her wear the scanty costume she wore aboard her ship, she would be a magnificent fantasy come to life as she wielded the whip!

The first grappling hook was thrown aboard the spectral, black frigate, and moments later it was lashed to the galleon and Chaezar's men were boarding her decks. When the last of his men climbed aboard, Chaezar followed. It was pointless to take unnecessary risks, he reasoned, one could never be too careful around the Sea Siren. Right this very minute, she could be watching for her chance to kill him. She could be hiding in some dark cranny of the ship waiting for him to show himself. When he was satisfied that his men had the situation in hand, he ordered the woman brought on deck.

Sirena looked blearily at the coarse man who grabbed her arm, yanking her from a sound sleep in her hard bunk. "My captain wants you on deck, now!" For a brief moment Sirena panicked, thinking herself back in time with Blackheart's scurvy crew.

"Take your filthy hands off me. Who are you? How did you get aboard this ship? Loose me, I say!" she cried shrilly. Her answer was to be dragged, half stumbling and half falling, up the ladder to stand on deck. "Chaezar! What are you doing here? What is this?"

"Would you like an embroidered lie or the plain, simple truth?" he asked gallantly as he made a low, swooping bow in her direction.

"Plain truth will serve for now," Sirena said bluntly.

"I plan to kill your crew and take you with me to my kingdom."

"And if I choose not to go, what then?"

"There is no choice. You will come with me, it's as simple as that."

"Never!" Sirena cried passionately. "I wouldn't cross the deck with you, let alone stand next to you."

"Then I shall force you to watch as your men are drawn and quartered, one after the other. When your decks are rivers of blood, you'll reconsider," he said cruelly.

Sirena blanched at the Spaniard's words. From the look in his eye he clearly meant what he said. Merciful God, help me, she prayed.

513

"Why must you kill my crew? What have they done to you?"

"It's not a question of them doing anything. I want no tales carried back to the islands. You might say I'm making my escape. Men with tongues will talk. I can't afford that in my position."

"You would kill as cold-bloodedly as that? What kind of evil man are you?"

"Am I so different from you, Sea Siren? You killed and reaped rewards for what you did. I'm merely doing the same."

"I never killed for the sake of killing," Sirena spat viciously. "Your thinking is warped, Chaezar. It is you who deserve to die, not these old harmless men. I'll strike a bargain with you. Let them go and I will go willingly with you. My word as the Sea Siren."

Chaezar groped for words. It would be better to have her come with him willingly than to have to use force. "Your word that there will be no tricks?"

"My word."

"Very well, climb aboard my galleon. Bring nothing but yourself. Understood?" Sirena nodded, and was gracefully swinging herself aboard the galleon as Frau Holtz emerged from the stairs with a blunderbuss in her shaking hands and a frightened look on her face. In the blink of an eye the weapon was dashed against the tackle box and the woman stood, tears streaming down her ruddy cheeks, the point of the cutlass at her throat.

"Hold!" Sirena shouted. "She's my companion, leave her to come with me. I'm not asking you,

Chaezar, I'm telling you."

"Very well . . . I've no stomach for killing old women. You may have your companion. Just remember that is one more favor for which you have me to thank. Order your men to remain silent of these doings or you will find this rapier coming out your back! *Comprende?*"

"Willem, you heard Señor Alvarez. You will do nothing to jeopardize his sailing. He has guaranteed me safe sailing, as well as Frau Holtz. You will do me one small favor perhaps." Willem nodded carefully, his eyes peering deeply into those of the woman across from him on the other ship. "See to it that the *Sea Siren* is repaired and her proper name restored to the bow. Be sure that my little brother receives her in good condition. Will you do that for me?"

"Aye, Capitana, I'll see that the boy gets the frigate." He raised his hand to his forehead and gave her a jaunty salute as he watched the heavy ropes being cut, separating the galleon from the *Sea Siren.*

Sirena turned to Fran Holtz, tears in her eyes. She clenched her teeth so as not to show any emotion before Chaezar.

Unable to contain herself, Frau Holtz screeched, "Heathen swine, dirty cutthroat pigs! Bastard at birth and bastard till the day of your death. The Lord should have you choke on your heathen tongue and swallow it."

"If you don't close your mouth, dear lady, it shall be you who chokes on your tongue."

Frau Holtz, her face as crimson as a passion fruit, closed her mouth into tight, grim lines.

"May the devil carve your heart from your skinny body and hang it on his fork!" she muttered beneath her breath.

"Take the ladies below to their quarters and lock them in," Chaezar ordered brusquely. "It's time to change course and head for my new kingdom!"

Chapter Thirty-two

Regan's heart ached when he looked at the morose boy at his side. A hard, bitter look crossed his face and he smarted at the idea that a child so young should be experiencing such feelings. Words were of little comfort, he had discovered. Caleb had one thought and one thought only, and that was to find Sirena and bring her home.

"She goes too slow, Father. At this rate of speed we'll never find Sirena! There must be something you can do. Don't you know any shortcuts to save time? Sirena always said if one looked hard enough one could solve any problem. And we have a problem. What if we never find her?" he cried brokenly.

"I have no control over the winds, son," Regan replied patiently. "You must trust me."

"If Sirena doesn't want to be found then she won't. Not you, not the Spaniard, not even I will be able to find her," Caleb said dejectedly.

"I told you I'll sail these waterways till I find her, what more can I do?"

"Sirena is like a wounded animal now, she hurts inside, not just for herself but for the baby," Caleb said in a suddenly adult voice. "What if she's taken to land? She doesn't care anymore, that's why I'm so worried about her. She's given up, nothing matters to her. I saw the look in her eyes and I tell you, Father, she's not alive anymore, just a shell."

517

Caleb's words cut Regan. It was almost impossible for him to imagine the forceful Sea Siren and the compassionate, lovely woman he called his wife stripped of her vitality and determination. A shudder coursed through him as he turned his eyes to Caleb. No matter how brave his father's words, Caleb read fear in his cold, hard eyes.

A week passed, then two, and then three. Caleb was openly discouraged and antagonistic toward Regan. Regan, his nerves as tightly strung as the guitar Sirena had strummed, could only look with pity into the eyes of his son.

"Sail ho!" came the cry from the rigging. Caleb leaped to the rigging and climbed to the topmost sail, his eyes hopeful and alive for the first time in weeks.

Regan lowered the spyglass from his eyes, a thoughtful look on his face. It was the *Sea Siren* and she carried a Spanish flag atop her mast. To the naked eye she sailed as if she were heavy with cargo. Caleb's jubilant cry made him raise the glass again.

"It's the *Sea Siren*," Caleb shrilled as he slid down the rigging. "It's Sirena, Father, it's Sirena!"

There was something wrong, Regan could feel it in his bones. He put a gentle hand on the boy's shoulder and tried to quiet him. His touch held no comfort. Caleb was off and running to the stern, his hands shielding his eyes.

"I see Jacobus and Willem. Sirena isn't on deck, she must be in her cabin," he cried excitedly.

Even at this distance Regan could see the grim lines on the faces of the two men on deck. He was right, there was something wrong!

"Ho! *Sea Siren*," he called loudly. "Call your captain to the decks."

"This ship carries no captain," Willem called harshly. "What is it you want? We carry no cargo."

"What happened to your captain? I speak of the Sea Siren, if you lie to me I'll carve your tongue from your mouth."

"Willem, Jacobus, it is I, Caleb. Where is Sirena? Answer my father, he means her no harm."

"Ay, boy, if I could make our capitana stand before you I would. She is no longer aboard. The bastard Spanish devil, Alvarez, attacked our ship shortly after the Sisters erupted. He took her prisoner, along with a woman we rescued from the wharf at Port Batavia. Her name was Frau Holtz. Our capitana made a last request as she left the ship. She entrusted the crew to bring the ship to port and to have her repainted and hoist a white sail. She was to be turned over to her little brother. We gave our promise. We could do no less as she saved our lives. The Spaniard was bent on killing every man aboard. She said she would go with him if he let us go free to bring the ship to port. There was no way we could fight. We were outmaneuvered and outmanned. The Spaniard's ships were heavily armed and he had an escort of two."

"Where did he take her, Willem?" Caleb called shrilly.

"If I knew I would have sailed after the stinking bastard," Willem said viciously as he spat in the water. "My guess would be Spain, but I'm not sure. I heard one of his crew mutter something about there being no welcome for him there, so it's possible he heads in another direction. I wish there were more I could tell you, young Caleb. Unfortunately, we weren't within earshot for long, the Spaniard took her aboard and immediately set sail. I didn't think he would keep his promise to let us sail free, at any moment I expected a good broadside to this frigate."

"How . . . how was . . . Sirena, Willem?"

"She was . . . ill. The woman will look after her. There's nothing more I can tell you. With your permission, Captain, we'll continue with our journey to the cove where the *Sea Siren* is to be careened and repainted. When you next see her, lad, she'll carry her true name. She's yours now, with the wishes of the Sea Siren." With a low, flourishing bow, Willem made his way to the wheel to relieve Jacobus and to continue his mission.

Tears of frustration pricked the boy's eyes as he gazed upon his father. "Even at the last she thought of me. Now do you see why I must find her? Tell me, Father, what captain do you know who would do as Sirena did to protect her men? Not one, I'll wager," he cried hoarsely, his young voice rising and falling shrilly. "Not one. Each would only want to save his own skin at the expense of the others. I told you, Sirena is like no other. She made a promise and she kept it."

Something strange and sad fluttered in Regan's chest as he stood at the rail. The boy was right. There wasn't one man in his employ who would have given of himself to let another go free. The sun-bronzed hands gripped the rail he leaned on, a new determination coursed through him. "And

I," he said quietly and with deadly calm, "will find your . . . sister. I may be many things in your eyes, young Caleb, but this I implore you to believe. I'll find her, for you and for myself."

Caleb looked at the tortured face opposite him. Gently, he lay a darkened hand on his father's arm. "We'll find her . . . together."

"You must stir yourself, Mevrouw, it's been weeks since you last walked on deck. You must have fresh air and move your muscles. Laying abed won't do you or the baby any good. I beg you, Mevrouw, come on deck with me. The winds are brisk and the spindrift is lovely."

"I can't bear to look upon that devil Alvarez. I'll want to kill him with my bare hands. If there were only some way that I could . . ."

"There is no way. You must also get that notion from your head. Day and night there are two guards outside this door. The Spaniard knows you couldn't fight in your condition."

"In my condition! I'd fight the Devil himself in my condition if I thought it would do me any good. You're right, Frau Holtz, it's useless to even dream I could overpower the bastard. However," she said viciously, "I won't always be in this condition."

"Mevrouw, at that time you will have an extra burden, one you do not have now, the babe."

"Ah yes, the babe. You'll care for the babe while I carve the manhood from the Spaniard's body," Sirena said conversationally.

Frau Holtz's eyes protruded at her calm words. There was no doubt in her mind that Sirena would

521

do exactly what she said she would.

"I think you're right, Frau Holtz, a brisk walk on the deck would do me wonders. Shall we go?" she asked, getting up from the hard bunk.

The two women strolled along the wide decks, the brisk trade winds ruffling Sirena's hair, bringing a glow to her pale cheeks. "It's been too long." Sirena sighed as she stopped to peer over the rail. The clear, azure waters brought a lump to her throat. A small school of fish swam beneath the surface — how effortlessly they moved beneath the sparkling water. Heaving a sigh, she stirred herself and moved from the rail to rejoin Frau Holtz.

"So, you decided to join the living," Chaezar said urbanely as he leaped to their side agilely. "Perhaps I'll join you, it's a beautiful day."

"If you so much as take one more step," Sirena said, stopping in midstride, "then I shall go below. I don't want your company now, or at any time. If you must walk, then walk alone. I warn you, Chaezar, stay out of my sight."

"Very well, Sirena, I've no wish to force myself upon you."

"It's well you've learned your lesson. The last time was a freak circumstance." Angrily, she turned on the Spaniard. "You drugged me, in my heart it was Regan no matter what you want to believe."

"I'm a patient man. I map every detail before I make a move. Bear that in mind. When next you sleep with me the only drug in your veins will be passion and desire." With a slight nod of his head he backed off a step, and Sirena, seething inwardly, continued her stroll along the deck.

Sirena looked at Frau Holtz, despair in her eyes. "It was all I could do to keep my hands still. I wanted to choke the life from his body and watch his face turn blue."

Her quiet voice sent a chill through the house-keeper as she laid an arm around the girl's trembling shoulders. She spoke soothingly of the warm weather and the sultry breeze, hoping to take Sirena's mind off the brief encounter with the Spaniard.

Chaezar impatiently paced the close confinement of his cabin. The child she carried within her was his! He knew it in his heart. Why did she persist in saying it was Regan's? He knew the marriage was never consummated. Even Regan would never go back on his word. How could he have reneged on her period of mourning? No, the child was his. Still, if it made her happy to think of it as Regan's, if fooling herself kept her content, let her. She would be due for a rude awakening when the baby arrived. The child would be olive-skinned with dark, glossy hair. What more proof could a man want? There was no way she could deliver a golden-haired, blue-eyed baby, of that he was certain.

It was two months since Regan sighted the frigate, *Sea Siren*. Since that time, he had questioned every ship he encountered. There wasn't one that had seen the Spaniard. Despair would have engulfed him time and time again were it not for Caleb. Each time he let his shoulders slump or his eyes grow weary, the boy was there to bolster him.

A strength which knew no bounds surged in Caleb's slim, youthful body.

"I think I'll weigh anchor at the next port and add fresh provisions. Perhaps we can learn news from some of the merchants."

"I'm sure we'll find something we want to hear. I feel good today," Caleb said jauntily.

A pall of gloom settled over Regan as he made his way back to his cabin, a dejected Caleb trailing in his wake. It was almost as if the ocean had opened up and swallowed Sirena.

One weary day followed another as the ship continued her journey to Spain. Caleb became fretful and openly defiant and constantly apologized for his behavior. Regan was fast becoming a man obsessed with the thought that the Sea Siren was dead. There was no other explanation. Two more days, he told himself wearily, and he would dock at Alvarez's home port.

"The Spaniard told me this morning that we are near land. By sundown," Frau Holtz said grimly.

"It's just as well, Frau Holtz. My time is almost here. I want a fresh bed and a soft pillow for my head. Where is this place we are landing, do you know?"

"I know as much as you, Mevrouw, the northwest coast of Africa."

Suddenly Sirena grasped the old housekeeper's hand. "Have I told you how grateful I am that you're here with me, Frau Holtz? I don't know what I would have done without you. I'll never be able to repay you."

"I want no payment." The women clasped hands and the housekeeper was the first to disentangle herself. "I must gather together the few belongings we have and be ready when Señor Alvarez gives the order to disembark."

"I think I'll lie down for a while, my head pounds with the thought that I'll be forced to live in the same house with that bastard Alvarez and that my child will be born under his roof."

Frau Holtz clenched her teeth. If there were only something she could do, but what? She was an old woman and old women were useless. Would the Spaniard guard her as he had done these past months aboard his ship? Nodding morosely, she thought he would take no chances that the woman called Sea Siren might escape him. Where was Mynheer van der Rhys now? Would he search for his wife or would he think she had died when the Sisters erupted?

Her small tasks completed, Frau Holtz sat down on a hard chair to await the Spaniard's orders to disembark. From time to time, she dozed off only to be jerked awake by some loud noise on deck or some slight stirring Sirena made in her cramped bunk.

A hard rapping on the door startled her. Still, she heaved a sigh of relief. It would be good to see trees and houses and have solid ground beneath her feet again.

Gently, Frau Holtz helped Sirena to her feet. She moved clumsily, her added weight a burden as she climbed the ladder with Frau Holtz's help.

The two women stood on deck as the galleon glided effortlessly into her slip at the wharf.

So, Sirena thought, this is to be my temporary home. There was no doubt in her mind that the word temporary meant just that.

Caleb and Regan disembarked onto the busy dock in Barcelona, Spain. Leaving orders with his crew to lay in stores, Regan immediately asked directions to the harbor master's offices.

Caleb watched his father's jaw tighten and his eyes narrow expectantly. He knew Regan believed he was close to his goal of finding Sirena and the scoundrel Chaezar. Not many nights ago, at the ship's wheel, Regan had confided to his son: "Sometimes, Caleb, I feel as if that bastard is so close I can smell his greasy hair oil and garlic breath!" It was merely wishful thinking, Caleb realized. Somehow the boy felt that Sirena was no closer to him than she had been when they left Java.

The dignified harbor master extended every hospitality to Regan and Caleb. It was an honor to receive the Dutchman who, if rumor was correct, had a very good chance of being named governor of Java — a post the Burghers of Holland had deemed necessary. During the leisurely midday meal which they were invited to share, Regan adhered to Spanish protocol and refrained from discussing business. It was over steaming cups of coffee that Regan broached the subject of Don Chaezar Alvarez.

Disbelief darkened Regan's features at his host's response. "You're sure of your facts, Señor? It isn't that I don't believe you, it's just that Alvarez painted such a glowing picture of his superiors' opinion of him here in Spain that I doubted he could ever fall out of favor. Now you

526

tell me there's a price on his head and that for years he's been smuggling unlimed nutmegs to some far-off place where he's going to retire and reign like a king."

"It is sad but true, Mynheer van der Rhys. We've only discovered this recently, and allowed him to stay on in the Indies till another of our men was properly trained. If he hadn't taken matters into his own hands he would have been relieved of his duties one month from today."

"Your new man will have his work cut out for him," Regan sympathized. Briefly, he told the aging Spaniard of the devastation the Sisters had brought to Port Batavia.

"*Via con Dios*, Mynheer. The most encouragement I can offer you at this time is purely speculation. The African coast is the only place Alvarez could hope to plant his unlimed nutmegs. If you have no success, then it would be wise to forget the matter for the time being. Alvarez will eventually poke his head out, much the way a turtle does. And when he does, you'll be standing by with a stick."

"Thank you for all your help, Señor, but I can't give up now!"

Back aboard ship, Regan cursed himself a fool a thousand times. Why hadn't he thought of the African coast? Even if he had to search the entire length of Africa he would find Sirena.

"What do you think, Father?" Caleb asked excitedly.

"I think the old harbor master was right. Alvarez has gone to Africa. If only I had thought of it, we could have saved ourselves months at sea. Soon, I'll feel that skinny bastard's neck beneath my fingers," he said, flexing his sun-darkened hands.

"Soon, Father, soon we'll have Sirena back with us."

"Yes," Regan answered, his thoughts spinning to Sirena. Could it have been almost nine months since that night aboard the spectral, black frigate when he had fulfilled both his obsessions: the possession of the Sea Siren and the consummation of his marriage.

Chapter Thirty-three

Frau Holtz lay in her bed listening to the soft moans that came from the bed adjoining hers. She decided she would pretend to be sleeping until her Mevrouw called for her. Sirena would prefer to be alone with her pain for as long as possible. Instinctively, the German housekeeper knew this and would defer to Sirena's wishes.

Frau Holtz was, for the first time in many years, frustrated by her helplessness. Not having had a child of her own or even attended at a birth, she was uncertain and unsure of her ability to help Sirena. Preparing for this moment, the housekeeper had inquired of Chaezar's staff and had located a midwife. The woman on which Sirena must depend to see her through the birth was far from the fastidious housekeeper's liking. Ebony-black, old and cronelike with a shocking gray mane of wiry hair, the woman appeared stupid and slow and exceedingly dirty. Even her name was unpronounceable; it sounded to her Germanic ears like Tsuna Muub. Whatever, the Mevrouw needed her and hers was the only knowledgeable assistance available.

The only fact Frau Holtz was certain of was that the baby would be healthy and strong. Hadn't she seen to it herself that Sirena ate properly, hadn't she insisted Sirena take daily walks to keep fit? Since coming to this godforsaken hole in the universe, she had made Sirena sit outdoors in the shade of the trees. The fresh air had been a boon to the pale-faced Sirena, and despite her constant objections, she had thrived under Frau Holtz's relentless care.

The moans were increasing and Frau Holtz sensed a struggle in the next bed. Quietly, she got up and slipped downstairs to the vast kitchen. She roused the shiny, black cook and through sign language was able to convey that the midwife Tsuna Muub was needed. The ebony-faced cook smiled her understanding and roused her sleeping husband to fetch the skinny, crone-like midwife. Without being told, the cook set to work heating water in her heavy kettles, humming a strange, toneless melody in her deep, throaty voice. Believing her message understood, Frau Holtz returned to Sirena, stopping only to take a fresh pile of clean bedding from the chest in the linen room.

"Frau Holtz, I'm so glad you're awake. I didn't want to disturb you, but I think my time has come," Sirena gasped, her hands grasping her swollen middle. Perspiring from the heat and exertion, she wiped her forehead with the back of her hand as the pain subsided, a trembling yet brave smile on her face.

"I've sent for that witch, Tsuna Muub, God help us."

Sirena laughed. Poor Frau Holtz, how she hated to admit she needed anyone's assistance, least of all a black-as-night, emaciated African's. And the way she pronounced the old woman's name!

A few moments later, the door swung open and

Tsuna Muub stepped across the threshold author-itatively, her yellow-rimmed black eyes darting around the room evaluating the situation. Frau Holtz stood near Sirena, as if to protect her from the old woman, whose appearance did nothing to instill confidence. Her skinny, almost skeletal form was draped with evil-looking trinkets and what appeared to be human teeth and bird feath-ers. Tsuna Muub padded to the bed on bare feet and faced Frau Holtz defiantly, daring the Ger-man to keep her from her patient.

With a grim face and low, disapproving grunt, Frau Holtz stepped aside. Another contraction squeezed a grunt of pain from between Sirena's clenched teeth. Alarmed and feeling useless, Frau Holtz stepped aside.

Tsuna Muub threw back the light sheet cover-ing Sirena and expertly placed her hands over her protruding belly, pressing and feeling. Speaking in what Frau Holtz called gibberish and through signs, the old midwife told Sirena it would be a long while before the child was born. Then Tsuna Muub, with surprising strength, pulled Sirena into a sitting position and mumbling insisted Sirena get to her feet.

Frau Holtz, her maternal protectiveness over-whelming her, began to protest in emphatic Ger-man. Tsuna Muub, proud of her craft, argued back in her own dialect. Sirena practically had to prevent the two women from strangling each other.

"Frau Holtz, Tsuna Muub! Stop this at once!" Still they persisted in their argument. Only with the onset of another contraction during which

Sirena clutched the bedpost did the women direct their attention to her.

Tsuna Muub rushed to Sirena's side and, taking her arm, led her at a quick, shuffling pace back and forth across the room. The contraction eased more quickly this time and Sirena smiled her relief. "I think the old witch just may know her business after all; that pain was stronger than the others and yet it was easier to bear. My legs didn't cramp up and it subsided more quickly." Frau Holtz's glance rested on Tsuna Muub, and while it wasn't friendly or even approving, there was a kind of relief behind it and perhaps a glimmer of respect.

Through the long hours before dawn, Sirena walked miles back and forth across the carpeted floor, the last hour leaning heavily on Frau Holtz's arm.

The German woman's hair was escaping the long braid which hung down her back, her nightdress and wrapper were damp with perspiration, and worry and fear crept from her eyes. Tsuna Muub, after raising the foot of the bed on two stacks of books and changing the bedding, had ensconced herself on Frau Holtz's bed and directed the pace Sirena must keep during her labor pains. Between contractions she allowed Sirena to sit on a hard straight-backed chair to renew her strength for the next pain. Every so often she would break into a low chanting, a satisfied expression that bordered on smugness playing about her thin-lipped, toothless mouth.

Even when Sirena protested she couldn't walk

another step, Tsuna Muub insisted, her hard, surprisingly strong hands prodding Sirena to her feet.

Once, when her protests overcame the spindly native, Sirena lay down on her bed in exhaustion, with Frau Holtz mopping her brow in tender sympathy. Another labor pain seized her in a grip of unrelenting agony. As soon as she was able, Sirena struggled to her feet breathlessly explaining to Frau Holtz that as much as she hated to admit it, Tsuna Muub was right. Walking did help.

Half an hour later, when the pains were coming hard and fast, Tsuna Muub motioned to Sirena that it was time to take to her bed. The midwife's wizened little monkey face bent close to Sirena and her hands pressed low on Sirena's abdomen. Issuing a knowing grunt, she began to prepare Sirena for the birthing.

Frau Holtz leaned close and whispered to Sirena as if Tsuna Muub could understand her. "Mevrouw, if you want I could ask Señor Alvarez for some laudanum. Just a drop or two if the pain becomes unbearable."

"No!" Sirena exclaimed, grasping the Frau's strong wrist, "I'd die before I asked him for anything! Under no circumstances are you even to consider it. Promise me!"

It was the most difficult promise Frau Holtz ever made. Each pain Sirena suffered the Frau suffered; she shared each long moment of anxiety with the mistress she had come to love. "*Ja,* I promise, Mevrouw."

Tsuna Muub had busied herself by tearing a strip of sheeting and twisting it into a thick rope. Quickly, she slipped it over the top bedpost and tied the ends in a thick, bulky knot. She then demonstrated the use of the rope to Sirena. When a pain began, Sirena was to take a deep breath and pull herself upward to the top of the bed. Then she was to release her breath in quick, light pants.

"Like a dog, Mevrouw," Frau Holtz said incredulously, "the witch wants you to behave like a dog!"

"And they never seem to have as many problems giving birth as we humans. I'll try her method, she was right about walking," Sirena said, perspiration wetting her cheeks. "Frau Holtz, my friend, if you see I'm about to scream will you place your hand over my mouth? Please! So far Chaezar doesn't seem to know what's happening. I don't want him to know. Promise me, a woman's promise to another woman," she gasped as a pain gripped her and she pulled on the rope.

Sirena lay gasping, consciously trying to follow Tsuna Muub's instructions. Her thoughts whirled in her head. What if she should die? What would become of the child? What if the baby died? How could she go on without Regan's child to hold and love, to give her a reason to live?

A small bird-like cry escaped Sirena as her frightened, anguished eyes sought those of Frau Holtz. "Remember your promise to me. That was the worst so far," she said, using both hands to grasp the rope to her. With all her strength she pulled, trying to move her heavy body to the top of the slanted bed. Her teeth were clenched, her hair was wet and shiny with sweat. "God help me," she groaned.

Tsuna Muub began to lift Sirena's nightdress.

"You'll not touch her with those filthy hands!" Frau Holtz snapped harshly, slapping the black woman's hands away from her mistress. Not understanding, Tsuna Muub again reached for Sirena, and again the German slapped her hands away. Having little patience remaining and fraught with worry, Frau Holtz pulled the spidery little woman to the washstand and motioned to her to wash her hands.

Tsuna Muub acquiesced, realizing she must placate this nervous, bossy woman if she were to get about her business. Frau Holtz handed her a bar of fragrant soap and Tsuna Muub took such delight in its creamy texture and heady scent it seemed she would never stop and the baby would birth itself. Frustrated, Frau Holtz watched Tsuna Muub stop once more to sniff the fragrant lather. The scrawny native then motioned for Frau Holtz to bring water from the kitchen. Hesitant to leave Sirena alone with the crone, the Frau left, realizing the only way to get the water to the room was to go fetch it herself.

When she returned carrying a heavy cauldron of water, Tsuna Muub was prancing about the room, shaking her amulets and chanting. Sirena was pulling on the rope of sheeting, her eyes rolled back in her head.

Suddenly Tsuna Muub stopped her chanting and rushed to Sirena's side, taking the rope from her and indicating she was to push. Sirena needed no instruction, nature was her teacher. Low in her back a curl of pain began, and her body responded to an ancient, instinctive response. With a low, animal grunt she began to bear down, down,

down, her body arching and pushing with a will of its own. She bit her tongue, she tasted blood. God in Heaven, would she ever be able to unclench her hands? Then, blessedly, the pain was gone and she was aware of Frau Holtz's gurgle of laughter as she held aloft a tiny red baby emitting a lusty yowl.

"A boy, Mevrouw. A golden-haired boy!"

A smile on her lips, Sirena watched the Frau bathe her son with gentle, adoring hands. Her last conscious thought was, now Caleb has a brother.

Chapter Thirty-four

Daintily, Chaezar dabbed at his mouth. His narrowed eyes raked his lavishly appointed dining room and a smug look crept into them. It was his and his alone. If Sirena chose to share it with him then it would be theirs. Slowly, he lowered his eyes to the gold-crested plate resting before him. A slight smile tugged at the corners of his mouth. Gold plates were something he had promised himself for many years. When he had the merchants dine with him they would be impressed with his apparent wealth. When they saw how huge his nutmeg plantation was, they would be even more impressed and hasten to make him the supreme ruler of the coast. With Sirena to grace his drawing room and sit at the foot of his table, there was no way these peasants could refute his authority and his dominance. He would be the supreme ruler. Some of his nutmeg trees were four years old. Another few years and he would safely control the entire trade in this commodity.

His actions were slow and deliberate as he folded the napkin in a precise triangle. Carefully, he lined it up with the knife at the side of his plate. He took one last sip from the gold-rimmed goblet at his side and then centered it in the middle of the gold-crested plate. There was no use prolonging the moment. It was time to see the new addition to his household. He had deliberately let days go by so that Sirena could regain a little of her strength. He had refrained from asking for a description of the babe. In his heart he knew the child would have a wealth of dark hair and olive skin. He had feigned indifference till he thought he would choke on his own saliva. Now he would confirm his belief.

Gracefully he slid back the high-backed cane chair from the lace-covered table. He stood a moment to look once more at the perfectly appointed table. Satisfied, he strode from the room, a fragrant cigar in his hand.

The door of Sirena's room was slightly ajar. He stopped short, his hand poised to knock. Frau Holtz, in the process of crossing the room, noticed his form in the doorway and quickly walked over to the slight opening and peered out. "What is it you want, Señor?"

"I wish to look upon the new addition to my household. Be so good as to open the door."

"The Mevrouw is resting now, Señor."

"It is not the Señora I wish to see but the babe. In the future, you will address her as the Señora and not the Mevrouw. I find the term offensive to my ear."

Frau Holtz inclined her head a fraction and opened the door wide for him to enter. "The babe lays near the window," she said harshly.

Chaezar hesitated a moment, then slowly walked to the cradle which held the new babe. All he could see was a mound of bunting. He was about to bend over for a closer look, when Frau Holtz pounced on the cradle and literally scooped the small bundle into her arms. A smile on her face, she peeled back a layer of bunting to expose a small pink face crowned with a mass of golden fuzz. Slyly, she watched as hatred danced in the Spaniard's eyes. The black pools were murderous as he nodded his head for the housekeeper to replace the baby in its cradle.

"A fine specimen, wouldn't you say, Señor? The babe will be robust and healthy. He thrives by the day, giving his mother much happiness. It is a pity the father isn't here to share her joy," Frau Holtz said craftily.

Gathering his wits together, Chaezar merely nodded and hurriedly left the room. Outside in the dim corridor, he let his eyes fall to the mangled cigar he held clenched in his hand. He let it fall to the tile floor and slowly ground it beneath his booted foot till the fragrant tobacco was nothing more than a mass of pulp. It was such a tiny head, one good stomp and all that shimmering golden fuzz would resemble the tobacco at his feet.

So he had been misinformed. Regan *had* bedded his wife. Perhaps the situation was not lost yet. If Regan were to be informed that he held not only his wife but his new son in captivity, he would come here and then he would have his final revenge on the man he had hated all these years. If necessary, he would make him watch as he took his wife right under his eyes and then make him watch along with Sirena as he killed the golden-haired bundle that lay in the cradle. He had to be the victor! Too long he had come out second to Regan. Not this time! Not ever again! He must find a way to send a message back to Port Batavia even if he had to send a fully-manned cargoless ship.

Casting a last hateful look at the tobacco at his feet, he pulled a fresh cigar from his waistcoat and, without a backward glance, left the corridor for his offices.

"Mevrouw, the Señor finally came to look upon the babe while you rested," Frau Holtz said, a smile on her wide mouth.

"And what did the Señor have to say about my robust son?" Sirena asked.

"He said nothing. His eyes held murder, your son's murder, if we don't guard him day and night. Never have I seen such hatred in a living person. He will do something that only God will know. He's a vengeful, hateful person, Mevrouw."

"I've known that for many months. You're right, Frau Holtz, he was expecting to see a dark-haired baby. We must guard the little one with our lives."

"Listen to those lusty bellows, your son wishes to eat again."

Sirena smiled at the baby's cries. His lungs were magnificent, one could almost believe he was heard all over the house.

Day after day, Sirena nursed the baby and then would rest, Frau Holtz always at her side. Wearily, Sirena would move and stir herself at the old housekeeper's prodding. She knew the woman was right, it was just that everything was becoming too much of an effort. Dread seemed to enter through every pore in her body. She had a particular horror of the visits Chaezar made to the small nursery. He would come many times and stand looking down at the small bundle, sometimes with hatred in his eyes and sometimes with no expression at all. Sirena feared the blank unreadable looks the most. She felt he plotted her son's death and her own. If only he would say something, anything was better than those moments when he entered unannounced and sent fear scurrying through her body, not for herself but for the small son she loved.

One brightly sunlit day, Sirena had just finished nursing the baby and was about to place him back in his cradle for a nap. She looked up to notice Chaezar leaning against the door frame, his eyes thoughtful as he watched Sirena remove the baby from her breast and arrange her wrapper before getting up to place the baby in its cradle.

"I have been inquiring for a wet nurse for you," he said urbanely.

"You what?" Sirena's tone held outrage.

"A wet nurse," he repeated. "You are fast resembling a sow and I find the sight offensive to my eyes. As soon as a suitable nurse is found you will turn the child over to her." The emerald eyes glittered dangerously but Sirena said nothing. "The reason I'm having a wet nurse for you is that it's now time for you to take on the duties for which I brought you here."

"And what are these . . . duties?" Sirena asked coldly.

"You will act as my hostess and be a charming wife. Everyone believes you are my wife. It wouldn't pay to dispute my words. It's two months since the birth of the babe, and time to wean him from your breast. You'll have much to occupy you without some squawling brat to worry about. Besides, I don't wish to see all the lovely gowns I purchased for you destroyed by dripping mother's milk."

"And if I refuse your . . . offer of a wet nurse, what then?"

"Then, dear lady, there will simply be no babe for you to worry about at all. It would be wise if you did as I suggested. Lately, I find that I have little . . . patience," he said, smiling cruelly.

"You have the audacity to hold me prisoner, tell your friends that I'm your wife — and that this is your son, no doubt — and you want me to act the loving wife. Your stupidity amazes me, Chaezar. I would kill you in a moment if I could. How do you expect me to carry on this farce?"

"My dear, something brilliant will occur to you, of that I'm sure. After all, we do have the child's best interest at heart, don't we?"

"You are a bastard pig, son of a whore!"

"And, dear lady, what does that make you?" A lecherous smile lit his face as he gazed at her protruding breasts. "The wife of a bastard pig, son of a whore. How would you ever prove differently?"

"As long as I know that I'm not your wife that will suffice for me. There is no way in this whole world you could ever make me your wife."

"As I said, I'm a patient man. With the health of your . . . son at stake, I think we both understand each other. Tonight there will be an intimate dinner for a dozen people. One of the servants will bring you a gown and appropriate jewels. Afterwards, I expect you to behave like a wife should.

"Dinner will be served at sundown. I wish you downstairs a good hour before. We shall toast your son's health with a glass of wine. Until then, my dear," he said, his eyes opaque in the dim afternoon glow.

"Frau Holtz, Frau Holtz, did you hear that? Did you hear what he has ordered me to do? Sow! And he wants to bed me tonight after his dinner. What am I to do?" she wailed. "If I don't do as he says one of his murderous guards will surely kill the little one. And you too, Frau Holtz. There's no choice open to me, is there?" At the compassionate look on the housekeeper's face, Sirena nodded. "I thought so," she murmured, "I swore to myself a long time ago that I'd never again be used by anyone. I meant it then and I mean it now. I won't crawl into his bed like some yearning whore. I won't do it!"

"But the —"

"I'll think of something. I still have several hours left. I'll think of something," Sirena said confidently.

Even from aboard ship Regan and Caleb could see the layout of the harbor town. The slips at the wharf were new and numerous, the raw unweathered wood bespoke the port's recent burgeoning. It was said that all the harbors along Africa's coast were undergoing this surge in trade. Unlike the sophisticated harbors of Europe and the Indies, the African ports were crude and rustic.

The commerce here was not spices and silk and foodstuffs, but a new resource that filled the merchant's pockets. It was called black gold or black ivory, but both terms meant the same thing: the

African slave trade. The dirtiest, most sordid and obscene cargo ever carried in a ship's hold. Slaves.

Regan jumped to land, Caleb behind him. As their feet touched the dock, a jumble of small children ran to them laughing happily. Regan squatted and gathered a dark-eyed, black-skinned little boy to him. He spoke slowly and through gestures asked his questions. The child smiled shyly and grasped Regan's hand and took him along the planked walkway that led into one of the buildings. Shyly, he pointed out a white-haired man and then ran laughing from the building, the other children close behind.

Quickly, Regan explained his wants and the old man nodded. "There is one such as you speak of. I myself have not met the man, but he resides at the southern end of town. He has built a magnificent house and they say he is wealthy beyond anyone's dreams. He brought a wife and son with him. I have heard just this morning that this evening is to be his first entertainment. It's said he's sort of king and she is his queen. I fear," the old man said gently, "that I do not understand such talk. To introduce her to our people is one thing, but to proclaim oneself king and queen is beyond my comprehension."

"How do I arrive at the . . . king's house?"

"It would be best if you went by horse. I can allow you the use of two of mine if you return them to me. Ride to the clearing and follow the trail to the very edge of the jungle. There you will see a walkway carved through the dense foliage. Follow that till you again come to a clearing and there you shall see a mansion beyond your wildest dreams.

That is the home of the man you seek, the one who calls himself a king."

Regan thanked the elderly gentleman and climbed astride the beast he was shown. Caleb followed suit, his eyes glassy in anticipation.

"Does this mean it is the end of the journey, Father? The man he spoke of is Señor Alvarez, is he not?"

"No one, save Alvarez, would appoint himself a king," Regan said coldly.

"Then he must mean Sirena is his queen," Caleb cried jubilantly.

"A more unwilling queen I could not imagine," Regan replied harshly as he spurred the horse beneath him. Now that he was so close he didn't want to waste even one second. Caleb found it hard to keep his seat on the massive beast beneath him. His head reeled giddily as he held onto the reins.

Within an hour, Regan reined in the horse and sat looking at the three-tiered house in front of him. The old man was right, it was a house fit for a king. Was it best to march to the front door or wait for cover of darkness and then stampede the dinner party? He looked at the shining eyes of the boy opposite him and slid from the horse.

No sooner did his feet touch ground than he was pinned by strong black arms. He looked up to see hard black faces peering down at him. A look to the left was all he needed to know that Caleb was in the same predicament. So, the bastard was afraid he might turn up on his doorstep; otherwise, why the guards? What was he protecting? His newly found queen and son? Then the son would be a prince. Regan forced the laughter back in his throat as he strained to free himself from the powerful arms that held him prisoner. Seeing that it was a useless effort, he relaxed and told the boy to do the same. They were literally dragged by the giant men to the rear of the house, where one of Caleb's captors picked up a heavy hammer and hit a stinging blow to a round metal shield hanging from a tree. Within seconds, Alvarez was framed in the doorway, an evil smile on his face.

"So! You have decided to pay my little kingdom a visit. I must say, Regan, you have the manners of a barbarian. A gentleman never comes uninvited." He clucked his tongue in disapproval.

"Your manners make me want to retch, you fop," Regan said acidly. "I've come for my wife! Or should I say your queen?" Suddenly he laughed. A sound that set Chaezar's teeth on edge. "Did Sirena willingly become your queen or did you . . . ?"

"Or did I what, you crude lout? I only had to make her the offer and she all but fell at my feet. Why are we standing here, come inside and let me show you how a gentleman of breeding presides over a kingdom. You do know how to behave indoors, don't you?" Chaezar asked caustically.

"I can hardly spill your blood all over your carpets when I'm hampered as I am. Have no fear, Chaezar, I won't stink up your . . . kingdom." Again he laughed, a cruel mocking laugh that made Chaezar uneasy.

Chaezar turned aside and spoke quickly and softly to one of the servants waiting in attendance.

Sirena finished dressing, a grim look on her face. With a grim warning to Frau Holtz, she had her hand poised to open the door when two servants entered the room. One of them thrust Sirena aside and immediately rushed to the cradle and deftly picked up the small bundle in one hand. With a wild screech of rage Sirena was on him, digging her nails down his bare back with Frau Holtz attacking him from the front. The second guard rushed to help the first and threw Sirena across the room, where she lay stunned with the force of the impact. Frau Holtz was gouging and kicking the guard who held the baby and screaming at the top of her lungs. Effortlessly, he shoved her aside and she landed in a heap next to Sirena, the breath knocked from her body. Sirena was on her knees, shaking her head trying to clear it when the door closed behind the men.

Rage and fury like nothing she had ever experienced before ripped through her as she stood and tried to calm her trembling, shaking body. She would kill the bastard with her bare hands if she had to. Swaying dizzily, she helped Frau Holtz to her feet and raced from the room and down the long, dim corridor. Where would they have taken the baby? To the first-floor level and Chaezar's study, or to the kitchens. She half fell and half ran down the winding stairway and arrived at the bottom panting for air. The sight that met her eyes was one she never expected to see. Regan and Caleb held prisoner by four black giants. Her eyes raked the room and came to rest on the guard who held her son in one arm.

Breathing raggedly, she shouted, "Return my baby to me, this instant!"

"Go back to your room unless you want to be a witness to the murder of your husband and your son," Chaezar said coldly.

At the cruel words, Sirena backed up a step out of Chaezar's reach and let her eyes go to Regan's. God in Heaven, what was that look in his eye? Murder, rage, despair, and . . . was it love? Swaying with her new knowledge, she then looked at Caleb. She smiled at the boy and spoke softly, "So, little brother, you could not let me go to my homeland without you. I'm sorry that you find me in such a strange house with such a strange man." Her tone was purposely light and gentle as she moved a step closer to the breakfront behind Chaezar. She flicked her eyes to Regan and noted the slight nod. She sidled up to Chaezar and said in a soothing voice, "I'm his queen, did you know that, Regan? Chaezar appointed me his queen. I was to assume my duties today. Tonight at dinner, as a matter of fact. What does this mean, Chaezar, is the dinner party canceled?"

Chaezar frowned at this strange conversation. Why hadn't the guard returned her to her room? Now he had to make a choice. She was in the way.

"I have to kill Regan and that snotty-nosed brat of his. And then the baby. I find that I won't be able to live in my new kingdom with ghostly reminders of Regan. Guard, remove the blankets from the babe. Let van der Rhys gaze upon the child."

Regan struggled to free himself but found that with each movement the hold on him became tighter.

Sirena watched his agate eyes widen in incredulous shock at the realization that Sirena could never have birthed this fair-skinned baby if the father had been dark and swarthy like Chaezar. What he had hoped for had come true, the child was his.

Too late the truth of the child's paternity dawned on Regan. Sirena had seen his doubt change to certainty as his eyes acknowledged the child's fairness. He had expected to see Chaezar's child, never his own! His expression was branded on her heart. She would never forget the incredulous shock on his face just as she would never forget Isabel's screams.

A film blinded Regan's eyes as he gazed upon the small golden head. But his eyes were glazed with fear when they turned to Chaezar. "You'd kill an innocent child and have no remorse? What kind of devil are you? You must be insane! Let the boy and the infant go free and kill me instead. Send them to the Indies and my people will care for them. In the name of God let them go!"

Sirena was now almost abreast of the crossed rapiers that hung behind Chaezar and over the breakfront. With panther-like speed, she had the rapier free of its hook and had shoved Chaezar out of her way.

Armed now with a weapon, she danced her way over to the dark-skinned guard who held her son. The tip of the rapier nicked the small of the man's back and skirted around to his frontal regions. While the man might not understand her language, he understood which direction the rapier was moving. With a nod to Frau Holtz, the woman ran to the perspiring guard and clasped the baby to her bosom in such a fierce grip he squealed his outrage at such rough handling.

Sirena waved the rapier and shouted for silence. "It is you against me, Chaezar. Tell your guards, in whatever language you prefer, to stay out of this battle. For, if you don't, your tongue will never help you to offer another word."

Chaezar mumbled a few guttural words and the guards quietly left the room.

"Regan, Caleb," Sirena said quietly, "you are not to interfere, is that understood? Even if I am coming out second best, you are not to lift one hand in my direction. If you do, I shall cut you down as I did the others who stood in my way." Regan's tortured eyes nodded agreement and Caleb's held confidence as he fought to keep from clapping his hands. He knew who would be the victor, so he could promise anything.

Sirena backed off, hampered by the length of her gown. With a few deft movements, she had it slit and hanging in kneelength tatters.

"It is a fight to the death, is it?" Chaezar asked.

"To the death. Make your choice, Chaezar, a quick clean death or mutilation?"

"Mutilation! Before you die, I want you to have the supreme pleasure of watching your son's blood run over this tile, then your husband's and then, lastly, when you beg for death, I shall leave you to die a slow and painful death."

There was no need for Sirena to answer in words, the message was in her eyes. Chaezar blanched a moment and blinked before he brought up the rapier.

"En garde!" Sirena called, and the battle was on. Chaezar feinted to the left, bringing up his rapier to slice thin air as Sirena nimbly sidestepped him and swiveled to bring her rapier down across the length of his back. She pivoted with lynx-like grace and brought up her arm with such force, she drove Chaezar back as she jabbed again and again. The Spaniard was perspiring freely as he tried to meet steel with steel. Each time he raised his blade, she would sidestep and jab at his legs. Both of Chaezar's legs were bleeding profusely as she again raised the rapier in a high wide arc and brought it down across his chest. Breathing heavily, she backed off and gasped, "Do you want it clean and quick or is it still mutilation? Answer me now, for I wish to see how much blood runs in your traitorous veins."

"I told you, mutilation, I want to see you weep over your son's blood!" Hate emanated from his eyes as he jabbed and the tip of his weapon drew blood from Sirena's bare arm.

"Neither of us will live to see my son's blood on this tile. The only blood that will drop on this floor will be yours, and if you aren't careful they will need a jolly-boat to row you out of here," she said viciously as she landed a wide slice to the man's chest. "Already your blood runs in many places. Look about you . . . King, and see what is happening to the marble floor in your castle," she taunted as she knicked the tip of the blade across his cheek. No matter what he did, he couldn't make the rapier touch her flesh, she was always one step away from him and his weapon would flounder in empty air, giving her the advantage time and time again. He was tiring and she knew it as she kept up her rapid-fire movements, a jab here and a jab there and then he would feel the warm stickiness trickle from his wounds. Sirena feinted to the right and slipped in a small puddle of blood, losing her balance. Caleb screamed as Chaezar bore down on her, the rapier posed over her neck. Sirena rolled away and sprang to her feet, her eyes hate-filled. "So, cut my neck off, would you?" she shrilled. She lashed out and pinned him to the wall, her breathing ragged. "Your last chance, Señor, quick and clean or the ultimate end?"

Insanity glistened in his wet, dark eyes. "Someday you'll love me," he murmured, "just as I love you."

Sirena never knew what happened. One moment she had him pinned to the wall and the next he had moved, jerking her backwards, the tip of his rapier at her throat. The baby uttered a high-pitched wail and Caleb shouted as she lost her balance and her rapier sliced downward, keeping the promise she had made.

Chaezar's screams rang in the room, vying with the infant's high-pitched cries of hunger and fear. A wide puddle of blood formed on the tile and trickled near her feet. Sirena imagined she could hear the drops as they fell. Chaezar's eyes remained open and glazed as Sirena stood over him, the rapier hanging loosely at her side. "I told you many times that a woman is not a thing to own and possess. She's a creature of God with a free will of her own. It was you, Chaezar, who made me kill you. You should have realized that this rapier I hold in my hand was a scythe of vengeance.

It was your choice, Chaezar."

"You win, Sea Siren, take your . . . son and go . . . home." A bubble of blood rose to his mouth and dribbled down his chin. The glazed eyes closed as Sirena dropped the rapier and fell into Regan's outstretched arms.

Chapter Thirty-five

The baby's high-pitched wail startled Sirena. With a quick movement she sprang from Regan's arms and was across the room near Frau Holtz with her arms extended. "Give me my son," she said, her voice husky and edged with desperation.

"Yes, I would like to see the infant myself at close range," Regan smiled.

"No," Sirena said coldly, clutching the baby to her breast. "This is my child! He's hungry and needs a fresh change of linen. All this excitement isn't good for him." Slowly, she backed away from Regan as he advanced toward her, his intent clear. He meant to see the baby at close range and nothing would stop him.

A vision of Regan's startled look when he noticed the golden head was all that Sirena needed to remind her of which side of the fence the Dutchman sat on. He'd been shocked when he saw the rich golden hair and fair skin, since it was jet hair and olive skin he expected to see. Men, bah! Bastards, the lot of them. Ignorant beyond insult. One would think he'd have the decency to mask his feelings. He was closer now, almost upon her. Lynx-like, she literally tossed the baby to Frau Holtz and spun around the rapier in her hand. "I told you once, Mynheer, that this rapier could move as fast as the bird takes to the wing. I meant it then and I mean it now. One more step and you'll join Alvarez in a similar death. Breathe easy, Dutchman, the choice is yours."

Regan laughed harshly, the sound grating in her ears. "You'd deprive your husband a look at his own flesh and blood? You would kill me for this?" His harsh voice sounded incredulous to Sirena.

"The child is mine, he goes back to Spain with me," Sirena spat.

"Your child! Would you have me believe this was a virgin birth? It's only on the whim of nature that the child is mine. He could very well have been Chaezar's."

"Bastard! Son of a whore! Pig! Animal!" Sirena screeched at the top of her lungs. "Not another step or I'll kill you. Move!" she raged, her eyes glittering angrily.

"Not till I look upon my son," Regan said calmly as he advanced still another step. Her rapier came up with such speed Regan backed up and matched her cold, frozen look. "Enough of this foolishness. Frau Holtz, bring the baby to me. His mother doesn't wish me to move another step."

"No." The one word was an iron command and Frau Holtz stopped in her tracks. "Remember the talk we had aboard ship, Frau Holtz? That's my child you hold in your arms and I tell you to take him to the nursery. I'll follow you and feed him shortly."

"And I'm telling you to bring the child to me this minute. If you don't then you'll feel my wrath," Regan said briskly.

Frau Holtz looked at the glittering eyes of the woman before her and at the mocking eyes of the man next to her. She lowered her own eyes to the small bundle and squared her shoulders. Who was Mynheer van der Rhys to command her to give the child to him? He wasn't paying her wages. Come to think of it, there had been many months with no wages. If he had only asked instead of demanding. Her head high, her cheeks suffused with rosy color, she opened her mouth and uttered, "No, the baby belongs with his mother."

"So, she has worked her magic on you also, Frau Holtz," Regan said sadly. "Is it too much to ask to let a father see his own child?"

"Yes," Sirena spat, "you ask too much. One moment you're convinced the child was the Spaniard's and the next you're convinced he's yours. What if I were to tell you he belongs to Captain Dykstra? What would you say to that? Speak up, Regan, I can't hear you!"

Regan stared into her angry eyes. He wanted to grab her by the hair and drag her to his lair like a prehistoric caveman. His stomach muscles knotted as she returned his stare, her eyes mocked him as Frau Holtz backed away from them and headed for the nursery. How could he allow her to best him in this issue, that of his son? There was no way she would win this battle. He had lost one son and he wasn't going to lose a second! Before he could help himself the words were out of his mouth: "I haven't forgotten those lengthy luncheons with Chaezar and the sparkle in your eyes when you returned. The whole island was talking of your affair with the Spaniard. Deny it, now this minute, that you never bedded the Spaniard! I want to hear your denial. I can't hear you,

Sirena," he almost sing-songed.

Sirena cursed herself for allowing herself to be placed in the position of having to make a denial. She could not, she would not lie. Her cheeks flushed with color and her bottle-green eyes turned murky as she gazed into his. How could she say she had bedded the Spaniard but only because she was drugged? Would Regan believe her? Would he believe it was his name on her lips when Chaezar had his way with her? Not likely.

Regan waited for the answer he dreaded. His agate eyes implored her to refute his accusation. When she remained silent, her eyes glittering and her face still as if carved from stone, a chain of steel closed around his heart. Why did he think she would deny the allegation? Was he hoping against hope that the charge was false when he knew it wasn't? Why did he care? Why was he standing here next to her making demands and why was she holding a rapier over him threatening to slice his manhood from his body? The child was his and he meant to have him. And he would have her too . . . when he was ready. The woman hadn't been born who could resist him.

He shrugged elaborately and backed off still another step. The agate eyes warmed and he smiled slightly to show her he was bowing to her demands. Sirena sighed inwardly and thanked God she could lay down her weapon. One killing was enough. She had wrestled with the question of whether she could harm Regan once before. Then she had decided she could never pierce that beloved flesh. Now she knew she would have carved the heart from his body if he had attempted to take

557

the baby from her.

Regan watched her through narrowed eyes and decided he had been magnanimous enough for one day. "Go, see to our son," he laughed. "Caleb and I will see that a meal is prepared. You'll be called down for dinner. We sail for Batavia the first thing in the morning, the crew will have set in stores by then."

Sirena didn't bother to answer him. She had no intention of going anywhere with him, least of all to Batavia.

His mood jovial, Regan clapped Caleb on the back. Caleb wasn't fooled, not for a minute. Regan was a wounded lion. This was a show of bravado and he would brazen it out to the death. Sirena was right. Men did think with their loins. That it was his father made no difference to him. She had won again. But only for the moment. Regan would have the baby. He had the law on his side. What could Sirena do in the face of the law? She couldn't kill everyone with that deadly rapier of hers. Besides, she was a mother now and mothers didn't do things like that.

A horrible vision of Sirena fighting a duel with a baby clutching at her leg made him gasp. His father cast a disapproving look in his direction. He had to talk to her. There had to be a way to get her to stop and listen to Regan. She loved him and he loved her. Why couldn't life be simple? Why did there always have to be problems? If it wasn't for that oily Spaniard everything would be all right. His eyes fell to the streaks of blood on the marble floor and he winced. So much blood! For a skinny man, the Spaniard had bled a lot. He shrugged.

He deserved to die and if Sirena hadn't killed him, then Regan would have.

"I know you want to see your new brother and I'm sure Sirena won't have any objections to your looking at him — go ahead, boy," Regan said kindly. "I'll see to having . . . this removed and the blood cleaned up. We don't want to dine with congealed blood at our feet."

Caleb shuddered at the words and bolted from the room in search of Sirena and his new brother. He skidded to a stop, not knowing which direction to take in the enormous house. Caleb bellowed at the top of his lungs, "Sirena!"

Frau Holtz stuck her head out of the door and beckoned him in as she craned her thick neck first to the right and then to the left. Satisfied that her former employer was nowhere in sight, she held the door wide and Caleb scooted through. He couldn't help but hear the bolt slide across the heavy door after he was inside.

"Little brother, so we meet once more. Come here," Sirena said, holding out her arms to the boy. Shyly, Caleb let her embrace him without flinching. He was too old for this motherly display of affection. Mothers always wanted to do that to children. Now that Sirena was a mother she would be wanting to kiss and hug him all the time. He grinned slightly and decided he could bear with it. He could never deny Sirena anything. "Come and see your brother. I think he has your eyes. What do you think, Frau Holtz, does little Mikel have Caleb's eyes?"

"*Ja,* he has the boy's eyes and the jaw of his father and the hair of his father, and soon his hands and feet will grow to the size of his father's," the old woman said dourly. "At the moment his disposition is his own, but for how long can only be a guess."

Sirena smiled in spite of herself. The housekeeper adored the infant and would die to protect him.

Caleb stood fidgeting on first one foot and then the other as Frau Holtz pulled back the blanket and he gazed at the small pink face crowned with golden fuzz. Caleb frowned — what was all the fuss? It didn't look like much of anything. He shrugged elaborately and said something polite to Sirena.

Sirena laughed, "I know exactly what you're thinking, that he looks like a plump, dried fig, right?"

"I . . . I didn't say that," Caleb stammered.

"You didn't have to, little brother. I fear I taught you too well. But I told you to speak the truth, the infant looks like a dried fig at the moment. Soon he'll be beautiful and grow to be a handsome, sturdy boy like his brother. I hesitate to say this, but you resembled the little one yourself when you were little. All babies look like this when they're first born."

Caleb gulped with emotion, "I'll teach him everything I know."

"I'm sorry, Caleb, that won't be possible. I'm taking the baby back to Spain with me. You'll be leaving with your father to go back to Batavia. Perhaps one day you'll come to Spain and then you can visit with your little brother. It has to be," she said sadly at the look she read in the boy's eyes. "I told you a long time ago that this could never be. Too much has happened for me to go on with Regan. Chaezar and Gretchen would always lay between us." She shook her head sadly. "No, it can never be."

"Sirena you must listen to me. Regan is downstairs pretending to be jovial. He doesn't fool me at all. We've been to Spain and back searching for you. He'll have the baby and that's all there is to it. The law gives him complete control over his son. You of all people know that. What are you thinking of to deny him the sight of his son?"

"The right of . . . never mind. It doesn't matter. The child is mine and I'm taking him to Spain."

"The baby is Regan's too, and he says he's taking him to Batavia. He'll use the law if he has to. I think he'd kill you, Sirena, if you tried to take the little one."

Sirena blinked. The boy's words didn't shock her, it was the certainty in his voice that sent fear coursing through her veins. "He's mine!" she shouted.

"And Regan's," Caleb said quietly. "Think about what I said, Sirena. Regan's not thinking with his loins now. His mind is crystal clear and sharp as an ax. The baby has a father."

Sirena and Frau Holtz watched the slender boy's retreating back as the baby Mikel fell into a quiet sleep. He had a father, true, but one who did not love his mother.

Regan had little trouble in bringing the black-skinned household staff under his command. They were terrified of this tall, golden-haired sun god but they followed his pantomimed commands faithfully. Chaezar had instilled fear in them, but was incapable of commanding their respect.

Within moments the servants removed Chaezar's battered, bloody body, and pails of steaming soapy water were coursing down the marble stairs. Soon there would be no trace of the scarlet blood which stretched across the floor like gay streamers at a pagan festival.

Satisfied that his orders were being carried out, he headed for the kitchen regions and managed to make himself understood. Dinner would be served at eight and a messenger was sent to tell the guests who were to arrive of Chaezar's untimely death. After seeing the messenger dispatched, he gave the order for bath water and sent Caleb to the horses for clean clothes from his saddlebag.

An hour later he rapped smartly at the door of the nursery and waited for admittance. He was not surprised when Sirena herself opened the door and stood aside for him to enter. She pointed to the small wicker cradle and watched as Regan gently pulled aside the coverlet. She heard his indrawn breath and smiled to herself. The bastard *would* take the sole credit for the small miracle of Mikel's birth. Regan bent over the basket and picked up the tiny babe. Sirena watched, her face passive. She saw the love in his eyes, felt the tenderness as he cradled the small bundle to his chest. Their eyes locked in a fleeting moment of understanding.

"His name is Mikel," Sirena said quietly.

"Mikel is a good name. It's a strong name. I approve of your choice," Regan said seriously.

"He has your chin," Sirena said.

"And your feet and hands!" Frau Holtz blustered.

"*Ja,* I see all these things, I'm satisfied," he said, placing the baby tenderly back in its cradle. He straightened the thin covering and placed his sun-darkened hand on the golden head for a moment. "A son is the greatest gift a woman can give a man," he said quietly, almost as if he were talking to himself. At first Sirena thought he meant her to hear the words but changed her mind when he straightened from the cradle and, without looking at her or Frau Holtz, left the room. His eyes were far away, focused on some other time and place, perhaps reliving the moment he first looked at Caleb. A stab of pity forced Sirena to blink and bite into her lips to prevent herself from crying out.

Regan, Caleb at his side, walked through the lush tropical gardens as dusk settled around the massive, ornate house that had been Chaezar's palace. He squinted into the semi-darkness and clenched his teeth at what he saw. Row upon row of nutmeg trees as far as the eye could see. The bastard! How could he have betrayed his own country as he did? The trees must be destroyed.

Caleb, sensing his father's mood, spoke softly in the gathering dusk: "Father, what will you do? If we sail at dawn as you said, there's no way for you to do anything about the trees."

"After dinner I'll either set fire to the groves, or along with the servants from the house, I'll rip every tree from the ground with my bare hands."

"There must be thousands," Caleb said dubiously. "If you set a fire it could easily get out of control."

"Not if it's done properly. I'll think on the matter while we look upon this . . . kingdom. Tell me, young Caleb, have you ever seen anything to equal this?"

Caleb shook his head as he craned his neck to look at the house behind him. "It is fit for a king. Señor Alvarez must have spent fortunes to have this built."

At the mention of the Spaniard's name Caleb felt the stiffening in Regan's arm and wished he hadn't spoken. Thinking to take his mind off the dead man, he spoke of the baby: "And do you think he looks like a dried fig, Father?"

Regan laughed, a happy sound in the quiet evening. "Now that you mention it, he did resemble a dried fig. But then so did you. Before long he'll be a strapping young man much like yourself. His name is Mikel. What do you think of that?" he asked proudly.

Caleb rolled the name around on his tongue and smiled. "Yes, I like the name, my brother Mikel," he laughed.

"You'll have plenty of time to get acquainted with the little one on the voyage home."

Caleb looked at his father, a puzzled look on his face. "You know a lot about babies, Father. I thought men left that to the mothers and nurses."

"That's true in some households. My children are important to me. One day all that I have will go to my sons. Many a night I myself walked the floor with you when you had a fever. Your mother

564

and I took turns sitting by your side and taking care of you. We wouldn't trust you to a nurse." The harsh voice had softened and was almost humble.

"Does Sirena know you feel like this, Father? Perhaps if you explained she wouldn't hold such bitterness toward you. She says the baby is hers and she'll take him back to Spain."

"The child belongs to both of us. She won't take him back to Spain. She'll sail with us in the morning to Batavia. The baby will need her. She has no choice in the matter. There are laws that govern matters such as these and Sirena knows she must do as I say."

Caleb spoke hesitantly: "A compromise . . ."

"There will be no compromise. She'll sail with us."

"She'll kill you if you try to take her baby," Caleb said nervously. "I saw it in her eyes."

"And I'll kill *her* if she tries to take him from me. An impasse, wouldn't you say?"

"A compromise, Father, that's the answer." A feeling of doom settled over the boy's shoulders as Regan swung him around to face him.

"I said there will be no compromise. The child is mine!"

"He belongs to Sirena, too, she gave birth to him."

Regan dismissed the boy's quiet words as if they had no meaning. "The child is mine," he repeated coldly.

Caleb shook his father's hands from his shoulders and backed off a step. "A baby should stay with his mother," he said stubbornly, his eyes angry and unforgiving.

"If it comes to a decision, which ship would you sail, boy, mine or Sirena's?"

Caleb ground his teeth together while he clenched his fists at his side. He met his father's cold blue eyes and clenched his teeth even tighter.

Regan knew he would get no response from the boy. In his heart he knew what the answer would be if the boy chose to reply. His shoulders slumped and Caleb gulped back a sob which threatened to choke him.

Why couldn't they solve their differences and start a new life, Caleb agonized inwardly. He was torn as never before and now he had more cause for worry. Perhaps he should take the new baby and run away and then they would see what fools they were. Dejectedly, he walked back through the sweet-smelling gardens and into the house.

Regan poured himself a generous glass of wine from Chaezar's bountiful wine cellar and sat down to think. He had to think! His eyes burned and his arms ached, for Sirena, for the Sea Siren. He was a fool! Why had he said the things he did? Why couldn't he get the picture of Alvarez and Sirena out of his mind? She didn't deny his allegation, so therefore that meant she had bedded the bastard. It was true the child could have been Chaezar's. Still there had been no need for him to say the cutting things he had said. For a moment, a tiny brief moment, he had read something in those glittering green eyes. Sadness, remorse? Whatever, it was gone too quickly for him even to be sure he had seen something. Caleb was right, she would kill him if he took the baby from her.

Yet, there was no way on this earth he would let her take the child from him. She would have to come back to Batavia with him. The child would need its mother at this tender age. Perhaps if he promised her something she would come willingly. What could he promise that could ever make her come willingly? Nothing. There was nothing she wanted from him except her son and that was the one thing he could not, could never, give her.

Then he would have to trick her somehow. Caleb said she never lied. He would trick her and then make her promise him she . . . Wearily, he shook his head, his mind whirling. What could he say to this cold-eyed woman who carried his name and was the mother of his son? There had been a time aboard ship when he swore she felt the same about him as he did for her, and then that time in her room when he had behaved like a wild animal. Would she forget that so easily? Now that he knew she had bedded the Spaniard he would never be able to get it out of his mind. Visions would always float before his eyes. Would he be able to make love to her like a husband and not let thoughts of Alvarez come between him and the woman he wanted to love? Why did he even want her, why did he still lust for her? What was there about the green-eyed witch that could set his blood to a boil and make him light-headed with desire? He wanted her as he had never wanted anything in his life. He wanted her at his side with his children. He would love her as no man ever loved a woman before. Why couldn't she see that? Why did she have to hate him and torment him as she did? Was she being torn as he was? No. She felt nothing for him, she had made that clear from the start. The question was, could he live without her? Could he live in the same house with her and not go near her? Never!

Angrily, he kicked a teak chair and cried out with pain. It wasn't the pain in his booted foot that caused him to cry out but the pain of his own inadequacy. What in the name of God was he to do? If he wasn't careful he would be lying in a pool of his own blood while his wife and two sons and that damnable housekeeper sailed off on his brig. She couldn't kill him, not the father of her child — or could she? For the first time in his life he was alone, truly alone, and he didn't like the feeling. This was a time in his life that he wanted to share. That also was strange, he had never had the desire to share anything with anyone, not even Tita. Why did Sirena have this effect on him?

Angrily he drove his clenched fist into the softness of the brocade sofa on which he sat. If he told her he didn't believe the things he said about her and Chaezar, that he just said them to make her angry, would she then . . . ? He drove his other fist into the softness of the shiny sofa and knew the answer. It was too late. There was nothing left in her now but love for her son, and soon he would take that from her too. There was no answer for him anywhere.

He poured himself more wine and drank it in a gulp. He poured another and then still another glass. By the time the servant went to fetch Sirena to the table he was roaring drunk and Sirena watched him through narrowed eyes and felt saddened.

"Are you packed for the trip tomorrow?" he asked, his speech slurred. Sirena didn't bother to answer but picked daintily at the fish on her plate.

"Answer me, damn you! I asked if you were packed," he enunciated clearly, to be sure she understood. Receiving no reply, he stood up and glared at her. Still she didn't answer, only toyed with the food on her plate.

Regan picked up the decanter of wine resting next to his plate and waved it in the air. "Damn you, answer me! I don't talk to hear myself. If you aren't careful," he said, his eyes gleaming, "you may find yourself on the floor and me atop you."

Sirena raised her eyes to meet his and smiled slightly. "They will be ready when you are, Mynheer," she said softly.

Sirena was fully aware of the effect she was having on Regan. She had utilized the hours before dinner in a hot bath, scrubbing the imaginary vestiges of Chaezar's blood from her body. She had dressed her long, dark hair in soft, wide waves with the heavy curling ends caught up in a shell comb at the top of her head; so different from the severe, slick knot at the nape of her neck he was used to seeing.

Chaezar had filled her clothes presses with gowns of indescribable beauty. Light silks, heavy brocades, cloth of silver and cloth of gold. Gossamer gauze creations to adorn a goddess and beaded satins fit for a queen . . .

"You're to wear these," Chaezar had proclaimed while Sirena was still heavy with child.

"After the birth, of course, to celebrate the birth of my son," he added confidently.

"Then I shall never wear them," Sirena spat in retort, "for there's nothing to celebrate. This child is Regan's!"

". . . nothing to celebrate," she had told Chaezar. But she had decided to wear one of his lavish offerings this evening to impress Regan who, aside from seeing her near-naked in her Sea Siren costume, had never seen her dressed in anything but the black dresses of mourning and heavy, concealing mantilla.

Seizing a gown of rich, vibrant topaz from the clothes press, she had muttered angrily, "You were right, Chaezar. The gowns are to celebrate . . . your death!"

Now, when Regan looked at her, she knew he was excited by what he saw. The jewel-toned topaz brought yellow cat-like glints out in her green eyes. Her skin paled against the vibrant color to the hue of buffed ivory, set off by her shimmering dark hair. Her breasts, always high and full, blossomed over the top of the trim-fitting bodice with a new voluptuousness.

"They! Who is they? I asked you if you were packed? You speak in riddles," he said, drunkenly eyeing her cleavage. She didn't fail to see him wet his dry lips as he forced his eyes to look into hers.

"They. Frau Holtz and the baby. I assume Caleb can take care of his own needs."

"Are you packed?" he thundered as he brought the wine bottle crashing against the side of the table.

"There's no reason for me to pack. I'm not going with you. You have the right to claim the child. I, too, know the laws. Frau Holtz is this minute securing a wet nurse for Mikel. Now if you'll excuse me," she said, rising from the table. God in Heaven, if she didn't get away from him she would be blubbering like a baby. Baby. She was giving up her baby to Regan and would never see him again. What kind of God are you, she implored silently, to force me to make still another decision that will haunt me for the rest of my life?

"What do you mean you aren't coming?" Regan shouted, all signs of drunkenness gone.

Sirena was halfway around the table and blinking rapidly to hold her tears in check. A glistening drop lay on her cheek as others formed in the emerald eyes. Regan looked at her in awe, his heart thundering in his chest. He had never seen her cry. The effect was devastating! He felt deeply ashamed and guilty. He weakened in the face of her tears. "The child needs you, Caleb needs you," he said huskily. "Won't you reconsider and come with us?"

Another tear fell to her cheeks and her shimmering eyes pleaded with him, as her heart leaped in her chest. Say it, Regan, say you need me, she silently implored. That's all you have to say and I would follow you to the ends of the earth. But you must say the words! Her lips trembling, she bit back the words. She waited a moment and then, blinded with tears, she raced from the room.

Regan slumped in his chair and cursed loudly and clearly. What did she want from him? If she had told him to crawl to her he would have, didn't she know that? God, what did she want? Those tears! His heart ached with the thought that he had caused them. Why hadn't he told her he loved her? What was wrong with him? Why couldn't he say the words?

Sirena raced to her room, racking sobs making her body shake from head to toe. She flung herself on the bed and howled like a banshee. She knew in her heart that he would never be able to forget that she had been ravished by pirates and, he suspected — correctly — by Chaezar. He wouldn't allow himself to love her. She had always known that her past would come between them. Their loving time on the *Sea Siren* and the time in her room were just accidents — animalistic actions. There was no love involved, just lust. On his part, she sobbed to herself. "I love him!" she cried into the softness beneath her. "I love him!"

Frau Holtz entered the room quietly and heard her Mevrouw's words. Her own words caught in her throat. So, Sirena did love Regan after all. Frau Holtz hadn't been sure for the past several hours. Gently, she brought the crying woman to her chest and cradled her much the way she held the small baby who lay in his cradle.

"Cry, Mevrouw, don't hold it in any longer." Sirena cried and cried as the old housekeeper stroked her dark head. Finally, she could cry no more and raised her face to meet the old woman's. "Tell me," she said shakily, "have you found a wet nurse for Mikel?"

Frau Holtz chose her words carefully lest the woman next to her find out she was lying. "There was no one. I couldn't get my idea across. Anyone capable of nursing Mikel has a family of their own and does not wish to leave Africa. I did the best I could, Mevrouw, I'm afraid that you'll have to go with the baby; otherwise, he'll surely die," she said ominously.

"How can that be, Frau Holtz? Did you offer money? Isn't there one among the natives who would make the trip? Are you sure you did everything you could?"

"Everything, Mevrouw. I did everything, Mevrouw," she said piteously. "You must go back to Batavia."

"I can't go, don't you understand? The longer I stay with the baby the harder it will be for me to leave in the end. Already my heart is in shreds. Every day will make it that much worse."

"You can do it," the housekeeper said sharply. "You have done harder things in this life than this. It is your child we speak of, you must do it. There's no other way!"

Sirena failed to see the old eyes dance with delight as she nodded. She would go with the baby. When he was old enough to be weaned she would leave him in Regan's and Caleb's capable hands. Nothing mattered anymore. Life was over for her.

It was nearing dawn as Sirena sat by the window nursing the baby. She let her eyes go to the window and was not surprised to see a roaring fire rip across the fields of nutmegs. So, Regan would burn Chaezar's magnificent kingdom and it would be no more. If the wind shifted the house would go also. Perhaps it was best. Another hour and she'd have to be ready to leave. Sorrow cloaked her body and tears again welled in her emerald eyes. Dear God, help me! she cried silently. I'm tired, help me, there's nothing more I can do. A glistening tear fell on the small golden head and the baby sighed contentedly. Was she carrying some invisible cross that said she was to go through life in torment? Was she never to find happiness? Wearily, she placed the small bundle in his bed and went about the business of preparing to leave.

Dawn had barely come when Sirena walked through the door of Chaezar's palace without a backward glance. She avoided looking at the scorched fields and the heavy smoke that lay to the west of her. Caleb trotted next to her like a happy puppy. He didn't know what made her change her mind. All that was important was that she was sailing with them to Batavia. He sighed in relief because now he was spared from making a hateful decision. From time to time he had pestered Frau Holtz for "just one more look" and constantly asked to hold his brother. He had known he could never leave Sirena or Mikel.

Regan's face, too, wore a look of sublime relief. He had sent for Frau Holtz and his new son, Mikel, hoping against hope for a last look at Sirena. He prayed that she would at least come downstairs to say goodbye to Caleb. It was almost beyond his belief when Sirena announced she was returning to Java with her son. Regan's eyes lighted and a smile spread across his face. Sirena's face wore a chiseled look as she carefully picked her way over the cobblestones. There was no way she would acknowledge Regan's smile.

Sunlit days and star-filled nights aboard Regan's brig were almost a balm to Sirena's spirits.

The three-month voyage was uneventful as far as Sirena was concerned. She spent long sunny days on deck with Mikel in his small cradle. He grew by leaps and bounds in the warm, salt air. In his spare time, Caleb would look at the baby fondly and make inane sounds in an attempt to make him laugh. Mikel would oblige and Caleb would rock on his heels in delight. Regan himself made daily morning pilgrimages to her quarters to play with his son and eye him adoringly. From time to time he would pick the baby up and make faces at him. Mikel would regard him solemnly and at times his face would pucker up and lusty yowls would be forthcoming. When this happened Regan would rapidly hand him over to Sirena, a sheepish look on his face. No words passed between them at these times. It was enough that she was aboard ship and Regan seemed content to leave things as they were.

Only once, when a particularly heavy fog rolled in, did Regan search her out at the rail and help her back to the cabin. The touch of his hard callused hand on her arm sent her to trembling and she was not oblivious to his heavy breathing. He explained away his concern for her by saying he didn't want her to get disoriented and fall overboard thus depriving his son of his nourishment. Sirena grimaced at his words and cursed the Dutchman under her breath.

His grip on her arm became more secure as he

led her to the steep ladder below. His touch was fire on her cold, damp flesh. Her foot betrayed her on the flimsy ladder and she fell against Regan, crying out in alarm. Regan himself emitted a small groan as she fell against him. Suddenly his hands were in her hair, his lips crushing hers. He wanted her as never before and she was responding in a like manner. Moans of ecstasy escaped her parted lips as Regan's mouth sought her throat, her breasts. Her senses whirled, her passion bordered on wanton lust. Sirena arched her back and opened her eyes to look at Regan and noted that the fog had shrouded everything in its gray, ghostly pallor. They seemed abstracted from their surroundings. Two lovers lost in a moment of time, isolated in a magical cloud of mist that seeped and swirled around them as their arms entwined around each other. Scorching lips met hers in a desire so fierce Sirena became dizzy. She felt her gown being ripped at the throat and immediately felt the mist wrap itself around her nakedness. Regan ground his lips against hers as his hands caressed the tautness of her breasts. His lips left hers for a moment, and he moaned huskily, "I have decided to overlook your affair with Alvarez. I knew that your passion would never be cooled by any other than me."

Regan's hands cradled her head gently as he again brought his mouth crashing down on hers. From some deep recess in her mind she heard his statement, but she was drowning in a pool of her own passion, her animal lust drawing her further and further: *Decided . . . overlook . . . affair . . . only he could . . .* All he had to do was wait . . .

"Bastard!" she shrieked, dragging herself from his arms and tumbling down the ladder. "Lusting bastard animal!" she shrieked. "Pig fodder and dung are only equal to your rottenness! Whoring bastard!" she continued her tirade. Regan stood with his arms extended and a stunned look on his face. "I'll slice that manly organ from your body when you sleep! I'll kill you yet, you whoring bastard pig, may vermin nest in that white thatch you call hair!"

"What . . . I don't —"

"Animal! You think of nothing save that which rests between your legs, bastard. You'll not use me again to salve your lust. I'll pray that dry rot settles on your organs," she spat.

Regan blinked. What had happened to her? One minute she was a passionate, lusting woman and the next she threatened to slice his manhood from his body. What did he do, what did he say?

Caleb said she never lied and she never broke a promise. He would secure his door at night. Visions of Chaezar laying dead, his manhood severed from his body, set Regan's teeth to a near-rattle.

Chapter Thirty-six

The orange ball of sun was just dipping into the cool waters of the horizon when Regan brought the rig into Port Batavia. He let his eyes scan the new wood at the wharf. His captains must have returned unharmed and started the business of rebuilding. Most of the trees were gone. Those that remained resembled ghostly specters in the deepening twilight. The office buildings were being rebuilt or repaired. Many strong backs would be needed before the harbors and wharves would be ready for the everyday life the islanders were used to.

Vaguely, he wondered how many of his good friends had gotten away safely and how many would never return to feel the warm easterly breezes and watch the graceful breadfruit trees as they dipped and swayed. He was saddened by his thoughts until a lusty yowl broke his mood. He looked toward the stern and saw Sirena holding the baby. He had no time for sadness. He had much to be thankful for. Two sons! Who could ask for more? He would do his share of rebuilding the island and hope that his sons would come to love it as he did.

Sirena walked to the bow, the baby secure in her arms. He bobbed his head trying to see everything. A motherly smile on her face, Sirena cooed gentle words to him. Seeing Regan advance on her, the smile left her face and she clutched the baby tighter. Not a word had passed between them since the fog-shrouded night on the ladder. Regan had avoided her deliberately. And just as deliberately she had sought him out time and time again. She would stand and stare at him with a strange look on her face. She smirked to herself as she watched him betray himself in many small ways. A forgotten word to the crew, a sharp tone with Caleb, a nervous jerk of his usually steady hand, a telltale twitch of his cheek. There were more ways than one to skin a cat, and when she was finished with this cat he would not only be minus his fur but his tail as well.

A rich bubble of laughter wafted across the deck and Regan bristled. She was always either laughing or smiling and there was never anything for her to smile about. Was she trying to drive him out of his mind? If indeed that was her purpose, she was almost succeeding. Not for the world would he admit, even to Caleb, that he slept with a bolt on his door. Many times he had caught her eyes on his lower regions and a strange smile on her lips, and then all through the night, visions of Chaezar would haunt his dreams.

"We're home," Regan said curtly. Sirena ignored him completely as she let her gaze travel over the wharf and the various stages of rebuilding. She wondered how much damage was done to the house and if it was habitable. She would sleep under a tree if necessary. Once inside Regan's house, she would be at his mercy. The rules would be his and she would have to abide by them. Or else, she thought coldly, she would kill him. She looked fondly at the baby in her arms and sighed. A few more months and he would be weaned. A sob caught in her throat as she watched Caleb lower the jolly which would take them to the wharf. A few months would pass in the blink of an eye. She had to decide on a course of action and make the most of it. She would live one day at a time and then she would be ready when Mikel was weaned. She would walk to the wharf, not look back, and cut the island of Batavia and all its inhabitants from her heart.

Standing on the wharf, dry land beneath her, she decided she hadn't missed solid ground at all. The hot dusty streets were busy with men and children. Everywhere there was noise of hammering and construction. These people were rebuilding not only their town, but their lives. New, raw wood glistened in the still twilight. Torches were being lit so the men could continue to work in the cool of the evening. At this rate they would have the island to its former condition before long.

"Regan! I thought you would never get here," Captain Dykstra shouted to be heard above the hammering. "We've been busy, as you can see. Your house is habitable but needs repairs. We've been doing one house at a time. The offices are intact and ready to be opened for business." He lowered his voice slightly. "There's a message for you from the Grand Pensioner himself. Your personal presence is requested in Holland. Wouldn't be surprised if you don't become the next governor," he said jovially.

Regan nodded. "How many were . . . ?"

"Too many. The Medrics, both of them. Helga

Kloss, Gretchen Lindenreich, scores of others. Mevrouw Kloss died helping the children get away. With Gretchen, no one seems to know what happened. And you know the Spaniard left before the holocaust."

"He's dead," Regan said coldly. "Fetch me a wagon, Daan, so I can take my family home."

Sirena's heart leaped at the mention of Gretchen's death. Foolish woman, she chided herself, there would always be another whore to take Gretchen's place.

Within a week of settling in, Regan announced at the evening meal that he would be leaving for Holland the following morning. Caleb was to stay behind and look after his little brother. Regan said he would return as soon as he could, but he expected to be gone for five or six months. Sirena blanched at his cold, impersonal tone and managed to finish her dinner somehow. Caleb seemed oblivious of the undercurrents that passed between them. Frau Holtz hovered near the double doors leading to the kitchen, a sour look on her face. For a bridegroom, her employer left much to be desired: at times the temptation to let him feel the toe of her stout boot was almost more than she could bear. Couldn't he see the haunted look in the Mevrouw's eyes. Was he blind?

"I wish a discussion with you, in private," Regan said coolly as he rose from the table. Sirena nodded and followed him to the cool, dim library he called his home office. He motioned for her to sit down and offered her a glass of wine. She declined both, her eyes roaming around the room and coming to rest insidiously on his lower regions. Regan faltered a moment and gained control of himself. She would no longer make a fool of him.

"I want your promise that you will not leave this island until I return. If you fail to give me your word I shall have a guard posted at the front entrance and one at the back." The green eyes were the color of a grassy meadow, quiet and tranquil. She uttered not a word as she waited for his next demand. She knew there would be others, there were always more demands.

"When I return you will have settled yourself in my chambers. Mikel will be in Frau Holtz's care. I plan to exercise my rights as a husband. I don't wish to hear yea, or nay, at this time. You will do it, understood?" Sirena smiled again and let her eyes travel to the window and the lushness outside. She couldn't care less about his demands. Let him demand till the end of time and then some.

"Caleb tells me you never lie or break a promise. It would be a shame for the boy's idol to have feet of clay. Your promise, Sirena."

Caleb would have to learn sooner or later that she wasn't perfect. How could she have let him build such a perfect image of her in his mind? "I'll make no promises to you, Mynheer. The boy is just that, a boy. He has no right to expect me to be perfect, I'm human. No promises. You have the right to Mikel, I recognize the law. But, you don't own me and I shall do as I please."

"We're married," Regan said harshly.

"Bah, a piece of paper that says we're man and wife. Fool! Look at your paper again. It says Isabel is married to you. The contracts were signed by

Isabel and you. The wedding is a farce. I'm a fallen woman, a disgrace. I am like your whore, Gretchen. Don't talk to me of marriage rights and what you expect, for if you do, then you may get more than you bargain for. If I wanted I could take the child and leave here, now this minute. Prove that you are married to me! Prove that Mikel is your child!" The green eyes were murderous as she spoke in a dangerously controlled tone. "I also know that one way or another I would lose. I have no desire to do battle again. Mikel is yours. But not me. Never me. I won't be owned, not now, not ever. And even if I were married to you I wouldn't allow you to own me. I'm not some object that you can boast about. If you have nothing further to say then I'll get back to my child — excuse me, your child, the one I'm caring for. I'm only his mother. I don't count for anything. Good-bye, Regan, and don't do me any favors by hurrying back."

Rage boiled in Regan as he watched her turn her back on him. With a long arm he spun her about. His eyes were vicious as he clasped her arm.

"This has gone on long enough! You come into my house full of lies and deceit and make a fool out of me in front of my friends and business associates. You wreak havoc on my ships and send my cargos to the bottom of the sea. You marry me under the name of your sister and have the gall to continue to live the lie. You carry on a blatant affair with my rival under my nose and go off to Africa with him and when you tire of him you kill him! Is that what you have in store for me? Dead men lie at the bottom of the sea because of you. You bewitched my son till he thinks you are a goddess and then you birth my son. Not my son, you conceived him alone! You can do anything, or so Caleb says. You allowed me to make love to you aboard your ship and then again here in my house. Ah, I see that you are about to protest. Think, lovely lady, you laid willingly in my arms and enjoyed our union as much as I. What do you want from me?" he asked brokenly. "Tell me, do you want me to crawl across this room and hang on your skirt, to grovel for your attention? Tell me, what is it you want from me?" The agony in his tone ripped at Sirena's heart. Even if she told him how much she loved him he would never believe her.

"Love is giving entirely of oneself," Sirena said quietly. "It's true I allowed you to make love to me and it's also true that I enjoyed it as much as you. I gave of myself entirely. Something I never thought I could do, not after . . . not after . . ." a lump rose in her throat as she tried to find the words.

"What can I do? What can I say? There must be some way to reach you. Just tell me. What do you want from me?"

"My son. Will you give me my son?" Sirena asked, holding her breath as she waited for his answer.

Regan eyed the woman in front of him. "And if I were to give you your son, then you would share my bed, is that it?"

Sirena smiled. "Believe what you will," she said lightly, "I can always kill you when I'm ready. I'll stalk you at night the way a wild animal stalks its prey. I'll tell the child you died, glorious in battle — if he should ask, that is." Her tinkling laughter bounced off the walls and Regan felt a shudder

584

ride up and then course down his spine. He raised his hand, gave her a stinging blow to the side of the head. Sirena saw the blow coming, but stood still, taking the attack fully on the side of her head. She reeled, stunned with the force of the blow. He had actually hit her! She staggered away from him and shook her head. Deliberately, she let her eyes narrow and then lower to a spot six inches below his belt. She forced her eyes to remain open for a full minute and then she knew nothing more.

When she woke she was alone in her room and the baby was wailing his head off. Dazed, Sirena climbed from the bed and picked up the crying baby. Gradually, she relaxed as her mind quieted. This was all she needed, this small warm bundle, her son. She wouldn't think about the past hour and what had transpired downstairs. It didn't matter. Regan would leave in the morning and she would never see him again.

Tears glistened in the sea-green eyes as she laid the baby in its wicker cradle. Time would heal her wounds. Time had a way of taking care of everything. Why should she care? Why should she feel sorrow? Time and time again Regan had flaunted his lust with Gretchen and every available female on the island. That was the worst humiliation of all. Sex! Was there anything in the world besides sex as far as men were concerned?

Storm clouds gathered in the green eyes as she walked to the small balcony and watched Regan stride around the courtyard, a cigar clenched in his strong, white teeth. He looked murderous. Would he trust her alone on the island now that he was leaving? While Mikel was his son, he had no right to Regan's name. Regan had no legal claim. Mikel was hers. In her heart she knew that there would be some way for the Dutchman to force his will. He would have the guards posted around his house and she would never be allowed to leave. He didn't care, all he wanted was his child. Would Caleb help her? Whether he would or wouldn't, she couldn't ask him. Those days were gone forever. This was a new time and a new place.

Regan stopped his long-legged strides and looked up at her balcony. He stood for a moment and slowly and deliberately brought the cigar to his lips. She watched his eyes narrow as he squinted at her through a haze of blue-gray smoke. Angrily, she walked back into her room and lay down on the bed. She was so tired. She couldn't remember a time when she had been so bone tired. All she wanted was to sleep. Sleep, the great escape. Her eyelids became heavier and heavier as she let thoughts of Regan float away on the warm gentle breeze that wafted through the wide windows. Sleep was an escape, a balm to the soul.

Frau Holtz woke her shortly after sundown and brought the baby to her. As the infant nursed at her breast, Frau Holtz casually mentioned that the Mynheer had left the house a short while ago. "He went to his ship and he'll sail at dawn. He was in a killing mood! He goes to Holland!" Still she received no reaction from Sirena, and she frowned. "He left instructions a mile long," Frau

Holtz said sourly. "There are guards positioned around the house and around your frigate, and if you attempt to sail her Mynheer's orders were to gut the ship."

Carefully, Sirena lowered the sleeping baby to the cradle. Here at last was the reaction Frau Holtz was waiting for. "Are you sure of what you say? You didn't make a mistake?"

"No, Mevrouw, no mistake. In fact, I think the Mynheer wanted me to hear his orders to Captain Dykstra. You're his prisoner!"

Sirena nibbled on her full lower lip, her thoughts racing. One day the guards would grow weary. Sooner or later they would become lax and then she would do as she pleased. She would not be held prisoner, not ever again. Regan should know that.

With Regan gone, the house took on a new emptiness. Caleb was quiet and a wary look had come into his eyes. Mikel seemed more fretful in the late morning, the usual time of Regan's daily visits. Frau Holtz grumbled constantly, trivial things rattled her as never before. She also took on a wary look as she went about her household chores. It seemed to Sirena that all eyes were upon her.

There were men, strong, forceful men, who worked outside, supposedly making needed repairs. She wasn't fooled. As soon as she set foot out the garden doors all work stopped and she could feel their eyes watching her every move.

Several weeks after Regan's departure, Sirena walked to the stable, her intention to ride as far as the eye could see. She wasn't sleeping well and she had to do something to tire herself. She would ride to the *Rana* and let her eyes feast on the sleek lines of the frigate. While she saw no one following her, she could hear distant hoofbeats behind her. Regan's men would follow her to the ends of the earth if they had to.

She reined in her horse and sat quietly drinking in the sight of the freshly painted frigate. She looked to the bow and was pleased to see the name *Rana* painted in bold white letters. It looked ghostly in the gathering dusk. When would the frigate travel the seas again? Would she be taken care of and careened and who would see to it, surely not Regan — or would he? He did appreciate the maneuverability of the frigate, perhaps he would lay claim to the ship and hold it for the boy. Sirena became saddened as she thought of her ship laying dormant in the bright blue waters. At the moment, it looked as dead as she felt. It needed a hand on its wheel and someone to hoist the sail just as she needed the caress of Regan's hand and a kind, loving word to make her whole again.

A group of men came out onto the *Rana*'s decks and stood watching Sirena. So, Regan was as good as his word. He had posted guards everywhere.

Willem stood on the deck, Regan's men behind him as he watched the slim figure astride the tall horse. Somehow he had thought she would return before this. He watched her, a knot in his throat. How could the Dutchman do this to her? He had heard Regan give the orders to his bully men. He had said in clear, cold tones that his wife was not to set foot on the ship while he was away. If she did then they would be dead, even if he had to search the world over for them.

Regan had looked at Willem and old Jacobus and had lowered his tone. "My wife wishes you to see about careening this ship and putting her back into shape. If you obey my orders, you can continue to stay aboard. One false move and your death will be fast and fierce!" The Dutchman had then lowered himself into the jolly-boat and headed back for the wharf.

Willem had whispered to old Jacobus and then laughed. They knew in their hearts when their capitana was ready, those burly men of Regan's were as good as dead. They placed a small wager between themselves and settled back to wait. The day would come soon, they were sure of it.

Sirena shielded her eyes from the low-lying sun and frowned. Was that Willem and Jacobus on deck? The reins in her capable hands, she felt the horse rear backwards, but still she didn't take her eyes from the tiny figures on the quarterdeck. She had to know! She brought her gloved hand to her forehead in a jaunty salute and was rewarded with a greeting of waving hands. A smile touched her lips as she spurred the horse beneath her. They had seen her and that was all that was necessary.

The blood raced in her veins as she rode the horse at a fast gallop. Regan had been wise in not forcing her men from her ship. At last he was beginning to understand. It was her ship and her men. It was well he hadn't tampered with either. Perhaps there was hope for him after all. She knew now that she had to do something. She had to fill her days with something meaningful. She had started to wean the baby gradually and now she had more time to herself. One couldn't just idle days and weeks away foolishly when there was so much to do. Tomorrow would be the first day of a new life, a new life that she would have to fashion for herself.

Sirena greeted the faint pink dawn fully dressed, a pail of soapy water in her hands. To Frau Holtz's horror, she worked till noon and then stopped to feed her squawling baby. She then had some breadfruit and marched out to the gardens where she hoed and weeded. When she finished, she picked baskets of fruit and vegetables and carried them into the massive kitchens. Frau Holtz rushed to her, but when she saw the determined look in her mistress's eyes she continued with what she was doing. She fed the wailing baby his evening meal and then rode out of the clearing, her destination, the quay where she could gaze out on the *Rana*.

Day after weary day passed with Sirena working tirelessly. She knew that her child's destiny could only lie with Regan and she felt she must do her share to help build that destiny before she left for the last time. She worked in the house, getting it back into shape for the Mynheer's return, she worked in the gardens and the fields carrying rubble to the big drainage ditches to spare the men for more important work. Literally falling asleep on her feet, she would feed her baby in a trance-like state and only come alive when it was time to take her daily ride to the quay where she could look down at her *Rana*. She would then ride back to the house and fall into bed and sleep like the dead. Frau Holtz grew more concerned as the days wore on. The Mevrouw was too thin and her milk was fast drying. There were deep hollows in her cheeks and dark smudges under her lusterless eyes.

Sirena was walking through the courtyard to the house when the groom met her and explained that her horse had lost a shoe and advised her against riding it. Sirena agreed and decided to walk through the gardens. The beautiful, sweet-smelling flowers that she had tended annoyed her, the graceful breadfruit trees grated on her nerves. She closed the iron gate of the garden and started out across the fields. Here her footstep quickened and her eyes lit up in speculation. She let her foot scuff the dry gray ash. In a moment she was on her knees and digging with her bare hands — down, down through the ash. Was it possible? Could it be? Again she dug frantically, her mind racing with her discovery. She moved further on and once more dug with her hands. Her eyes were shining as she stood and looked around her. She, and she alone, had the power to secure Mikel's future. Swiftly her mind calculated the time Regan had been gone and the time left before he would return. There would be time she decided, time for her to secure her son's destiny. Could she do it? She had to do it!

Racing back to the house she sought out Frau Holtz and explained her plan. The old house-keeper looked at her in amazement. "But Mevrouw, you are only a woman, how can you do it? You will drop dead in your tracks. Will you, at least, allow me to help you? We can leave Mikel with Caleb and work from sunup to sundown. I'll be at your side. It is time these men on this island looked at us with something besides . . ."

Sirena laughed. "Were you about to use the word lust?"

"*Ja,* but it was you I was thinking of, not myself. It has been many years since I saw lust in a man's eyes for me."

Sirena clapped her hands in glee. "Arrange for the flat wagon to be in the courtyard at dawn tomorrow. We'll ride out and be back by late afternoon. On second thought, we'll need two wagons. You, Frau Holtz, must drive one of them." The old housekeeper nodded, a look of battle in her eyes. Sirena wasn't sure who she was going to do battle with, but never had she seen the old woman so animated. Together they would arrange Mikel's and Caleb's future! She thought with irony that Chaezar's treachery would aid her. Perhaps they would think kindly of her in the future when the nutmeg trees were thriving and their harvest was rich. It was something she had to do. She knew she couldn't let the ground lay fallow, not when she had it in her power to make it rich again. Regan's heart must have been near to breaking when he had to set fire to the groves of nutmeg trees in Africa.

Late that night when she went to bed at last, she fell asleep almost instantly. Visions of Regan, riding through the rows and rows of nutmeg trees that she and Frau Holtz had planted, plagued her dreams. He rode endlessly, calling her name over and over again. She woke in the morning with tears in her eyes and a salty taste in her mouth.

She dressed comfortably, it would be a back-breaking day for her. She hoped fervently that Frau Holtz was up to the hard labor.

Hot, sweat-filled days passed, each more tiring than the one before. They were clumsy at first, these two women filled with one purpose, but gradually they managed to get into the rhythm of their task and worked without wasted motion. They started at sunup and worked till dusk was low over the hills. They trudged home in clouds of gray dust with only one thought in mind: tomorrow was one day closer to finishing the task they had started.

"There's one barrel of nutmegs left," the housekeeper said tiredly. "We should finish by dusk."

"I think, Frau Holtz, that we should be proud of ourselves, we have accomplished a tremendous job. There were days when I thought my back would break, and my arms fall off. And you are more tired than I am, I can see it in your eyes. It was foolish of me to allow you to do such hard labor. If anything happened to you, I would never forgive myself."

"There is no need for worry, Mevrouw, I did what I did for you and the child. If I had to do it again, I would. A few days of rest and I'll be fine. What of you? You're thin, the sparkle of life is gone from your eyes."

"I'll survive, Frau Holtz. I think I'll bathe and go riding."

"You torture yourself!" Frau Holtz said sternly.

"Why do you ride to the quay every day and look upon your ship? You plan to leave when the baby is weaned? I read the decision in your eyes many days ago. The days are numbered," she said sadly.

Sirena had to continue her evening rides to the quay regardless of how tired she was. She knew Willem and the others well. Each night they waited to salute her. Each night she returned their greeting. It had become a ritual. One night soon she would not appear on the quay and her men would deduce that they should make ready to sail, for the next time they would see her would be when she had made her escape.

More days passed and Sirena lapsed into a state bordering insanity as the fruits of her labor failed to make a showing. Was the ground ruined forever? Had all the back-breaking plowing been in vain? Day after day, she rode out to the fields to oversee the cultivation. The men Captain Dykstra had been able to secure for her were practiced plantation hands. Had she been insane when she turned over the earth in the hopes the nutmegs would grow once more? They should have sprouted by now.

Another week passed and Frau Holtz came on the run, her thick arms waving wildly. She grabbed Sirena by the hand and dragged her through the house and out to the fields. Triumphantly, she pointed to a miniature sprout peeking from the black soil. "Your son's destiny," she said happily.

Sirena smiled as she let her eyes travel the neat rows of planting. Tiny green shoots sprouted as far as the eye could see.

Chapter Thirty-seven

The baby Mikel was fully weaned. The nutmeg trees were a foot high and thriving in the warm, humid air and daily rain. Caleb had just returned from the wharf and told her that a ship had just pulled into harbor and they had sighted Regan two days out of port. Sirena's heart leaped at the words and immediately turned into a hard lump that made breathing difficult.

So, tonight there would be no ride for her to the hills. Martin and Willem would be in readiness for her arrival. In cool, brisk tones devoid of any emotion, she ordered Frau Holtz to pack her trunks and have them sent to the wharf where the *Rana* was secured. The old housekeeper went off to do her Mevrouw's bidding, her watery eyes stormy with anger.

Sirena argued with herself. She had made no promises and she was a free woman. Regan had no hold on her. She would leave her son in his hands and . . . Why did she even think of these things? This part of her life was over. Somewhere, someplace, there was a new life waiting for her. In time the wound in her heart would heal — if she managed to live that long. For days now she had felt like the very life within her was draining away. She had seen the concern in the housekeeper's eyes and how she had forcefully held her tongue to avoid a confrontation. She meant well, Sirena knew this and held only respect for the old woman. But Sirena had made her decision and she alone would have to live with it.

Sirena awoke, her ears alert to a strange sound in her room. She opened one eye and saw Regan standing over the baby. She forced her breathing to remain calm and even. She waited patiently for him to leave the room, her heart fluttering madly in her chest. She felt rather than heard him move, and she knew he stood next to her bed. She remained still, and eventually he left as quietly as he had come. When he closed the door behind him, Sirena turned her face into her pillow and sobbed.

The following morning, Frau Holtz entered Sirena's room and helped her dress. "Your trunks have been loaded in the wagons. Caleb still sleeps. Is it wise for you to leave without telling him good-bye?"

"I cannot bear another good-bye. The boy will understand. The little one will never miss me, not with you in charge of him. You will take good care of him, won't you, Frau Holtz? she asked anxiously.

"I shall care for him as if he were my own," the old woman said brokenly.

"Regan is back so I must leave. I'm sure that after he satisfied himself that I was here as well as the baby, he will have gone to sleep. This will be the best time for me to leave. I don't know why I waited so long. I should have gone weeks ago."

I know why, the housekeeper thought sourly, you could not bear to leave without one more look at the Mynheer. No matter what you tell yourself,

596

that is the answer.

"Quietly now, I don't wish anyone to know of my going. What do you think, Frau Holtz, a trip down the vine or through the front door?" she asked impishly, trying to make the old woman smile.

The woman shrugged, no humor in her eyes. The Mevrouw was leaving, what did it matter how she left? One way was as good as any other.

"I'll leave by the front door. There is no reason or cause for anyone to stop me. I'm free as the birds. I belong to no man. Good-bye, Frau Holtz, I shall remember you in my prayers. Take good care of my son."

The old woman couldn't restrain herself. "What prayers? I haven't heard or seen you pray in a month of Sundays. Pray that the little one survives without you."

"He'll survive." She descended the stairs and came to an abrupt halt at the bottom. Regan was towering over her.

"Good-bye, Regan," she said quietly. "Please, allow me to pass." Her eyes were pleading as she spoke. "Your son is upstairs, waiting for your return." She moved to go around him.

Regan fought the bellow that threatened to choke him. She was leaving and there was no way he could stop her. She didn't belong to him! She had never belonged to him! He had been proud to receive the appointment of Governor of Java, and knew Sirena would be a perfect first lady for him — but now he would rule Java alone. Miserable and alone. His eyes implored her to give him some sign that she cared, some faint look, anything.

How could he allow her to walk out of his life?

Sirena, her heart thumping so madly in her chest she was sure he could hear it, begged him with her eyes to say the words that would make her stay. Why? Why couldn't he say what she wanted to hear? Was she so repulsive that he couldn't wait to be rid of her? This couldn't go on, she couldn't continue to torment herself. With one last imploring look that Regan met with bewilderment, she walked through the door.

Regan's shoulders slumped as the door closed. The sun was gone from the room, the life from his body. On lagging feet, he walked to his office and sat down, the rum bottle in his large sun-bronzed hand. He would get drunk. He would drown out all feeling in him. No sooner had he downed his first drink when the door burst open and Caleb burst into the room, his eyes pools of fright and anger.

"She's gone! Father, she's gone! Why did you let her go? And," he shrilled hopelessly, "she left Mikel behind. She didn't tell me good-bye! Why did you let her go? After what she did for you, how could you allow this to happen? You lied to me!" he accused vehemently. "You told me you loved her. Why did you lie to me?"

Frau Holtz, not to be undone, pranced into the room and picked up where Caleb left off. "What am I to do with this child? I am an old lady. I know nothing of small babies. This child needs a mother, already he wails," she said, pinching the soft flesh underneath the blanket. The baby let out a lusty yell and Frau Holtz immediately placed him in Regan's arms, but not before she gave him another gentle pinch. "You are his father, see to the child. Perhaps you can convince *him* he needs no mother!"

"What is this conspiracy you have laid for me?" Regan sputtered, his grip on the howling baby precarious. "Both of you will stay out of my affairs from this moment on!"

"Bah!" the housekeeper snorted. "What affairs? You have none with the Mevrouw gone."

"You lied to me!" Caleb howled, tears forming in his dark eyes. "I'm leaving your house. I'll go and stay with Captain Dykstra if he'll have me. You said you loved her, that's what you said. Those were your exact words, Father, that you loved her!"

Was there no peace for him anywhere? What were they doing to him? Why couldn't they see that Sirena didn't want him. He couldn't force her to stay in his house.

"I didn't lie to you, Caleb, I do love her. But I cannot, I will not, force her to live in my house if she doesn't want to."

"If you love her why didn't she stay?" Caleb asked, puzzled now where a moment ago he had been angry.

Frau Holtz stood erect and spoke imperiously. "Because he chose not to *tell* her he loves her. He takes these important matters for granted. He thinks because he is a man, she will *assume* that he loves her!"

"Then this is what Sirena meant when she said men think with their loins. I wasn't sure exactly how that applied to you, Father. Thank you, Frau Holtz, for explaining the matter to me."

Regan choked back a gasp of rage at these words.

"I think perhaps, Father, Sirena is doing something else that I never fully understood before. She is being a wily woman. You do know what that means, don't you?" Caleb asked anxiously.

Frau Holtz, angry now beyond human feeling, spoke harshly: "When did you tell the Mevrouw that you loved her? When did you tell her that you couldn't live without her? When did you tell her her eyes were like the stars and her skin like . . . ?"

"Enough!" roared the harsh voice.

"Enough. No, it is not enough. Look through the windows and let me know what your eyes see, Mynheer."

Regan strode to the wide windows and gasped. Nutmeg trees, a foot high!

"The Mevrouw and myself planted those trees. She said it was to secure the destiny of her son and young Caleb. She planted those trees for you. For you, Mynheer! Who but a woman in love could do that for a man? What woman could give up her son to a man she didn't love? You have much thinking to do, Mynheer. When a man needs a woman, he shouldn't be afraid to tell her so. If you hurry you may still catch her!"

Regan eyed the rum bottle stubbornly. What did some cranky old woman and a boy not yet dry behind the ears know of love? He would think on the matter — after he finished the warm rum. "Leave this room!" he shouted. "And take this squawling child with you."

"What am I to do with him? Without his mother he is lost," she said, giving the infant still another pinch. Fresh yowls of outrage split the air in the tension-filled room. Regan, a look of despair on his face, looked to Caleb and told him to go play with his brother.

Caleb flatly refused and strode through the doorway, a smile on his face. The baby's cries continued to waft through the house, and finally he heard the door slam shut and the wails stop.

Regan drank greedily. Were they right? Was that what she wanted, to hear him say he loved her? Were women so foolish that they had to hear those soft words? He had never spoken them and he wasn't about to start! A devil perched itself on his shoulder and whispered dark words into his ear. What did a few words matter? It was true he had never said these things. She should have known that he loved her after they . . . Why did he have to say the words? The rum bottle found its way to his lips and he downed the last of its contents in a fast gulp. Quickly, he uncorked a second bottle and drank greedily. He set the bottle on the desk with slow, precise movements and stood looking at it. He could do two things. He could stay here and continue to drink or he could go after her. If he went after her he would have to tell her all the things that were burning in his heart. He would have to tell her he loved her, that he was dead without her. He would have to say he needed her, that he wanted her at his side when their child grew to manhood. He would tell her he wanted many children to romp and laugh through his house. He would tell her Chaezar Alvarez and Gretchen Lindenreich were things of the past that they would put behind them. Could he say all these things to her? A vision of the rows and rows of nutmeg trees made his eyes blur. And the lusty howls of his son rang in his ear. What kind of woman was she? She was . . . his. He eyed the rum bottle again and then knocked it to the floor.

At best, his seat upon the horse was unsteady. He cursed the rum bottle and then he cursed himself. When he was finished he felt no better, so he cursed once more; this time, Frau Holtz was the recipient of his verbal abuse. Dull-witted old hag, what did she know of love? He cursed the fact that upon his return the night before he had stopped at the wharf and set the guards free to do other chores for him. Now that he was home he thought there would be no need for guards. What a fool he was. Would he never learn to listen to his instincts? Some tiny little thing had needled at him as he told the men to go to his offices and make themselves useful to his captains. He hadn't missed the smile that passed between Jacobus and Willem. At the time he merely thought they were glad to see the last of the big, burly men that had lived on the ship these many months.

He wiped the sweat from his brow as he spurred the horse faster and faster. If Sirena had set sail immediately she would have a two-hour head start on him, and with the brisk breeze she would make excellent time. By the time he stored a few provisions and got underway he would lose another two hours. Where would she go? Spain? Or would she ride the lonely sea until they were one?

A worm of fear crawled around his belly and inched its way up to his throat. The pain was so real he had to gasp and fight for breath. Where had that thought come from? Was it the empty look in her eyes? Did she somehow convey to him that she no longer cared to live? Would giving up her son to him make her want to die? Why, in the name of all that was holy, hadn't Frau Holtz thought to say something about that? It was his gut that told him something was wrong. Sirena was not a woman to give up her son. Not to him, not to any man. And why had she planted those damnable nutmeg trees and where in the hell had she gotten the fertile nutmegs to begin with? His mind whirled with these thoughts as he continued to spur the horse forward.

Sirena climbed aboard the frigate and greeted her small crew warmly. She gave the order to hoist the anchor and went below. There was no point in looking toward the town of Batavia. She never wanted to see it again. All she wanted from now on was to stare at the water till her eyes fell from their sockets. The sea was her only friend. It would never betray her. Her mind wandered to the time when she was a child playing with Isabel under the trees. She had been so happy then. Now there were no more happy days. Only days filled with vengeance, hatred, and sorrow.

Old Jacobus quietly entered Sirena's quarters several hours later to convince himself that his Capitana was still alive and well. There was no doubt that she was different. She was a shell of her former self. He wished there was something he could do for her. Too many times he had seen that same look in the eyes of men who went to sea and never returned. Feeling helpless, he withdrew from the doorway.

Hours later, Sirena stirred fretfully and finally woke. For a moment she was disoriented as she looked around her quarters. She rubbed her temples and blinked her eyes. She had a raging headache and it was stifling in the close quarters of the cabin. She longed for a cooling bath and some fresh, tingling cologne. She would settle, instead, for removing her heavy clothing and wearing the abbreviated costume she had worn as the Sea Siren. At least she would be able to breathe, to move, and the spindrift was all she needed in the way of cologne.

It was close to midnight when she relieved Willem at the wheel. The air felt heavy and oppressive, they were on the brink of a storm. She was proved right moments later when a vicious bolt of lightning ripped across the sky and a doom-like roll of thunder split the air. The waves beneath her churned and rolled the frigate. As bolt after bolt of lightning lit the sky Sirena thought she saw a ship on her stern.

It was old Jacobus who heard the grappling hook find its mark. He blinked as he saw Regan van der Rhys climb aboard the frigate, alone. Delight danced in the old man's eyes as Regan made his objective known. Willem joined Jacobus on deck and listened to Regan, smiles on their lips. They nodded slightly as Regan motioned for them to go aboard his brig.

Regan watched the men as they swung aboard his brig. The taut ropes holding the ships were straining in the fierce storm. He pulled his cutlass from his belt and looked at the rope that held the two ships together. He threw the grappling hook to Willem and slashed at the rope, his face grim and purposeful.

Sirena fought the wheel and was about to fall in weariness when she felt a presence behind her. "Willem," she shouted, "take the wheel, I've had enough!"

"Do my ears deceive me?" Regan shouted to be heard over the crashing waves. "You've had enough!" His voice was incredulous.

"Regan!" she gasped. "How . . . what . . . ? Get off my ship," she spat. "Who let you aboard? Where are my men?" She fumbled for her rapier and was stunned to find it missing from her belt.

"It would seem that we must fight with words this time," Regan grinned. "I have things that must be said to you. Things you must listen to!"

"I'm past the stage where whatever you have to say will be of interest. Get off my ship!"

"You'll listen to me if I have to lash you to the wheel. I haven't come this far to have you make a fool of me."

"Very well, say whatever it is you have to say and leave. This is my ship!"

Regan looked at her and was amused at her tone. He loved to see her when she was spitting and fuming and snarling at injustice. She would demand her rights as a person, as a woman. She was the kind of woman with whom a man could build a future. A woman who would endure. She was his woman! She had been his from the moment he first saw her on the bow of her ship. She was his future!

"Did the cat get your tongue?" Sirena taunted. "Why do you look at me that way?"

"What way?" Regan asked mockingly.

"Like . . . like . . ."

"Like I love you? I do. I love you as I never thought it possible for a man to love a woman, Sirena. I need you to make me whole, I can't live without you at my side. Chaezar and Gretchen are in the past —"

"No, they're not! They're standing here between us as if they were living and breathing." He motioned to interrupt her, to tell her she was wrong, that all their pain and torment and suffering was behind them. He loved her, that's all that mattered.

"No . . . Don't stop me, Regan, you have to know." The words welled up in her throat, almost gagging her. "Chaezar," she began hesitantly, her voice barely audible, "Chaezar seduced me!" It was out. She could see the pain in his eyes. She knew he didn't want to hear this, she was hurting him, but there was no other way. If there could ever be love between them, the truth must be known.

"Listen to me, Regan, Chaezar's attempts to bed me were fruitless. All his flattery and pretty phrases were in vain. I think I knew even then that I loved you." Sirena saw a slight lifting of the pain in his face. He raised his gaze and looked long and deeply into her eyes.

"Chaezar even tried the direct approach and invited me to become his mistress. When all else failed he drugged me." Her shimmering green eyes met Regan's in direct confrontation. "He

606

made love to me. In my drugged state I imagined Chaezar was you. I really believed it was your arms about me, your lips on mine. Chaezar was with me but I was making love to you. Loving *you!*"

The pain cleared entirely from his eyes and the gaze that met Sirena's was free of all doubtful shadows.

Sirena had never loved him more than at that moment. He had been ready to accept her, to love her, to share his life with her, without any explanations. It would have been enough for him to know that she loved him. He had let the past bury the dead and had come to her for one reason only. *He loved her.*

"Sirena, nothing is important. Nothing but you. I loved you from the moment I set eyes on you. I loved the Sea Siren and then I came to love Sirena, my wife. Somewhere along the way they merged and became one. It's you I want to carry my name. It's you I want to share my house. It's you I want to be the mother of my children." Why wasn't she saying something? Why was she looking at him with such horror? Had he been a fool to listen to Frau Holtz and Caleb?

Sirena listened to the words and couldn't believe her ears. Was that God she prayed to finally, after all this time, answering her prayers? Would she really be released from the nightmare of her shattered spirit, of her broken heart?

It must be a trick, she thought frantically. Or else she was dreaming. Regan would never tell her these things. How could she believe she wasn't dreaming? Her eyes widened and her hands went slack on the wheel as Regan came closer and closer. She wasn't dreaming, his touch was real, beautifully, ecstatically real.

As suddenly as the *Rana* had entered the squall, just as suddenly they had left it behind. So could the past be left behind. They knew this with a sureness neither of them had ever felt before.

The air was cool and fresh. No fog spun its disguising, isolating web between them. The moon came out from behind dark clouds and shone down on Regan and Sirena. In the clear, silvery light they gazed at one another and saw the longing and love in each other's eyes.

Regan pulled her to him, his lips burned into hers, igniting their flames of passion. Hungrily, she answered his kiss, her body pressed tightly against him. She could feel the life re-enter her soul. He made her alive with his touch, with his kiss. She was warm and loved and happier than she ever dreamed possible.

He pulled the bandana from around her head. The wind lifted the dark, curling tresses and whipped them about her face. "Why did you do that, Regan?" She smiled, her eyes glowing with happiness, her tinkling laugh sailing across the water.

Enfolding her tightly in his arms, he whispered, "I wanted to see the Sea Siren just once more."